BADD LOVE

A BADD BROTHERS NOVEL

Jasinda Wilder

BADD
LOVE

PROLOGUE

Dane

I HONESTLY CAN'T QUITE BELIEVE THIS IS HAPPENING. MY BIG bro, Duncan, is getting married.

What a tool.

I mean, look—Rune is fucking great. I like her. I love her for him. I love them together. Honestly, I do. She inspires him to be better—and he is.

But my god, what a try-hard.

Twenty-three and you're getting married *and* having a baby *and* moving out of Mom and Dad's?

I have no interest in any of that. Marriage, babies...nah. Not for me. I have no problem with marriage and children as, like, an idea. But for now, at least, it's just not for me.

And I really don't understand how all this happened so fast. One second, he was hanging out with some random tourist chick, hooking up, and being the bro I know. And then suddenly he's all serious and *in love* and moving in with her and she's fucking *pregnant*…

Sure, I might be projecting my own issues onto Duncan. I'm in no way ready for or interested in a serious relationship, let alone the fast and furious assault of adulthood he's going through.

You can miss me with that shit.

A certain memory nibbled at the edges of my awareness, but I pushed it away as I stood next to Jax at an angle near the altar in our backyard. *Our* being Mom and Dad's, the place I at least still call home. Delia's moved out, Emerson's moved out, and now so has Duncan, which means I'm the last one still living with my mommy and daddy.

It's fine. I'm fine.

The subject of said memory stood opposite me, and my damned eyes were having a hell of a time staying away from the wondrous vista that is Lindsey Snelling's epic cleavage.

The woman has incredible tits.

Her ass is divine.

Her hips that definitely do not lie.

Legs for days.

Snatched waist.

In a word, she's fucking gorgeous.

Piercing sapphire eyes, platinum blonde hair cut with razor precision at her shoulders, swinging loose around her perfect, heart-shaped face.

And yet, after what happened several months ago, she still won't even look at me.

Her eyes were fixed on Rune as she wafted gracefully down the aisle in her white wedding dress, which was an admittedly amazing piece of fashion, being created almost entirely of a spiderweb of sheer lace, with a stripe of silk covering her from chest to thigh, highlighting rather than hiding her belly bump. The result was sexy as hell. Rune's hair was loose around her shoulders, her bangs braided back and held in place with a strip of blue silk donated by Mom as something blue, according to that "something borrowed, something blue" business.

Duncan, unsurprisingly, has eyes only for his about-to-be wife, and his eyes were shining. Uncle Canaan, Uncle Corin, Aunt Aerie, and Aunt Tate form a four-piece band playing the wedding march. Opposite Jax, Rune's other best friend, Raquel, was positively beaming.

Lindsey…also beaming. But every so often, her eyes flicked to me, and her expression went carefully blank.

I still don't understand what happened.

I pushed that out of my mind yet again—as I've done multiple times a day every day since that incident occurred. She won't talk to me about it, and I'm stuck in some sort of limbo, wondering if I'm the asshole for reasons I'm not self-aware enough to understand, or if there's something in Lindsey's past that created the situation.

It's put a serious cramp in my style, to be honest. I hooked up with a girl a few weeks ago—or tried to, but I kept thinking about Lindsey and what happened, and had to pull the cord on the poor girl I was with. She was understanding and didn't seem too upset about it, which was cool of her, but it's messing with my head. I haven't been able to even think about being with anyone since.

Fuck—I'm spacing out at my brother's wedding. Focus, jackass.

I put Lindsey out of my mind as best I can—a big ask, considering she's standing a few feet away wearing a pale blue dress that cups her epic tits, hugs her killer hips, and leaves bare her fucking endless legs.

All of which I've had the immense privilege of having seen naked. And can't stop seeing...

I daydream about her. I dream about her at night and wake up hard as a damn rock.

"And now the bride and groom will exchange vows," Papa Lucas said. "Hit it, Dunc."

I shook myself like a dog in an attempt to clear my wandering brain. It mostly worked, and I tuned into Duncan's vows.

"...To say the events of the last few months have been unexpected is an understatement," Dunc was saying. "I definitely didn't have 'meet the love of my life, get engaged, and find out she's pregnant' on my bingo card, especially when things didn't exactly happen in that order."

This got a smattering of laughter from the gathered audience—the entirety of the extended Badd Clan, plus Raquel and Hamish, Lindsey, Rune's parents, and a handful of Rune's social circle from USC, most of whom were just up here for Raquel's wedding a few months ago.

"I wouldn't trade any of it," Duncan said. "My life was on a specific track, and this…none of it was in my plans. And I honestly couldn't be happier that my plans got derailed when a certain black-haired spitfire with the bluest eyes I've seen asked me to be her fake date for a wedding, specifically for the purpose of making her douchebag ex jealous." His eyes flitted to Ricky, Raquel's brother, who was said ex's best friend. "Sorry, Ricky, but he's a cheating jack-hole."

Ricky just held up his hands in a gesture of surrender, laughing. "Hey, I told him he was making a mistake when he first started flirting with that chick. He didn't listen, obviously."

"I don't think we need to go there, Dunc," Rune said, laughing.

Duncan just grinned. "I've never been so glad to be anyone's fake date. That weekend changed my life in so many ways. I can't imagine my life without you, Rune. I'm excited for our future together. I know being young parents won't be easy, but we've got a hell of a support system in place. I love you with every last part of myself, and I vow to you in front of everyone we know and love that I will spend every moment of the rest of my life trying to be worthy of your love, making you feel cherished, supported, and protected. I promise that I will always try to put you first. I probably won't succeed at that all the time, but I sure will try. You're the best thing that's ever happened to me. I love you. You're my everything." He sniffed, shook his head. "Um, yeah. That's it. Do I say, like, amen?"

"No, you doofus," I said. "You're not praying."

"Dane Badd, you cannot call your brother a doofus while he's getting married," Mom hissed at me, while Dad endeavoured to not look like he was stifling laughter.

"Do *not* encourage him, Sebastian Badd," Mom snapped at Dad.

"Guys," Duncan muttered, narrowing his eyes at me, Mom, and then Dad. "Can we not?"

Rune's shoulders were shaking with laughter, and she wiped a tear out of her eye—tears of laughter, tears of wedding emotions? Who knows.

Feelings are not my specialty.

Papa Lucas sent a warning glare at us offenders and then gestured to Rune. "Now that my family is being rude, it's your turn, Rune, my dear."

"Thanks, Papa Lucas." Rune takes a deep breath, focusing on Duncan. "Dunc, my love. Falling in love with you was definitely not in the plans, but it's absolutely the best thing that ever happened to me." She covers her slight bump with one hand. "Becoming a wife and a mother were always someday goals for me. But life has a funny way of throwing twists and turns at you, and now, suddenly, I'm getting to be both of those things, and I could not be more excited. We get to discover life together, Dunc. I'm so incredibly grateful to have found you." She looked to Lindsey and then Raquel. "Linz, you encouraged me to stop hiding and running and get back out there after certain things took a very wrong left turn. Raquel, if it wasn't for you and Hamish planning your wedding here, I'd never have met Duncan."

"Good thing the Old Toby burned down then, eh?" Hamish called out, to much laughter.

Rune took another deep breath, held it, and squeezed Duncan's hands. "I promise to love you as hard as I can, Duncan. I promise to always forgive you when you're a jackass, and I promise to never run when things get hard. Or, if I do, I promise to at least let you catch me again." More laughter. "I can't promise to obey you all the time because I've never been good at that, but I'll definitely try to listen to you. I love you, Duncan Badd, and vow, here and now, in front of everyone we know and love, that I will spend the rest of our lives learning how to love you more perfectly."

"If anyone has reason to object," Papa Lucas said, with a dramatic pause, "keep it your damn self. These kids are gettin' hitched. Now. Rune. Do you promise to love, honor, cherish, and at least try to obey Duncan for the rest of your days, no matter what?"

Rune sniffled, nodded. "Yes. I do."

"Duncan, grand-nephew, do you promise to love, honor, cherish, and at least try to obey Rune for the rest of your days, no matter what?"

"Absolutely, I do," Duncan said, blinking hard.

Oh god, he's crying.

Shoot me.

I glanced at Lindsey, and I guess I must have rolled my eyes or something because she was glaring daggers at me. Or maybe the glaring-daggers was for some other reason. I honestly wish I knew.

Maybe I can corner her fine ass and get some answers out of her at some point this evening.

"Well then, by the powers given to me by the good ol' internet and the great state of Alaska," Papa Lucas said, with a big old grin, "I now pronounce you two beautiful kids married as hell. Kiss'er, kid."

Duncan yanked Rune against his chest, hooked one arm around her waist and the other around her shoulders, dipped her backward, and kissed her stupid.

I couldn't help myself. "Get a room, you two!"

"That's the plan," Duncan said, lifting his wife to her feet. "But first, we party! Let's get it, Badd boys and girls!"

Cheers erupted, and white roses were thrown at the couple as they walked down the aisle together toward the Passage, Aunt Eva snapping roughly a hundred photos every few seconds. As choreographed, Lindsey and I were next, meeting at the front of the aisle and pausing so Aunt Eva could get a portrait of us together. At the very last second, as my aunt was crouching to get the right angle, I snagged Lindsey's hand and stepped closer to her, angling my body toward hers as if we were not just standing up in the wedding together, but actually were together.

"Aww," Aunt Eva crooned as she snap-snap-snapped. "You two are adorable together! Lindsey, sweetheart, turn toward Dane a touch. There you go. Perfect!"

Aunt Eva stepped out of the way and snapped again as we walked hand-in-hand toward where Duncan and Rune were waiting.

Lindsey, the second Eva turned to focus on Raquel and Jax, yanked her hand out of mine. "What the *hell* was that?" she hissed, sounding absolutely furious.

"I don't know what you mean," I said, trying to sound innocent. "Just posing for the photos."

"You made it seem like we're together," she said, still hissing her words with serpentine venom. "We are *not* together, and you know it."

"We aren't?" I said, faking shock—gasping and clapping a hand to my chest. "My god, if only I'd known….oh wait, that's right." I snapped my fingers. "We fucked exactly once, after which you freaked the fuck out, bolted without a word, and haven't so much as acknowledged my existence since, let alone offering me some kind of an explanation."

She stomped with blatant fury radiating from every pore. "Maybe it just wasn't that good," she snapped, "and I'm just not interested in a repeat."

"And maybe you're full of shit." I leaned toward her. "It was goddamned fantastic, and you know it, Lindsey. You owe me an explanation."

"I don't owe you shit," she answered, now speaking through gritted teeth as we reached Duncan and Rune. She left my side and hurried to Rune. "Congratulations, bitch. I can't believe you're married *and* pregnant!"

The girls embraced, and I sidled over to Duncan, wrapped an arm around him, and shook him. "Congrats, I guess." I bumped my head against his. "For real, bro, I am happy for you. You snagged a winner."

He turned to me and pulled me into a hug. "Thanks, Dane. I know I did." He put his mouth near my ear. "When are you gonna tell me what the actual fuck is going on with you and Lindsey?"

I blew out a frustrated breath, squeezing him closer and embracing him hard. "Soon as I fuckin' know, man. She won't talk to me."

He laughed, the bastard. "Ah. So…what'd you do?"

I frowned at him. "Why do you assume I did something, asshole?"

"Because you're my little bro and I know you.

You'll shoot yourself in the foot before you even know you're holding a gun and then put that foot in your mouth."

I shoved him away, laughing even as I bitterly recognized the nugget of truth at the center of his teasing statement. "Shut up, jackass."

"For real, though, man, what happened? I know something happened."

I shook my head. "Not the time or the place, Dunc." I clapped his shoulders. "Today's about you and Rune. We'll talk later."

He nodded. "Heard, bro." He playfully shoved me. "So, you gonna be lonely all by yourself up there. Last kid in the house."

I snorted. "Yeah, I think I'll be okay."

Jax and Raquel joined us then, and the opportunity for private talk was gone as we were ordered by Aunt Eva into roughly forty-seven billion different poses and configurations with the wedding party—which consisted of me and Lindsey, Raquel and Jax, Mom and Dad, and Tom and Kelly Rigby. Why Duncan and I had to pose with Tom and Kelly, I wasn't sure, and neither did they, I didn't think, but you didn't argue with Aunt Eva. She was the sweetest, most soft-spoken woman you'll ever meet, but my god, she had a core of pure titanium. I mean, she'd been married to Uncle Baxter for something like twenty years, and god knows that man is more than a bit of a handful. Takes a hell of a strong woman to tame a man like Baxter Badd as much as she has.

While photos were happening, several party buses were transporting the rest of the wedding guests to Badd's Bar and Grille for the reception, and then a stretched limo took the rest of us once photography was over.

The irony of the reception was that Duncan, in solidarity with his pregnant wife—that's gonna take a while to get used to, my big bro being *married*—didn't drink any alcohol.

Nine months without drinking? Yikes.

I, obviously, didn't have that hindrance, so I went after it. A DJ had been hired so Canaan, Corin, Aerie, and Tate could enjoy the reception rather than pro-vide the music, and I spent a lot of time dancing with my various cousins, doing shots, and avoiding Lindsey.

Avoiding didn't mean I didn't think about her, though. Or, more specifically, her claim that the sex hadn't been that good.

My response had been automatic—I'm patholog-ically incapable of filtering myself. But after the fact, it was haunting me.

My memory of that night was crystal clear. After Duncan and Rune had gone upstairs to Rune's room to talk, Lindsey and I, having spent the better part of the day flirting, had gone to dinner together. Dinner had led to drinks at a bar near her apartment in West

Hollywood, and drinks had led to us going to her apartment.

The sex, according to my memory, had been goddamn spectacular. I know for a fact that she'd had at least one orgasm—unless she was faking it, but she'd need to be an Oscar-winning actress for that to have been faked. I *felt* her pussy spasming while I was inside her, for fuck's sake. I don't know how you can fake that.

We'd passed out together. Woke up. Pillow talk about nothing in particular. And then I'd gone down on her. Eagerly. For a very, very long time. And skillfully, I like to think. I certainly have never had any complaints. And again—unless she was a world-class actress, she hadn't faked the orgasms I'd given her.

Once she'd recovered, she started returning the favor. Now, admittedly, we'd had a good bit to drink, and I was a bit hazy from that and having just woken up in the middle of the night. But I definitely don't remember doing or saying anything that could be construed as pressuring her to do *anything*. I wouldn't. I may be a horny jackass and bona fide hookup artist, but I'd never pressure a girl to do anything. Lindsey had gone down on me of her own free will.

And then, after I came—and I gave her plenty of warning beforehand so she could choose how to let me finish—she freaked the fuck out. Rolled away from me, hyperventilating, locked herself in her bathroom, and screamed at me to get the fuck out.

I remember being confused as hell. Like, what

just happened? Did I do something? I've scoured my memory of that night obsessively, and I can't think of anything. I hadn't held her head down, hadn't forced her down or anything like that, and I gave her lots of lead time before I let go. I hadn't begged or demanded or insisted or cajoled. The second I'd finished making her come, she'd seemingly eagerly moved to suck me off. Great, I love it. But if she had some sort of an issue with it, I'd *never* have let that happen.

In the words of a somewhat overrated hero, I may be an asshole, but I'm not a hundred percent a dick.

With no other option, since she just kept screeching for me to get the fuck out, I'd gotten dressed and left, going back to the hotel Duncan and I were sharing.

She'd refused to speak to me since. She blocked my number. Didn't answer texts, didn't return voicemails. I even talked to Rune about it privately—without explaining what happened, just asking her to have Lindsey get ahold of me—and had been told that Lindsey wasn't talking to her about me either.

She'd shut everyone out when it came to me.

Which made me think that whatever had happened in her head wasn't about me.

But it just doesn't seem fair that I get punished for it.

Fuck, I'm thinking about it again.

I took a fresh bottle of beer through the kitchen, pressing the dewy, icy-cold bottle to my sweating forehead and cheeks. I'd long since lost my suit coat and tie, had my sleeves rolled up, and my shirt undone so my tank top peeked through the gap of my open shirt.

I emerged in the alley behind the kitchen, taking a long slug of beer. Which, honestly, should have been water, considering I was pretty tipsy. But fuck it. Your brother only gets married once.

I hope.

I leaned against the brick wall next to the door and held the bottle against my cheek, trying to quiet the chaos in my mind.

I'm ADHD, so that's a losing game, but right now, the crazed squirrel on a treadmill that is my brain is going a little haywire, and I needed a moment alone in the silence to bring down the noise in my head.

Which is when I heard it.

A sniffle.

A shuddery sob.

And damn me, but I recognized the voice, somehow.

I looked left and saw Lindsey in her baby blue bridesmaid dress, leaning against the wall a few feet away, head tipped back, weeping.

Fuck.

"Um, hey," I said. "Uh, you...you good, Lindsey?"

She snorted. "Yeah, Dane. I'm peachy. I'm out here bawling my eyes out for fucking fun."

"Jesus, dude, I was trying to be nice. Fuckin' shoot me for having the teensiest bit of compassion, even though you won't fucking tell me what the fuck I did wrong."

"NOT EVERYTHING IS ABOUT YOU!" She shrieked and collapsed to her hands and knees.

Stunned by the outburst, I stood frozen for a moment and then went over to her and knelt beside her, recognizing an emotional breakdown when I saw one.

"Hey, whoa, Linz. Take a deep breath, okay?"

She shook her head, hyperventilating. "C-c-can't."

I rested a hand on the smooth, warm skin of her back just above her shoulder blades. "Keep trying. Take a breath. Slow it down."

"Don't—d-don't…don't *touch* me," she hissed.

I removed my hand immediately and sank to my ass on the dirty ground beside her. "Okay, no touching."

"Go away."

"No."

"Dane. Fuck off."

"When you can stand up and breathe normally again, I'll leave you alone. Not until then."

"I d-d-didn't a-a-a-sk for your h-h-h-help."

"Too damn bad, Killer. You got me anyway."

So I sat next to her as she knelt in a quasi-fetal position on the dirty alley ground, her sobs and body-wracking shudders slowly subsiding.

Eventually, she stood up and began pacing back and forth. I remained on the ground, sipping my beer and watching her pace.

She came back to where I was and leaned against

the wall. Didn't look at me as she spoke. "I don't owe you any explanations."

"I disagree. I've spent the last several months trying to figure out what I did to make you freak out like that. And I've come up empty. I don't think it's too much to ask for you to tell me what I did."

She didn't answer for a very long time, and I waited in silence for her response, sipping beer and occasionally stealing glances at her long, smooth, tanned legs.

When it felt clear she wasn't going to even respond, I stood up, tossed my empty bottle into the dumpster, and paused at the door to the kitchen. "Fuck me. Got it. Well, have a nice fucking life, Lindsey. And for what it's worth, I'm sorry for whatever it was I did. I mean that. I don't expect you to give a fuck, but it's true."

I held my place for another beat, but she still said nothing. With a huff and a headshake, I left her there alone and went back to the party.

By three a.m., everyone over thirty was gone, leaving only the younger crowd—my boatload of cousins. And we can fuckin' party. Duncan and Rune had long since left as well, with an encouragement to us to keep the party going. Which we did.

Lindsey rallied, but stuck mainly to Raquel's side,

hanging out with the handful of LA kids who were Rune's friends.

By four, I wasn't hammered, but I was pretty damn sloshed, and ready to call it. Rune and Duncan had taken their honeymoon to Hawaii—a last getaway before she was too pregnant to fly, which I hadn't realized was a thing, and before they had a baby and wouldn't be taking any vacations for a long damn time.

Which meant the guest room upstairs was open—Duncan had given me blanket permission to crash there when I needed, as long as I understood that they weren't going to be quiet on my account.

Noted.

Fortunately, they were on the flight to Hawaii, and I wouldn't have to hear them boning.

Thank god for that.

I shuffled, dizzy and unsteady, upstairs. Bounced off half a dozen different walls, found the guest room. Took a five-year-long piss in the en suite bathroom, stripped out of my clothes, and collapsed in the bed.

I woke up wrapped around a soft, warm, naked female body. Her bare ass was pressed against my groin, which was throbbing with a giant boner.

Um.

I went to bed alone. I *know* I did.

I cracked an eye open, saw a tangled haze of

blonde. She shifted, and I caught a glimpse of a medusa tattoo at the base of her neck, usually hidden by her hair. She flung her arm aside, showing a semicolon tattoo on the inside of her wrist.

Lindsey.

Confused, I rolled to my back, away from her.

She twisted, rolling to follow me, and put her head on my chest. Huffed, nuzzled.

My heart clenched, flipped. What the fuck was going on?

I held still, frozen by sleepy indecision and confusion.

Her hand slid up my chest, found my mouth, and covered it. "Don't," she mumbled. "Just…shush."

"I…"

"Dane," she whispered. "*Please*. Don't say anything. I need this. Just this. Please."

"Okay, Linz. All right."

I kept still, my arm around her shoulders, her soft breath slowly evening out as she fell back into a deep sleep.

I was a lot longer in returning to slumber.

I dreamed of Lindsey screaming, "GET OUT!" Dreamed of her on her knees, shaking, crying, but refusing to let me so much as touch her.

I dreamed a memory of that night we spent together—silver moonlight streaming through her window, bathing her naked body in quicksilver light, highlighting her lush curves, glinting off of her eyes as she smirked up at me while slipping sensuously down my body, mouth opening as she neared my aching cock…

The dream ended then, and I woke up with a start, seconds from coming.

"FUCK," I snarled, covering my face as I dragged myself back from that edge.

When I had myself under control, I glanced at the space beside me.

Empty.

On the pillow was a sheet of paper towel, scribbled on in neat, female block letters with a Sharpie.

There were three words: *It wasn't you.*

Wow, what a relief.

I'm saved from my obsession.

Not.

I'm more confused and worried than ever, especially after her meltdown last night, or this morning.

I had to find her and figure out what was going on.

My phone rang—I slapped at the nightstand blindly, found my phone, and stabbed at the answer button without reading the caller ID.

"H'lo?"

"Dane?" It was a female voice I didn't recognize.

"Yeah? Who's this?"

"Raquel. Rune's friend?"

"Oh, right," I said, sitting up, confused yet again. "Uh, what's up?"

"So, Lindsey never came back to her room last night."

"She, uh, slept here with me. Not *with* me, with me, but with me." I slapped my forehead. "She was here last night. She's not here now, though."

"Shit. Her phone's going right to voicemail."

"Well, she's had me blocked for months, so I dunno."

"Dammit. I'm worried about her. She's not been herself lately."

I cleared my throat. "Honestly, I'm worried too. She, uh, she had a bit of a breakdown last night, around three."

Raquel was silent for a second. "She…she did?"

"Yeah. Big one. Hyperventilating, crying, the whole nine yards. Wouldn't tell me shit, but what else is new."

"Not good," Raquel said. "Not good at all."

"Where would she go?" I asked.

"That's just thing—I dunno. But we have to find her."

"Let me call my cousin, Jax. He can help."

"He can? How?"

"Well, he's my Uncle Xavier's protegé, which means he's sort of a world-class hacker. He can find her."

"Is hacking even a thing anymore?" she asked.

I laughed. "Y'know, that's a good question. I

dunno. I just know he can do just about anything that involves a computer. He can help find her."

"Can you guys meet us at our hotel? We're at the new Old Toby."

"Yeah," I said. "We'll be there ASAP."

Well…shit.

This isn't good.

ONE

Lindsey

Threads of guilt and shame were tangled up in my gut with germinated seeds of hope and deep roots of suspicion and anger. I sat in my window seat—28A—staring out at the glittering sea rippling thirty thousand feet below like a wrinkled blue-gray blanket. Hating myself. Hating Danny more than ever. Hating Dane—unfairly. Hating everything and everyone with the fire of a thousand suns.

There were reasons for my generalized hatred; not all of them were *good* reasons, but they were reasons. One, I was seconds away from starting my period, but it just wouldn't fucking start, and it was making me feel stabby, like a gory version of a stuck sneeze but in my vagina. Sort of; sorry, TMI, I know. Two, I was running away from my problems like a pussy-ass bitch, and I knew it, I just couldn't seem to stop myself.

And by the way, did you know that "pussy" as an

insult for cowardice is not, in fact, a reference to the vagina? True story. It's actually a very complicated situation, and not every linguist agrees with this take, but the short story is that calling someone "a pussy" is rooted in the word "pusillanimous," which does, in fact, mean weak or cowardly. I could give you the longer version, which explains the connection between Old Norse "puss" meaning "pouch" or "purse" for the female anatomy, and a truly sexist usage of calling a man a pussy, but that's a long digression, and people tend to get annoyed at my tangents. So there you go: #themoreyouknow.

So yeah, here I am on a plane making its descent toward LA, feeling miserable and angry and full of self-loathing and a whole hell of a lot of self-pity.

The one thing I'm not is tired. You know why? Because I slept better last night than I have in months. Years, maybe. Possibly even *ever*. And why is that, you ask? Excellent question.

The answer?

Dane Badd.

The sexy bastard did exactly what I asked of him, despite how shittily I've treated him. He found me in his bed, in his hotel room, naked, and he just *held me*.

ALL—NIGHT—LONG.

With his thick, hard, beefy arms wrapped around me like the world's heaviest weighted blanket. With that absurdly sculpted chest of his pressed against my bare back. With that long, hot, thick salami of a cock pressed up against my naked ass, teasing and torturing. I know, I know—I did it to myself.

I slept like a damned baby. He held me. He didn't try anything, even though I felt the full glory of his hard-on wedged between my ass cheeks. He just fucking held me, exactly as I'd asked, even though I was a rank bitch who ghosted him without explanation for my freak-out, blocked him, snapped at him at the wedding…and *then* demanded he comfort me without any kind of reward.

Yeah, you'd feel like shit about yourself, too, so shut up with your judgment.

Fuck, I'm the worst.

Tears burned behind my eyes, and I dialed up the anger a bit just so I didn't start bawling right there in the ass end of economy class.

I mean, how dare Dane Badd be hot as fuck, funny as hell, incredible in bed, *and* understanding *and* forgiving? For real, where does he get off being all that?

The bastard. Save some winning for the rest of us, you damn glory hog.

Furthermore, I can hear you saying, "But Linz, wouldn't it be easier to just…I don't know…*give the man an explanation?*"

Yes. Obvi. That would be *simpler*…just not *easier*.

Explaining my freight train full of emotional baggage is a losing proposition, where men are concerned. Me being kooky, independent to a fault, vulgar, foul-mouthed, and hypersexual as hell is all good and well when he thinks it's just a fun hookup, a friends-with-benefit situation, or just a low-key situationship. But when he gets a whiff of the traumatic fuckery that gestated all that fun weirdness? *Poof.* He's gone. Buh-bye.

"Don't stick your dick in crazy," they tell their buds, and *I'm* the crazy. It's fine to stick your dick in my crazy when there's no drama and no obligation, but if they catch a hint of me having feelings, suddenly it's not so fine to stick their dick in my crazy.

So I don't explain. No trauma dumping from this loon. I get what I need, and I bounce before they get a chance to so much as crack off a morning fart. I mean, why invite more pain? I've had enough of that, thanks. I'll take my orgasms with a side of emotional unavailability, please. And most guys are perfectly happy to oblige. "I'll be gone before you wake up," I tell them, "so don't bother calling." Mainly because I don't give out my number, and if I *did* give a number to a guy, it was probably to a Chinese restaurant in San Francisco, or a massage parlor specializing in off-book happy endings.

Yes, I gave my real number to Dane. It was a lapse in sanity, I think. I'm not sure. I don't remember giving it to him. Probably because I was in a post-orgasm fog at the time and probably would have agreed to give him my firstborn, had he asked. Not that I plan to ever have kids, but you know what I mean. When a man dicks you down so good you forget your own name and need help walking to the bathroom afterward—legit, I did—you tend to go a sorta addle-brained for a minute. Sort of like how guys get after you've sucked their brains out through their dicks.

Ugh, now I'm thinking about his dick. About the sex.

God, it was *good*.

Rune and Duncan had been up in her room hashing their shit out, and then they came down and had it out with Rune's parents, which is when Dane and I made our escape. I don't think anyone noticed that I left with him. We had dinner and too many drinks, flirted with each other over tiramisu, shared a joint on the balcony of my apartment, and then he kissed me.

It was an epic kiss. The man knows how to use his mouth for a lot more than sarcasm and crude jokes, that's for damn sure. The man kissed me like he fucking meant it, all tongue and heat and hunger. He kissed me so damn good my panties were soaked before he even slid his hand up my shirt.

And then it was *on* like Donkey Kong. We fucked like porn stars, and he rode me hard and put me away wet. God, the man's cock was...*chef's kiss*. Gorgeous. Just big enough to make me question my life choices, but not so big I'd need an episiotomy beforehand. He was also blessed with the rare combination of having a massive dong *and* knowing what to do with it. I came so hard I saw the Lord. No, really—the stars bursting behind my eyes as I came left afterimages on my retinas that resembled White Jesus. Don't ask me to explain it any better, because I can't.

That was great. Love it. Ten stars, would recommend. We both passed out, because I like to think I gave as good as I got. When he got up to take care of the condom, he had to move from bed to chair to doorway, holding onto any available surface for balance like a gym rat who hit leg day a little too hard.

Yeah, my pussy got game.

If he can still walk after you're done fucking him, are you even doing it right? Asking the real questions, here.

I woke up to find him looking at me with a curious, speculative expression. We talked about nothing for awhile—bands, favorite concerts, movies, the random shit you chit-chat about with someone you don't really know but are naked in bed with.

This was followed by the most epic, mind-altering, pussy-shattering cunnilingus I've ever received. The tongue? The fingering? Fuck me. I must have come two, if not three times, in less than ten minutes, and he kept going until I had to make him stop because if I came any more, I'd...I dunno. Pass out again? Have a stroke?

Can you orgasm too many times or too hard? He pushed the limits, that's for damn sure.

Once I stopped quivering and wasn't seeing double, I started returning the favor. I felt obligated, y'know? Like, the man just introduced me to the fact that I could, apparently, come while still coming, and I felt like that deserved a reward.

Under the right circumstances, I can be induced to enjoy giving head. It's just…a fraught proposition, laden with minefields of uncertainty: will I suffer a total mental breakdown while his cock-tip is playing tonsil-hockey at the back of my throat? No one knows! Not me, not you, not him, probably not even God, who I hope doesn't actually watch us fuck, by the way. That'd be weird.

Anyway.

I started going down on him. It was all good and well for the first minute or two. I was just getting started, really—establishing a nice thick base layer of saliva, some tongue-swirling, all the good stuff. No worry, no hurry.

And then?

PANIC!

ANXIETY!

FLASHBACKS!

Did you know you can experience a panic attack *and* an anxiety attack at the same time? It's really, really, really fun, ya'll. And to be clear, Dane did absolutely *nothing* to trigger it. He's innocent, I tell you. It was all *gobble gobble gobble, yum yum, ooh taste that sweet, musky precum*…and suddenly, for no reason whatsoever, I was thirteen again and Danny Cohen—my shitstain older brother's best friend—had my hair gripped in his fists, and he was ramming his cock down my throat so hard

Mia Khalifa would have sympathy-gagged. Once that happens, there's no going back. It was a blip—a fragment of a partially-repressed memory that haunts me like the Ghost of Christmas Past. That's usually when it starts going downhill.

I started sweating, felt dizzy, my heart started pounding, and my breath came in short, sharp gasps, and my lungs felt constricted by iron bands. For the uninitiated, those are the symptoms of an anxiety attack. I tried to breathe through it, but it's hard to breathe when you can't breathe, y'know? Lungs don't work, and no amount of mentally chanting "breathe, bitch!" will make them inflate. The anxiety swelled and boiled until I was caught in the maelstrom of physical symptoms, and when you can't breathe and can't see straight, and you've got a dick in your mouth, things get tricky, especially when the dick in the mouth is the source of the anxiety. That's when the anxiety explodes into full-blown panic.

Because—again for the uninitiated—anxiety is the precursor to panic. Put another way, anxiety is Panic Lite™.

That's how you have both at the same time. Because when anxiety turns into panic, you don't just go from anxiety to panic—oh no. You get anxiety *and* panic—when you're me, at least, and suffer from Complex PTSD and Generalized Anxiety Disorder.

When it struck me, I'd locked myself in the bathroom and tried to cope. Breathing. Counting. The usual tricks: five things you can see, four things you can feel, three things you can hear, two things you can smell, one thing you can taste. Tapping. Rocking. Humming. None of it worked.

And then Dane started pounding on the door, demanding to know what the fucking problem was, understandably, since I'd gone from nomming his dong to crying and screaming for him to leave me the fuck alone in less time than it took to tickle the man's balls.

That didn't help.

I felt bad. I felt fucking terrible, honestly. If you've never totally and utterly ruined perfectly good sex with your emotional hangups, you can't know the guilt, shame, anger, and confusion you feel. It fucking *sucks*. Compound that with some serious confrontation avoidance issues?

I screamed and screamed for him to get the fuck out, and he had.

He had inadvertently left his white undershirt behind—it had been underneath my dress. I may or may not be wearing it right now, because it smelled like him.

So now you're all caught up: he fucked me until I couldn't walk, ate my pussy like a champion, and then had me freak-out mid-BJ, screamed at him to get the fuck out, got ghosted, blocked, and treated like shit at his own brother's wedding, and then had me sneak into his room and demand he hold me, naked, in his bed, *and then* I ghosted him *again* the next morning.

And the only explanation he got from me was three words: *It wasn't you.*

Nice, huh? Yeah, I'm a real winner. Wonder why I'm still single.

"Ladies and gentlemen, this is your captain speaking. We're beginning our final descent into Los Angeles. We expect to land in approximately ten minutes. It's a beautiful eighty-five degrees and sunny down there. Please check that your seatback is in its full and upright position, your seatbelt is securely fastened, and that your tray table is stowed. We hope you had a pleasant flight, and on behalf of the whole crew, we thank you for flying with us today. Safe travels."

Out of habit, I took my phone out of airplane mode—it erupted with an avalanche of alerts, mostly missed calls, voicemails, and texts from Raquel. I'm sure I'd have them from Dane, too, but he was still blocked.

Raquel: *WHERE THE FUCK ARE YOU?????*

Raquel: *Lindsey, srsly. Answer your damn phone.*

Raquel: *Im gettnig seriously pised, Lnz!!!!!!*

The misspellings from Raquel were an indicator of her temperament—she's normally a full punctuation, no abbreviations, and checks her spelling texter, who only uses slang, abbreviations, or shorthand when pissed or in a hurry. The six exclamation points were another solid indicator that my girl was gonna murder me when I eventually contacted her.

That's a problem for Future Linz. Today Linz is

going to continue to avoid everyone I know. I'm going home, getting on my Peloton, and doing a Cody Rigsby ride until I either pass out or my period starts, or both. And then I'm taking a boil-me-alive hot shower and going the fuck to sleep, and I'm not getting up until things stop sucking or a solution dick-slaps me across the face, or both.

If the dick-slap was from Dane, that might answer both. But then, that's not happening, ever. Right? He's done with me, surely. Going along his merry way to dick-dazzle the lucky ladies of Ketchikan, Alaska with his gigantic, magical peen.

He doesn't want me anymore.

He wouldn't try to find me—not after this all-time great performance of self-sabotage.

The man can't possibly be *that* much of a glutton for punishment, can he?

TWO

Dane

MY PHONE RANG, AND I SNATCHED IT UP; THE SCREEN told me it was Jax calling, and I glanced at Raquel and Hamish, who were sitting on the loveseat in the den of the apartment above Badd's Bar and Grille. "It's Jax," I told them, and then swiped to answer. "Jax, buddy, thanks for calling back."

"Let me up, jackass. I'm at the back door."

"You didn't need to come here, dude, we could've done it over the phone."

"I'm an in-person kinda guy, Dane. You know this. I hate being on the phone more than just about any-thing on the planet. Now come down here and open the fuckin' door."

"Coming, coming, keep your shirt on, Jesus." I hung up on him and trotted down to the bar and through the kitchen, unlocking and opening the door to the alley, which was the door the family always used to enter the building.

Jax's vintage Chevy Li'l Red Express pickup was parked in the alley, twin vertical exhaust pipes sticking up above the cab. He had a messenger bag slung over his left shoulder, and he was wearing pressed khakis and a Geek Squad polo; he was a freelance web designer and all-around IT pro, moonlighting as a Geek Squad tech to make ends meet when his freelance gigs left income gaps.

As Uncle Xavier's protégé, he could have his pick of positions within Xavier's tech empire, but he was determined to do so without nepotism, which meant logging a rather morbid and masochistic amount of hours slaving away over piddly jobs from Fiverr or wherever simply to build out his resumé. He has the talent, undoubtedly, and to be honest, most of the family has, at one point or another, told him to just ask his uncle for a damn job, but Jax is stubborn. He's even talked about applying under the name Jax Quinn—his mother's maiden name—to avoid any possibility of nepotism.

Jax pushed past me through the kitchen and upstairs, plopping onto the couch and whipping a laptop out of his bag. He glanced at Raquel and Hamish. "Hey, guys. I'm Jax Badd, Dane's smarter and better-looking cousin. So, I hear we're looking for someone."

Raquel clenched her hands together between her knees, giving him sad puppy dog pleading eyes. "Yeah, my friend, Lindsey Snelling. She took off early this morn-ing or late last night and isn't answering her phone."

Jax frowned. "So, just to be clear, here: how wor-ried about her are we? Like, does she have a history of self-harm? Because if that's the case, you need to contact the authorities, not a sexy nerd with a laptop."

Raquel shrugged. "I know she's had issues in the past, but this doesn't seem like that."

"She does have a semi-colon tattoo on her wrist," I said.

Jax sighed. "Well, I'll see if I can track her down, but if you have any concerns for her well-being, don't wait to send someone with real authority to locate her." He opened his laptop and did something that involved a lot of typing. "Okay, let's start simple. Phone number?"

Raquel rattled off Lindsey's cell number, and Jax went to work. A map popped up on the screen, and a red dot blipped. A second, and a third, and then after a few minutes of processing, the three dots became a triangulation, putting a fourth dot in the center.

"Looks like the last time she had her phone on, she was in…LA. Near…let's see, let me zoom in…" he named some cross-streets that meant nothing to me—I'd been at her apartment, yes, but we'd taken a cab from Rune's parents' house to the restaurant where we had dinner, and then another cab to the bar, and then had walked to her apartment, and I hadn't paid atten-tion to street names. I'd been too focused on her, and on the delicious prospect of getting her fine ass naked.

Raquel sighed. "That's her apartment. She went *home*? The crazy skank-ass ho is *home* and not answering calls or texts? I'm gonna *kill* her!"

"Raquel," I said, going for a placating tone, "she seemed really upset. I don't know what about because she wouldn't tell me shit. I don't know her well enough to know if her level of upset is within normal bounds or not. I just know she wasn't okay. I won't be able to relax until I know she's safe, at least. She doesn't have to talk to or see me, but we *have* to see her face-to-face."

Jax did more computer shit. "Looks like she shut her phone off a few hours ago." He glanced at Raquel. "Want me to sweep her feeds?"

"Sweep her feeds?" Raquel echoed.

"Check her socials," Jax clarified. "If you know her handle on Instagram, I can start there."

Raquel gave him Lindsey's IG handle, and Jax did more computer shit, then leaned back, frowning with a sigh. "She's killed everything. Her Insta is offline, so is her TikTok, Snapchat, everything. She's gone dark."

Raquel covered her face with both hands. "That's not good. She's always been super active online. She basically lives on Instagram."

Hamish was on his phone. "We can get flights out of Ketchikan tomorrow morning at the earliest," he says, his thick Scottish brogue rendering "tomorrow" as *tuh-MOHR-uh* and "earliest" as *EARRRR-Leest*, with a thick, juicy roll of the R.

"Book'em, baby," Raquel said, patting his thigh.

"Get me one," I said. "I'll Venmo you back."

"Three in business, departing at seven…" Hamish muttered under his breath as he booked the flight.

A few minutes later, I had my digital boarding pass on my phone, and had paid Hamish back for the ticket. It burned like hell to have to sit around the rest of the day, worrying, but it was still faster and cheaper to wait and fly tomorrow morning than to leave now and spend three days driving.

Raquel, it turned out, is not much of a morning person. She's not cranky, she's just a zombie. Dressed in a matching crushed pink velvet Juicy Couture track suit, she had her feet stuffed into a pair of Ugg slippers and a silk hat/bonnet sort of thing on her head and giant bug-eye sunglasses on her face. She clung to Hamish's arm with both hands, her backpack-style purse on her back while Hamish and I dragged the luggage; I had a single duffle bag across my back and nothing else, so I willingly helped Hamish with their suitcases—it didn't look like Raquel was even aware of where she was or what was happening, but was just blindly going along with her husband.

We reached our gate with time to spare, and as soon as her ass hit a seat, Raquel tipped her head onto Hamish's burly shoulder and was asleep within seconds.

I grinned at the Scotsman. "She's not much for mornings, huh?"

Hamish chuckled. "Nah, she's no. Gettin' her sweet wee arse out the tent on our honeymoon was always a bit of an ordeal."

"Kinda seems like you could lead her anywhere and she wouldn't notice."

He snorted. "Oh, aye. I could walk her into the fires of Mount Doom with the One Ring, and she'd no notice if it was before noon." He shot me a look. "You're invested in this wee guddle, are y'no? Got to be if you're flyin' all the way to LA to clap eyes on the thrawn lassie."

I stared at him. "Yeah, so I have not a clue what the fuck you just said."

Hamish passed his fingers down through his long red beard. "Guddle means a messy or complicated situation, and thrawn means difficult or hard to please."

I hummed thoughtfully. "I dunno, man. I don't think Lindsey is difficult or hard to please—I think she's just been through some gnarly-ass shit. I just wish she'd talk to me about it instead of blowing me off and ghosting me."

"Get yo ass in line," Raquel muttered, sounding more asleep than awake. "She'll talk to Rune about that mess, but no one else. I don't know much more than you, and I've been her friend for almost four years." She nuzzled closer to Hamish. "And boy, if you walk my half-asleep ass into a volcano, I'll haunt you into the next millennium. You'll *wish* your ass was Gollum by the time I'm done with you."

Hamish sniffed a laugh and kissed the top of her head. "You know I'd walk into the volcano my own self before I let you come to harm."

"Mmm-hmmm," she hums. "I know that's right. Now, if you'll excuse me, my *sweet wee arse*," and here she adopted a funny impression of Hamish's thick burr, "needs a nap. Wake me up when them bitches start boarding." She slides down to rest her head on Hamish's lap, pulls the voluminous hood of her tracksuit hoodie down over her eyes, and was very swiftly snoring with a delicate *huff-snurk*.

Hamish rested one hand on her hip, and with the other toyed with the end of one of her braids, his expression idly affectionate as he watched her sleep.

We sat in silence for awhile, Raquel sleeping, Hamish dozing off while occasionally reading a few pages of a dog-eared Ludlum paperback.

For my part, I let my thoughts wander, and they inevitably wandered back to Lindsey. To that night. It's where my idiot, caveman brain goes, all the time, on repeat, like a tongue probing a sore tooth.

What did I do? Was it something I said? How I said it? How I did it?

I know, I know—the note; *It wasn't you*. Wow, that really clears shit up, thanks a fucking ton, *Lindsey*.

Not.

So then, what was it? Something she went through

at some point in her life, obviously. But why wouldn't she just tell me? Literally *anything*—any amount of explanation at all would help. I don't need her life story, although I'd gladly hear it.

I also found myself revisiting that night for more… prosaic reasons. Or perhaps a better way of putting it is for less emotionally-charged reasons.

It was some seriously top-notch, grade A sex. I mean, look, I…get around, okay? I'm not a man-whore. I don't usually have sex on the first date. I only hook up with randos and tourists once in a while. Maybe "once in a while" is a bit of a stretch, sure, but the point is, I don't go around thinking about individual sex sessions this long after the fact. I might think to myself, "That was hot," the next day. I might tell Dunc about a particularly good night. But still going back to that night *months* later?

Unheard of.

I think I'm trying to figure out what about it was so damn good. Sex is sex, right? We've all got the same parts. The act is the same. Details differ, sure. The particulars of foreplay, the intensity, the duration. It's changeable, mercurial. It's chemistry, right? Some people you just click with, some you don't. Some girls I can read easier than others—their responses, their subtleties of expression, things like that. I dunno. I've turned this over in my head more times than I care to count, also. Why can I not move on from Lindsey? Is it just the abrupt, jarring shift from the hottest sex of my life to being screamed at? Possibly.

The problem is that I have no answers to any of the questions, and that is driving me absolutely fucking batshit insane.

"Now Boarding Zone One," the gate agent announced over the intercom, jarring me out of my thoughts and Raquel from her nap.

We shuffled through the gate, down the jetway, and found our seats—I took the window, Raquel was in the middle, and Hamish was on the aisle.

The flight was much like the wait—quiet, thoughtful. Maddening.

I see her eyes again and again—bright, clear, hypnotic, azure, stunning in their intensely electric blueness. I see her kissing her way down my chest, palms roaming my pecs and shoulders. I see her swiping her tongue teasingly over my hipbone, along the no-man's-land below my navel and above the tip of my cock, my other hipbone. I see the way she grins at me, seductive and eager, as she teasingly flits her tongue against my shaft here and there…and then wraps her mouth around me.

And holy fuck, for the ninety or so seconds before she lost her goddamn mind, that was a stellar fucking blow job. All lips and tongue and saliva, soft and hot and wet, with just the right usage of her hands.

And then?

Screaming.

Hyperventilating.

Inconsolable, angry, terrified—*traumatized*.

Someone hurt her.

Badly.

I don't truck with anyone who hurts women. I was raised to respect women, to protect them, take care of them. Not just my family, not just a woman I happen to be seeing or whatever, but all women. Shit, *all people* deserve respect and basic decency. No one should be hurt or manipulated or disrespected or used. My family has very strong feelings when it comes to men's treatment of women. You hurt a woman in our orbit, we hurt you.

It's very fucking simple.

That's the baseline, the benchmark.

When I think about some faceless shithead doing something horrible enough to Lindsey that she has episodes like that?

I see red.

Fury boils inside me.

I want to punch someone's fucking face in—the shitstain who hurt her, in particular.

It'd be great if I could just focus my memory on the sexy parts, like when she rode me like the penny pony at the grocery store, those big juicy tits bouncing like Jell-O. And to be clear, I fucking love Jell-O.

FUCK.

I have to get some answers. I am fully aware that

I may very well hate the answers once I get them, but that's still better than this total ignorance.

We clambered out of the gray Toyota Sienna driven by Arjun H—a small, quiet Sikh man with a red turban, a fucking fantastic beard, and a wizardly ability to weave through traffic. He thanked us as he handed off our bags, doing that funny little bobble of his head that seemed to mean something I was too ignorant to understand.

Raquel slung her purse over her shoulder and gazed up at the four-story apartment building in a section of West Hollywood inhabited largely by the starry-eyed service industry and gig workers hoping for a shot at glory in the film industry.

She sighed. "Let's get this over with."

Hamish and I followed her to the main entrance of the building—a freakishly good-looking, jacked Black guy in expensive athletic-wear held the door open for us with his brawny brown shoulder, cell phone to his ear as he *uh-huh*'ed his way through a conversation. He gave Raquel a friendly chin-jerk of recognition with an absent-minded smile, and then he was gone in a swirl of cologne and Central Casting charisma.

I recognized the street and the building, but only vaguely; we'd both been pretty tipsy by the time we got back here.

Hamish eyed Raquel as she stabbed the elevator call button. "Y'know him, then?"

Raquel gave him a droll side-eye. "Seen him around a few times, but I don't know him." She arched an eyebrow. "Jealous, baby?"

"Of his perfectly sculpted, hairless, Adonis physique? Nae, love, not hardly."

Raquel snorted and patted his belly. "If that's what I wanted, I would've married that. Guys like him are a dime a dozen in LA, baby. I married *you*—a burly, hairy, red-haired Scotsman with a heart of gold and just enough padding to be the cuddliest man on the planet."

Hamish grumbled something under his breath, but it was in such a thick Scottish slang-laced brogue that I understood precisely none of it.

Raquel just snickered. "You gonna repeat that for the class, my love?"

Hamish just shook his head and mumbled something about showing her padding, which got her giggling breathily and had me wondering if I needed to wait for another elevator, or maybe just take the stairs.

The elevator opened onto a dark, low-ceilinged hallway with gray industrial carpeting on the floor and builder-grade wall sconces that were likely meant to "elevate the aesthetics" or some shit but which really just screamed "lipstick on a pig."

Raquel led us down the hallway, around the corner, and to the farthest end unit, all by itself in a strange corner-nook at the rear of the building.

There was a sheet of printer paper taped to the door, with *"GO AWAY!!"* in size 100 font, bolded, italicized, and underlined.

Hamish chuckled. "Well, I think we know she's here. Unless she has this up year-round?"

Raquel shook her head. "No, this is new." She sighed. "Just…let me do the talking, okay?"

She hesitated, lifted her fist to the door, hesitated again, and then rapped three times.

"READ THE SIGN!" came Lindsey's voice.

"Linz, baby girl, it's Raquel. Let me in, please? I just wanna talk."

"NO!" Lindsey shouted. "GO AWAY!"

"Lindsey, c'mon, honey, it's me. I just want to make sure you're okay."

"I'm not! Go away!"

"Lindsey!"

Silence.

And then a ripped half-sheet of lined notebook paper slid under the door. Written on it in black Sharpie: *I'm alive. I'm not suicidal. I don't want your help. I'll be fine eventually. Go away.*

Raquel dug in her purse, found a pen, flipped the paper over, and wrote on it: *Just let us in, Linz. Talk to us. Please.*

She slipped it back under the door.

Seconds later, it slipped back to us.

She'd scrawled *NO* across Raquel's note in huge, angry block letters.

"Lindsey Snelling, open this damn door!"

"FUCK OFF!" Lindsey screamed. "GO AWAY!"

Hamish squeezed Raquel's hand. "I think maybe she just needs some time and space, my love. She's being pretty fuckin' transparent about that."

Raquel sighed. "You may be right, Hammy." To Lindsey, then. "Girl, you know I love you, and you know I'm here for you. When you need to talk, you know how to find me."

No answer.

"Just go away, Raquel. You too, Hamish." Her voice was quiet, just on the other side of the door.

Raquel gave another heavy sigh and nodded. "Alright, alright. At least I know you're alive and not gonna do anything stupid."

"It's not like that, Kell," Lindsey murmured. "Promise."

"Linz—"

"Kell, please. Just leave me alone. And *do not* bother Rune with this. You know she'll come back early, and I won't have that. Not on my account."

"As long as you promise you'll call me if you start feeling—"

"I won't feel that way, but if I do, I'll call you. Promise."

"Fine. Then we're going. But girl, you owe me *some* kinda answers, someday."

"Get in line, Kell."

"There's just one thing you should know before we—"

"RAQUEL!"

Despite a door between them, Raquel held her hands up, palms out, in a gesture of surrender. "Alright, alright. Have it your way."

Hamish patted me on the back. "I'll text you later, laddie," he whispered. "Good luck with that bird. You'll need it."

Raquel squeezed my arm. "Maybe just leave her, Dane. She clearly doesn't want to talk about it." This is whispered as well.

"I can hear you whispering!" Lindsey shouted

"I'm good," I whispered back. "Just go."

Hamish and Raquel took their leave, and I was alone in the corner/hallway.

"Kell?" came Lindsey's voice a solid minute later. "You still there?"

I sat down on the floor, put my back to the door. "Nope. Just me."

"Dane?"

"The one and only."

"Did you miss the part where I said to go away and leave me alone?"

"Nope."

"So, if it applies to one of my best friends, why would it not apply to you?"

"Oh, I'm sure it does," I said. "I'm just choosing to ignore that."

"Dane—"

"Lindsey, I'm not leaving."

"Dammit, Dane. I'm not letting you in. I want to be alone."

"Fine. You can be alone in there, and I'll be alone out here."

"Fuck me," she muttered.

"I did. It was fantastic. Wanna go again?"

"DANE!"

"No? Okay, then."

"Dane."

"Linz?"

"What do you want?"

"A million dollars. A Ferrari. Peace on Earth and Goodwill Toward Men."

"Dane. Please. Just answer the fucking question."

"I did."

"WHAT DO YOU WANT FROM ME, FUCKNUT?" she shouted.

"To talk."

"Answers. You want answers."

"Yes. But I'll settle for just a civilized, adult conversation."

"No."

"Then I'm not leaving."

"I could have you arrested for loitering or harassment or something."

"Fine. Do it. Hamish and Raquel will bail me out, and I'll be right back here."

"Dane Badd. Don't be impossible."

"It's too *LAAAAATE* to apolog*iiiiize*—" I sang, intentionally off-key.

"Oh god, please don't sing."

"Then let me in."

"NO!"

I queued up "I'll Be Watching You" by Sting and the Police, played it, and sang along, loudly and again terribly on purpose, just to be an annoying fuck.

"Jesus H Christ," she muttered. "You sound like a dying donkey."

I cackled. "You can stop it anytime you want, babe."

I launched into "Hit Me, Baby One More Time" in a falsetto that could get me indicted for attempted murder.

"JESUS, DANE! Shut the fuck up already!"

"Then let me in so we can talk."

"Not happening!"

"Okay. So, a rabbi, a priest, and an imam walk into a bar—"

"Ohmygod," she murmurs. "Shoot me now."

"What is this? says the bartender," I continued, "some kind of joke?"

"Jesus fucking Christ, Dane. I *will* have you arrested and hancuffed."

"How'd you know I have a bondage kink?" I asked.

Her silence was conspicuously loud.

"That was a joke," I said. "Please don't tie me up."

"Dane, for real. I'm fine. Just go away."

"Well, I'm not fine," I answered. "You got me fucked up."

"Dane, that's not fair."

"Not *fair*?" I couldn't stop the rant from tumbling out. "I've spent every day since that night wondering *what the fuck* I did wrong. What I could have done differently."

"Dane, I left you—"

"A note," I interrupted. "I know. "It wasn't me. But pardon me if that doesn't help *at fucking all*."

"Dane—"

"You can tell me it's not me all you want, doesn't mean my subconscious is going to fucking listen. I get that you're a woman, so this might be difficult for you to understand, but when a girl has a complete nervous breakdown mid-blow job, it tends to make you wonder what it is about you that caused the breakdown."

"Dane, it wasn't—"

"I fucking *know*, Lindsey. Try telling it to my psyche."

"Goddammit," I hear her hiss. "Now you're guilt-tripping me?"

"Yup."

"Asshole." A long pause. "What if I'm incapable of giving you the answers you want?"

"How do you know if you won't try?" I countered.

She didn't answer. I settled against her door, turned on a playlist of my favorite music to annoy people with: black metal. Lots of screeching and other fun noises that most sane people can't stand, but I, being less than sane, happen to enjoy.

"What the *fuck* is that sound?" she demands.

"'Cradle of Filth', obviously. Nymphetamine is a classic banger."

"Turn it off, Jesus fuck, man."

I turned my volume all the way up and put the speaker to the gap between the door and the floor.

"DANE!"

"That's not how you were saying it that night," I quipped.

"Really, asshole?"

"Really, bitch."

"You did not."

"I did."

"You can't call me a bitch."

"But you can call me an asshole?"

"Yup." A sigh. "You're really, actually going to sit outside my door and be as obnoxious as possible until I let you in, aren't you?"

"You've guessed correctly!" I said in my best game show announcer voice. "Tell her what she's won, Bob!"

"An all expenses paid trip to a remote desert island where I can be LEFT THE FUCK ALONE?" she said. "Perfect!"

"Nope, just me being an obnoxious piece of shit."

"So your natural state, then?"

"Yup."

"Dane, please. All jokes aside. I really just need some time."

"I hear you," I said. "I really, really do. I just happen to disagree."

"You disagree with what I need?"

"I disagree that that's what you need."

"But—but—"

"You can refuse to give me word one of an explanation for what happened, my fault or not. That's your right. It's my right to feel like I should get *something*. If you never want to see me again, that can be arranged. *After* you let me in."

"You do realize *you're* the reason I ran away? Not because of what happened—that's not your fault. You didn't do anything wrong. But this—what you're doing right now. *This* is why I ran away. I don't know how to give you the answers you want, even if you do deserve them."

"Then we're at an impasse." I took pity on her and turned off the playlist, trading it for the Canary album from a few years ago that won all those Grammys.

"Oh, now that's just mean," Lindsey groaned. "Busting out Canary? Really?"

"It's a good album!" I said.

"No shit it is," she mutters. "It won like six Grammys. That's not the point."

"Then what, pray tell, *is* the point?"

"Pray tell? Okay, Shakespeare."

"The point is," she grumbles, "I listened to this album on repeat every day for a month. It got me through a seriously hard time in my life."

"Wait, really?"

"Yeah. A breakup."

"Oh, shit. It was supposed to be funny. They're my aunt and uncle."

Silence, then: "Funny, Dane. Good one."

"Um, I'm not kidding?"

"You're not?"

"That's a weird thing to make up, isn't it?"

"Well, yeah. But have you met you?"

I laughed. "Good point, but Canary really is my aunt and uncle. Canaan and Aerie—Canary."

"So? Everyone knows where the name came from."

"What, I need to prove who my relations are?"

"Yeah. I mean, what's next? More famous relatives?"

I laughed uncomfortably. "Well…?"

"Shut the fuck up." A pause. "Who?"

"Harlow Grace is my aunt, and her husband is my uncle, Xavier Badd."

A heavy sigh. "Oh, come on. Really?"

"Rune didn't tell you? Dunc got Uncle Xavier and Aunt Low to let Raquel and Hamish sleep on their yacht before my other uncle flew them to Anchorage for the wedding."

"It must have slipped her mind," she deadpanned. "The bitch. Keeping piping hot tea like that to herself?"

"I don't think it was intentional, Linz. There was sort of a lot going on."

"She spent the night on a yacht owned by HARLOW GRACE and Xavier Badd?"

"Yes."

"She could have told me."

"I believe you know about my sister Emerson marrying Hunter Hawkins."

"We're not talking about that. I've never met this Emerson person, but she stole my dream man."

"You and most of the women in the country, and more than a few of the men," I said, laughing.

"What the fuck is with your family, though?" she asked. "Every male I saw or met at the wedding was fucking hot as hell. Even the old dudes were silver foxes. The one with the salt-and-pepper beard and all the tattoos in the front row? Mmmmm-*mmmm*! Yummy."

"My *father*, you mean?"

"Oh. Um. Sorry, not sorry, your dad is hot A-F, for an old dude. The women all made me feel frumpy, too."

I just laughed. "You could never be frumpy." I paused as something occurred to me. "Literally, my entire family was there. How did you not realize that they're related to me?"

"Honestly? I just thought they were guests, like someone knew someone well-connected or something. I didn't realize they were your relatives."

"It was a family-only wedding, Linz."

"There were dozens of people there! How was I supposed to know you have the world's biggest family?"

"I guess that's valid."

A long silence.

I felt her on the other side of the door. Heard a

sniffle. "Dane, I…" A sigh. "You're really not gonna leave me alone, are you?"

"Nope."

"Fuck. *Fine*."

I heard a deadbolt thunk, but I was too slow in reacting to stop myself from slumping backward as she opened the door—my head hit the floor with a thud.

I looked up—bare legs. More bare legs. Jesus, so much leg—bare, curvy…and a little prickly from being unshaven, if I'm honest. Not that I cared, mind you. She was wearing a plain white T-shirt that looked sort of familiar—it was too big, hanging just low enough to cover all the good stuff. The oversized bagginess of it couldn't hide the monstrous size and melon-shaped perfection of her glorious tits, though, swinging free and unhindered behind the shirt as they were.

"Hey, that's my shirt," I said.

"Not anymore." She backed up, pressing a hand over her crotch. "And stop trying to see up my shirt, Dane."

"Why? Because I haven't seen it already?"

"Not the point." She put a foot on my chest and applied a tiny amount of pressure. "Come on, perv."

THREE

Lindsey

H<small>E WAS *IN MY APARTMENT.*</small>
Where I eat and sleep and poop and walk around naked and talk to myself out loud in terrible accents and *do not ever ever ever* have boys over.

It's my sanctuary. My safe space. My home.

Boys do not come here. Boys do not cross the threshold. Shit, no boy even knows my address. Or, didn't. When I lived with Damian, we lived in an apartment we shared, new to both of us. When we broke up, it just happened to coincide with the end of the lease, so I let him take over the contract and found this place.

Look, it's not a sexy loft in Echo Park or a Brentwood condo with soaring ceilings and acres of natural light. It's a shitty West Hollywood one-bedroom that I can still barely afford on a cocktail waitress's income. But it's *mine*.

Dane Badd should not be here.

Yet there he was, lying partly over the threshold, staring up at me with those stupid, big, deep, brown eyes in that stupid, angular, rugged, handsome face.

I'm only panicking a little.

Or a lot.

Turning away, I scanned the apartment for anything embarrassing—which was…oh. Oh boy.

Everything.

It's a marker of how fucked up I was that my place was this messy —I'm normally a clean freak. Yet since coming back less than seventy-some hours ago, I've done precisely dick other than DoorDash myself chimichangas and binge *Love Is Blind*. Granted, my version of messy is most people's version of spotless. But, there were dirty panties on the floor of my bathroom, literally all my bras were hanging off the doorknob of my bedroom, and a Styrofoam clamshell full of day-old tortilla chips was on the kitchen counter.

I think that's all.

Guess we'll find out, because if I know anything about Dane Badd, if there's something embarrassing, he'll find it.

With a grunt, he went from lying down to standing up without using his hands, which is harder than it sounds. He stepped inside and shut the door, and then scanned the place.

Thrift store couch, a tan fake suede thing that sagged in the middle in such a way as to suck you in and never let you go. Mismatched thrift store recliner and love seat. A sweet 72" flat screen that was a Christmas gift to me from Mom and Dad Rigby last year. A truly, shockingly shitty coffee table, a 90s relic of that ugly oak they made literally everything out of—on which was a clutter of clamshells, empty Spindrift cans, and a partially empty box of wine.

Yes, I said box. It's cheap, plentiful, and not half bad. And I'm sad and lonely and desperately fighting off a real, actual emotional, existential crisis.

"Sweet place," he muttered, settling onto the couch. "Whoa. Okay. Guess I'm sitting in the middle." This last was because the couch sucked him down, as it does.

"Sorry about the couch, it has a mind of its own," I said. "And you don't have to pretend. I know it's a shithole."

He picked up a juice glass that had an inch or so of wine in the bottom, sniffed it, sniffed it again, and then shrugged. "Fuck it." He tossed back the dregs and refilled the glass a little more than halfway, and then sat back, kicked his feet up, and grinned at me. "It's a sweet place. Wasn't lying."

"Okay, buddy," I said in a deep, mocking voice.

He frowned at me. "What? It is. It's yours. It's clean, dry, and seems to be free of mice, rats, and roaches." He gestured at my little cluster of succulents on the windowsill across the room. "You've even got some greenery."

"Oh. Uh. Thanks I guess?"

"I still live with Mommy and Daddy, so." He shrugged.

I stood with my back to the door, wondering if he was really that oblivious to my inner turmoil at having him in my space. My hands were clammy, my chest felt tight, my eyes burned, and I wanted to curl up in a ball at the bottom of my bathtub.

Instead, I just sort of stood there like an awkward ditz, staring at the gorgeous male on my couch, who was currently sipping my cheap box wine and inspecting the contents of a bag of Doritos with his hands.

"Make yourself at home," I muttered. "No problem."

He grinned at me, the cocky dingdong. And yes, despite my tumultuous, trauma-addled state of mind, that grin still moistened my panties. "You know what we're gonna do?"

"I shudder to ask," I said, deadpan.

He grabbed my remote, turned on my TV, pulled up Netflix, and turned on a cheesy, early-aughts rom-com. He tossed the remote aside, stuffed my bag of Cool Ranch Doritos in the V of his manspreaded thighs, rested my juice glass full of my wine on his big, hard, beefy thigh, and settled in to watch a movie—on my couch, in my apartment.

What the fuck?

"Um, Dane?"

He patted the couch. "You can't watch the movie from over there."

"But I—"

He poured wine into a different, pre-used glass and held it out to me. "C'mon. I don't bite...in this context."

I rolled my eyes at the innuendo but didn't otherwise acknowledge it—with Dane, it's best not to encourage him. "Sure, Dane, come on in, make yourself at home, help yourself to my wine and chips. Yes, yes, this is what I need. You know me so well." This was all said monotone.

He smirked at me. "You jest, I realize, but sometimes we don't actually know what we really need."

I arched an eyebrow at him. "He says to the woman with a degree in psychology."

"Oh, is this your office where you have your practice?"

I narrowed my eyes at him. "I wanted to be a researcher, not a therapist."

"Wanted, past tense? Not anymore?"

I sighed and sat beside him, finally taking the cup of wine. "You know it's not even noon?"

"Yeah, well, fuck it. YOLO or some shit, I dunno. Who fuckin' cares? Sometimes, we just need to day drink."

I sipped and watched as a hot young girl fresh out of grad school wafted adorably around her million-dollar Manhattan condo that she somehow afforded on a fashion magazine intern's non-salary. Oh, look at those dorky glasses, she's so ugly, she needs a hot, funny, charming guy to make her see her own self-worth, so she finally gets contacts so she can be attractive to anyone at all, because she's so ugly in those *spectacles*, you ugly fat loser.

Fuck, I hate rom-coms.

I made it until our plucky heroine bumped her silicone G-cups into the square-jawed hunk's chest, tittering like a demented songbird.

"You actually like this shit?" I asked.

He frowned. "Fuck no. It's lame as hell. I thought you would."

"What, because I'm a chick, I have to watch romantic comedies and pine about the love life I don't have?"

He pulled a face. "Well…yeah?"

"Wow. Nice. Sexist fuck."

He nodded. "Cool, cool. So what do you want to watch?" He widened his eyes. "Please, *please* don't say reality TV."

I put *The Bachelor* on, just to fuck with him. "You barged into my place, jackass. You don't get to complain about my choice of entertainment."

He made it through a cocktail party and half a dozen confessionals before groaning. "The rom-com was better. Can we settle on something else? Golf? The Paint Drying channel? Adam Sandler movies? *Saw Three*?"

I frown at him. "You did not just put Adam Sandler in with that other shit, sir. No, you did not."

"What? He's not that funny."

"SACRILEGE!" I shouted.

"He's not! He's just himself in everything."

"And himself is fucking funny, *DANE*. It's not his fault you're a lame ass loser with shit taste in movies. You probably don't like Will Ferrell either."

"*Anchorman* is a classic."

"Fine. You can stay. But don't diss my boy Adam. Have you seen any of his newer, more dramatic stuff? He's a damn good actor."

Dane groaned. "Please god, no."

"Oh yes." I picked a recent Sandler release and started it. "You watch this with me and give it an honest chance, and I'll let you pick the next one, no questions asked."

"You've got yourself a deal," he said.

Which is how I found myself shoving my hand between his legs for the next four hours. For Cool Ranch Doritos, granted, and not his big fat salami, but hey, you gotta start somewhere.

No, no, no—bad girl, Linz. You *do not* want Dane's big fat salami. Not now, not ever. Off-limits.

As if on cue, while I was scolding myself, he adjusted his junk, reaching down his pants and shifting said girthy kielbasa off his thigh.

Gah, fuck me. Stop thinking about the penis, woman. It's not that hard.

Not yet, it's not. Let me get my hands on it and—

NO.

Bad.

Bad girl.

Spank me, daddy.

FUCK.

I shot to my feet abruptly, inadvertently knocking Dane's wine all over his faded, perfectly fitted blue jeans that had just the right amount of rips, and which cupped his beefy thighs and rock-hard ass like a second skin.

So now he was on his feet, staring down at the red wine stain on his crotch and thighs.

"I…shit, sorry. My fault." I hurried into the kitchen, snagged half a dozen sheets of paper towel, hurried back, and started patting at his groin.

He grabbed my wrists after a second. "Linz?"

I realized what I was doing—rubbing at his dick with paper towels—and leaped away. "Sorry, sorry. Sorry. I'm a spaz."

He indicated the dark brown leather duffel bag on the floor just inside the doorway. "I'll just change real quick. Maybe Mom can get the stain out later."

"Really?" I asked. "Mama still does your laundry?"

He stuck his tongue out at me. "No, Lindsey. I do my own laundry. But she's better at stains than I am. She can get just about anything out. So if I have a bad stain, yeah, I let my mother help."

"I suppose that's valid." I gestured at the door to my room. "Bathroom is through there."

He rummaged in his bag and came up with a

folded article of clothing, vanishing into my bathroom. A moment later, he emerged wearing a pair of gray sweatpants.

Yes, really.

The cruelty is real, I tell you.

Big fat salami? Outlined. Swaying heavily with every step. Was he even wearing underwear? The way that monster sausage of his pushed against the material, I couldn't believe he was.

Why do you hate me, God?

I snatched his jeans out of his hand, took my stain-removing basket from the closet where I kept it, and sprayed the stain with multiple products. I caught his look and rolled my eyes. "I'm not your mother, but I too deal with stains, Dane."

He frowned. "Okay?"

"Period blood? Every woman deals with it, Dane. We're experts at bloodstain removal. That's why you shouldn't fuck with us."

"Oh, right." He shook his head. "You don't have to do that. I'm not worried about the jeans."

One of the primary reasons, aside from cost and location, that I picked this apartment was the in-unit stacked washer and dryer. Having laundry capability in your apartment is the peak of luxury, I tell you.

Towel warmers? For peasants.

Marble floors? Plebeian bullshit.

In-unit stackable washer and dryer? Gold standard in luxury.

I ran his jeans and then went to use the facilities myself.

Which is when I saw it.

My clit stimulator. Right there on the counter next to the sink, where I left it after washing it last time I used it…an hour ago, along with a box of tampons from when my period *finally* started; it had, fortunately, been abbreviated, as well, likely due to my emotional stress level, lately.

While thinking about the very same big fat salami currently wiggling a jaunty hello at me from the confines of his gray sweatpants.

Oh, god. Shoot me now.

I did my business, washed my hands, and put the toy away in the drawer beside my bed. Sat beside Dane on the couch.

"I didn't know I left it out," I heard myself blurt, apropos of nothing.

He didn't have to ask what I was talking about. "None of my business. I wasn't gonna say anything."

"But you saw it."

"Well, yeah." He frowned at me. "To be honest, I wasn't sure what I was looking at, at first."

I pulled a face at him. "You've never seen one of those before?"

He shrugged. "Nope. My sisters were both pretty vicious about Dunc and me staying out of their rooms growing up, so if they had them, I wouldn't have seen them—and thank god for that, because I *do not* want to have that visual in my fucking headJesusCriminy-it'stoolatefuckme." The last sentence was uttered all in a rush, head in his hands. "God*dammit*."

"It's a clitoral stimulator, Dane," I said.

"It's a vibrator," he said, snorting.

"No, it's not. It's a clitoral stimulator."

"What's the difference?"

I held up one finger, went into my room, brought out the device in question, and my other favorite toy, Mr. Big—a giant purple vibrator the size of a county fair first prize-winning zucchini with nine different settings, including one that made the whole thing rotate, for some reason. Like, to imitate a dick that can... umm...swivel around inside you? You know, like real dicks do?

I tossed said vibrator at Dane—he caught it instinctively, and then, realizing what it was, fumbled in pure horror.

"JESUS FUCK, woman!" He quickly recovered from his horror and held the device by the bottom end, examining it, turning it this way and that. He powered it on and started cycling through the settings—low vibe, medium vibe, fast vibe, pussy-punisher vibe, and then a series of baffling staccato patterns. Who uses the S-O-S pattern, anyway? I tried it once, and my orgasm got confused and ran away like a bitch, and I spent the rest of the day in a sour, climax-denied funk.

When he got to the setting where the whole slightly-curved silicone device rotated like a beef frank on one of those gas station heaty-rolly dudes, he arched an eyebrow at me. "The fuck is this supposed to do?"

I cackled. "Honestly, I have no idea." I pointed at the device in his hands. "The point is, *that* is a vibrator." I held up the clitoral stimulator. "*This* is not."

"So what's the difference?" He asked.

I blinked at him. "You're genuinely asking?"

He shrugged. "Yeah? Why wouldn't I be?"

"Guys get weird about women and their sex toys, in my experience," I told him.

"Really?"

I snickered sarcastically. "Uh, yeah."

"How so?"

"Again, you really want to know?"

"Again, yeah."

"Okay, well, to answer your second question first, a vibrator is a dildo that vibrates—it's a fake penis that jiggles really fast, more or less. It goes inside my vagina and feels good when it goes buzz buzz. Sort of like sex, but not exactly." I held up the stimulator. "This is a clitoral stimulator. It uses suction, basically, to stimulate the clit. Thus the name. It feels more like having someone go down on you, but not as wet. And honestly, not quite as good, if you compare it to a guy who knows what he's doing."

Dane didn't have to say anything, but I could tell he was thinking the same thing as me: that I knew, and he knew, and I knew that he knew that I knew that he very, very, *very* much knew what he was doing.

I think I confused myself with that one.

Point is, I took one look at him, and the only thing I could think of was the screaming, quivering, jelly-legs orgasms he gave me with his mouth: stellar. Ten out of ten, would recommend.

If only there wasn't such a fraught, emotional freight train of baggage between us; if only I wasn't such a disaster; if only I was capable of the slightest, most infinitesimal amount of emotional vulnerability.

"So, back to the first question," Dane prompted. "Dudes being weird about sex toys."

I pointed at him. "Well, you proved it just now. I tossed you that vibrator and you reacted like I'd tossed you a live grenade—or more to the point, a real, live dick. It's not an actual penis, Dane. You're not gonna suddenly be gay and want to put in your butt because you touched a fucking vibrator for point-two seconds."

He frowned at me, but it was a thoughtful frown. "I see your point."

"Let me ask you this," I said. "Have you ever incorporated a sex toy into sex with someone?"

He shook his head. "No. I guess…I guess I've always thought of sex toys like vibrators or clit stimulators to be for solo play. Like, we've got each other, so why would we need extra gadgets?"

"Which is totally valid. But let's say you're hooking up with a girl and she's hot, she's into you, things are going well, but…she just can't quite reach orgasm."

"I'd be asking what I was doing wrong," he said.

"Sure, of course. But what if she says you're not doing anything wrong—it's legitimately not you, it's just that she has a hard time reaching orgasm. What if she asked how you'd feel if she used one of these," I gestured with the stimulator, "during sex?"

He frowned again, and—to his credit—spent a while truly considering the question. "Hmmm. I guess…yeah, I like to think I'd be willing to try it and see how it goes. A part of me would probably feel like she was pandering to my ego by saying it's not me, though. Like, making my partner feel good is low-key more important to me than me feeling good. Like, I know I'm going to come, and I know it's going to be good. But it's not a guarantee with women."

I laughed. "Yet you'd still take it personally if you couldn't get your partner off, even though you know that to be true."

He chuckled. "Yeah, you caught me in that one." He sobered, eying the dildo. "Now, if I'm honest, I'd probably feel weirder about it if she wanted to bust that monster out during sex. Like, yo, babe, where the *fuck* do you think *that* thing is going?"

"Awww c'mon, Dane," I said, giggling, "you mean to tell me you're not into being pegged by a dildo the size of a horse's cock?"

"Yeah, no. Nope. Not into that. No shade to anyone who is, but I'm not."

I patted him on the arm. "That's my point. You're more open to it than other guys I've talked to about this, and you're still weird about it. Most guys I've talked to about this wouldn't even *consider* letting me bring out a toy during sex."

"Why not?" Dan asked.

"Why did you hesitate when I asked?"

A pause, and a slow exhale. "I guess…" a clearing of his throat. "The brutally honest answer is feeling threatened. Which sounds really fuckin' pathetic when I say it out loud. Jesus. But…yeah, that's it."

"Threatened by an inanimate object?" I asked, not even attempting to not sound derisive.

He shrugged. "It's not jealousy, exactly, not like I'd be jealous if you were ghosting me and fucking some other dude. It's…god, how do I put it? You wanting to bust out a vibrator during sex triggers a feeling of inadequacy. Like why am I not good enough? We as men feel like our manhood, our *virility*, is the core of our identity. That's why erectile dysfunction is so debilitating."

I arched an eyebrow at him. "Because you've experienced ED?"

"Not ED, no, but I've had the li'l fella not work before. It sucks. It's embarrassing. Makes you feel like a useless sad sack of shit."

I blinked at this revelation. "Whiskey dick is all too common, and unless the girl you were trying to hook up with was a class-A bitch, she wouldn't rag on you about it."

He actually flushed. "Not talkin' about whiskey

dick, as a matter of fact. And I'm confiding in you, Linz. This shit is seriously hard to talk about."

I felt a heat in my throat, a thrum of panic in my belly. "Oh. I…oh."

He stood up and paced across the room, and went to stand by the window. "To this day, I still don't know the exact cause of what happened. Just stress, maybe?" He sighed. "It can be hard, sometimes, being in my family. Delia and Duncan both know and have always known what they want out of life—they love the bar. They love bartending. They love being part of the family business, the history, and all that shit. I just…don't. It's not for me. I'm proud of the family business, and I can, have, and will pitch in and help when I'm needed, but tending or managing one of the Badd bars is just not my career path. The shitty thing is, I don't know what my path *is*, just that it's not that." He glanced at me. "This is relevant, I promise. Sunni, my sister Emerson, is the same, but she has talents, you know? She's a badass. And then there's me. No clue what I want. No obvious talents. Like, sure, I'm pretty athletic, but I'm not a football hero or some shit. I'm not going pro is my point. I'm taking classes at UAS Ketchikan. Gen Ed classes, mostly. I was in the middle of studying for finals, and I had this algebra class."

I fake gagged. "Fuck math."

He snorted at my reaction. "Exactly. Fuck math. My other classes weren't hard, exactly, but I still had to study to pass the finals. Not like I had to cram for the algebra final, but still a lot of studying. I was stressed the fuck out because I just couldn't get this one set of problems. I'd worked through them half a dozen times, and I was just missing some step or some shit, I dunno. Didn't have the answer in my notes, and I didn't have any phone numbers for anyone in my class. So I was freaking the fuck out. If I fucked that whole section, I'd fail the final *and* the class. And my family? We do *not* fail. It's not like Mom and Dad are breathing down my neck threatening to crucify me if I fail a math class, but you just…everyone in my family is so goddamned *successful*. It was fucking my head to pieces. So I thought, eh, fuck it, I'll take a break. Wound up at a party on a houseboat, chatting up this girl. She was backpacking North America or some lunacy like that. She'd hiked from LA to Ketchikan and was planning on hiking east across Canada. I dunno. Sounded pretty fuckin' ambitious to me, but whatever. She was leaving in a day or two, so it felt like a pretty good way to relax, y'know? Blow off some steam."

"Makes sense to me," I said. "I'd do the same thing."

"I wasn't drunk. I was barely even tipsy. I was into her." He eyed me, hesitating.

I rolled my eyes. "Just tell it like I'm a bro, Dane."

He chuckled. "Fine. She was hot as fuck, okay? Nice body, pretty face, great hair. She was interesting, too. I *genuinely* liked her, like as a person, not just because she had a great rack but when we started making

out, I just…my dick didn't work. I…even after getting her top off, nothing. Not even a twitch behind
the zipper—nada. She tried to help, god bless her. But
I just…I felt like I was gonna cum, but I never even got
to a half-chub. It was fucking mortifying. I had no excuse. Wasn't drunk, hadn't even been drinking booze,
just a few beers. I was intentionally not getting lit because I had finals. I just…*fuck*, it was *horrible*. She was
a sweetheart about it, though. I promised her it wasn't
her, and she was nice as hell about it. Didn't say a word
of criticism or whatever. She did cut out pretty fast,
though, and I'm pretty sure she ended up with someone else on the boat. I went home and went back to
studying, feeling like a complete and total loser." He
exhaled roughly, scrubbing his face with both hands.
"Never told anyone about that, not even Dunc." He
glanced at me. "Not sure why I told you, to be honest."

I couldn't help myself—I stood behind him and
up close on his left side. "I think if anyone can get how
that feels, Dane, it would be me."

He shot me a look over his shoulder. "Oh yeah?"

"Look, I get what you're saying about sex and
identity. More so than you can know. Men and their
penises, right? Just going back to the sex toy topic real
quick—I get what you're saying. If you take pride in
being able to please and satisfy your partner, her needing or wanting something more than you, I can see
how that would be a little…threatening. But that's not
what it is, for me."

He frowned at me. "But that night, Linz. Unless you were faking it, and I really don't think you were, you had no problems getting off with me, and you didn't use a toy."

I swallowed hard. "I wasn't faking, I promise. I've never, *ever* faked an orgasm. I wouldn't. I'm not here to protect some dude's fragile little ego by pretending he made me come when he didn't."

"I know," he murmured. "That tracks with what I know about you."

"You…" I bit my lip, started over. "I didn't have any problems with you. Maybe I'm just more comfortable with you? I dunno, Dane. That's…that's partly why I bolted. It was intense—too intense, almost. You made me feel like no one else I've hooked up with ever has. It scared me. But I do have trouble reaching orgasm during sex. Not all the time, but pretty frequently. I don't always know why, either. You'd think it'd be a chemistry thing, like some guys I feel better with than others, right? But I've had trouble with guys I felt pretty safe with, and no trouble with guys I felt…I mean, safe, but not…not as strong of a connection, I guess."

"Sex is complicated—the human body is complicated," Dane said. "And I know with women, especially, it's super connected to your emotional or mental state. Or maybe emotional *and* mental state is a better way to put it."

"Facts," I said. "I wish I had more answers, but I don't. I just know that there's been quite a few situations where I would have liked to have been able to use a toy during sex. I'd have been able to finish instead of feeling stuck and frustrated. And it's not about you—meaning, who I'm with." I frowned. "I mean, maybe it is, in a way. But it's *me...my* body. And if I want to use a toy, it's not a statement about *your* lack of performance or ability. It's not that I'm not enjoying it. I just...sometimes it's hard for me to get there, and a toy would help. And honestly, in those situations, a toy would benefit both of us. I'd come faster, and maybe even more than once. I wouldn't feel frustrated, and I'd want it again. Which means more sex with me for you."

Dane spent a while considering this. "That... makes sense," he said eventually. "You've definitely given me something to think about." He laughed. "You know, I don't remember how we got on this topic." A wave of his hand. "Doesn't matter."

I waited—expecting questions. Demands for answers. Instead, he turned, took my hand, and returned us to the couch. Handed me the remote. "I know you picked that show just to be a dick, Linz. Now pick something you actually want to watch."

"You won't like it," I warn.

"You don't know that."

I sighed. "Fine, but don't say I didn't warn you."

I put on *Love is Blind* because I had four episodes left in the season before the reunion aired in a day or two, and I wanted to be caught up. But, of course, I had to pause it and explain the show to him so he'd have a clue what was going on.

"So…they never saw each other, just talked to each other in the cubicles?" he asked.

"The pods, yes."

"And *then* they get engaged, which is when they meet in person for the first time?"

"Right," I said, "And then they live together to see if their relationship survives."

"Does it work?"

I shrugged. "I think they have a better percentage of successful relationships than other dating shows, but most don't, so no, not really."

"Interesting," he said. "Well, play that shit, babe. You've got my interest."

"Wait, really?"

He nodded. "Yeah, it's an interesting premise. I still think dating shows as a genre are sadistic bullshit, but this sounds kinda different."

We talked as much as we watched. We drank box wine, ate junk food, and talked about dating shows and reality TV in general. He told me some stories—which seemed highly unlikely to be true—about his family history when it came to relationships.

"Wait, so…your Aunt Joss fell into the Passage in the middle of the winter, your uncle Lucian jumped in and saved her…and *that's* their meet-cute? *That's* how they met? And they're still together?"

"I mean, there's a lot more to it, but yeah. All my

aunts and uncles have these crazy, interesting stories. Shit, Delia met Hunter when he came up here to try and buy out our company."

I groaned. "Can we not talk about Hunter Hawkins, please?"

He cackled. "And why would that be, Lindsey?"

"Because I've harbored a not-so-secret crush on the man for years…as in I used to make collages of cut-outs of him from magazines back in his billionaire playboy days." I covered my face. "And now he's married to my best friend's husband's sister. It just feels like a cruel, cosmic joke."

Dane, to my surprise, didn't make fun of me. "Yeah, I get it. Hawk is…he's even cooler in real life. It can be hard to not feel a little inferior around the pretty bastard, to be honest."

"Hawk? You call him *Hawk*?" I groaned. "Come *on.*"

"It's his nickname for friends and family. Although Dee doesn't call him that." He laughed. "You really do have it bad, don't you?"

"I do. It's embarrassing. I know it's dumb. I've always known it was just a stupid, childish celebrity crush. It's just a funny irony that he ends up in the orbit of my life."

The conversation tapered off, then, as I got more and more drowsy. I felt myself slipping toward sleep and then nodding off. At some point, I became vaguely aware that the TV sounds had shifted from my show to what sounded like a nature documentary. Something firm was under my cheek. Warm, firm, and more comfortable than any pillow.

Three-quarters asleep, I found myself wondering at something: at no point since he'd been here had Dane made any kind of move or play. Even his flirtation was restrained, and I had a feeling flirty was a core trait for him. He hadn't touched me. Hadn't asked any hard or deep questions. Hadn't demanded answers as to why I'd behaved like I had, even though he'd been pushing for those answers when he was on the other side of the door.

He'd just…hung out with me.

"Dane?" I mumbled.

"Yeah, Linz?"

"I thought you were going to demand answers."

"Changed my mind."

"I thought you'd try to kiss me or something."

"Much as a big part of me wants to more than anything…no."

"Why? To both."

His arm encircled my shoulder, held me against him. "Because that's not what you need right now, Lindsey."

I felt a hot bubble in my throat. Turmoil in my heart. Confusion in my mind.

I let him in, fully expecting to have to explain why I'm not in a frisky mood. I expected to have to unearth all my shit for him, because he absolutely deserves an explanation.

Instead, he was just…my friend.

When it would appear, that's exactly what I needed.

Dane rotated ninety degrees on the couch, taking me with him as he stretched out. My face was on his chest, his arm slung low over my back. He snagged the blanket off the back of the couch and draped it over us both.

"…the albatross pair will spend the next sixty to eighty days taking turns incubating the single, precious egg. The female will lay her egg and immediately fly away to find food while her mate incubates the egg. When she returns, it will be the male's turn…"

Sleep dragged me under, then, and it was a deep, sound, dreamless sleep.

FOUR

Dane

I WOKE UP SWEATING AND THIRSTY BUT REFRESHED. AND confused.

Where the fuck was I?

There was an unfamiliar weight on my chest. Warmth. Softness. Someone snoring softly—a nearly silent inhale and a long exhale at the back of the throat.

I opened my eyes—Lindsey Snelling was fast asleep on my chest. One hand was cupping the side of my neck, her nose nuzzling my throat. I felt her breath huff hot on my skin.

Then, as my gaze traveled south, problems arose.

Her T-shirt—mine, which she had found and kept—had rucked up in her sleep and was now crumpled up above her hips. Which revealed the fact that she hadn't been wearing a damned thing under it. As in, that sweet, big, juicy, firm, plump, round ass was bare in all its magnificent glory.

And my hands were cupping it. I squeezed—god-damn, it was perfect. I groaned softly, not wanting to wake her but unable to stop the sound of appreciation from emerging.

Hands off the ass, Dane, I told myself.

I didn't listen to me, naturally.

No, instead, I copped another feel. A slow, petting caress of its roundness, a gentle exploration of its delicious, delectable expanse. Fuck, fuck, *fuck*, she had a great ass.

For a fraught moment, all I could think about was having her on her hands and knees as I pounded into her hot, wet pussy from behind, feeling this ass—which I squeezed again and then immediately gentled my grip to a soft caress—smash and squish and jiggle as I crushed my hips into it. I'd take a double handful as I fucked her, and then as she started coming, I'd spank her.

Fuck!

My cock was an iron rod behind my sweatpants, throbbing with arousal. What a way to wake up, good lord.

Lindsey stirred, snuffled sleepily. Hummed. Wriggled on me. Rubbed her naked pussy against my erection.

I had to move—I had to get out from under her. If she did that again, I was gonna pop my load in my pants like a fourteen-year-old virgin watching porn for the first time.

Which was a firm "hell no" for me. Not happening.

I slipped as slowly and carefully as I could out from under her, trying as hard as I could to not rouse her. I think I succeeded—I reached my feet and she was still out, albeit making more waking-up noises.

I limp to the bathroom—my left leg was half asleep and tingling. I stopped at the toilet and lifted the lid, but I had a major problem: I was rocking a monster hard-on. For the non-dick-havers in the audience, pissing with a hard-on was a physics problem: erect dick point up—toilet down, peepee go wrong direction.

Now what? Wait for it to subside? I had to piss *now*. Do a handstand? I wasn't a gymnast, and how did you aim? Stand halfway across the bathroom and arc the stream? You'd get piss literally everywhere. Sit and lean forward? Maybe. Stand in the tub and let 'er rip? I would, but this isn't my place.

Maybe I can just bend it down enough to get the stream into the toilet?

"Dane?" Lindsey's sleepy voice comes from behind me.

"Oh, uh…" I had my sweatpants down in front and my dick in my hand as I tried to angle it downward.

"What…uhhh…what are you *doing*?"

"Trying to piss," I growled, annoyed at how embarrassing this was.

"Trying?" I heard her shuffle forward, and then she was beside me, staring down at my erection. "Oh." She giggled. "I see the issue."

I had no words—my mind is blank. I let my dick go and tugged my sweatpants back up. "You go. I'll just…wait."

I left the bathroom and closed the door behind me. I went into the kitchen, located her coffeemaker and supplies, and started a pot. While it brewed, I braced my hands on the counter and breathed, focusing on nothing, willing my erection to go away so I could relieve my screaming, aching, burning bladder. Normally, when I woke up with morning wood, it was gone by the time I reached the bathroom, because normally, morning wood wasn't about arousal, it was just a physiological thing, and often because of a full bladder. This was not that, and the bastard was *not* going away.

Mainly because my stupid monkey brain kept unhelpfully supplying me with a montage of erotic images involving Lindsey and that perfectly plump peach and all the sinful things I want to do to her.

"Still having your…ummm, problem?" I heard and jumped, startled.

"Shit!" I gasped. "Yes. I am."

She stood behind me, hesitated. "I…um. I don't know what to say."

"Nothing to say," I growled. "I have to piss, but the hard-on won't go away."

"Think about dead kittens and naked nuns?" she suggested.

"That doesn't work," I mumbled. "Nothing is working."

"Morning wood usually goes away on its own pretty fast, I thought. That's what my ex always told me."

I sighed. "Not morning wood."

"Oh. Ummm…"

I turned on her—which was a mistake. That shirt barely cleared her crotch, and now I knew she was naked under it. Her nipples were hard, poking against the material. I felt my cock twitch—going harder rather than softer. "It's your fault."

"M-*mine*?" she squeaked. "How is it *my* fault?"

I advanced on her, erection first. "Ask me how I know you're not wearing any panties, Lindey."

Her face goes white and then red. "Oh. I…um. You—I—"

I stepped closer again, until we were not quite touching—you couldn't fit a sheet of paper between her tits and my chest, but we weren't touching. I tugged the hem of her shirt up, keeping my eyes firmly on hers. "Ask me how I know you have a triangle of freckles right…here." I traced a triangle on her right ass cheek, near the top on the outside, just below that sexy fucking dimple, where the freckles were, according to my very vivid memory.

"Dane," she whispered.

"I woke up with my hands all over this gorgeous ass of yours," I murmured, palming both cheeks. "And now all I can think about is what I'd like to do to it."

She whimpered, leaning into me, crushing her tits

against me, gazing up at me with her mouth hanging open, eyes wide. "I can't."

"I know."

"You have to know it's not because I don't like you or that I'm not attracted to you," she whispered.

"I *don't* know that, as a matter of fact," I said. "I don't know anything for sure, at least when it comes to what you're thinking or feeling." I slid my hand up and pinched her erect nipple. "Is this because you're cold?"

"No," she breathed. "I do want you."

"But?"

A hard swallow. "If you were anyone else, I'd help you out, Dane. But it's you. And I can't."

"I don't understand."

"I'm fucked up right now, and it's because of you. Not that you did anything wrong—you didn't. I just… it's *not* you, really. It's…ah, shit, I'm not making any goddamn sense." She rests her forehead on my chest, sighing. "I *want* to help you, Dane. But I…if I did, I'd… it'd be…I just can't. I'm sorry. It wouldn't be fair to you."

I turned away. "I get it."

"I don't think you do. That's no shade to you, Dane, I just don't think you can." Soft hands rested on my shoulders. "Go in there and take care of it."

"No."

"Why not?"

"I'm not jerking off in your bathroom."

Her lips brushed my ear. "You want a pair of my panties to jerk off into?"

"What? Fuck no, that's weird."

"Dane, I'm trying to help. I want you, but right now, if I touched you, we'd do stuff. And if we did stuff, it would confuse things for both of us."

"I'm not asking you to do anything, Linz," I murmured. "I believe you. I'll be fine."

I wasn't fine.

The damn erection was a stubborn motherfucker, unhelped by her scent, her proximity, the soft press of her breasts against my back, the memory of her bare ass in my hands, the memory of that night we shared flashing through my brain like a PowerPoint slideshow of our greatest moments—which was all of them.

I felt her chin on my shoulder. "Not going away, huh?"

I almost told her it wasn't going to until she left me alone, but I didn't want her to leave me alone. "No," was all I said.

She pushed me toward her room. Into the bathroom. Had me face the toilet. "C'mon, Dane."

I pivoted to face her. "I will if you will."

"At the same time? Watching each other?"

"Yes."

She bit her lip. "That's a dangerous, slippery slope."

"I want to see that toy in action," I said.

She turned away, left the room, and came back

with the clit stimulator, went to her bed, settled on it, knees drawn up and pressed together—providing me with a teasing glimpse of her ass. She pressed the power button, and the white silicone surrounding the opening glowed pink, and she pressed the button that cycled through the settings until it was buzzing softly.

I grabbed the waist of my sweatpants, but hesitated. "This is a little crazy, Linz," I muttered.

"I know," she answered, gripping the hem of the shirt. "I wish I could just…do what I want to do. But it wouldn't make anything better. Only worse."

"You don't need to keep explaining," I said. "I get it."

"I don't know if I can," she whispered. "No one has ever watched me masturbate before."

"Me either," I said.

But the situation was untenable. Just the thought of watching Lindsey orgasm had me harder than ever, and the bladder situation was still an issue. I wasn't even sure if I *could* come while I had to pee, but I guess we'd find out.

I peeled off my shirt and tossed it aside; Lindsey's eyes widened and I watched her pupils dilate, watched her knees press together harder. She let her knees drop, legs extending. Without taking her eyes off mine, she leaned forward to tug the hem of the shirt out from under her butt, and then stripped it off.

"Goddamn, Linz," I whispered. "So fucking hot."

She blushed. "You too."

Her tits, man. Just fucking perfect. My cock twitched at the sight of them as they swayed, pert pink nipples standing on end, begging for my lips, my tongue.

"Dane," she breathed. "Let me see."

I swallowed hard, weirdly nervous, even though we'd been naked together already. I scolded myself for being stupid and slid my sweatpants down past my ass and then stepped out of them. Now Lindsey's eyes widened to the size of platters, and she bit her lip. Splayed her thighs apart, baring her naked pink folds to me. Fuck, fuck, fuck. She had a scrim of blonde fuzz covering her sex, the stubble of someone who normally keeps herself shaved or waxed but hasn't recently. I could almost feel it on my tongue, rasping against my cheeks, my lips.

I could almost taste her juices.

The thought of her pussy against my mouth had me grabbing my cock and stroking it.

"Fuck me," Lindsey breathed. "Your cock, Dane."

"What about it?" I growled, squeezing and stroking my length slowly.

"So fucking big. So thick." She drew her knees up to her butt, touched the toy to her clit, and immediately gasped. "Oh—oh god. I hope you won't take a long time, because I'm gonna come so fast."

The pulse of arousal throbbed through me, the straining ache painful. My balls boiled, and my cock felt like it could explode any second.

Yeah, I wasn't taking a long time.

Not when she was already gasping and writhing, making those fat, gorgeous fucking tits jerk and jiggle. Not when I saw arousal quite literally leaking out of her pussy. Not when she was gazing at me through slitted eyelids, biting her lower lip, and keening in her throat. She had two fingers splaying her pussy lips apart so she could press the toy to her clit, angling it this way and that until she found the perfect angle, and then she cried out loud, arching her spine to press her tits to the ceiling. I watched her thighs quiver, and I stroked my length, unable to stop myself from speeding up as she drew closer and closer to climax. As did I. Too soon.

I slowed, gritting my teeth to hold back.

"Oh!" she whimpered, "Dane! Fuck, oh god, yes— jerk that dick, Dane. Harder. Jerk it like you're fucking me."

"Goddammit," I hissed. "I'm close. Come for me, Linz. I can't come till you do."

My knees threatened to give out; I hated jerking off standing up. I dipped and straightened while pumping my length, and Lindsey didn't so much as blink. Neither did I, for that matter, not wanting to miss a second of Lindsey's beautiful bare body bucking and bending as she quivered and quaked closer and closer to release.

"Fuck, Linz," I growled. "You're so goddamned beautiful. Wish to fuck it was me making you come."

"Oh god, Dane," she whimpered. "Don't tease me.

I fantasize about your mouth every fucking night. All I can think about is you."

"So why are we doing this, then?" I demanded.

She didn't answer—she couldn't; she was too busy coming. Her eyes clenched shut, and she bucked upward and quivered that way, breasts shaking and rolling in circles as she thrusted against the toy, arched off the bed. She keened in her throat as she came, and then screamed, biting down on the scream and crying out through gritted teeth.

"DANE!" she shrieked.

"Fuck, Linz," I snarled. "Hottest thing I've ever seen."

I felt my own release building, and I had to speed my strokes. Had to meet her in orgasm.

She wrenched her eyes open as she kept the device on her clit. "Come here," she breathed. "Dane, come here."

I staggered toward her on shaky legs, crossing the dozen or so feet from toilet to bedside.

She patted the bed beside her. "Lay down."

"Thank fuck," I muttered as I collapsed onto the mattress next to her.

"Now come for me." She bit her lip again.

I closed my eyes for a moment as I found the rhythm again, stroking my erection in a loose fist—faster and faster as I neared my release. I heard her whimper, and my eyes flew open—she was watching me raptly, toy on her clit, and she was seconds from coming again. Her pink folds were soaked, and I could smell her arousal. My mouth watered, and my cock pulsed. I need to taste her. Need to feel her orgasm against my mouth.

"Fuck this." I rolled over and wedged my shoulders between her shaking thighs, and lapped at her folds.

"DANE!" she cried out.

She clutched my head, dropping the buzzing device, and guided my mouth to her clit. I growled wordlessly as she detonated beneath me, shrieking as her orgasm wracked her into paroxysms. The sex toy was buzzing away at my elbow; she was still shaking through her orgasm, so I pressed the opening to her clit, slid two fingers inside her clenching, clamping, hot, tight, wet channel, and fucked her with them while sliding up her body to suck her nipple into my mouth.

"FUCK!" she screamed, bucking violently as her climax seemed to implode, making her come so hard she was paralyzed, arched and quivering all over as her pussy squeezed my fingers.

Hot wetness flooded my fingers as she squirted through her orgasm, weeping and sobbing and bucking.

Ravenous for her, I kept going. Kept the toy on her clit and kept fucking her with my fingers and suckling her nipples until she was a limp, boneless, silently weeping puddle on the bed.

"Stop—" she panted, the word a ghost of a

whisper. "Stop, stop, please stop, I can't—I can't take another one."

I acquiesced, even though all I wanted was to keep her coming, just so I could have her body under my hands, her taste in my mouth, her breasts shaking for me.

I rolled away, cock throbbing and bobbing against my belly as I flopped to my back, pausing to catch my breath before I tried to finish myself off.

A soft, small hand wrapped around my cock.

"Linz," I whispered. "Don't. I know I shouldn't have done that. I just—"

Warm skin and the soft press of her tits against my ribs made my breath catch. Her other hand covered my mouth. "Sssshhh," she shushed.

My eyes met hers. "Linz," I whispered, the word muffled behind her hand.

She pressed her palm more firmly against my mouth, leaning into me while gently pumping my cock. "Hush, Dane." She nuzzled my cheek with her nose. "Shut up and enjoy it."

FIVE

Lindsey

DANE'S COCK SLID SLOWLY THROUGH MY FIST. HE groaned as his tip mushroomed up through my fist, his length sprouting up and up as my fist slid down and down.

This was irresponsible. Foolish. Hot as fuck.

I can't seem to stop myself—mainly because I wasn't trying. I should have known we couldn't just mutually masturbate—our chemistry is too fucking real for that.

It was difficult enough keeping my ass on the bed beside him instead of slapping against his belly as I rode him. Which is what I really wanted to do—I could almost feel his huge, hard, hot cock inside me.

Fuck.

I'd have to settle for giving him a handy, because if we had sex right now, this already-complicated situation would get even more complicated. Shit, what we're doing right now is going to complicate an already complicated situation.

Not that I was about to stop—no way. Not when I had Dane's lovely penis in my hand, oozing precum as I stroked his improbable length and unlikely girth. The man was *hung*. And listen, I'm no size queen. I've had guys with relatively small dicks give it to me good, and men with monster dongs perform poorly. It really is about the individual. But Dane? He had both—size *and* technique. And the size? *Oooohhhh* lordy, any bigger in length *or* girth and he'd be too big; he had a slight emphasis on girth, which was preferable.

He groaned again, arching his back as I gave him a few short, shallow pumps at the base. God, I really wanted him inside me. It'd be so easy. Swing a leg over his waist and *boop*, I'd be a happy girl, getting dicked down by Dane Badd.

I focused—exercising self-control for once in my life. Twisted my fist around his plump cockhead, smearing precum over the round tip with my thumb. He growled, a soft, quiet hiss in the back of his throat, flexing his ass muscles to push his cock into my hand.

I slid my palm away from his mouth, gazed at his lips, remembering the way he kissed me on my balcony. My god, he can kiss.

Fuck it.

I draped myself over him, clutching and stroking his cock with one hand and his balls with the other, and I kissed him. Like the dumb, irresponsible, horny-ass ho that I am, I kissed him: all tongue, no chill. He groaned into my mouth and clasped the back of my head, dug his fingers through my hair, swept his tongue through my mouth, and clamped a hand on my ass cheek.

Fuck, this is dangerous.

I was *this* close to hopping on that dick.

Fuck, fuck, *fuck*.

I wriggled higher so he could get a better grip on my ass, which he seemed to be somewhatobsessed with—and lemme tell ya, that's a damned nice feeling. I shoved my tongue into his mouth and pumped his cock faster, harder, palming his balls, massaging them, teasing and tickling them with my fingertips. He broke the kiss with a moan, head tipping back as he thrusted into my hand.

"Fuck, Linz," he snarled. "I'm close."

I slid my finger along his taint, pressed my finger into it, massaged, and dared further toward his asshole.

"Linz?" he questioned. "Whatcha doin'?"

"Anyone ever do this?" I asked.

"No."

"Never had your prostate milked?"

"No?"

"Say yes, Dane. You'll like it, I promise."

I slowed my strokes, pressing my finger against him a little more firmly, waiting for his consent—this wasn't something you just sprung on a guy.

"Linz…"

"Trust me?"

Yes, I'm all too aware of the cruel irony of me asking him to trust me.

"Yes." He whispered it.

"Yeah?" I asked, excited—for him.

I don't do this almost ever, because again, it's something most guys I've hooked up with balk at for obvious reasons. But Dane is different. He didn't just allow me to use my special friend; he used it on me. He's open-minded and willing to play. To experiment.

Fuck, this is bad.

Stupid. So, so stupid.

I'm just confusing myself.

But I can't stop. I don't *want* to stop. I want to make him come so hard he forgets his own name. After all, he just made me come three times in less than five minutes, and each orgasm was more intense than the last one, and by the end, I was seeing stars and actually sobbing.

So yeah.

I'm gonna give the guy a handjob for the ages.

Including a little light fingering of his prostate.

I dripped a little saliva onto my fingers and smeared it over him, pressing my fingertip against the opening. I caressed his cock with slow, loose strokes, applying a little more pressure to his asshole with each stroke. Within a few seconds of this, he was arched off the bed, hands fisted in the quilt as he alternated between arching up and dropping down to thrust into my hand, groaning and growling all the while.

I wasn't even inserted. Just you wait, big boy… you're gonna *love* this.

I think.

Now, to be clear, prostate milking is a whole actual thing, and a very specific thing, and what I was doing to Dane wasn't really that. I was just playing with his back door a little while giving him a handy. Still, I had it on good authority that this *greatly* increases the intensity of his climax.

He seemed to agree, based on the way he was reacting—eyes screwed shut, jaw clenched, gasping raggedly and shaking all over as he bucked into my hand, desperately riding the edge of orgasm.

Now for the really fun part.

I circled his cock at the base with my index finger and then squeezed—*hard*. He grunted, doing an ab crunch to give me a *what the fuck* look—which is when I slid my fingertip inside him, just a hint.

Enough that he shouted: "Oh—FUCK!"

"Yeah?" I murmured. "You like that?"

"I…I don't—Oh fuck, oh god. Maybe? I think?" He was squirming and writhing helplessly, like a worm on a hook. "Oh fuck—I need to come, Linz."

"Oh, honey-boy, you will. And I expect you to scream my name when you do."

I loosened my grip on his cock a little and he gasped when I gave him one slow caress of his pulsing hot length, the gasp becoming a ragged groan as I gripped him tightly once more and wiggled my fingertip a little further in. He tensed all over.

I leaned toward him, whispered in his ear. "You gotta relax, Dane. I won't hurt you, I promise."

"It's…fuck. It's just…a little…weird," he panted through gritted teeth.

I pulsed my grip around his cock while simultaneously pulsing my finger further in, millimeter by millimeter. "Breathe, Dane. Relax. Breathe and relax."

To his credit, he listened. He inhaled deeply, filling his lungs, and then let it out slowly while consciously relaxing his muscles. Bit by bit, his body unclenched— toes uncurled, thighs unbunched, abs went slack…and his asshole loosened, allowing me a little deeper, up to the first knuckle. His cock jumped as I curled my finger inside him, pressing against his taint from the inside.

"Linz!" he shouted. "FUCK!"

"Yeah?" I crooned. "*Now* you get it?"

"Yes!" he rasped, his voice hoarse and ragged. "Please, please let me come."

I squeezed his cock tighter while rhythmically pulsing my finger in and out—not really moving very far, just giving the impression of it. Enough to stimulate him for his first time. I felt him throb in my hand, his cock swelling as he reached the point of no return, his abs tightening and relaxing as he tried to thrust.

His eyes flew open and met mine. "Linz—fuck,

please. I'm begging. I can't—I have to—fuck, please. Please. I'm literally begging."

I grinned as I squeezed his root once more, pulsing my finger a little deeper and pressing against his prostate. His groan started loud and quickly turned gravelly and raw as his desperation mounted, every muscle now tensed all over again as his body tried to release but couldn't, prevented by my grip.

"Ready, Dane?" I whispered, ghosting my lips against his. "Open your eyes, big boy, and watch this."

His eyes snapped open and he glanced at me first, his gaze fraught with emotions I refused to acknowledge or name. "Linz—Jesus. I—oh god, oh god!" A gasping, writhing arch of his body. "Lindsey…."

I released my grip at that exact moment when he whispered my name. His whole body bucked upward as his climax blasted through him, starting with a tightening and pulsing of his taut, soft ball sack, followed by an isometric clenching of his muscles from head to toe. His teeth clenched so hard I saw his jaw ticking—I could swear I heard his molars creak under the strain of his clenching. I watched his beautiful, hard, shredded body writhe and flex, watched his gorgeous, rugged face go through a myriad of emotions.

And then…I pumped his cock. Hard and fast, merciless and rough. I spat into my hand and coated his thick shaft with nature's lubricant, and now my fist slid easily slick on his cock and he arched, jaw open, eyes fluttering as he tried to watch, fighting his body's natural inclination to shut his eyes.

"Watch, Dane," I whispered. "Now. Come for me, big boy. Gimme all your cum."

Groaning raggedly, he obeyed me like a good boy. Furiously pumping his cock, I pulsed my finger inside him, felt him grip my finger as he tensed tighter yet, his whole body locked in a paroxysm of release.

A hot ribbon of cum jetted out of him, laying in a thick white stripe over his belly—he came with such force that it splashed over his diaphragm and onto his chest. "Linz!" he shouted, his voice raw and wild. "Lindsey!"

"Yeah, baby," I whispered in his ear, pumping his cock as fast as my hand would move, blurring up and down on his shaft. "Who's making you come so fucking hard?"

"You are," he growled. "Lindsey! Oh fuck, Linz. Linz!"

"Yes," I hissed, smearing my fist around his head as he shot another load of cum through my fingers, smearing his own hot, viscous cum over his shaft. "Good boy. This is *my* cock."

Jesus, what's wrong with me? Why would I say that? Fuck, I'm so screwed.

"Yours," he agreed, arching off the bed to spurt again, just as hard and just as much. "Oh fuck, honey, please don't stop."

I claimed his mouth, slashed my lips over his,

sucked his tongue into my mouth, and slid my finger out of him—making him grunt abruptly, jerking as he came yet again, all over my fingers and his belly. The puddle of cum was becoming rather voluminous.

He relaxed a little, panting as if he'd run a mile flat-out, growling quietly with each gasping breath. I kept milking his cock, pumping his length slowly now, rifling a series of short, fast, twisting strokes around the head and then giving him a full-length caress. I palmed his heavy balls as I stroked him, then squeezed, traced the seam of his cock from taint to root, and then squeezed again—and got another hot load of thick cum out of him.

He tried to meet my gaze, but his eyes were crossed, and he couldn't seem to focus, groaning quietly as he went boneless on the bed, eyes rolling into the back of his head as I kept massaging his balls and gently caressing his cock even as it began to slacken and lose its rigidity, leaking the last dribbles of cum.

Finally, he was done.

I kept his now-flaccid cock in my cum-coated hand, rested my chin on his chest, and grinned at him like a very self-satisfied Cheshire Cat, watching him as he slowly regained his senses.

"Holy motherfucking shit," he mumbled, his eyes opening and slowly focusing on me. "I mean—goddamn, Linz."

"Figured I owed you at least *one* good orgasm, right?" I said, trying to keep my tone light.

"Wrong," he said. "Don't owe me anything. Now or ever." He blinked, groaning, and rolled to the edge of the bed, working to his feet like a stiff-jointed old man. "Oh fuck, fuck, fuck, I'm gonna pee everywhere in a second."

"Please don't."

He staggered around the foot end of the bed, wobbling on unsteady legs like a newborn colt, toppling against the bathroom door frame, and caroming off it. He reached the toilet and sat down heavily, and I heard him cut loose with a sigh of relief. He pissed for what seemed like a solid two minutes. I heard the sink go as he cleaned himself up.

During that time, panic filled me.

It started as a tightening in my belly. And then my hands went numb and started tingling, and my mouth went dry, and my throat tightened so I couldn't swallow, and I broke out in a cold sweat, breath trapped in my lungs and below the hot knot in my throat.

What did I just do?

I let him eat me out. I let him give me *another* orgasm—*three* of them, each one so intense I was still shaky.

I jerked him off. I put my finger in his asshole.

Stupidest of all, I *kissed him.*

He's gonna want things, now.

Answers.

History.

Feelings.

I let him into my home.

I slept with him—cuddled. Was comforted. I slept like a damn baby.

We were *intimate*.

I'd almost have been better off just fucking him, I'm starting to think. That may have been less intimate than what we just shared.

What I just did.

Fuck.

I heard him moving, but my eyes were hazed with hot tears, and I couldn't breathe and couldn't move. This wasn't a BJ panic attack; this was a full-on emotional meltdown. Again.

The poor man has seen me like this more than he's seen me normal.

"Linz?" His voice was soft and concerned.

A warm, wet washcloth cleaned my hands, my folds, tenderly, gently, softly.

I shook my head. "No. No. No."

"No, what, Linz?"

"Don't. Don't. You can't."

"Can't what?"

"Be sweet."

"You'd rather I be a jerk?"

"*Yes*," I hissed.

"Sorry, babe. No can do." He lifted me, and then I was curled up in a ball in his arms.

I was naked, he was naked. It didn't matter—my only thought was to get away.

But I couldn't.

His arms around me, his hot, hard muscles firm and warm—the comfort I felt at being held by Dane Badd was all-consuming. I couldn't move if I tried.

"I've got you, honey. Just breathe."

"Not your honey."

"Okay."

"I'm a bitch."

"Hard disagree."

"We should have just fucked."

"Maybe. That felt pretty goddamned spectacular to me, though."

"I shouldn't have let you in."

"But you did. And I'm here, and I'm not going anywhere."

"I c-c-can't—" I was suddenly cold, chattering. "I c-c-can't—t-t-talk…a-a-about it."

He drew the blankets up over us, tucked them around me. Wrapped me tighter in his embrace. "I've got you."

"Don't."

"Not like that."

"We shouldn't have done that, Dane."

He blew out a sigh. "I'm sure you think so."

"I can't…" I had to fight the words past my teeth. "I can't give you what you want."

"How do you know what I want?"

"I can't be what you need."

"You don't know what I need."

"DANE!" I snapped, trying to squirm out of his arms. "You don't know shit about me!"

"Nor you me."

"I'm not telling you shit."

"Have I asked?"

"Before I let you in, you said I owed you answers."

"Maybe I changed my mind."

"We shouldn't have done that, Dane," I whispered. "I'm just more confused."

"I'm not confused."

"I am."

"About what?"

"Everything."

"Start with one thing. Maybe I can help clarify things."

"Not fucking likely."

"Try me."

"No."

"You're so goddamned stubborn, you know that?" He sighed, and his hands roamed soothing circles around my shoulders, back, hips, buttocks, and thighs. His touch was tender and affectionate.

My soul strained toward his; my heart tried to open.

Alas, my heart was atrophied and shriveled and black, and my soul was locked away in a lightless, airless box—safe from trauma, perhaps, but from everything else as well.

"Why won't you ask?"

He sighed again. "Because you have to choose to tell me. I realized at some point that demanding answers was cruel and unfair and wrong. I want you to *trust* me. I want you to know that you're safe with me." He gripped a fistful of my hair and gently yet firmly tugged my head back so I had to look up at him, had to meet his gaze; my eyes were blurred with tears I refused to let spill over, so all I could see of him was a wavering, ghostly outline. "I know something awful happened to you, Lindsey. I don't know what and I don't know when, and I don't need to know, right now. It's enough to know that there's something that I don't think has anything to do with me that's got you fucked up about a lot of things."

"I'm fucked up about everything," I murmured.

"But sex and intimacy especially. I don't know if going down on me triggered it or if it was something else, but it's got something to do with sex."

"Yes," I whispered. "I can tell you that much, at least."

"What we did just now, did that trigger you?"

"No."

"So this is different than what happened that night?"

"Yes."

"But related."

"Yes."

There was a long silence. "I just want to be there for you, Lindsey."

"I *know*, goddammit," I hissed. "I fucking *know*. I just don't know how to let you."

He let out a frustrated rumble. "I'm sorry, Linz. I shouldn't have let that happen. I should've…I dunno. I feel like I pushed you into something you didn't want to do, and I'm sorry."

My heart clenched at how distraught he sounded. It pulled me out of the miasma of self-pity and panic, a little. I twisted so I was lying on his lap, staring up at him. "No," I whispered. "It's not your fault. None of this is your fault."

"I was only thinking about myself," he muttered. "Thinking with my dick. I pressured you into doing things, and now you're panicking."

I dug my fingers into his chest. "No, Dane. *No.* That's not what happened, I swear." I looked up at him, summoning enough strength to sit up on his lap, straddling him, facing him. "It was just as much as me thinking with my pussy."

He shook his head. "It's okay to put the blame on me, where it belongs."

"Goddammit, Dane, you're not listening to me." I cupped his face in both hands. "I *want* you. I've *always* wanted you. I was fighting the urge to jump you all damn night. And when I saw that gorgeous dick of yours all hard and begging for me to play with it, I couldn't stop myself. I tried. I thought maybe we could just mutually masturbate."

"Until I lost control."

"And went down on me," I said. "You didn't hear me complaining, did you?" I let him go, sat back. "You didn't ask me to do anything. I did what I wanted to do."

"So why are you so upset?" he asked.

"Because I'm more confused than ever!" I shouted. "I don't *want* to want you, Dane. And I swear on all that's holy, that's not about *you*, it's about *me* and my fucked-up psyche. I'm scared. I'm—I'm fucked up. And you—you make me feel things. Big things. Scary things. Things I don't have the emotional bandwidth to deal with right now."

He was quiet for a long time. "Linz, I…I guess I don't really know what to say to that. I want you to trust me. But I know how much easier that is said than done."

"Honestly, Dane, a big part of me wishes you were more of a cocky asshole. It'd be way easier to fuck you again just to get you out of my system so I can be done with you."

"But it's not that easy, huh?"

"Shut up."

He huffed a laugh. "Are you saying that I'm not out of your system yet?"

"Dane, seriously, shut up."

"Because if you give me another ten or fifteen minutes, we can go again." He paused. "A big black bug bit a big black bear, and the big black bear bled black blood."

"The fuck?"

"Warming up my mouth."

I slapped his chest. "Shut up. No. We aren't going again."

"Awww. You sure?" he held a hand up in front of my face, index, middle, and pinky fingers extended, his ring finger tucked. "Now that ass-play is in the picture, I could see if I can make you come so hard so many times you pass out…again."

"Ass-play is *not* in the picture."

"My asshole disagrees."

"You liked it."

"Fuck yes, I did. You're welcome to do that to me anytime you want." He laughed. "You're telling me two in the pink, one in the stink doesn't interest you?"

"Not when you phrase it like that."

"Fine. You're telling me that you would not, in fact, allow me to gently finger your delicate little rosebud while I eat your pussy?"

"Rosebud?" I echoed.

"I dunno. Just go with it."

I sighed as I finally found the wherewithal to leave the all-consuming comfort of his arms—it felt like leaving a warm bed and jumping straight into a cold plunge. "Dane…" I shifted away to sit upright in the bed beside him, tugging the blankets up and tucking them under my arms.

He sat upright and gave me his full attention. "Lindsey?"

"I'm stuck, Dane." My voice was low, quiet. Shaky. "Yes, I'm wildly attracted to you. Physically and emotionally—as hard as that last part is to admit. I see you. You're a good guy—a *great* guy. You deserve better than you've gotten from me, Dane—no, no quips about what just happened. For once, I'm being serious."

"Hi, serious, I'm Dane."

I rolled my eyes at him, vainly trying to suppress a grin. "Dane, fuck off with the jokes."

He scrubbed his face. "I'm trying, I swear."

"I can't give you…anything, really. I just—I don't know how to open up about what happened. If I…if I were to start talking about it, I'd fall apart, and I'm terrified that if that happens, I'll never be able to put myself together again. I've seen therapists my whole life. I've done work on myself. I'm trying, Dane, I swear to God I'm trying. And—and if I could open up to *any* man about what happened, it'd be you."

"Does anyone know?" he asked.

"Aside from the person who—" I shook my head. "Only Rune knows the details."

"What about your parents?"

I shook my head. "I tried telling my mother, but she basically just victim-blamed me. My parents are the worst. I haven't spoken to either of them in years and have no intention of changing that."

"Your father?"

"Hasn't been in the picture since I was, like, seven. They separated when I was five or six, I think, and I saw him every other weekend for like a year, maybe a year and a half. And then he got engaged to a stripper named Flossie and moved to Miami with her. They're married, living in a trailer, she's still stripping, and I'm pretty sure he's a raging alcoholic. Dunno, don't care."

"Hey now," he said. "There's nothing wrong with living in a trailer *or* being a stripper."

I laughed at this, despite myself. "No, there's not. He's just a useless piece of fuck."

He snickered. "Piece of fuck, that's funny." He glanced at me. "Also, *Flossie?*"

I shrugged. "I dunno."

"And your mom, currently?"

Another shrug. "Last I checked, she was still in the same shithole apartment I grew up in, and still parading a constant revolving door of losers through her bedroom. And no, it wasn't one of them." A pause. "She's just weak-willed, selfish, and lazy, and has fucking *terrible* taste in men, my father most of all. She's worked the same shitty, dead-end job at a department store for twenty years. There's nothing wrong with the job in itself, it's just…she's…fuck, I dunno. She drinks a lot but isn't an alcoholic; she isn't, like, a meth-head or anything. She never hit me or let her asshole boyfriends hit me. One did, once, and she brained him with a frying pan. So at least there's that. She's just…" I shook my head. "I don't know how to explain my mother, honestly. I think maybe she didn't want kids and ended up with two, so she resented us. When shit with my father blew up, it made her more bitter than ever, which is saying something, because she was a mean, bitter hag to begin with."

"Old?"

I snorted. "At heart. She had my older brother at sixteen, so she's actually not that old; she's just one of those people who always just seemed...*old*. Weary, haggard, and run down and...I dunno. Thin? Like, I don't mean thin physically. I mean thin as a personality trait. Fuck, how do I put it? There's just not that much to her as a human other than bitterness, resentment, and laziness. Most of the shit in her life is her own fault. She could live a better life if she tried to improve herself, but she's got zero interest in that. She's content to work at the department store, live in her shitty two-bedroom roach-infested fuck-shack surrounded by drug dealers and petty criminals, and screw any loser with a dick and a car and a rap sheet."

"Wow. You really don't think much of her, do you?"

"Nope. I left home at seventeen."

"Left home, meaning...?"

"Ran away. Couch-surfed with friends for a while. Let me tell you, though, being homeless in Boston in the winter sucks hairy assholes."

"Linz, Jesus."

"It was better than being in that house with her and her creepy fucking boyfriends. Better than spending another minute in that house with the woman who told me to my face in so many words that I must have asked for it." My voice broke. "When I was fucking twelve."

"Jesus. Jesus."

I looked at him. "Starting to get the picture?"

"Yeah," he whispered. "I think I am."

"How'd you end up here in LA, if you grew up in Boston?"

"Hard fucking work. When I was fifteen, I had this friend, Abby. She was a senior, and I was a freshman. Some jock dick was picking on me during gym class, and she ripped him a new asshole for it. It was glorious and inspiring, and I wanted to be like her. She had a similar background as me—shitty home life, no prospects for a future that didn't involve taking her clothes off. I guess she and I were kindred spirits, sort of. We lived near each other, so we walked home together. I idolized her. She gave me a piece of advice that I never forgot, advice that I followed, and it changed the course of my life. She told me I had to rise above my circumstances. I couldn't let the life I was born into determine my future. The only way out for girls like her and me was college so either I worked my ass off, stayed out of trouble, stayed away from boys, and got into a good college far, far away from there, or I'd end up dead of an OD, hooking on the street corner, or stripping at Deluca's, where my father met Flossie."

"So you got into college."

I nodded. "It wasn't exactly that easy, but yeah." I

sighed. "I went through a rough patch the next year—
Abby graduated and left Boston, and I had no friends.
The person who…he got put away, and I…I went a little crazy. Got into trouble. Drinking. Drugs. Parties.
Bad crowd, bad choices. Did a lot of irresponsible shit.
But one night, I was wasted at a party. This girl and
I had been hanging out, talking, and whatever. She
ditched me for some guy. Left with him and never came
back. Vanished. Everyone assumed he'd done something to her, but he swore he didn't, and he actually
came up with an airtight alibi. Said he dropped her off
at home after they smashed, then went home, spent the
rest of the night playing video games online, and his
gamer friends validated his alibi. She turned up a few
months later, after the snow melted. She'd wandered
off after he dropped her off, got lost or fell or passed
out in the snow, froze to death, got buried under a fresh
load of snow, and…" I shrugged. "That could've been
me, I realized. And I remembered Abby's advice—stay
out of trouble, keep your grades up, join a sports team,
and get the *fuck* out of Southie."

"And you did?"

I nodded. "Yup. Even homeless, I stayed on top
of my grades. I'd study in the public library until
they closed, and I'd ride the T all night, doing home-
work, studying, sleeping. I was friends with one of
the school janitors—Yuri, a sweet little old Ukrainian
guy. I think he understood my situation. He couldn't
do much about it, but he was a sweetheart. He'd let

me in before the faculty arrived so I could shower in the locker rooms. He spent his own money to buy me a little shower caddy with shampoo, conditioner, and body wash, and he'd hide it in the janitor's closet and get it out for me when I arrived. I'd hide in the locker rooms until people started arriving, and then I'd act like I was just a goody two-shoes eager to get to class early. I'd hang out in the library after school until practice started or I got kicked out."

"What sport did you do?" He asked.

"Softball. I was a pitcher."

He grinned. "Couple of my cousins are softball athletes. I used to go to their games all the time."

"To support your cousins or to ogle the other girls?" I asked, grinning.

"Bit of both. Softball girls have *spectacular* asses."

I snickered. "You have an ass obsession."

"Maybe. I just appreciate a nice big butt."

I frowned at him. "Are you saying I have a fat ass, Dane Badd?"

"Abso-fucking-lutely."

I glared at him. "You're lucky you're hot and that I'm not insecure. Tell just about any other girl that she's got a fat ass and you're likely to end up with a split lip."

"To be clear, though, I didn't say 'fat', I said 'big.' They're not the same thing."

"Not any better, in our minds. Hate to break it to you."

"Plump?"

"Bzzzzzt. Wrong again."

"Juicy?"

I tipped my head to one side. "That I can accept."

"Linz," he started, his tone serious.

"No."

He snorted. "You don't know what I'm going to ask."

"You can't eat my asshole, Dane."

"I mean, let me get you in the shower and I'll wash that thing till it's squeaky clean and then eat it till you beg me to stop." Pause. "But that's not what I was going to say, you nasty girl."

"*I'm* nasty?"

"*You* brought it up."

"I was joking."

"I wasn't."

I frowned at him. "You really would?"

"Sure. I mean, I'd try it once, at least. You don't know if you'll like something till you try it. I never thought I'd let anyone put *anything* in my bungus, but here we are. I let you put your finger all up in there, and I liked it. So yeah, if you asked me to, I'd eat your ass."

I shook my head. "Good to know, but no. Fingering? Yes. I'd let you finger me. But eating it? Nah. Even clean, that just seems like a good way to get, like, pink eye or...dysentery or whatever it is."

"I don't think it's dysentery. That's what you die of in *Oregon Trail*, and something tells me people weren't eating ass until they died on the Oregon Trail."

"Oregon Trail? Are you a fucking millennial now?"

He rolled his eyes at me. "When I was ten or eleven, Papa Lucas cleaned out a storage unit he'd been holding onto for, like, twenty years. Lots of old shit in there from when Rem, Ram, and Rome were kids, including this old desktop computer. He found out that it still worked, and he had all these old computer games, like on the big floppy disks from the olden days. He brought it over to our house and showed us how to use it, and me and Dunc used to spend *hours* every weekend playing those old games. Oregon Trail, Carmen San Diego, and this weird typing practice game with a rocket ship or something."

"Okay, hold on. Who's Papa Lucas, and who are Rem, Ram, and Rome?"

"Oh, right. I forgot you don't really know my family. Papa Lucas is…um…technically my…great-uncle? I think? I gotta think about it. He's basically my grandpa. My actual grandparents are all long gone, dead before I was even a twinkle in Dad's eye."

"Ew."

"Why ew?"

"Because a twinkle in your dad's eye means his eyes were twinkling because he was thinking about putting you inside your mama through his dick."

"Dude, Linz, what the fuck? That's *not* what that means."

"Sure it is, in a roundabout way."

"Well I'm not using the roundabout way." He

shuddered. "I do not need that in my head, woman, Jesus. It's bad enough that my parents are all over each other like white on rice without you putting shit like that in my head. Thank fucking *god* I've never walked in on them."

I laughed. "I walked in on Mom once. Although, in my defense, she had her bedroom door open, and it was three o'clock in the afternoon in July, so she *knew* I was around, she just chose to let Barry Godwin bend her over her bed, anyway. I walked in to see this skinny little bald dude with the dangliest ball sack I've ever seen in my life pounding her from behind. That shit is seared into my brain. She was all splayed out over the foot of the bed, and skinny fuckin' Barry was drilling away at her like Ramjet the Rookie. Mom turned to look at me, must've heard something, and just gave me the finger. Barry didn't even know. Just kept on fucking."

"Good lord."

"I swear, his balls hung halfway to his knees. It was like watching a pair of tube socks stuffed with baseballs swing back and forth."

Dane winced. "Thank you *so much* for that visual."

"He could've tossed them over his shoulder. Legit."

"Lindsey!"

"They were pink and hairy."

"Fuck me, woman, I *get* it. Shut the fuck up about the man's balls."

I dissolved into laughter. "I wish I was kidding! I just felt like if I have to have that in my head, then so do you."

He groaned. "You're demented. I could've gone the rest of my life without knowing that." He paused. "Wait, though. If he was facing away from you and standing up, then how could you see his balls?"

"He had his legs really far apart. They swung so far back each time he fucked her that they smacked him in the asshole."

"Dear god."

"I called him Long Balls Barry after that. He stopped coming around after a couple of weeks. Couldn't take the heat, I guess."

Silence.

"Linz, I…" he looked at me, frowning, sighed, and started over. "So now what?"

"Go home, Dane," I whispered. "You deserve someone who can…" I swallowed. "Someone who's not me. Someone that doesn't have a freight train a mile long full of trauma and baggage and bullshit."

"I don't like that answer," he murmured

"I know. But I can't be what you need. Not now. Maybe not ever. What I went through, Dane? You don't just get over it. You don't just…forget. It'll fuck me up the rest of my life."

"Maybe I'm willing to stand beside you anyway."

My eyes burned. "I don't know how to let you. I've

told you more than I've ever told anyone other than Rune, and I'm barely keeping my shit together as it is."

"Linz, I—"

"I don't *do* feelings, Dane. I don't do tender and sweet. I don't do lovey-dovey."

"Recent events lead me to believe otherwise."

I rolled out of bed, taking the quilt with me, leaving Dane naked on the bed. "I'm trying to be nice about this, Dane. I'm trying like fucking hell to be nice to you. If you were anyone else, you'd be gone already. Most likely, you'd be on a plane back to Alaska, and you'd probably be crying because I was such a vicious bitch to you. I can be like that. I'm kind of like a praying mantis or black widow. Once I fuck a dude, I turn mean. That way, they leave me alone before I get hurt."

He followed me across the room to the window, where I was standing with the blanket around my shoulders. I saw him in the reflection—huge and hard, all sun-browned skin and rippling muscles and messy, sexy, I-just-had-my-hands-in-it hair. "News flash, darlin'." He wrapped his arms around me from behind. "You were mean to me for *months*. You screamed at me. Ghosted me. Blocked me. Avoided me. Ghosted me again after the wedding. Yet I *still* hunted your ass down despite all that. And here I am, willing to keep taking the punishment."

"Why?" I asked. "Because we had some good sex?"

"Was it *really* just good sex, Lindsey?" His voice

was deep and commanding, now. "Was that *really* all it was?"

"No," I whispered, unable to lie about it.

"No," he agreed. "It was the best sex either of us has ever had, by an exponential factor. You know it, and I know it. But it was also more than that, Linz, and you know that too. I'm not here hoping for a repeat of the sex. If that was the case, we'd have fucked just now instead of what we did."

"Don't," I whispered, the word a breathy whine.

"You know it's true. If I'd given you the slightest hint, we'd have fucked." He put his lips to my ear. "You know you want it again every bit as much as I do."

"*Stop*, Dane. Please just—just fucking stop."

"But we didn't fuck, did we?" He wasn't stopping. "We just fooled around. But you wanna know something, sweetheart?"

"Not your sweetheart," I growled.

He ignored this too. "Fooling around with you, just now? That was more intimate and real than an all-night fuck-a-thon with anyone else." He nipped my earlobe. "Tell me I'm wrong."

I said nothing—and that said it all.

"Say I listen to you," he said. "Say I walk out that door and go home. You think this would be over between us?"

I was breathing hard, now. Swallowing a hot knot. "Shut up."

"You can't forget me. You can't get over me."

"Shut the fuck up!"

"I'm under your skin. I'm in your heart, Linz. You fucking know it."

"You're wrong."

"I'm not. You can lie to yourself, but you can't lie to me." He grabbed me by the shoulders, spun me around, and pushed me back against the window, the sill biting into the small of my back.

He cupped my face in gentle, powerful hands. His lips touched mine, teased, touched, slid—claimed. Hard. Fast. Deep. Just when I was about to soften into his kiss, he broke away.

Kept his hands framing my face. "You felt that, didn't you?"

"No."

"Liar." He slashed his mouth onto mine again, and kissed me until my heart pounded frantically and my knees shook and my belly flip-flopped. "Lie to me, Linz. Tell me you felt nothing."

"I felt nothing," I lied. "Not a single butterfly."

He yanked the blanket off of me and hurled it aside. His erection nuzzled my seam. "You want to try and fuck me out of your system, Lindsey?"

I whimpered. My hands lifted on their own and gripped his shoulders; I rested my forehead on his chest. "No."

"No?" He cupped my breast, bent, and sucked on my nipple until I gasped. "You sure?"

I shoved him away roughly, violently. "STOP IT!"

I screeched. "So the fuck *what* if I'm falling for you, Dane? What aren't you understanding?" I stomped toward him and shoved him again; he let me push him, stepping backward, fully in control. "I can't love you! I've never been loved! I've never been anything but used and abused! Rune and her parents took care of me, sure. But that was as much pity as anything else. I have nothing to give you. Nothing!"

"Lindsey," he started.

I bent over the bed. "Is this what you want? Take it. Take me! Fuck me! Use me, just like every other man has." I straightened and whirled on him. "Or no, wait—I've got that backward. I use *them*, Dane. You know why? Because some fucked-up part of my brain thinks if I have enough sex with enough random dudes, maybe I'll somehow get over what Danny fucking Cohen did to me every fucking day for *four fucking years*! I know I won't, but I do it anyway because I'm a dumb fucking whore! I'm a dumb fucking whore with a useless fucking degree from stupid fucking Stanford. I'll never amount to anything. I thought I could escape Boston, but I just brought my shit with me." I stepped into his space. "Hear me when I say this, and hear me well, Dane Badd: *I—cannot—love you*. I know that's what you want. You want what your family has. Good! You deserve that. You're a damn good man, Dane Badd. But you won't get it from me. So yes. Go home and try to forget me."

He gazed at me in sad silence for a long, long time.

And then he bent, picked up his T-shirt—the one he was wearing yesterday—and tugged it over my head. Numb and confused, I let him put my arms through the sleeves. Helpless to stop myself, I lifted black cotton to my nose and inhaled his scent.

Fuck.

My nose stung.

My eyes burned.

"Go home, Dane," I whispered. "Try to forget me. Maybe in a different universe I could be what you want me to be, but…here and now? I just can't be that girl for you."

He let out a long breath through pursed lips. Nodded. "Okay. Okay."

He stepped backward, face crushed by sorrow, regret, wistfulness, anger, and hurt. Without looking away from me, he got dressed. Boxers, jeans, socks, shoes—last of all, he put on the white T-shirt I'd kept all this time. The white T-shirt I'd been wearing for three days without washing—because it smelled like him. It must smell like me, now…but B-O and pussy stank, not perfume.

He shoved his phone into his back pocket, swept his hand through his hair, messing it up even more. "I'll just ask one question."

I swallowed hard. "Fine. I'll answer one question. *One*."

"Why—or how—did it stop?"

"He got arrested for rape and went to prison."

"Good riddance, then." He let out a breath. "Lindsey, I…" he covered his face with his hands for a moment, and then tried again. "I'll go. For now. But I'm not giving up on you. On this—on us."

"There is no us and never will be." My heart broke when I said that, because deep down, that's all I wanted.

I was telling the truth, though: I genuinely did not feel capable of love, giving or receiving. It was too scary. Too big. Too much for the pathetic ruins of my heart, which hadn't survived the trauma of my youth.

He stepped into my space, closer and closer until he occluded the whole world.

"Don'tkissme," I hissed, all in a rush. "Please. I can't take it."

He didn't respond. Cradled my face. Stared into my eyes. My heart broke and broke and broke and broke as I met his gaze, seeing the vast, incomprehensible scope of his feelings for me.

Still, he spoke not a word.

Instead of kissing my lips, he kissed my forehead.

Infinitely worse.

I shattered, then.

Wept.

Sobbed silently.

"Fuck you," I hissed.

"I know."

"You're ugly and stupid, and you have a tiny

penis, and you couldn't find my clit with a map and a flashlight."

His laugh was a quiet sniff. "I know."

"I hate you," I breathed, chin on my chest, tears dripping down my cheeks. "I really, really, really fucking hate you, Dane Badd."

"I know. I hate you too." He kissed my forehead again, which was cruel and mean and horrible.

I watched his feet as he walked backward away from me. He reached the door, paused. I shut my eyes so I wouldn't risk looking at him. I might break again if I looked at him.

I'm doing this for him, after all.

"This isn't over, Lindsey."

"Fuck you," I whispered, barely managing that much. "I hate you. Leave me alone."

If this was a Disney movie, he'd be the wild wolf that followed me across the wilderness and protected me from other wolves and I'd be the plucky heroine throwing sticks at him to make him go back to his pack, yelling at him through my tears, but only because I loved him, and when you love someone, sometimes it means letting them go.

Alas, I'm no Disney heroine, just a stupid whore with a broken heart. Dane did remind me of a wolf, though. The shaggy brown hair, the deep brown eyes. Dangerous. Wild. Unpredictable.

I heard the door open, and my stupid whore eyes slid open.

Damn me, he was beautiful. So fucking beautiful. So kind. So funny. So sexy.

Such a lovely penis.

I really must be stupid, running him off like this.

It's for his own good, though.

Stupid whores don't deserve love.

He stood in the doorway gazing at me. His liquid brown eyes were soft and warm and full of sentiment. Affection. Understanding.

"I love you, Lindsey Snelling."

Click.

He closed the door and was gone, after dropping that nuclear bomb in my lap.

I collapsed to the floor, sobbing.

I miss Rune.

I hate my life.

I hate Dane Badd.

I hate everything.

Fuck.

SIX

Dane

I STARED OUT THE WINDOW OF THE JET, WATCHING CLOUDS scud past thousands of feet below, heart aching, mind blank.

The trip to the airport had passed in a hazy blur. I don't know how long I sat in the lounge, waiting for my flight. I don't remember boarding.

And then I was jolted as we landed. I barely saw my surroundings as I boarded the ferry from the airport to the mainland.

"Dane, over here."

I turned in place, looking for the voice—Jax. "Did I text you?"

He clapped me on the back, guiding me toward his Li'l Red express. "Nope. Been keeping an eye on your location."

"You're stalking me?"

He eyed me. "You're sharing your location with me, Dane. Remember?"

"No."

"Couple months ago? We had that stupid cousin scavenger hunt party for Kieran's birthday, and we all shared our locations so we could cheat?"

"Oh, yeah!" I exclaimed, chuckling. "Whose dumbshit idea was that, anyway?"

"Uncle Bax, I think."

"Why did he think a scavenger hunt party was a good idea for his son's twenty-first birthday?"

Jax cackled. "Fuck if I know, bro. He's Uncle Bax. He's a fuckin' spazzy-ass weirdo." He socked my bicep. "It *was* low-key kinda fun, though, you gotta admit. Tweak the format a little, and it could be a killer tradition."

I frowned at him. "We spent four hours wandering around the greater Ketchikan area looking for dumb, random shit, Jax."

"I know! But think of the possibilities! Instead of random shit like a specific road sign or something, you make it things like…shit, I dunno…graffiti in bar bathroom, or a specific strain of weed at a dispensary or…or…well, you get the idea."

"Yeah, maybe."

He cranked the big diesel engine and let it warm up for a second, glancing at me. "You good, cuz?"

I let out a breath that was far too shaky for my own comfort. "To be honest, Jax, no. Not really."

"You wanna take Dad's boat out into the Passage and get spaced? I've got some killer flower."

I did not. I wanted to go home and cry like a bitch; I use that term in a strictly gender-neutral sense, by the way—men can be bitches, too.

But also, the thought of going back to my parents' house alone and…what, sit in my room feeling sorry for myself because a woman who was—I'm 99% sure—sexually abused at some point in her life is too emotionally vulnerable to be with me?

Grow the fuck up, Dane. Jesus. Pussy.

"Sure," I said. "Just…don't expect me to be my usual obnoxious self."

Jax laughed and whacked me on the shoulder—for a computer dork, he's strong as hell. "It's okay, cuz, I can be obnoxious for the both of us."

"Or we could just chill and *not* be obnoxious?"

Jax pretended to consider this notion for a second. "Nahhhhhh," he said. "That's lame."

And so, an hour later, I was lying on my back on the bow of Uncle Zane's fishing boat; Uncle Z calls it a fishing boat, but it's actually a former Coast Guard Defender-class Response Boat. How he got his hands on one of them, I have no idea. Former Navy SEALs get sweet boat connects, I guess.

The waves rocked the boat gently, and the sun was shining; the sky was clear and blue. Overhead, an eagle circled, banking around on a wingtip, occasionally giving off one of its strange, thin, chirpy little squawks.

No, the glorious and haunting *SCREEEEEE* call they use for bald eagles in the movies is not what they actually sound like—that sound is a red-tailed hawk. Eagles just sound like annoying little shits.

Lying beside me, head and shoulders aligned with our feet facing opposite directions, Jax puffed on the joint—which was big enough for two more people to smoke with us. When Jax says he wants to get "spaced" you'd better be sure you know what you're getting yourself into. The guy has a wild tolerance for cannabis. Pretty sure he could smoke ol' Willie under the table. Okay, maybe not, but he'd hold his own.

As for me? I'm more than just spaced, I'm on another planet; when a stoner gets so stoned he or she or they can't get off the couch, we call it "couch-lock." Well, I'm deck-locked.

Jax doesn't seem high at all. He could probably re-code an entire website right now. I'm pretty sure I've misplaced my feet, and I don't remember what color my hair is.

"Bro." It came out elongated: *BROOOOOOOOOOO*.

Jax laughed. "Bro?"

"What color is my hair?" I pinched a lock, but it was too short to see. "I can't remember."

Jax cackled, taking another long hit and then speaking while holding it in his lungs. "Purple, bro. Remember? You dyed it purple yesterday."

"Dude, what?" I rolled my head side to side, trying to see if he was telling the truth. "I did?"

"Yup."

I looked at him, and his shoulders were shaking. "You're a dick," I said.

"Just fuckin' with you, Space Cadet Badd."

"Yeah, and whose idea was it to take your dad's boat and get stoned? I have no tolerance, Jax, you know this."

"Yeah, that's why it's fun."

"Can you get us back? I don't think I can move."

"Yeah, I'm straight."

"I'd still love you if you weren't."

He elbowed me. "Shut up. I mean I'm not too stoned to drive the boat back."

"If you're not stoned out of your gourd right now, man, then you smoke *wayyyyy* too much pot," I told him.

"I've always had a high tolerance. First time I smoked pot with Jimmy Hansen, Colin Cray, and Kajuk Wilson, I didn't get high at all. They rolled another joint and I smoked the whole thing myself before I felt anything." He shrugged. "Just how I am."

"How *is* Kajuk, anyway?" I asked. "Haven't seen him in a while."

"Me either," Jax answered. "Not for a year or so. Last I heard, he was living in the interior somewhere near Fairbanks. He had all that trouble with Jess or whatever-her-name-was, remember? After that, he was just like, fuck this, and went native."

I snorted. "Dude. He's Inupiak. He *is* a native."

"Oh, right. Maybe I am a little high. But you know what I mean."

"Uncle Ink would cuff you upside the head for that ignorant ass bullshit."

"Fuck off. It's Kajuk. He'd laugh at me. And you know what I mean—the old ways or whatever."

"He was always talking about doing that, wasn't he? Getting away from everything."

"Jess really did him dirty," Jax said. "I know he wasn't innocent in that whole thing, but she did him dirty. I think it was more about starting over than anything else."

"I never liked Jess." I closed my eyes and let the world float around me.

"What happened in LA, Dane?" Jax's voice was quiet.

"And now we come to the real reason we're out here. Get me stoned and make me talk."

"Well, yeah. You're a tough nut to crack, Dane. You don't like talking about the real shit. You joke and act a fool to hide how you really feel about things."

"And you're so open?"

"About what? My life is about as interesting as a cardboard box. I code, I work for fucking Best Buy, I get stoned with friends, go for hikes, go fishing…there's no drama to talk about."

"You're telling me there's no part of you still pining after Sunni?"

He lurched upright in a swift, violent sit-up. "Oh fuck you all the way off, asshole."

I cackled. "Wow, some big-time metaphor mixing happening, there. I think it's either fuck you or fuck all the way off. It's never fuck you all the way off."

"Thanks for the cursing lesson, oh wise one."

"I notice you're not answering the question."

He groaned as he lay back down. "Pining? No. Do I still feel a little funny in my no-no zone when I see her? Maybe."

"See? Jokes about the real shit. It's not just me."

"I was in love with her for like half my life, bruh." He let out a long sigh. "You don't just get over that. I knew it was hopeless the whole time, you just can't help how you feel. I really have tried to move on. She's married. Her husband is a real one, and I genuinely like him. I'll never, ever do anything to make it weird. But is there a part of me that still has some residual feelings for her? Sure." He rolled to his side, taking a hit from the joint that he had in his fingers the whole time, smoldering. "Your turn."

"I don't know where to start."

"Anywhere."

"I told her I love her."

Jax burst into a hacking coughing fit. "Fuck. Jesus." Eyes watering, voice hoarse, raspy, and phlegmy, he blinked at me. "You fucking *what*?"

"I told Lindsey Snelling I love her. And then I walked out and came home."

"Harsh."

"It's what she wanted."

"Which part?"

"The walking out part."

"And the L-bomb part?"

"Probably not as much."

"I feel like there's a whole middle piece missing."

I tried to hold back, but it came tumbling out anyway. "We smashed, back when I went down there with Dunc when he went to get Rune back."

"No shit? She's fine as fuck. Was it epic?"

"Well, I'm in love with her. What do *you* think?"

"Those are separate things, Dane. You can have epic sex and not fall in love."

"Yes, it was epic. Up until she had a complete and total emotional breakdown mid-BJ."

"Dude, you never go for the deep-throat without asking first. Chicks *really* don't like that."

"Fuck off. I would never."

"I'm teasing."

"Well, it's not fucking funny to me. She went from acting like she was into it—into *me*—to having a screaming fit in the space of, like, ten seconds. No reason. I didn't do anything. I didn't even ask her to go down—she did it on her own. She just fucking lost it. Ran into the bathroom and screamed at me to get out, get out, get out." I groaned. "Fuck me, I am so sick of talking and thinking about that shit. I've gone in circles about it mentally a billion fucking times."

"Did she ever tell you what it was about?"

"Nope. Well, sort of. Indirectly. And I'm not sharing even the little bit she did tell me, because it's not my story to tell. But after she freaked out and I left, she blocked my number. I didn't see her again until the wedding, and she was...icy toward me. Avoided me. Then I found her having a breakdown in the alley and tried to comfort her. She wasn't having any of it. Fine, whatever. So I left again. Woke up in the guest room over the bar with her naked in bed with me."

"Nice. Round two?"

"Nope. She asked me to just hold her."

"Mean. Hot body like that, naked, all up in your shit, and you can't have it?"

"She was clearly so upset about whatever the fuck that it wasn't as difficult to deal with as you'd think. When a woman is that fucking upset, I'm not exactly thinking about smashing."

"I guess that's valid," he said. "So...then she, what? Vanished? Which is when you called me in?"

"Pretty much, yes. I woke up, and she was gone. Number still blocked. Fine, whatever. But then Raquel called me, saying she couldn't find her, and she wasn't answering her calls or messages either. And when a girl won't answer her bestie, we have a problem, especially if said girl is clearly going through some kind of crisis."

"Understood. So you showed up in LA, and she was, what, just chillin' at home like, why the big deal?"

"No. I mean, yes, she was at home. But she

wouldn't let us in. Wouldn't let Raquel in. If Rune had been there, she'd have let her in, maybe. Raquel and Hamish took the hint and left."

"But you're a stubborn-ass bitch, so you badgered her into letting you in."

"Pretty much." I sighed.

"Did she take a lot of convincing for her to tell you what the deal was?"

"I told you; she *didn't* tell me what the deal is. She hinted at it, vaguely. I just…once she let me in, I realized the last thing she needed was to have me demanding she bare her soul to me. She'd ghosted not just me but Raquel. Rune is on her honeymoon, obviously, and none of us are about to tell her about this because she'd come home early, and Linz doesn't want that."

"So she wasn't, like, at risk of self-harm?"

"No, or I wouldn't have left."

"So what happened? How'd you go from 'little pig, little pig let me in' to 'Lindsey, I love you?'"

"She put her finger up my butt."

Jax had been mid-toke when I said this, and he lost it, cackling and coughing. "The fuck?"

I laughed. "We just watched TV and talked about nothing important, and then crashed together on the couch. Woke up horny, and she was in nothing but my T-shirt, and…" I shrugged. "We fooled around."

"You'd already fucked, right? So why only fool around?"

"She…I dunno where to start, man. It's personal,

what happened. It wasn't just messing around. It wasn't just sex, either. That first time, I mean. She…I think she feels things, but it scares her. She doesn't want to feel things for me—for anyone. Whatever happened to her left some serious trauma behind. She's a mess. She's trying to deal with it, but some shit isn't easy to heal, y'know?"

"In theory, yes. I understand the idea." He handed me the roach. "We've lived pretty charmed lives, you know. We have a lot of blessings—most significantly, two parents who love each other and us, and no significant traumas."

"Right, exactly. We…it escalated. I know I normally have no problem sharing details, but this is different."

"Dane, bro, you can't lead with 'she put her finger up my ass' and then not spill the tea."

"Let's just say that I saw Jesus."

"Should I give you a dildo for your next birthday?"

"Fuck you, no. And this stays between us. Everything. You got me?"

"It's in the cousin box."

I rolled my eyes, snorting out smoke. "Flashback to tenth grade."

"Lotta shit in that cousin box."

"Like when you broke your dad's framed photo of his SEAL unit while we were playing bop-sock in your basement?"

He cackled. "Oh…my…*god*! Bop-sock! I haven't thought about that game in *years*."

Bop-sock was a game we rambunctious, half-feral boy-cousins used to play all the time as kids. You take a pair of socks, stuff one in a ball into the toe of the other, and swing them around like weapons, whacking each other with them mercilessly, either using a pillow for a shield or dual-wielding. It was a fun, mostly harmless game, but sometimes it'd get out of hand, and someone would end up with a black eye, or we'd break something and get sent outside.

"We claimed Doo-Dee broke it, as I recall," I said.

He face-palmed himself. "Doo-Dee was six inches tall and weighed half a pound, and the photo was on the wall at head height." Doo-Dee was their mini-poodle/Pomeranian mix dog, now gone over the Rainbow Bridge. She was a sweet little dog; the idea that she could have broken a picture on the wall was a comically implausible claim.

"Dad didn't buy it, obviously but he couldn't *prove* it was us. We weren't allowed to play bop-sock in the basement anymore after that, though." Jax sighed. "So was it, like, just *whoooop*, finger up the butt, or…?"

I groaned. "I shouldn't have said anything."

"No, but you did. I'm not gonna let it go."

"Two words, and that's all you get."

"Okay?"

"Prostate milking."

He spluttered. "Oh fuck, man. She's into *that*?"

"Huh?"

"It's a whole thing. Like, a whole subgenre of kink."

"I dunno about any of that, man. It was, like, maybe the first knuckle while jerking me off. It wasn't even kinky. It just felt fucking incredible. Best orgasm of my life."

"For real?"

"Fuck yes. I couldn't walk straight for like ten minutes."

"Huh. Maybe I should try that sometime."

"I'll get you a dildo for your next birthday," I said, laughing.

"No, you won't."

"Are you seeing anyone?" I asked.

"We aren't changing the subject, Dane. Still not understanding how that led to a profession of love followed by a French exit."

"It wasn't a French exit. I looked directly at her, told her I loved her, and then left."

"Whatever. So *again*—how do you go from a butthole-fingering handjob to I love you?"

"It's complicated."

"Is it?"

"She…I…we…" I sat up slowly, with effort, worked unsteadily to my feet, and took a long piss over the side; I sat back down next to Jax and tried again. "We talked. She was…not freaking out but…I dunno. She was conflicted. We have chemistry. Real deal shit.

Not just physical chemistry. Deep shit. The unexplain-able thing our parents all have—we have that. She's just in denial because of whatever happened and how bad it fucked her up. Her words, not mine—'I'm fucked up,' that's what she says all the time. Like she...she doesn't think she can have..." I shrugged. "Anything real, I guess. I don't know, she won't elaborate."

Jax didn't reply for a while. "And you thought de-claring your undying love was the move, huh?"

I stared at him. "I don't like how you said that."

"Oh, like you're an idiot?"

"Says the guy who—" I clapped my teeth together, deciding against that particular dig.

"You were about to be a meany-head, weren't you?" Jax guessed.

"Yep."

"I'm not in love with Em anymore. It's residual affection and latent attraction, because she is objec-tively hot."

"She's legally your first cousin, now."

"I know. But we share zero genetic material, I wasn't raised in the same house as her, and also she's married to someone else."

"I didn't actually say anything. I was gonna say something dickish, but decided against it. You're welcome."

"Dane, you've completely missed my entire fuck-ing point."

"Which is? How is me telling her I love her—which is the objective truth—being an idiot?"

"Because she can't handle that. She wouldn't have P-I-V sex with you because she was afraid of being dragged into feelings. I'm inferring, here, but it really seems like she used quasi-kinky sex—or foreplay, or whatever you wanna call what you did—to distract you from everything she didn't want to talk about, think about, or feel." He shrugged, pulling a *there you go* face. "She did everything she could to protect herself from what she feels like is a threat to her emotional stability, which seems pretty damn fragile. She was trying to get rid of you so she could get a grip on her shit. And you go and drop the L-bomb on her…and then leave."

"Fuck. I hadn't thought of it like that."

"Clearly. You think after you left, she sat on her balcony plucking flower petals and gazing wistfully into the sunset, daydreaming about your ass?"

"My ass? No."

"Dane. This is real shit, man."

"Shut up. You do the same thing."

"And you call me on it."

I sighed. "I know, I know." I groaned, rubbing my face with both hands. "I don't know what to do, Jax."

"If it were me, I'd give her some time."

"This is a dance of months, Jax."

"So? Whatever she went through is deep, dude. Clearly, it's an open wound, not even a scabbed-over thing. That shit is still bleeding. If you really love her, which I don't doubt, you're gonna have to be patient."

"Patience is not my strong suit."

"We're Badds, man. None of us are exactly over-flowing with it."

I cackled. "I dunno. Your mom is kind of a saint. She deals with your ass."

He flipped me off. "I'm her precious little angel."

"Mommy's boy."

"Yup!" He leveled a look at me. "And you're not? You're still living with them. Ten bucks says she does your laundry."

"Does not. Unless it's really stained." I wasn't gonna mention the jeans LIndsey washed which were, as we spoke, still in my bag...laundered.

"No, but for real! Why are moms so good at stains?"

"Periods, apparently."

"Huh?"

"They deal with bloodstains every month. You think after that a little mustard on your Care Bears T-shirt is a big deal?"

He hummed thoughtfully. "Oh. Huh. Never thought about that." He glared at me. "Also, don't throw shade at my Care Bears tee. It's vintage and cool as hell."

"I wasn't throwing shade. It's a cool shirt."

"You really love her, Dane? Like for real? It's not just wanting another shot at epic sex?"

"If I had made a move, we'd have had sex. It's not that."

"You sound awfully confident in that."

"I am."

"You don't get credit for not doing something bad."

"That's not my point. My point is that it's not about sex."

"You do you, boo, but if it were me, I'd give her some time and see what happens."

"I think that's the only thing *to* do," I said. "You think I'm a tough nut to crack? Lindsey is on a whole other level of impossible to get through to."

Silence, except the *chuck-slap* of waves against the hull and the squawking chatter of gulls.

"Okay, but like, the finger in the bungus…was it your idea or hers?"

"I shouldn't have said anything."

"But you *diiiiiid!*" he turned "did" into a three-syllable sing-song.

"Hers."

"Right, right, right. So, then—"

"Jax? Shut up. Try it yourself if you want to know what it was like."

"I just might."

"You'd need a girlfriend for that. Or a boyfriend, I'm not judging."

"Ever hear of casual sex?"

"Hell of a thing to do on a one-night stand. Like,

hey girl, we just met, and this is crazy, but would you finger my butt while you suck me off?"

"You may have a point. And I'm not discussing this any further."

I stabbed the sky with a forefinger. "To shore, Captain Bungus!"

"Yes, sir, Admiral Hole Puncher."

I stared at him. "The fuck?"

He turned red. "Shut up. It sounded funnier in my head."

I snickered. "Admiral Hole Puncher. Guess who's got a new online handle, now."

"You do?" he asked, hopefully.

"Nope, you. I'm gonna hack into your Fortnite account and change your name to Admiral Hole Puncher."

"You couldn't hack into an open-source browser."

"I could figure it out."

"Dane, if you can change my handle in Fortnite, I swear to god I will give you my truck."

"You really don't think I could?"

"Nope." He grinned. "Mainly because I don't play Fortnite anymore. I got bored of owning everyone."

"Oh, come off it. I beat you every time."

"Try me in Apex."

"No one plays Apex anymore."

"There are more diehards left than you'd think."

"Wait, wait, wait. Remember our Goldeneye tournaments over Christmas break?" I grinned at him.

"Let's get the gang together and see if it holds up. I have my N64 in the basement, still."

"You mean *my* N64?" he corrected.

"No, mine."

"I got it for Christmas."

"Yeah…from Merrick, who stole it from my house while I was at hockey camp and gave it to you."

He blinked at me. "Wait, *what*? You're fucking with me."

"Nope. He confessed at a barbecue last summer. You were too busy flirting with Isaac's girlfriend to hear him."

"She's out of Isaac's league."

"Uh, yeah. She's in New York modeling for, like, Givenchy and shit. How he snagged her in the first place is the real mystery."

"He *is* funny," Jax said. "Like, really funny. I think it's a Pete Davidson sort of thing."

"What, like B-D-E?"

Jax waved both hands. "Why are we talking about this? Are we calling everyone for a Goldeneye tourney or what?"

"Wait, like *everyone*?" I said. "Not *everyone* everyone."

"No, not literally all thirty-six of us or whatever it is," he said. "Marco, Isaac, Kieran, Merrick, Lucas, and Lennox. And Donovan. That's the crew who used to do the Goldeneye marathons."

"You think the dads would want in?" I suggested. "Bax, Brock, Canaan, and Corin all used to get in on it."

"It's from their generation, so we should probably invite them, yeah." He pointed at me. "You text the cousins, I'll text the dads. And bro? Keep it short and spell check your shit. You're high as a motherfucker and you know the cousins will say shit, and I don't have enough to smoke down all of us. I'm broke till payday—that joint was the last of my flower."

I clapped him on the shoulder. "I appreciate you, Jax. Thanks for this. I needed it."

He pinched my cheek. "I know you did. Now—whose house? You have the best basement."

"Let me make sure my folks are cool with us all dropping in."

"Yeah, good plan. I don't wanna walk in on Uncle Bast and Auntie Dru gettin' freaky...*uhhhh*-gain."

I lowered my phone and stared at him. "*Again?*"

"Unfortunately, yes. I thought I'd swing by and say hey to you one afternoon—this was, like, two years ago. I thought you'd be home 'cause you usually were at that time on that day. They always said the door is open, we're all family, just come on in. So I did."

"Oh god."

"Yup."

"Don't tell me anymore. Please. I'm begging you."

"Couch. Reverse Cowgirl."

"FUCK YOU! I said *don't* tell me anymore, you ass-clown!"

"If I have to know that, so do you."

"Those are my fuckin' *parents*, Jax. Jesus." This was feeling like déjà vu.

"They're my aunt and uncle! You gotta admit, though—it's inspiring. I want that for myself, some-day. A relationship where we're still fucking like porn stars after twenty-some years, you know?"

"Yes, yes, yes, I agree, me too, but we can not talk about my parents and their sex life anymore, please? I swear I'll name my firstborn after you if we can change the fucking subject."

We bantered all the way back across the Passage to shore, but my mind was only partly on the conversation.

The rest of me was back in LA, wondering what Lindsey was doing, how she was feeling...

And more than anything, whether or not Jax was right that me professing my love was a shit move.

As Mom used to say to us kids all the time when we were arguing and started saying mean shit:

Just because something is true doesn't mean you have to say it; sometimes the kindest thing you can say is nothing at all.

SEVEN

Lindsey

*B*AMBAMBAM. "LINDSEY NOREEN SNELLING! OPEN THIS fucking door right this goddamned second!"

Oh dear. Rune was using the full name—she knew how I felt about my middle name: hate, hate, hate, *LOATHE ENTIRELY*.

"No!" I shouted. "I'm not home."

"Do I have to have Duncan kick the door down?"

"Hey, now, don't bring me into this," I heard Duncan say. "I'm just here for moral support."

"You just can't kick down a door, can you?"

"No," he muttered. "It's harder than it looks."

"Which means you've tried?"

"Long story. Short version is Dane locked me out of my room when I popped out to pee while doing a loot run in Diablo Four."

"So you tried to kick your door down?"

"I was fourteen and didn't pause it, just kept a passive effect spell going that killed all the minor minions."

"Dunc, baby—"

"You don't care about Diablo, I know."

"CAN YOU TWO HAVE THIS CONVERSATION ELSEWHERE?" I shouted. "I'm not home."

BAM! My door rattled with a shuddering impact.

"RUNE RIGBY BADD! Stop kicking my door!"

"I'm not—" *BAM!* "Kicking it." *BAM!* "I'm—" *BAM!* "Shoulder charging it." *BAM!* "Ow."

"Babe, stop. You're gonna dislocate your shoulder. Trust me when I say that shit *really* hurts."

I shuffled to the door, undid all three locks, opened the door a crack, and shuffled back to my couch, where I plopped back down, tossed my blanket back over my bare legs, and resumed eating Boom Chicka Pop chocolate sea salt drizzle popcorn and watching a *Teen Mom* replay marathon.

Duncan took one step inside, looked around, looked at me, and turned right back around. "I'm gonna… ummm….go do…things. Elsewhere."

"Good plan," I mumbled, mouth full of popcorn, which I washed down with a swig of…you guessed it, box wine.

Once Duncan had shut my door, Rune re-enacted Dunc's survey of my place: it was a pigsty. Not just for me, for anyone. Dishes were piled up in the sink, there was a carryout container that probably contained a lifeform NASA would be fascinated to study, and we're not going to talk about the pile of empty wine boxes by the garbage can.

Or the sex toys on the coffee table.

Or the fact that I was still in Dane's T-shirt, and hadn't showered since he left…. *mumbles inaudibly under her breath* days ago.

With a heavy, long-suffering sigh, Rune tossed her purse on the table by the door, kicked off her shoes and socks, took off her bra from beneath her T-shirt, shucked her yoga pants, and climbed pantsless under the blanket with me.

She ate my popcorn and watched a good fifteen minutes of the show with me without saying a damn word.

That, my peeps, is the definition of a bestie. She's the girl who yeets her bra and takes off her pants, no questions asked.

Finally, I poured myself more wine and muted the TV, which was a shame because Amber and Gary were about to really get into it.

"How was your honeymoon?" I asked.

She spied a six-pack of mini Diet Cokes on the floor under the coffee table—don't ask—and snagged one. "Fantastic. We swam in the ocean, had romantic candlelight dinners on the beach, and had fabulous sex in just about every pregnancy-possible position you can think of on just about every horizontal and vertical surface in the room, including the balcony."

"Oooh, hotel balcony sex is fun."

"Not when you're our upstairs neighbor. They shouted at us to please stop strangling the cat."

I spluttered a laugh. "You *do* sound like a cat when you're coming, a little."

"You don't know that."

I swigged wine, which loosened my tongue—not that it needs loosening, the flappy bitch. "Um, hello? Was I or was I not in the next room when Hayes drilled you into kingdom come on that trip to Myrtle Beach, our sophomore year?"

Rune grimaced. "Oh. Right. Forgot about that."

"The boy was a class-A loser and ding-dong fuck-nut for the ages, but he sure could use that dick."

Rune sighed. "You're not wrong."

"Can I ask you something I've been wondering for a long time?"

"Obviously."

"You always told me that Hayes was the best sex you ever had. Is that still true, or...?"

She crammed popcorn into her mouth like it was going to run away and join a convent. "No. Not even close. Hayes wasn't the *best* sex I ever had; he was the most *consistently good* sex I ever had. Until Dunc, the *best ever* was Brutus."

I cackled, spluttering wine through my fingers. "Fuck me!" I coughed, gagged, and leaned forward, as I'd rather drip wine on my floor than my/Dane's T-shirt. Fortunately, I had a stack of brown paper carry-out napkins handy. Once I'd cleaned myself off, I turned on Rune. "Brutus? That giant beefcake you hooked up with before Hayes?"

"Yup."

"I remember you saying it was good, but better than Hayes?"

"Well, that's my point. Brutus was hit or miss. It was either pathetic and awful, or goddamned spectacular."

I arched an eyebrow at her. "Rune, he was bipolar."

"Wait, what? He *was*? How do *you* know?"

"Because while you were fucking him, I was fucking his buddy Clint. And Clint was a post-sex chatty Cathy, lemme tell ya. That boy *loved* gossip. If I didn't know better, I'd think he was gay, he loved the tea that much. And he told me that he knew for a fact that Brutus was diagnosed as bipolar but hated the meds. He'd go on and off them all the time. Sex drive issues is one of the side effects of the medication. Or some of the meds, at least."

"That would explain it. Why wouldn't he tell me, though? I feel bad, now. I never said anything to him, but I had a lot of unkind thoughts about it. He was a sweetheart…some of the time. Other times, he was either a ball of mayhem and chaos or freaking Eeyore. Bipolar makes so much sense of it all."

"It can be hard to talk about. My aunt was bipolar, and I overheard her talking to Mom about it a few times, about how much of a struggle it can be. Plus, we studied it for my degree."

"Why didn't you live with your aunt when you ran away?" she asked.

"Well, mostly because she was dead by then. Killed herself in a drunk driving accident the year before I ran away—drove into a tree doing sixty in a snowstorm."

"Shit, I'm sorry to hear that. I had no idea."

I shrugged. "I wasn't close to her because she wasn't close to anyone except Mom, and she and Mom would fight like cats and dogs, not talk to each other for months at a time, and then Aunt Delulu would show up drunk, and she and Mom would go on a bender for a week."

"Aunt Delulu?"

"Her name was Delilah. Mom called her Auntie Delulu to me, and this was *way* before 'delulu' was a thing." I sighed. "The other reason I wouldn't have gone to her was she wouldn't have taken me in. Or if she had, it probably wouldn't have been any better of a living situation. Auntie Delulu wasn't exactly responsible, as evidenced by her manner of death."

"You know," Rune said, "just when I think I know you, you pop out with something new. You've got more layers than Shrek, girl."

I chuckled. "Right now I'm more like an onion— stinky and no one likes me."

"Okay, well, first of all, that's bullshit on a number of levels, so no. Lots of people like onions, and lots of people like you."

I sighed and tipped sideways on the couch, so my

head was on Rune's lap over the blanket. "I know, I know. I'm just wallowing in self-pity."

"I can tell."

I frowned up at her. "What gave it away?"

She stared at me like I'd suggested we shave our heads and become Buddhist monks. "Um, I have eyeballs? You smell like a dead raccoon, also. Furthermore, your apartment resembles an abandoned science lab. Additionally, I talked to Raquel."

"Raquel. Well, Raquel doesn't know everything."

"She, Hamish, and Dane had to have Cousin Jax cyberstalk you because you ghosted everyone and gave them a suicide scare."

"I wasn't—"

"I know," she interrupted. "I know. I really do. If only because I hope and pray that if you *were* having thoughts of self-harm, you'd *call* me."

"I just needed to be home, alone, and not answer any goddamned questions."

"You could've just told them that," she said.

"Yeah, well, panic isn't rational, and I was having, like, an extended-release panic attack. I wasn't lucid or rational; I was acting like a fucking nutcase. I just wasn't at risk of self-harm."

"You're still acting like a fucking nutcase, honey, hate to break it to you." She gestured around. "This isn't just wallowing in self-pity; this is a few steps beyond that. And I say that with all the love in my heart for you—which is a fucking lot."

"I know!" I shouted. "I'm still panicking!" I couldn't stay still anymore; I shot to my feet and paced across the width of the apartment, stabbing my fingers into my knotted, greasy hair; I yanked my hand away and looked at it in disgust, and then pinched a lock of hair and looked at it in horror. "I should just start calling myself Oscar the Grouch, because I'm living that dumpster life, clearly."

Rune followed me across the floor, grabbed me, stopped me, and forced me to look at her. "Linz, what the *fuck* is going on? I know you didn't want to interrupt my honeymoon—"

"Because you'd have dropped your brand-new hubby and come running, and you deserve happiness, and he gives it to you."

"But if you're going through something serious enough that Raquel had my brother-in-law's cousin—my cousin-in-law, I guess?—cyber-stalk you because they were that worried about your state of mind, yeah, I need to be there."

"No, you don't, because I'm not a fragile little dumpling, Rune. Yeah, I'm going through some shit. It sucks. I'm in a bad place right now, I'm not gonna lie." I leaned in and wrapped my arms around her. "Yes, I need my bestie, but I love you enough and know my own limits well enough to know that I can deal until you're back. Also, why are you in LA? Why didn't you fly into Ketchikan?"

She shrugged. "It was cheaper to fly into LA with a totally separate flight to Ketchikan a few days later."

I arched an eyebrow at her. "So this was the plan all along? You didn't spend thousands of dollars to alter your travel plans on my behalf?"

"No?" She looked away when she said it, though, while rubbing her belly.

"You did!" I screeched, irate. "You fucking *did*!"

"We changed our plans *a little*, yes. But you really, seriously need to calm your tits, girl. It didn't cost us thousands of dollars. It actually works out better, if you must know. Dunc's Uncle Brock, as you know, is a pilot, and he has a friend who's a pilot for a private jet company—they sell seats at a discount to groups, and when they only have a few individual seats left, they sell those at a discount too. We changed our destination from Ketchikan to LA, and Brock got us a pair of seats on a private jet from here to Ketchikan for pennies on the dollar. This way, we get to stop by here and see you, spend time in LA with my folks, and help them pack up the house before we go back to Ketchikan and start our lives, *and* we get to ride in a private jet and pretend we're Heather and Terry Dubrow." She shook me gently. "It wasn't *entirely* about you, okay?"

"Fine. As long as you didn't do it entirely for me. That would piss me off."

"Oh no, someone cares for you," Rune said in a droll, sarcastic monotone. "How horrifying."

I groaned. "Rude."

"Something tells me that letting someone care about and for you is at the center of your current emotional… situation."

"Emotional situation, is it?" I muttered. "Funny way of saying 'total breakdown.'"

"But yet you'd be pissed off at me for going even slightly out of my way to be there for the person who is, for all intents and purposes, my sister?"

"Shut up."

"Linz. Talk to me. Tell me what's going on, *please*."

I tipped my head back and let out a groaning sigh. "Fine. But I need to shower first. I'm disgusting."

Rune, none too gently, shoved me toward my room. "Yes, please, dear Jesus, get clean. I'll work on…" she waved a hand at my apartment. "This."

"Rune, you don't have to—"

She flipped me off with both hands. "But I'm going to, bitch, so deal with it. Go take the hottest shower known to mankind. You smell like you just crawled out of a sewer."

I stopped on the threshold of my room. "Wow, nice. Fuck you too."

"As your ride-or-die, it is my prerogative—nay, my *obligation*—to tell you the unvarnished truth. And the truth, dearest friend forever, is that you look and smell so bad a fucking hobo would cross the street to avoid you."

I flipped her off without looking and then shut the door to my room. I slumped back against the closed door, sniffling. I was putting on a brave face for Rune, which I knew wouldn't last once I started talking. She could always get the dirty truth out of me, the bitch. I stared at my bed—still rumpled, sheets and blankets twisted and tangled…from Dane and me being in the bed together.

That's right: I haven't slept in my bed since he left because it'll smell like him and remind me of him and that'd just make it all that much worse, so I've been sleeping on my couch.

I'm that much of a coward.

First, I stripped the sheets off my bed and tossed them to the side so I *had* to wash them. Next, I peeled the shirt off and sniffed it, then gagged. Fuck, I have to wash it. I wonder how I can get my hands on another of Dane's articles of clothing without having to actually interact with him. Sneak into his parents' house like a big titty ninja who's clutzy and also not a ninja, steal a bunch of his T-shirts, boxers, and hoodies, and sneak back out? Getting to and from goddamned *Alaska* is a bit of an issue with that plan, aside from being fucking stupid.

I scrubbed my face and tossed the shirt on my pile of dirty laundry—which was so large I may have to consider hiring a sherpa to help me with it.

Sad day—no more boyfriend shirt.

Fuck me—it's *not* a boyfriend shirt. How do you scrub an errant thought out of your brain?

I turned on the shower and brushed my teeth—twice.

I took my time in the shower, scouring my skin until I was pink, and then shaved myself from pits to ankles, because nothing feels as clean as being freshly depilated. I washed my hair twice, conditioned it once, gave my pits and bits another scrubbing just because, and then rinsed off and got out. I dried my hair and brushed it until it was a voluminous mass of glossy glory, left it loose and wild, and dressed in a sexy thong, my most comfortable sports bra, the leggings that make my ass look stellar, and my favorite T-shirt, a V-neck that did spectacular things to my boobs, even with a compressive sports bra.

Sometimes, you just gotta look good to feel good, y'know? Not for anyone but you, but because you've been wallowing in self-pity like a hog in a mud puddle and it's time to put on your big girl panties and face the shittery that is your life. In my case, my big girl panties happen to be a scarlet thong that barely covers my yoohoo.

Ever so unhelpfully, my idiot brain decided to ask what Dane would think of me in the thong. The other part of my idiot brain answered that he'd salivate and then rip it off. And maybe stuff the thong in his pocket to sniff later.

Why do dudes like to sniff panties? I get eating pussy—trust me, I'm a fan. But sniffing old underwear is just weird. Like, I farted in those, bro. You really wanna sniff my farts? I guess some dudes would, but… ick. Good thing I don't have my phone in here, or I'd be tempted to call him just to ask if he's a panty-sniffer or not; I think not—I vaguely remember him saying something along those lines when he was here.

Clean, dressed, and feeling less like Oscar the Grouch, I went to the living room to find that Rune had turned into Tropical Storm Rigby while I was in the shower. There were several trash bags piled by the door, my coffee table once more had a surface other than trash, and she'd even done the dishes and vacuumed.

She was washing her hands when I entered the kitchen. "Hey. Feel better?"

I nodded, blowing out a breath. "Yes, much." I hugged her tightly from behind while she rinsed her hands. "Thank you, Rune. I don't know what I'd do without you. I was honestly so overwhelmed by the filth that I was sort of just accepting it as my new lot in life."

She shook her head. "Nah, you'd have pulled yourself out of it eventually. I just gave you a little jump-start." She dried her hands, draped the towel over the oven handle, and turned to grab me by the shoulders. "Now. I threw out your wine—you need to dry out, honey. Drinking isn't a coping mechanism; it just fucks you up worse. You know this—you are *not* your mother."

That fucking hurt, that last sentence. I yanked out of her arms and turned away, abruptly so furious it wouldn't have surprised me if steam was coming out of my ears. I had to literally bite my tongue to keep from cursing her out.

When I was more in control, I turned back to her.

"Rune, I hope you know that you're the only human being on the planet who could say that to me and walk away with all their teeth."

She gave me a soft, loving look. "I know, that's why I said it. I'm the only one who can, and it needed to be said. You know I'm right. I'm sorry it hurts, but you're engaging in the same self-destructive spiral. You worked way too fucking hard to distance yourself from her and that kind of life to go down that vortex of self-destruction now, honey. I love you too much to let that happen."

I had to face the facts: she was absolutely right. Whenever life didn't go her way—which was always—Mom would drown her sorrow, anger, and frustration in the bottom of a liter of sweet red wine. Sometimes, she'd finish one and walk to the corner store for another. I swore, growing up, that I'd never be her. I'd *never* use alcohol to cope.

Yet how many boxes of wine had I gone through in the last week? I refused to count, nausea and shame tangling in my gut.

"Fuck me," I whispered. "I'm turning into my goddamned mother."

"No, you're not," Rune insisted, shaking me. "You're recognizing the problem and taking steps to correct it. You only become your mother if you keep going the way you were. Is that who you are? Is that who you want to be?"

"No," I muttered.

"Louder."

"NO!"

"Then you're good. I'm down to get lit with you any time, you know that, but only if it's for fun, not escape."

"You're pregnant, dummy. You can't drink."

"I know. You know what I mean."

"And then you'll be a mother. You can't go around getting lit with your irresponsible best friend."

She sighed. "I'm sure I'll be able to finagle a tipsy Friday night out with you once in a while."

"You'll be in Ketchikan."

She nodded. "Yeah. But Rune, do you really, *actually* want to keep living in LA by yourself?"

"Raquel is here." When Rune didn't answer that, warning bells went off. "Right?"

"Um, actually, when I talked to her a bit ago, she told me that Hamish had gotten a job offer in Seattle, which is only an hour and a half by air from Ketchikan, and Uncle Brock flies to Seattle regularly."

I sighed. "Fuck. So I *will* be here by myself."

"Not if you come to Alaska with me," she said.

"Fuck Alaska. It's cold."

She laughed. "It's really not." A shrug. "Not in Ketchikan, at least."

"It's Alaska!"

"The winters in Ketchikan see more rain than snow—apparently, the weather there is more Seattle than Arctic Circle. Duncan and Mama Badd convinced me—that was a big hangup for me, too. I had this idea that Ketchikan winters were, like, arctic or something. Apparently not."

"What would I do there?"

She snorted. "You *do* know they have bars there? And you are currently a cocktail waitress, despite having a BS in psychology from fucking *Stanford*."

"There are no jobs here."

"Exactly! In Ketchikan, you can do what you're doing while paying less in living expenses and figure out what you want to do that's not serving booze." Her eyes narrowed. "Unless there's—*ah-HEM*—some *other* reason you may have for wanting to avoid Ketchikan."

"No!" I said, too immediately and too vehemently.

"Methinks the lady doth protest too much," Rune said.

"You just...shush." I said, pinching her lips together. "Shushy time for you."

She blew a raspberry at me, but it just came out the sides, along with some spit, which sent us both into paroxysms of laughter.

Once we'd regained our composure, Rune pushed me out of the kitchen toward the front door. "Shoes, phone, keys, purse."

"Where are we going?" I asked.

"To get you some fresh air and sunshine."

"But the daystar burns us."

"Lindsey."

I stomped a foot. "Ugh! You're mean. I don't *like* fresh air and sunshine."

"Oh, stop being dramatic. It's good for you, and you know it. Now get your shit, woman, we're going."

Which is how I found myself sweating like a pig as we hiked through hell—I mean, some ridiculous trail or other in the hills. I don't know. This girl doesn't *hike;* I walk where I need to go and no further. I know, I know, I used to be an athlete, I should be able to walk a slightly challenging and well-groomed trail without falling apart, but here we are. Duncan trailed behind us, earbuds in his ears and a happy smile on his face. Rune was waddling along happily as well. I was the only one with a murderous expression on her face.

Eventually, Rune, puffing, called a halt as we reached a bench on a crest with a sweet view of LA. We sat, and Duncan fished a pair of water bottles from his backpack and handed them to us, wandering away to sit by himself.

"Start talking, Linz," Rune ordered. "Leave nothing out."

"Well, it all started roughly six billion years ago, when an ape decided it wanted to be a homo sapien..."

Rune rolled her eyes at me. "Ha fucking ha."

"Rune—"

She stuck up an index finger. "NO! No excuses,

no rabbit holes, no bullshit. Tell me what happened and why is it Dane?"

I sighed. "God, pushy."

"I know you. You can squirrel out of conversations with other people, but not me. I know your tricks. Spill, bitch, or I'll have to get creative."

That usually involved bribery—I could be persuaded to do just about anything if you offered me high-quality gelato. Don't tell Dane, though.

Why did I think that?

Fuck!

"I see that brain doing things. Make word sounds, woman. You know you'll feel better. Talk to Mommy."

I reared back with a horrified expression. "No, no, no, no. Nope. Absolutely the fuck not. You wanna have Duncan call you mommy? Cool. But *we* are not doing that."

She grimaced. "I don't know what came over me. I'm sorry. That was weird, and it just sort of came out."

"Hopefully, the baby comes out as easily."

"No rabbit holes. We aren't talking about me being a mother. We're talking about what happened between you and Dane and why it led to you going full hoarder in your apartment."

I had to just tell her. She wouldn't let up until I did, and she really would get creative in making me talk.

"If you promise me gelato later."

She rolled her eyes. "*Fine*, I'll get you a fucking ice cream. Jesus, you child."

"It is *not* mere ice cream, you peasant. It's *gelato*."

"*Lindsey Snelling*."

"We fucked." It popped out of me like a hemorrhoid.

"When?"

"When Duncan and Dane came down here to get you back with Duncan. While you and your folks were getting to know Duncan, Dane and I left. We got dinner, drinks, and boned."

"Okay." She gave me a look, rolling her hand. "And?"

"I sort of freaked out."

I related the whole story—every gory, embarrassing detail. Even the fingering.

"Wait, he let you do that?" She asked, looking speculatively at her husband.

"Yes, ma'am. Claims it was an all-time best orgasm."

"How much of your finger was it?"

I indicated my first knuckle. "Just like that. It's not about plundering his booty, it's just a little added stimulation to increase the intensity."

She whipped out her phone and sent a text message, watching Duncan with hawkish intensity, a smirk on her face. A second later, Duncan tugged out his phone, tapped, read…and his eyes widened. He was mid-sip of his water and spluttered, coughing. He turned a look on Rune, who was cackling. He sent a reply without looking away.

Rune's phone dinged, and she read his message, biting her lip. "It's about to go *down*."

I snickered. "He's interested in the idea, I take it?"

"You could say that." She looked at Duncan with a sly, seductive look, licked her lips, and then mimed giving him oral—you know, moving your fist toward your mouth and sticking your tongue into your cheek. She also curled her finger in a come-here gesture.

Duncan turned beet red.

"Be warned, babe," I told her. "It'll turn him into a geyser, so if you do that while giving him head, be ready to swallow a gallon of his man-juice."

"Mmmm," she hummed. "Sounds good to me. I've legit been craving his baby batter as I enter the third trimester."

"Shut up," I snorted. "You do not."

"I do! My libido is through the fucking roof. He's gotten more head from me over the last ten days than in all the time we've been together since we met. He had to stop me from blowing him in the backseat of the Uber on the way here."

"I bet he's happy about that."

She laughed. "I've had to convince him that he doesn't need to match me one-for-one."

"Why on earth would you do a silly thing like that? Let the man nosh your taco as much as he wants."

"It takes me less than five minutes to make him blow his load, but it takes me twenty to get there. We don't have that kind of time. Plus, I don't crave that. I crave his dick. It's an oral fixation or something, I dunno. Pregnancy does weird-ass shit to you, man, I'm telling you."

"Not that I've known a lot of pregnant women, but this is the first I'm hearing of this side effect. Maybe you just like giving your man head."

"Oh, I do, no doubt about that at all. He just gets so pathetically, hysterically stupid and grateful. It makes me laugh. But it's not that. It's literally when I hit the third trimester mark that my libido got hit by an after-burner. I want his dick all the time."

"Lucky man."

"Lucky me," she countered. "He went out at three in the morning looking for Skittles and Frito-Lay corn chips because I got a craving. He rubs my feet whenever I ask. He doesn't bat an eye when my mood swings like goddamned Tarzan. He didn't ask a single question when I told him to put my pillow in the freezer."

I coughed, choking on a laugh as I took a drink. "I'm sorry, *what*?"

"I get hot, okay? Really, really, really fucking hot, especially at night. Our suite at the resort had a full fridge, so he got me an extra pillow and put it in the freezer. Then, when I got hot in the middle of the night, he went and got it and put the other one in. Boom, cold pillow."

"Never having a baby," I muttered. "Turns you into a fucking lunatic."

"Legit, it does," She agreed. "I find myself doing and saying things, and I'm like, is that me? What *the fuck* am I saying? But then you get a craving, and you just…there's no ignoring it. It's a kind of madness, I tell you. And the sex drive! Oh my *god*. I'm worried I'm gonna deplete him or something. Like, burnout from too much fucking—this trimester, at least. I couldn't even *touch* him until the second trimester, the poor guy. And we're not gonna talk about the pee situation."

"Pee situation?"

"Every ten minutes, all day, all night. More frequently if he or she starts dancing on my bladder."

"You don't know the gender?"

"We decided we don't want to know. When we have our baby shower, we're asking for gender-neutral gifts."

"Why wouldn't you want to know?" I asked.

She shrugged. "The baby was a surprise, obviously, so we figured what the hell, might as well keep the surprise theme going." She eyed me. "You know, the apartment over the bar where we're gonna be living has several bedrooms. We'll need one for a nursery, but I feel like you could have the other one. I'd have to clear it with Dunc, of course, but wouldn't it be fun to live together again?"

"You, your husband, your baby, and me, huh?"

"And Dane…?"

"Rune, no. I can't even handle the idea of having feelings for him. We are so far away from joking about living together, it's not even funny."

"Who's joking?"

"Did you hear *nothing* I said?"

"Yeah, I heard you." She shrugged. "I just think

you're fighting a losing battle. He told you he loves you, Linz. He's a good guy. He's perfect for you. He won't bat an eye at your craziness. If anything, your individual brands of crazy complement each other."

"You are spectacularly unhelpful."

"What, you thought I'd think you're being rational about this?"

I stared at her. "Of course I'm not being fucking *rational*. You think I *want* to be like this?" I rapped on my temple as if knocking on a door. "I feel as fucking nuts as I must seem. I *know* Dane is a good guy. He's sweet, he's funny, he's sexy, he gives fucking *incredible* dick, goes down like a pro, and isn't scared of how kooky I am. He's patient. He's understanding."

"You're not making a great case for having kicked him out of your life, Linz."

"I *know*," I groaned. "I don't *have* a good case for it. It's stupid—*I'm* stupid. I just can't seem to…" I shook my head. "I'm too scared. Too messed up."

"What's the worst that could happen if you were to try and be with him? Like for real."

"He would discover that I'm impossible to love. I'd be unable to ever enjoy a normal sexual relationship with him because of what happened. It'd last all of a month before I did what I always do and sabotage the whole thing before he had a chance to break my heart."

Rune leaned her head on my shoulder. "You do realize that's fear talking, right? That's not reality. None of that is a given."

My heart twisted, coiled, flipped on itself. "I recognize that intellectually, Rune, but convincing myself of it is a whole different thing, and I am nowhere even close to that." I stood up. "If there was a quick fix for what's wrong with me, I'd take it. But there's not. I don't know if there *is* a fix."

"What if the fix is what you're afraid of?"

"You can ask *what if* all day long, Rune. No amount of logic is gonna change anything. I wish it would. I really, really do. And now, if you please, I'm hot, hungry, and tired of talking about this. I'm tired of fresh air and sunshine. I want to go back to being a cranky recluse."

"I'm not letting that happen."

"I'm considering getting twenty-six cats and becoming a crazy cat lady with a collection of cute sex toys. I'll get all my food delivered and become a quirky best-selling romance novelist living in a tumbledown Gothic Revival mansion in Upstate New York, where I'll also have a pet hedgehog named Spike Flea. Except when a handsome city boy gets lost and ends up on my property, I'll run him off and go back to being a recluse, because Hallmark can go fuck itself with its false and misleading advertising."

Rune stared at me from the bench. "Are you finished?"

"Yes."

She extended her hands to me. "Good. Help me up—I'm a beached whale."

"You're not even that big yet."

"Goodyear Blimp, coming through."

She waited until we were back at the trailhead before grabbing both of my hands and facing me with a serious expression. "If you don't give Dane, and yourself, a chance, you'll regret it for the rest of your life. No, he can't fix you—because you're *not* broken. You've suffered a lot. You have scars and open wounds. He *can* help you heal, Linz, but if you won't give him a chance, he can't. And if you don't let him try, I promise you, you'll look back at this when you're a sad, bitter, lonely old hag with your cats and your hedgehog and you'll regret letting fear win. You'll hate yourself for it. You'll be your mother, Lindsey. I bet if you asked her, assuming you could get the truth out of her, she'd tell you the same thing. At some point along the way, she let an opportunity slip away because she was too afraid to try."

I had no response to this, but she didn't seem to want or expect one.

We went to her parents' house and spent the rest of the day helping them box up their lives. I faked cheerfulness and my usual spastic, inappropriate humor, but down deep, I had a pit in my stomach.

A hot knot of knowing that Rune was right.

I just didn't know where to find the courage to do anything about it.

EIGHT

Dane

"YOU NEED ONE MORE ELECTIVE, MR. BADD," THE counselor told me, after looking at my proposed schedule for the upcoming semester.

"I know, that's why I'm here," I said. "I can't find one that works with my schedule."

The counselor—a short, petite, pretty woman with salt-and-pepper hair and cat-eye eyeglasses—frowned as she reviewed my schedule and then the options. "Your options, if you want to leave the rest of your schedule as is, are…let's see…art history, ceramics, or choir."

I frowned. "Choir, huh?"

I looked away, thinking, music runs in the family, generally speaking, but I've never considered myself a musical person; of the three options, however, choir sounded the least lame. I don't really even know how well I can sing. I typically only ever sing out loud alone in the shower or the car, and everyone thinks they're fuckin' Lady Gaga in the shower. What if I join choir and discover I sound like a dying bullfrog or something? I *like* singing, I just don't know if I'm any good at it.

But the alternatives—art history or ceramics? Nah, fam. I'll honk like a goose before I sit around listening to someone yak on and on about Degas and Dali and whatever else. I'm not even talking about ceramics. What even is that? Like making shit on those spinning clay dudes? Maybe if a young Demi Moore is gonna give me a hands-on lesson, otherwise, again, nah fam.

"I guess I'll give choir a shot," I tell the counselor.

"Wonderful. I'll just add that in…" a glance at me. "So you've got your math credits, your science credits, language, history…and choir. Excellent." She peered at me speculatively. "Have you given any thought to a major? After this semester, you're pretty much done with your gen-eds and basic pre-reqs."

"Not really." I rubbed the back of my neck.

"Well, this is the semester to really start giving it some thought, Mr. Badd," she said.

"Yeah, I need to start dialing it in. So I'm set with my schedule for now, though?"

The printer on her L-shaped desk spat out a sheet, which she handed to me. "Yes, you are. Here you go. Anything else I can help you with?"

"No ma'am." I stood up and smiled, waving at her. "Thanks, ma'am. Have a great day."

I left her office perusing my schedule, which was

the biggest class-load I'd given myself since starting college: 17 credit hours across four days a week, with Wednesday being my biggest day, starting with a 9 am class and ending with choir until 9 pm, which was apparently a once-a-week class from 6 pm to 9 pm.

Long fucking day.

That's on top of working at the landscaping company full-time—it's a privately owned company, and my boss is all for me going to school, so he always works with my schedule. If classes preclude working during the day on a lawn unit, I can always go in after hours and clean the machines, wash the trucks, and do sundry maintenance jobs. It's not a career, but it's a good job with good people, and it pays well. In the winter, considering we don't get much snow, Doug shifts the majority of his employees to his other company: junk removal, specializing in garage and basement clean-outs. It's hard, backbreaking work, but it's honestly pretty satisfying to watch a cluttered garage or basement get tidied and usable.

I'd decided to take a bigger class load and work more just to keep my mind off of Lindsey. It'd been two weeks since coming home from LA, and there'd been nothing from her. Dunc and Rune were back from their honeymoon and were settling into domestic life together, running Badd's Bar. Rune had decided to go all in on the family and was stepping in as an administrative assistant; Delia and Hunter were busier and busier, what with kids and Hunter's empire and the much, much smaller Badd's Bars empire. Delia desperately needed someone to come in and help her with the deeply unsexy administrative work—which apparently was what Rune had been doing and was good at. Plus, it's work she can keep doing while pregnant, and much of it she can do from home after giving birth. Not to mention, we have the world's largest support system, consisting of a half-billion aunts and cousins who are, to a woman, more than a little baby-obsessed, so whenever Rune needs to get work done, all she needs to do is send a text, and she'll have a dozen women clamoring to cuddle and sniff little baby Badd.

What is it with chicks smelling babies, anyway? They just smell like a baby. It's weird.

Speaking of Rune, I've been avoiding going over there…because I'll ask about Lindsey. I know I need to see Dunc, but I just need some time and space from the whole shitshow, and I know they'll both ask me a shitload of questions, and I just don't know how to deal with it. I'm still pretty raw about the whole fucking fiasco.

I reached my car—a '98 Ford Ranger Dunc, Jax, and Lucas—Aunt Aerie and Uncle Canaan's son, named after the Big Fella himself—helped me fix up. It's not a show pony, it's a daily driver. No lift, no fancy tires, stock radio, crank windows, original engine and transmission—with over a hundred thousand miles—but it runs well, and it's mine. It's baby blue with a white stripe running around the lower edge and cheap steelies on the tires. As I climbed into the cab—I'd replaced the original tattered leather upholstery with saddle blanket upholstery—my phone buzzed with an incoming call.

I checked it as I cranked the engine. "Duncan, I was just thinking about you. What's up, bro?"

"When are you coming over? I feel like you're avoiding me."

"I am."

"Lindsey?"

"Yup."

"I get it. But look, I need some help. We're redoing the keg-room because it's woefully outdated and slow, we need a new pump system, and we have room to add some new taps, so we need to pull everything out and—"

"Yeah, yeah, I don't need the explanation. I get it," I cut in. "I'll be there in a few. I was just on campus nailing down my schedule for next semester."

"Just a fair warning, Rune is gonna wanna talk eventually—there's no getting away from it forever."

I groaned. "Why do you think I've been avoiding you guys? I don't want to talk about it."

"I know, I know. Just come help. I'll feed you beer and wings for your trouble."

"Jerk," I muttered. He knew I was a sucker for beer and wings slathered in mouth-scorching buffalo sauce.

"Gotcha!" he crowed. "So I'll see you in a few?"

"Yeah, I'm on the way. Just tell your dear wife that I'll only have the patience to answer a few questions."

"I'll tell her, but good luck getting my wife to listen. She's determined to get you two through this."

"It's not me she has to convince, bro." I paused. "Also, it's still weird to me that you have a wife."

"Right? I can't stop fidgeting with the ring." I heard distant, muffled voices. "I gotta go. See you when you get here."

When I got there, I parked in the alley and entered through the kitchen, studiously avoiding looking at the spot where Lindsey had been crouched. I followed the noise down into the cellar, where the keg room was. It was chaos. Dad was there neck deep in stacked kegs and a tangle of tap lines, while Uncles Bax, Brock, and Zane all crowded the space, playing musical kegs and cursing at each other. Duncan was sitting on the stairs watching, chin in hand, amused, as the brothers fought exactly the way Dunc and I do—with curses, insults, playful but hard punches and shoving, and a lot of inefficiency.

I sat next to Dunc. "So this looks like it's going well."

"Yeah, they showed up after I called you and took over. they're making a mess and getting nowhere, and I have a plan, but I can't get their OLD, DEAF, STUBBORN ASSES TO FUCKING LISTEN TO ME!" he shouted the last part.

Dad stopped, wiped sweat off his forehead with his wrist, and stared at Dunc over top of a stacked pair of kegs. "I'm not deaf, boy."

"But you are old and stubborn," Bax said.

"Fuck you," Dad shot back. "If I'm stubborn, I don't think there's a word for what you are."

"A literal saint," Bax answered, making a face I think was meant to look...pious? "A prince among men. A holy man."

Zane doubled over laughing, and Brock joined him. Bax looked around, offended. "Well fuck you all very much."

Zane couldn't breathe for laughing. "A h-holy man! Oh god, good one, bruh."

"Bruh? Bax echoed. "You gonna start saying skibidy next?"

"I've got about...*six-seven* seconds before I give up and go home," Brock quipped, to groans from everyone, including Dunc and me. "So cut the shit and let's hear my nephew's plan."

"If I never hear six-seven again, it'll be too soon," Bax said. "Finn's fucking *obsessed*. He thinks it's peak humor. I've threatened to toss every electronic device he has into the passage if he doesn't shut the everloving fuck up about the two stupid goddamned numbers. *IT DOESN'T EVEN MEAN ANYTHING!*"

At twelve, Finnian was Uncle Baxter and Aunt Kitty's youngest. Like all of us Badd boys, he was wild, rambunctious, incorrigible, hilariously inappropriate, and often so obnoxious you wanted to punt him across the Bering Strait and let the Russians deal with him.

They'd send him back in about ten seconds, though, so we keep him.

The dads finally shut up with their shenanigans, and, once everyone started listening to Dunc's plan, the keg-room remodel started to progress. Although it wasn't so much a remodel as an update of existing systems. Whatever. Point is, I spent the rest of the day down there, hauling kegs around, pulling and replacing and adding tap lines, and installing new taps. It was good, hard work made fun by my family's inability to not act like immature six-year-olds, even for dudes in their fifties.

By late evening, the bulk of the work was done—the job had been made a little trickier by the fact that we were working on the system while the bar was operating, meaning we had to make sure that most of the taps were running while working on others. The old guys went home, full of free beer and hot wings, leaving Dunc and me finally alone. We took fresh pints out into the alley and sat on the old metal folding chairs we keep out there for times like this.

"So," Duncan said, "You and Lindsey."

"No, *not* me and Lindsey," I answered, "which is the problem."

The door opened, and Dad stepped out, a pint in one hand and a chair from the dining room in the other. He plopped down on it, tipped backward against the wall with his long legs crossed at the ankle, resting his feet on an empty keg waiting to be picked up and exchanged by the distributor.

"Hey, Dad," I said. "Thought you went home."

"Was gonna, but I felt a disturbance in the Force." He indicated Dunc and me. "I've noticed you've been avoiding your brother for the last couple of weeks. Figured this powwow might have something to do with that."

"I wasn't avoiding Dunc," I said. "More his wife."

Dad shook his head. "My oldest boy is married. Fuckin' weird." He eyed me. "What'd Rune do?"

"Nothing, exactly. It's...complicated."

Dad snorted into his pint glass. "This got anything to do with the sparks I saw between you and Rune's best friend, Lindsey?"

"Not sure sparks is the right word," I muttered.

"Sure it is. Sparks don't just come from fire, they also come from friction."

I laughed at this. "That interpretation is accurate."

"So?" He tipped his glass in my direction. "Out with it."

I ended up spilling—most of it. Some things, my dad doesn't need to know about. Or my brother, for that matter; I hadn't meant to mention *that* little incident to Jax, it had just popped out. I was intentionally vague about Lindsey's background, and they both got it without having to be told—it's her story to tell, not mine...and I don't know the story anyway. All I would say is that she has some shit in her past that makes it hard for her to trust guys, and is scared of relationships.

Duncan looked at me over the top of his glass. "If she's so dead set against relationships and wants nothing to do with you, what are you gonna do?"

I shrugged. "Honestly, I don't know. I hung out with Jax when I first got back into town, and he thinks I should just give her time. What else *can* I do, anyway? I've made my case. I told her how I feel."

Dad tapped a thumbnail against the glass in his hand. "Jax is right. I know that sucks when you've got all this shit inside you, big feelings and all that, but sometimes, we gotta let people go, and if they come back to us, it's meant to be."

"What about fighting for what you want?" I asked. "What about proving that I'm for real?"

"If she's not in an emotional place where she can handle what you're offering, there's nothing to fight *for*, Dane." He gave me a sympathetic look. "There doesn't seem to be much you can do but give her time and space to sort her shit out on her own, like Jax said." He snorted. "Words of wisdom from that knucklehead—who knew?"

"Took me by surprise, too," I said. "He's got hidden depths."

"He still nurturing that crush on Em?" Dunc asked.

Dad answered for me. "Nah. Not gonna say it

was puppy love, but he knew it wasn't ever gonna go anywhere."

"I think it was deeper than that," I said. "I think his feelings for her went a lot deeper than any of us realized and lasted for a lot longer than we thought."

"But he knows—" Dad started.

"Yes," I cut in over him. "He categorically stated that he's not in love with her anymore."

"And you believe him?"

I nodded. "Whatever he may still feel, he hides well. He likes Hayden, he knows Sunni loves Hayden, and he wants her, and them, to be happy. I just think it was a lot more than a crush or puppy love."

"She shot him down *so* many times," Duncan said. "It almost hurt to watch, sometimes."

"Jax is more like his mom than people realize," Dad said. "Eva is quiet, but like your Uncle Lucian, still waters run deep. I know Jax presents as this hyperactive, outgoing computer nerd, but he's got his mom's depth of emotion. Eva doesn't love easily, but she loves deeply. Jax is the same."

I hated myself for this a little, but I felt jealousy for a second—my dad could recognize that in my cousin, but not me? People have this idea that I'm all jokes, a good time guy, and little else, directionless and shallow.

"He hides the depth a little too well, then," Duncan said. "Like somebody else we know."

Dad smirked at me. "I see you over there, son. I know you and Jax are more alike than anyone realizes."

I should've known better than to doubt Dad. "Yeah, yeah. I'm so deep. Real Marianas Trench of emotion, me."

Dad tapped the side of my calf with a foot. "Knock it off. Self-deprecation is for suckers." He transferred his crossed feet to my lap, which was weird—but kinda… nice.

Affection from your father, when you're a young adult trying to find your place in the world, occupies a complicated place. On the one hand, you wanna be cool and independent and manly. But on the other hand, I'm not so far from my youth that I've forgotten the comfort of my father's embrace.

"Dane, I don't doubt the genuineness of your feelings for Lindsey. And I don't know her pretty much at all—I barely even met her the day of the wedding. But *you*, I do know, and I know you're struggling with finding your purpose. I know that can be hard in a family like ours, with so many of your siblings and cousins seeming to know exactly what they want."

I nodded, head hanging. "Dad, did you…did you *want* to take over the bar when you did?"

Dad blew out a breath. "Askin' the deep shit, huh?" He sipped beer and thought for a while. "No, I didn't. I wanted to get outta fuckin' Ketchikan like the rest of my brothers had."

"So why'd you stay, then?" I asked.

"It'd be easy to say I had no choice, but there's always a choice—just not always a *good* one. Sometimes there's only one real possible choice to make. After your grandmother died, your grandfather…" Dad hesitated, hunting for the right word. "Basically, his body stayed alive, but the rest of him died with her. He gave up, more or less. Spent more time drinkin' than anything else, although he did his drinking behind the bar instead of on a stool in front of it. My last couple years of memories of Dad are of him leaning against the service bar, a rocks glass half full of Jameson in his hand, watching sports. He was a diehard Mariners and Seahawks fan and never missed a game of either team. He'd pull drinks for the service bar, but he'd do it one-handed. He never got wasted, and he wasn't mean or violent or anything like that. He just…drank and drank and drank all day, behind the bar, silent and brooding."

"What was he like before Grandma died?" Dunc asked.

Dad blew out a breath. "Really takin' a stroll down memory lane, huh, boys?"

Callie, one of the waitresses, popped her head out, asking Dunc to comp a ticket for her for a disgruntled customer; he came back out a few minutes later with fresh pints for all three of us.

"Pop was…honestly, a lot like Uncle Lucas. Big and strong as a fuckin' ox. He had a drier sense of humor than Uncle Lucas. It could be hard to tell if he was teasing you or being serious, and he played that up. He convinced your Uncle Zane once that if he didn't stop picking his nose, his whole nose would fall off and he'd be noseless the rest of his life. Now granted, Zane was like six at the time, but Pop played it so straight I almost believed him myself. Zane got so scared he quit picking his nose on the spot."

Dunc grinned at me. "Shoulda tried that with Dane, eh, Dad?"

"I have scratchy boogers, okay?" I said, flipping him off. "You gotta get rid of the crusty ones."

Duncan gagged. "Oh, fuck, that's gross. Crusty ones, bro? *Really?*"

"Like you don't pick your nose in the car?" I said. "Every guy picks his nose in the car."

Dad chuckled. "Just don't get caught wiping 'em on the seat."

"You flick 'em out the window, obviously." I shook my head. "Way to hijack the conversation, *Duncan.*"

Dad stared into space. "Pop was awesome, back in the day. He used to take us camping almost every weekend." He smiled faintly, remembering. "Xavier, Lucian, and the twins were too young to go, so Mom stayed home with them. Dad took me, Zane, Bax, and Brock. He had this giant canvas tent, like, I think it was legitimately used in the Boer War or something, an officer's tent, I think. It was *so* fuckin' cool, boys. It took for-fucking-ever to set it up, but as a kid, it felt like a palace in the wilderness. He'd dig a firepit right outside the front of the tent, and he always used a... shit, whaddya call it? Ram would know. An old native American trick where you dig the firepit and then you dig a little tunnel under it and away. The secondary hole pulls the smoke out and lets fresh air in, so the fire burns hot and the smoke is drawn away."

"Dakota firepit," I said.

"Yeah, that's it." Dad was quiet for a moment or two. "He'd bring a whole cooler full of hot dogs and fat-ass steaks and cans of beans, and we'd cook on the fire and go fishing, paddle around in the canoe, swim in ice-cold glacier-melt rivers. He'd always be up before us, always. We'd wake up, and there'd be Pop with his special camping mug, a battered old tin thing that he only used at the campsite. Still got it somewhere. He'd sit and fill that mug from the percolator that was always on the edge of the coals, all day long. We'd hike out into the bush, and Dad would teach us about plants and all that shit, point out animals we'd never have seen otherwise, stuff like that. Teaching us wood-craft, basically. We'd get back to camp and cook up the dogs and make hot chocolate." He shook his head, his voice thick. "Haven't thought about those days in fuckin'...*decades*."

He eyes Dunc and me, frowning. "Jesus. Just realized something—I'm older now than he ever was." He sat forward, pulling his feet down, tossing back the last of his beer. "Dane, son, I know this is gonna sound like bullshit, cliché advice, but you gotta follow your heart. Just don't leave your head out of it—your big head, I mean. The little head is a terrible decision maker."

"Are we talking about my purpose in life or Lindsey?" I asked.

He sniffed softly. "Both, I guess."

"And what about when your head and your heart say different things?"

A long pause. "I've found in circumstances like that, that situations have a way of making the choice for you."

"Not sure how I feel about that," I said.

"Hear that, for sure. Unfortunately, life doesn't ever really give much of a shit how you feel about it."

"What was your mom like?" Duncan asked.

Dad, forty-some years later, went misty-eyed, cleared his throat. "Mom was…Jesus. Everything Dad wasn't, which was a good thing, in both directions. She was an easy laugh. I think to this day, Bax's sense of humor comes from his incessant drive as a little kid to make Mom laugh—which he did, frequently and up-roariously. He got in trouble as much as he made her laugh, and sometimes she'd have to pass off discipline to Dad because she couldn't hide her laughter. She was *so* beautiful. Her hair was almost to her waist. I remember being super little, like, Zane must've been— shit, three? Bax was just a baby. It's one of those super dreamy memories, y'know? Like, it could very well be one of those memories you've partly invented." He cast his eyes toward the sky, blinking hard. "A band was playing downstairs—you could hear the hum and thump through the floor. The chatter of the crowd

under my feet, the sound of the band on the weekends. Zane had passed out on Mom and Dad's bed
with a sippy-cup—it had a red lid. Mom was sitting
at her vanity. It had the light bulbs around the frame
of the mirror. She was wearing one of Dad's flannels;
Dad was so big and she was so tiny that it was like a
dress on her. I think she actually did wear one of his
shirts as an outfit once,—there's a photo somewhere.
She belted it and left it partially unbuttoned. Anyway.
She was brushing her hair and humming some song.
Her vanity was the only light, so the room was dark
and warm. She had her hair down over her shoulder
and she was dragging this super old brush through it—
must've been an antique or…or an heirloom. I think
it might be in a box in the attic here. I wonder. She *always* had her hair up, braided, and in a bun. That was
her hairstyle, and she almost never varied it except on
special occasions. I think the memory is so distinct and
special because it was one of the few times I saw her
with her hair down." He sniffled, wiped at his face; Dad
didn't cry almost ever, but the few times I have seen it,
he didn't try to hide it or seem embarrassed.

In fact, the only other time I've seen him cry is
when our dog, Bomber, died. It was one of those classic cases of Dad didn't want the dog but Mom did and
so they comprised and got the dog. Bomber had been
a rescue—he was three or four when he got him, and
he was, fittingly, a mutt of indeterminate breed mix,
and a rambunctious troublemaker that drove Dad

absolutely nuts. Having a dog like that in a three-bed-room apartment over a bar was a pretty wild idea. We hadn't moved to the house, yet—it was almost done being built, as I recall. I think Bomber was at least part sheepdog of some sort, because he used to love herd-ing us kids around the yard, after we moved to the house, nipping playfully at our heels. He got sick pretty abruptly when I was thirteen or so, and passed pretty quickly thereafter. We were all devastated, but none more so than Dad, who, despite all his bitching about Bomber destroying his slippers and chewing on door-frames and barking his fool head off every time a sea-plane went overhead, loved the shit out of that dog. We never got another dog after that, if that tells you anything.

"Mom was quiet and mellow, for the most part," Dad said. "Where Dad was more…taciturn, a man of few words as a rule, Mom was more just quiet. Soft-spoken. She and Dad…I don't remember them having tons of conversations. I think their relationship was more about the quality of silence. Being content to just be near each other. They were super physically af-fectionate, though." He looked at me. "Dane, son. Just live your life. If this girl, Lindsey, is supposed to be in your life, she will be. I am not a religious or spiritual man, and I'm not sure how much I believe in fate either. Our lives are what we make of them. That said, shit happens. People make inexplicable decisions. People do shit that surprises us. And women…? Son, I've loved and lived with your mother for more than twenty years, and in that time, we've only spent a few weekends apart, total. And she's *still* a mystery to me, in some ways. Like, I know her inside and out. I know how she thinks. I know when she needs space and when she needs me close. I get to thinkin' I've got the woman all figured out, and then she does something that shocks the shit outta me, and I realize I don't know dick." He looks at me. "The reason I say that is you may have the most genuine feelings in the world for this girl, but you don't really *know* her. That's okay—love doesn't require you to know the person. Sometimes, you meet someone, and your hearts or souls or whatever just…*know* each other. I can't explain it, but I've felt it myself and seen it time and again. You don't know this girl. You don't know what she's thinking. Shit, I'm not sure you even know what she's feeling."

"I don't," I said.

"If she made it clear she's not in a place to deal with her feelings for you, there isn't much you can do except respect that. There's a time to fight for the woman you love—even if that means fighting her in some way. You ask me, this doesn't seem like that. It seems like a situation where you gotta let her confront her demons and hope she finds her way back to you. Which means there ain't shit you can do. I know that sucks dog balls, and I'm sorry."

Dunc and I aren't twins—we're Irish twins, born less than a year apart. Although something tells me that term is probably associated with some sort of negative stereotype about Irish people, and I shouldn't use it. The point is, even though we aren't real twins, we are close enough that we can sometimes communicate silently through looks. And sometimes, we can just feel what the other is thinking.

Point in case, I saw Dunc open his mouth, and I just knew he was about to say something about Bomber; I met his eyes and shook my head. We'd probed into enough of Dad's painful memories for one conversation.

As much as it sucked, I recognized the truth in Dad's advice. I'm convinced Lindsey has feelings for me—as strong as mine for her. But if she's unwilling or unable to face them or handle them or whatever, there's not much I can do to change the situation.

All I can do is go about my life and…wait.

Hope.

Dream.

If this is being in love, I'd like to unsubscribe, please and thanks.

NINE

Lindsey

I'M ALONE.

Raquel and Hamish were busily moving their lives to Seattle. Rune was officially an Alaskan. Even and Mom and Pop Rigby were gone—house sold, closed, and turned over to new owners, belongings stored in a locker, the pair off on an extended trip throughout Europe.

Leaving poor lonely Lindsey languishing all alone in the impersonal plastic hell of Los Angeles.

Fuck this.

But I'm too damn stubborn to let myself cave—to call Rune and beg her to find me a couch to sleep on and maybe a job. Mainly because Dane was in Ketchikan, and I still couldn't handle thinking about or seeing him.

I've been having nightmares about Danny. Flashbacks—visceral, physical memories that leave me nauseous, shaking, and weeping. They come at random times—this morning, I was having a cup of coffee on my little Romeo and Juliet balcony when one hit, and I dropped my mug on the sidewalk below, nearly crowning some poor dude. Yesterday, one hit while I was in the shower, and I couldn't get off the floor for almost half an hour.

I see his curly black hair, his pale skin, his flat, cold, greedy gray eyes the color of a dreary, sullen day. I feel his hands on my skin. His foul-smelling breath in my face, whispering about it being a secret and how if I tell anyone, the police will come and take me to jail. I remember being confused about that—I knew I hadn't done anything wrong, but the fear was irrational and the gut-wrenching, soul-destroying nausea of what he was doing to me overrode any sense I may have had that he was wrong, not me.

It felt wrong, and he put it on me, and I was scared and ashamed and sick, and he got me all twisted up inside.

Fuck.

"Linz?" I heard my name being called, but the maelstrom of thoughts and feelings paralyzed me. "Lindsey?" A hand shook me, firmly. "Lindsey!"

I jolted, sniffled, and wiped at my eyes. "Sorry, sorry. Yeah, what's up?" I turned to my boss, Saleh, who was looking at me with concern.

"You are okay?" he asked.

I shrugged. "Sure, sure. Fine. Just…stuff going on."

"Table twelve, please."

I glanced at the table in question—a pair of abutted four-top high tables in the bar area, which was my usual section. A group of studio exec types was seated at the table, laughing and elbowing each other and looking all chummy and bro-y…and handsy.

Trust me, I'm familiar with the type. They're experts at "accidentally" brushing my butt or boobs and then acting like innocent little lambs.

I've never spat in anyone's drink or food, but I have been tempted, and it's always tables like this. I once made a guy's drink with well vodka instead of Goose, just out of spite. Not that he noticed.

Saleh must have noticed and correctly interpreted my expression. "I can have Alicia wait on them, if you prefer."

"No, no. I got it. I need the money."

"If they are trouble, you let me know, yes? I will put into them the fear of God…and Saleh."

That was no idle threat—Saleh was a lovely, kind, soft-spoken man who was my favorite boss ever. He also happened to be six-foot-five, weighed three hundred pounds, and had fought alongside Americans against Saddam Hussein in the Gulf War.

"I know." I patted his arm as I breezed past him toward twelve. "Just keep an eye out. I'll let you know if they're a problem."

He caught my arm and spun me around. "You do not need to tell me what is wrong, but I hope you talk to someone. You are changed, in recent days. More sadder. Lost in your thoughts very often."

I winced. "I know. I'm sorry."

"I am only worried for you," he said.

"I'll be okay."

He sighed. "Okay. Go, now. Go."

I went. They addressed 99% of their comments and requests to my cleavage, but I'm a cocktail waitress in an industry bar. I wear low-cut tops on purpose, so that's nothing new or surprising; big cleavage equals big tips, and since I've got 'em, may as well benefit from 'em. They kept their hands to themselves, thankfully—the presence of Saleh glowering watchfully from the hostess desk may have helped.

They did tip well, though, so that's nice.

The evening progressed normally. A few tables shorted me, a few tipped generously. By the time the bar was getting ready to shut down, I was wiped out and ready to go home, rinse off the bar-stank, and go to sleep.

The feeling started fifteen minutes before the doors were set to close. Saleh was counting cash in the office with Sharon, the assistant manager, and the rest of us servers were doing our closing work—rolling silverware, filling condiments, counting tips, wiping tables, sweeping floors.

It was a feeling of disquiet, at first. A subtle

gnawing in the pit of my stomach. Women, you're familiar. It's the feeling you get walking to your car at night, a knowledge that someone is watching or following, even if you can't see anyone. You can just *feel* it, so you walk faster, grip your keys between your fingers, or have your taser or pepper spray in your hand inside your purse.

I looked around the bar, but saw no one unusual: Geoff, Tommy, Cal, and Carl, our "Cheers crew" regulars, were sitting at the far end of the bar as always, four in a row, sipping the last of their beers. The kitchen crew was banging around the kitchen as they closed up. The other girls were at table 1 rolling silverware while I stood at the bar, topping off ketchup, mustard, salt, and pepper.

"Connor?" I called out, addressing our busser, who was flipping up chairs onto the tables.

In the act of flipping a chair, he popped his head up. "Yeah, Linz?"

Connor was a cute kid—seventeen, gangly and long-limbed, eager to please, with all the signs pointing to an eventual glow-up into a hottie, one day. I knew he harbored an innocent little crush on me, and I was very careful to not encourage it.

"Have you checked the bathrooms?" I asked.

He shook his head. "No. Should I?"

"Would you mind? Please?"

"Sure!" He finished putting up the chairs at the table and then scurried to the bathrooms, popping into the men's room, and then poking his head into the women's and calling out before entering.

He returned a few minutes later, stripping off rubber gloves. "Clean and empty."

"Thanks. I just…" I scanned the bar again, uneasiness making me queasy. "Make sure the cooks don't leave the back door open tonight. I have a funny feeling."

"Maybe you just have to fart," he suggested, grinning.

I snorted. "'If it was me, Donkey, you'd be dead.'"

"Shrek! I love that movie!" He trotted for the kitchen, quoting the scene where Donkey talks about everybody liking parfaits.

Still, the feeling persisted, and I was getting freaked out by it. I'd experienced enough bullshit in my life to know better than to doubt this feeling. I tried telling myself I was safe in the bar, but with the recent spate of nightmares, panic attacks, and flashbacks, it was a hard sell to my poor, battered psyche.

Iris, Ash, Lola, Bettina, and CallyAnne finished their side-work, tipped out Connor, and left. Sharon was gone, dropping off the night deposit on her way home; most of the cooks were gone, too, as was Al, the dishwasher, leaving Saleh, Connor, and me to finish closing up.

I checked my phone—1:55 am. Saleh was a stickler for the rules, and never shut the doors before two, and if someone were to come in right now and want a drink, we'd serve him. He'd just have to chug it before the clock hit two.

I just had to kill the last five minutes.

I did so at the bar, watching talking heads debate some sportsball thing or other.

"'Scuse me. I know you're about to close. Any chance I can get a quick shot?"

That voice.

My entire body clenched instantly. Bile hit my teeth. My lungs seized.

No.

No.

No.

It was *him*.

Danny Cohen.

There was no question—I didn't need see his face to know. I knew that voice; I heard it in my nightmares.

Alicia, the bartender, met my eyes, questioning me silently. I couldn't respond, couldn't blink, couldn't breathe.

"Hey, sweetheart—" Boston accent: *'ey, sweeth-AH-HH-t.* "I'm talkin' to you." *T-AHHHH-kin' to ya.*

Yeah, he hasn't changed.

I was frozen in terror, horror, and an incandescent rage so potent I was almost more scared of that and what I'd do because of it than I was of Danny.

"We're closed, sir," Alicia said, recognizing my paralysis and moving toward Danny. "Sorry. Come back tomorrow, and we'll give you a free draft on the house."

It's a strange feeling, being frozen in terror yet so full of rage that I could explode all at the same time. I felt him move, scented him: a douche-bro amount of Axe body spray layered over the stale, ashy stench of cigarettes and the skunky aroma of cannabis.

"What'sa matter, sweetheart. Cat got your tongue?" *Whassa mattah.*

He was too close. Way, way, way too close. My hands closed around a silverware roll from the stack in front of me and tightened.

"Hey, man," Alicia said loudly, knowing Saleh had excellent hearing and left the office door open so he could hear what was happening out here. "I said we're closed. Time to go, okay?"

He ignored her. Sidled closer to me. Did he recognize me? I can't imagine he could; it's been a long time, after all.

"Got a nice ass on ya, don't ya, sweetheart? How's about you let me get a little bit o' that cake, huh, baby?" His tone was wheedling, sickening.

I had zero control over my actions then. It was like watching someone else. Like I was that little alien dude from *Men In Black*, the one who was sitting in a guy's skull, driving him like a mech. Bile at my teeth as my fingers pried the fork from the roll. Gripped it with white-knuckle intensity, tines pointing downward, away from my thumb.

Danny slid closer, one arm slithering alongside me. Alicia was saying something, but I couldn't understand it past the roaring in my ears.

His hand was in my frame of vision—scarred knuckles, tanned, weathered skin, faded prison ink along his knuckles and the backs of his hands, illegible.

With a sudden shrill shriek of awful hate that came from the pit of my stomach, I slammed the fork down into his hand as hard as I could. I'll never, ever forget the crunch of the metal tines scraping past bone, or the way it bit into the wood below his hand. He yowled, jerking his hand away—or trying to. I had, apparently, stuck the fork in him so hard it was fixed into the wood of the bar.

"FUCK YOU, YA CRAZY ASS BITCH!" he screamed, sagging down and away from the bar while trying to wiggle the fork free. "I'LL FUCKIN' *KILL YOU!*"

I pivoted slowly to show him my face. "Not if I kill you first, Daniel Cohen." I spat in his face, and when he reared away, howling in rage and wiping at his face, I closed my fist around the fork handle and used my hand like a hammer to drive it deeper, prompting renewed screams of agony from him.

"Remember me, *Danny*?" I was no longer frozen. Ohhhh no. Now I was caught up in a red haze of fury. "Surprised you're hitting on me, actually, Danny, now that I'm not a *FUCKING CHILD*, you rapist, pedophile *FUCK!*"

He looked stunned, trying to get away from me. "L-L-L-Lindsey?"

I wiggled the fork back and forth, felt the tines scraping against bone. "Shut the *fuck* up." I grabbed a stack of bar napkins and stuffed them in his mouth when he went to speak, shoved them in so far he gagged on them. "Did you get raped in prison, Danny? I gotta say, I really, really hope some big-ass motherfucker used your asshole like his own personal Fleshlight." I leaned over the bar, snagged the soda gun, clicked the first button my thumb hit—the lemonade button—and sprayed his eyes with it. "I bet you could fit a Louisville Slugger up your asshole, now, Danny. Kinda feel like we should try. My boss keeps one in the office." I stepped back while he was sobbing and clawing at his eyes and choking on the now-sodden napkins clogging his mouth… and kicked him in the balls as hard as I could. "Maybe I'll just use it to turn your pathetic little balls into fucking ketchup."

He gargled something muffled.

"Sorry, I couldn't hear that," I said. "Let me help you out." I sprayed him with the gun again, directly in his mouth, effectively waterboarding him.

And then I kicked him the nuts again, complete with a step back, wind up, and follow-through like I was a punter making a Super Cup winning football goal in the fourth inning, or whatever the right analogy is—I don't know, I don't sportsball.

I wound up to kick him again, but hands wrapped

around my arms and lifted me bodily off the floor, car-ried me away. I kicked and thrashed until I heard Saleh's voice in my ear. "Calm, calm. Calm. It is me. You must be calm now, Lindsey."

"I'll kill him!" I screeched, thrashing. "Let me go! I'll fucking kill him!"

"And then you will go to jail."

"I don't care! I'll kick him in the fucking balls until he dies! I don't care! Send me to jail, as long as he dies first!"

The red haze obscured my vision—I'd always thought seeing red was a figure of speech, but the edges of my eyesight were, quite literally, tinged red. I was thrashing, kicking, screaming, spitting. Saleh held me like he would a similarly-behaving feral cat, which wasn't far from the truth.

"Saleh, he's unconscious." Connor.

"Good. Leave him. I will deal with him." His voice was cold and hard and scary. To me, then, warmth and compassion in his voice. "Breathe, Lindsey. Breathe. You must try to breathe."

I wasn't breathing; my lungs burned.

I heard traffic. Fresh air hit my face—fresh air tainted with the sickly-sweet stench of old food trash from the dumpsters.

"He hurt you?"

I nodded.

"You were a child?"

I nodded again. "T-t-tw-tweh—twelve. Un-until I w-w-was s-s-s-sih—sixteen."

Saleh cursed floridly in Arabic. "Then what you have done was a kindness compared to what an animal like him deserves."

"N-n-not an animal," I whispered. "A m-monster. I l-like animals."

"Sit, sit." He guided me to the wall and helped me slide down to my butt on the filthy ground. "Put your head between your knees and breathe slowly in and out. You know the square breathing?"

I nodded, doing as he suggested.

"You stay here," Saleh told me. "I will return soon."

I kept breathing, trying to square breathe: Four seconds in, hold for four, four seconds out, hold for four, repeat. I kept slipping back into panic and had to start over.

That's it, baby. Keep breathing. I heard his voice—I swear to God I did.

"Dane?" I whispered, sniffling.

I lifted my head, looked around. The alley was empty.

"Dane," I whispered again. "Fuck."

I missed him.

God, I missed him so damn bad.

It'd been over two months since that night in my apartment.

I spoke to Rune almost every day, via text, calls,

voice notes, and video calls, but I never mentioned him, and neither did she. Duncan occasionally popped across the screen to say hi, and I could see tightness in his expression when he looked at me.

Angry at me, probably, for being the bitch who broke his brother's heart.

Too bad for me, only Rune seemed to understand how broken I was—what I was really struggling with.

It wasn't Dane.

It wasn't trust.

It wasn't even men.

It was me. My self-worth. My fear. Fear of what? Yes. Love. Sex. Intimacy. Vulnerability. I'd been a vulnerable child, a twelve-year-old girl who had had the misfortune of developing early and significantly—by the time I was twelve, my breasts were already bigger than most high school girls'. Yay—not. The jealous mockery from other girls, the looks and comments from the boys—my age, younger, older, even adults. *So* fun.

And then my figure caught the attention of my brother's best friend. My brother was ten years older than me, so at the time, he'd been twenty-two and still living with Mom and me. He was a troubled kid, unsurprisingly, but managed to avoid arrest, despite being involved in a lot of highly illegal shit, most of it drug-related.

Fuck. I have to get him out of my mind.

He hadn't aged well. That was some consolation, at least.

"Focus on me, honey." I heard Dane's voice again, soothing, calming, comforting. *"I gotcha."*

Can you panic so hard that you have auditory hallucinations? Or have I just finally, actually lost my mind? Because the alley was still empty.

I don't know how long I was in the alley alone, trying to gather myself, to slow my breathing. At some point, Saleh came back.

"Where is he?" I asked him.

"Do not worry about this, Lindsey. It is my worry, not yours."

"Did…did I…?"

"No. He will recover, unfortunately. Perhaps he will not be making any children, but I do not think this is any great loss for the world."

"Where is he, Saleh?" I demanded. "Please, tell me."

"I left him in the street outside the hospital."

"With any luck, he'll get run over by an ambulance. That would be nice."

"Sadly, I do not think that is what occurred." Saleh knelt in front of me, took my hands in his. "Will you please allow me to drive you home, Lindsey?"

"My car." It was a 2012 Dodge Neon; it was white, which means it was always dirty; the A/C tended to conk out when it was hottest, which is the most fun and helpful during the scorching Angeleno summers;

it was always leaking oil and the gauges on the dashboard only worked some of the time, so I could never be entirely sure how fast I was going, how much gas I had left, or how hot the engine was, which was an issue considering the oil leak.

"Connor said he would drive your car," Saleh said. "I will take him home."

I sniffled. "Okay. Thank you, Saleh."

"Of course, my dear. Of course."

I barely remember anything else past that—streetlights, stop lights, motion, Saleh having a quiet conversation in Arabic on his phone while driving; mostly, I had Danny's face, his voice, his hands, his everything vile flashing through my brain.

I remember Saleh escorting me upstairs to my apartment.

And then I was dreaming. I was fifteen. Danny and my older brother, Larry, had been gone all week on a bro trip to Baja. It had been great having them gone. It meant Danny couldn't corner me. In the dream-memory, I was in bed asleep. Something woke me up—a sound of some sort. My eyes had flicked open to see my door easing open. A tall, lanky frame filled the doorway, backlit by the nightlight from the hallway. I had scooted against the wall and curled up in a ball, already crying as Danny approached.

"No," I'd whimpered. "No. Please."

He'd shushed me, placed a hand stinking of cigarettes over my mouth. His belt had jingled as he fumbled with his baggy, oversized jeans. I'd worn a T-shirt and loose shorts to bed. He'd yanked the leg of my shorts aside, hand over my mouth, muffling my whimpers as he took what he wanted from me; the only good thing about Danny was that he never lasted more than a minute or two, so at least it was over fast.

"Keep your whore mouth shut," he'd hissed in my ear, breath stinking of vodka and cigarettes and halitosis. "If I can come in here and do this and no one knows, I could kill you in your sleep. You say a word about this to anyone, and I fucking will. You'll wake up with my hands around your whore throat."

I was a whore because he raped me. Makes sense, huh? Real sweet guy, Larry's BFF. Of course, Larry was a piece of shit himself, so it wouldn't surprise me if he was doing something similar to some poor girl somewhere. He'd left me, then, and I'd lain there awake for hours, weeping silently before I could summon the courage to sneak into the bathroom to clean up. Which meant getting in the shower and scrubbing myself till my skin bled.

I jolted awake, sobbing in relief when I realized I was twenty-two and alone in my apartment, not fifteen and waiting for Danny to sneak in again.

"Fucking fuck me," I rasped, sitting up and wiping my face. "How *the fuck* did Danny find me?"

I fixed myself coffee and tried to enjoy it, but every time I blinked, I saw his evil little eyes widening as he realized it was me. The nasty things he'd said to me even before he knew it was me.

My skin crawled, and I clawed at my forearms, my chest between my breasts, my stomach. Fuck. The crawling, creeping, slimy, grimy sensation coating my skin worsened with each successive heartbeat until it felt like I had spiders under my skin, slime mold growing from my pores.

I dumped my coffee down the sink and all but sprinted for the bathroom, ripping my clothes off as I went, keening through gritted teeth, fighting the mother of all breakdowns. I twisted the hot water on and climbed in before it was even hot—the abrupt cold shocked my system and the breath out of me, leaving me paralyzed and gasping until the water started to slowly heat up until it was just off a boil. Which is what I needed—to scald off the filth.

Yet even after scrubbing myself raw in water hotter than the fires of Mt. Doom, I still felt filthy and violated all over again.

I was afraid.

Sick to my stomach.

And I realized, as I stood naked in front of the full-length mirror on the back of my closet door, that I've spent the last several years hiding from this feeling. Running from it. Burying it. Ignoring it. Pretending that Danny didn't exist unless someone else brought him up, or what he did.

Last night made it agonizingly clear that this approach wasn't fucking working.

I have to face him.

I have to look him in the eye—without giving in to the urge to claw that eyeball out of his skull—and find a way to make peace with myself. Not with him. Not with what he did. With myself.

I chose my outfit with care. It started with my favorite pair of booty-lifting underwear and a matching push-up bra. My best leggings, which make my ass look great—with lifting underwear *plus* the leggings, Dane would take one look at my ass and spontaneously combust*WHY*the*FUCK* am I thinking about him right now? I put him out of my mind and pulled on the pièce de résistance of my outfit: a fitted V-neck tank top that took my cleavage to eleven. I styled my hair loose and wavy. Smoky, dramatic makeup.

Bombshell.

It was a fuck-you outfit.

I stuffed my shit into my purse and headed for my car; there was only one hospital within a thirty-minute drive of the bar where I worked, which is the only place Saleh could've taken Danny. I drove there, parked in the back of the lot, and made the long walk to the ER desk. Yes, they'd had a patient by that name last night; he had been admitted to the ICU last and was upstairs. I pretended to be his worried girlfriend and wheedled his room number out of the lady behind the desk. Which, might I add, was some god-tier acting on my part. There was a teary-eyed sniffle, a catch in my voice, and a wobble in my lip. I was *good*.

I marched down the hallways feeling like Beatrix Kiddo, just needed an eyepatch. I even whistled that jaunty melody as I catwalked toward his room, catching the eye of doctors, nurses, and orderlies alike. I reached room 1244 and hesitated outside.

I had no clue what I was going to say or do. I reminded myself sternly that I was there to *talk* to him, and *only* talk…no matter how tempting it was to steal a syringe and inject air between his toes.

"Do *not* kill him, Lindsey Snelling," I murmured out loud.

A mammoth orderly paused as he passed me, pushing a cart. He lifted an eyebrow in my direction. "I need to worry about what's gonna happen in there?" he asked me.

I faked a laugh. "Oh god, no. He's my boyfriend. He vanished last night, and I'm pissed at him. I spent the whole night searching the hospitals for him."

He peered at me, and I'm not sure he believed me. "Mmmm-hmmm." He pushed his cart full of cleaning supplies into motion again. "Hope you're not lying to me."

"I would never," I scoffed.

He lumbered off with more than one suspicious backward glance—I must be radiating palpable fury or something.

I pushed into the room. It was dark, the lights

dimmed, curtains drawn. A shape was at his bedside, doing something; when finished, the figure turned and saw me. The nurse was a young woman about my age, pretty, with black hair and lovely brown eyes. "Are you family?" she asked in a whisper.

"I'm his girlfriend," I whispered back. "What *happened*?" I endeavored to sound worried. "How is he? No one would tell me anything on the phone."

She winced. "He was assaulted last night, I'm afraid. Someone stabbed him through the hand with a fork. I know it sounds kind of like a joke, maybe, but I promise you it is no laughing matter. He will have permanent nerve damage to that hand. He will never have full use of it again."

"Ohhh, poor baby," I tutted, in a saccharine, concerned tone.

"Well, that's only part of it, unfortunately." She hesitated, leading me out to the hallway and speaking in a low murmur. "His testicles were…ummm… crushed. Very, very badly. No one saw what happened, as someone did a drive-by dump. Whoever did this to him must've *really* hated him. I'm no detective, but this was deeply personal."

I acted shocked. "Holy shit. Is he, ummm…will he ever…you know?"

She winced again, shaking her head with a shrug. "Unlikely, I'm sorry to say. The damage is pretty comprehensive. He'll almost definitely suffer permanent impotence and/or erectile dysfunction."

Fuck yes.

It was so hard to not pump my fist like Rocky at the top of the stairs.

Look, I'm normally not a violent person. I don't like horror movies or war movies or shoot-em-ups. I like reality shows where out-of-touch rich women yell at each other about transparency and starting a new chapter. I like dating shows where douchebags with jobs like "amateur donkey jockey" get drunk at each other and whine about everything.

But knowing I possibly, hopefully, please-baby-Jesus ruined Danny's ability to get a hard-on ever again?

Chef's kiss.

"Can I see him?" I said to the nurse.

She nodded. "He's on a lot of painkillers, so he won't be entirely lucid." She scanned me, looking perplexed. "Sorry, he just didn't mention a girlfriend."

"Well, he got his balls kicked in," I said. "I'm sure he wasn't entirely coherent."

"I suppose." She glanced back in at the still form on the bed. "Don't keep him up too long. He needs to rest."

"Forever," I muttered under my breath.

"Sorry, what was that?" the nurse said.

"Nothing." I patted her shoulder. "Thank you, nurse…"

"Joanna," she supplied.

"Thank you, Joanna. I won't keep him up too long."

When she was gone, I let out a breath, hesitated, and then entered the dark room. Closed the door behind me. Drew the curtain around his bed, blocking him from view from the hallway.

Drew a chair up to the bedside and sat back in it, one leg crossed over the other. Danny was sleeping peacefully, right hand bandaged. A thin hospital blanket covered his lower half, so I couldn't see what was going on down there. Spikes through the dickhole, with any luck.

I looked at him for a moment or two. It was the same face, just older. Same weak jaw and chin, same beady, bulging eyes. Same hooked nose, crooked from being broken multiple times. His face was pocked and scarred—acne, meth sores, scars from fights. He was actually decent-looking…at first glance. Look closer, and you saw the wear of age, and you realized he was much younger than you thought. He was only thirty-two, but he looked fifty. His hair was thinning at the widow's peak and crown, and the stubble along his jawline was salted with gray in places.

There was a pillow that had slid out from under his head and was about to topple off the other side of the bed. I had to sit on my hands to stop myself from holding it over his face.

My god, when did I become so murdery?

I watched him sleep peacefully for a few minutes, until my hate bubbled over. "DANNY COHEN, YOU'RE UNDER ARREST!" I shouted.

He jolted out of his sleep, scrabbling and gasping, looking around frantically until he saw me. He stopped thrashing, his face full of anger. I saw his hand slithering toward the little controller dude that would let him summon the nurses, and I took it away before he could push any buttons.

"Don't worry, fuck-bag," I hissed. "I'm not here to finish the job."

"You ruined me," he mumbled, his voice muzzy and stoned on opiates. "Balls're ruined."

"Less than you deserve."

He tried to look around—for some other way of summoning help, probably. "I'll call...th'p'lice."

"Oh yeah?" I opened my phone and dialed 9-1-1, handed it to him so all he had to do was hit the call button. "Do it."

He turned his head away. After a minute, he looked back at me. "Why're you here?"

"I don't know," I admitted. "Testing my self-control, maybe. It's taking a lot of it to not finish murdering you."

"Don't. Please. Please."

"Now that I know your pathetic little peepee is broken forever, I think it's a better punishment to leave you alive. You'll never be able to rape anyone ever again." I leaned toward him, and he shied away. "Every time you take a piss, you'll look at your sad, crushed little balls and you'll know *I* did that to you. I hope you piss razors every day for the rest of your pathetic existence. I hope you spend every second of your life in pain, Daniel Cohen. I hope your life is miserable. I hope you live to be a hundred and twenty years old, and every single fucking *second* is hell on earth."

I took my phone back and snapped a photo of him.

"Fuck…you…whore."

I laughed. It was forced, but still. "Whore. That's what you always called me. Did it make you feel bet-ter about raping a twelve-year-old *child*, calling me a whore, Daniel? You're a pedophile. The vilest scum on the planet. You're worse than scum, Daniel. You're less than the mold that grows on old dog turds."

"Did you…" he groaned, shifted. "Did you come here just to—just to insult me?"

"I had to see you face-to-face. You surprised me last night. You were the last person on the planet I ex-pected to walk into my place of work. I thought you were in prison for raping a grandmother or something horrible."

"Got out a few years ago."

"Still raping little girls and grandmothers?"

"Fuck you."

"You did. For four years."

He had the decency to look away, at least, look-ing ashamed.

"So, how's Larry?"

He shrugged, looking a little less hazy. "Dunno. Haven't been in touch in years. He joined the Navy after I went in." He blinked hazily. "He knew, you know."

"Oh, I know. So did Mom. I told her."

"You know she died?"

I swallowed hard. "She...she did? When?"

"Six months ago."

"How?"

"Some kind of cancer. Heard from a cousin who was neighbors with her. She got sick and was dead within a few months."

"Consider the floor spat on," I said, "but I won't do the orderlies dirty like that."

"She sucked my dick for coke," he told me. "All the time."

I laughed. "I'm not surprised. Is that supposed to upset me or something? I *hated* my mother. I've always hated her. I'm not sad she's dead, and the fact that she blew you for coke when she knew damn well what you were doing to me is absolutely unsurprising. If anyone in that house was a whore, it was her."

He shrugged. "Well, yeah. Literally. She whored herself out for drugs all the time. Rent money, too."

I shrugged back at him. "I don't give a fuck. Good riddance to bad rubbish." I sighed. "I needed to look at you and see how it felt, now that I'm not taken by surprise."

"And?" He seemed genuinely curious, so I thought about the answer for a while.

"The longer I sit here looking at your ugly fucking

face and listening to your horrible fucking voice, the more I realize I've been held hostage by a pathetic piece of shit. You violated me. You ruined my life, which was already spectacularly shitty. But you know what, Daniel? I *survived* you." The hate was still there, but as I spoke, I realized I was telling the truth—to both him and myself. "I *survived* what you did to me. I survived how you made me feel about myself."

He just stared at me, in pain as the opiates wore off, visibly uncomfortable at my presence.

I thought of something a professor said in a philosophy and ethics class I took in college: "Hate is the heaviest of emotions," she'd said. "Hate is the most destructive force on earth. Hate is entropy. Hate has mass and substance. Hate blinds. Hate kills. Hate is a poison, but it poisons only you and harms the subject of your hate not a whit."

I remember hearing my professor say that and knowing it applied to me. I had gotten up and left, deeply uncomfortable because I was consumed by hatred for the man in the bed opposite me. I have harbored that hatred for years. Nurtured it inside myself. And behold, my professor was right. It had poisoned me and had eaten away at me. It had caused me to push away a good, kind, honest man who cared for me.

While this festering puddle of diarrhea lived his life, blissfully unaware of my hate.

I hated and hated and hated, and only harmed myself.

I stared at him in silence for a long, long time, sorting through the swirling shitstorm of emotions inside me.

"What's the opposite of hate, Daniel?" I asked.

"Love?" He shook his head. "I don't fuckin' know. Why the fuck are you asking me that?" he demanded. "Can't you just fuck off, now? You've seen me. You got your revenge. You said your piece. Please, just leave me alone."

"No, I don't think the opposite of hate is love," I said. "They're totally different. I know a soulless monster like you can't fathom what love is, but it's totally unrelated to hate. No, I think the opposite of hate is forgiveness."

His eyes flickered. "Cool. Fuck off."

I stood up. Glared down at him. "What I'm about to say, I say for me, Daniel, not you. You can get fucked." I cleared my throat. "I forgive you."

He blinked a few times, surprised. "I—"

"Shut *the fuck* up, you ugly, stupid, dickless, shit-stained hemorrhoid. Fuck you until the end of time. I really do hope you live the rest of your life in agony. I will *not* forget, but I *will* move on, and I will live my life, and I *will not* be held hostage by hating you anymore. When I say that I forgive you, all I mean is that I am going to try and let go and move on. Put you in my past. Put what you did to me in my past. I do not mean it's okay, don't worry about it. It's not okay. Do not worry about it. Worry about what I'll do to you if I ever, *ever* see your ugly fucking face ever again."

"I didn't know you'd be there. I've been on oil rigs for most of the past few years."

"Shut the fuck up. I don't care. If you see anyone that even *looks* like me, you better fucking run the other direction."

At that moment, I heard the squawk of a radio in the hallway, and then two uniformed LAPD officers entered the room.

"Daniel Hezekiah Cohen?"

"Fuck," Danny muttered quietly enough that I almost doubted my ears; then, louder: "Nope. Not me."

The officer wasn't amused. "Daniel Cohen, you're under arrest for the violation of the terms of your parole and for the violation of a restraining order against one Elizabeth Gabardine."

I stood aside and watched, not bothering to hide my gleeful grin.

A second pair of men entered the room, these dressed in business suits that screamed FBI.

One of them, a Patrick Warburton lookalike, stepped toward Daniel. "Daniel Hezekiah Cohen, you're under arrest for—" he glanced at the LAPD officers. "Wait, you guys too?"

"Parole violation and violating a restraining order. What do you have him on?"

"Transporting Schedule One substances across state lines, possession of a Schedule One substance, possession of a firearm without a license, and tampering with a federal witness."

The LAPD gestured. "Please, be my guest. We can figure out custody for our charges later." He glanced at me. "Your boyfriend is not a nice guy, ma'am. I'm not trying to meddle in your life, but you're better off without him."

"Oh, he's not my boyfriend," I said. "He sexually abused me for four years, starting when I was twelve. I heard he was here and decided to…say hello."

The FBI agent who'd listed the charges gave me a speculative appraisal. "You wouldn't happen to know anything about what happened to him, would you? How he got here? The nurses said someone pushed him out of a moving car near the ER entrance."

"Me?" I put a hand to my chest. "No, sir, officer. Or…special agent, is it?" I gave him my best deer-in-the-headlights look. "Violence is never the answer, sir. That's what my mama always told me, at least."

The agent fought valiantly to suppress a smirk. "I see. Well, ma'am, once the hospital gives us the go-ahead, we're taking him into custody."

I patted the agent's dense, burly arm. "Thank you for what you do. And please, feel free to lose the key once you've locked him up."

"Ma'am, when the other inmates find out he's a pedophile…" he shrugged. "Well, let's just say that sometimes, with guys like that, justice comes *after* the law has had its say."

"That information has a way of coming out, does it?" I asked.

"Yes, ma'am, it does."

"Good." I did a finger wave at Daniel. "Too-doo-loo, Danny-boy. Enjoy prison...*again*."

He had sagged back against his pillows, face drawn, exhausted, and resigned. "Fuck off, Lindsey. You called 'em, I bet."

I laughed. "I wish I had. Honestly, though, no, I didn't. I didn't know you were wanted. I didn't know you were even out of prison. But this is the best possible outcome I could have hoped for. Goodbye forever, Danny. May your socks always be wet and your pillow always warm."

I heard a stifled snicker from one of the officers.

I breezed out of the room, feeling a lightness within myself so potent that when I reached the bright sunlight of the street, I felt like I could bound over the buildings like a Brobdingnagian astronaut.

I had to read *Gulliver's Travels* for a college lit class, okay? Just look it up, okay? Don't judge me; I don't typically use $10 words, but that's just a fun one: Brobdingnagian. Say that five times fast.

I didn't even mind that my car was a hundred and forty degrees inside and the AC was on the fritz again. I knew I had more work to do to heal from what had happened to me, but maybe, just maybe, this was a meaningful start.

TEN

Dane

I CLEARED MY THROAT, BUT NO ONE LOOKED AT ME, SO I tried again, louder and more dramatically. "A-*hem.*"

It was Sunday afternoon, a beautiful late fall day, and my family—Mom, Dad, Delia and Hunter, Sunni and Hayden, and Duncan and Rune, who was a billion weeks pregnant, or "overcooked" as she called it—were all sitting around our outdoor dining table.

"Somethin' to say, son?" Dad said, drawing everyone's attention.

"Um, yeah." I let out a breath. "So, I, uhhhh…I'm in a choir at the college, and our first concert is a week from tomorrow night. If, um…if anyone wanted to come."

Silence greeted this.

"Wow, don't everyone all get excited at once," I muttered.

Mom was the first to come up with a response,

unsurprisingly. "Choir? I didn't think you were interested in music."

"I needed to fill an elective, and that's what worked," I admitted. "But I'm finding I actually like it a lot. Our teacher or director or whatever, Mrs. Roslin, says I have one of the most beautiful baritones she's ever heard. She *is* roughly four thousand years old, though, so she could be senile. She's a funny old bat, though, and I'm fond of her."

Delia smiled at me. "That's really great, Dane. I'm glad to see you broadening your horizons. We'll be there."

"Broadening my horizons?" I echoed, muttering. "What's *that* supposed to mean?"

Sunni, on my right, patted my shoulder. "It's a good thing, Dane."

"But, what? I'm narrow-minded?" I said.

"No," Delia answered, drawling the word. "Just... less inclined to take risks or get outside your comfort zone."

Dad cut in, then. "We'll all be there," he announced. "I'll put the word out to the tribe."

I groaned. "I just meant our family, like us, here. I'm not sure the auditorium is big enough for our whole crew to show up."

"It's what we do, son," Dad said. "Best not to fight it."

"It's you, on stage, singing," Duncan said. "Of course we'll all be there."

"Sweet," I mumbled.

"Oh no," Emerson teased in a sarcastic monotone, "the support of my whole family, how tragic."

"Shut up, Sunni," I muttered.

I felt better, now that that was out of the way. I'd been oddly nervous to make that announcement. What I wasn't telling them was that I had a solo. I also wasn't mentioning that I had to wear a tuxedo with a jacket that had those long tails. I'd made it into some sort of higher-level sub-choir thing, because apparently there's not just one choir, but also lots of mini-choirs and groups and shit. I dunno. I just show up and sing.

Another thing I wasn't telling them was that I fucking loved choir. I loved singing. I'd feel myself hit the perfect note and get the shivers. I'm not sure anyone in my family has ever ever heard me sing, because I never realized I actually could—like, not well, I mean.

I wasn't sure what to do with this newfound love for singing, but I figured I'd take it one step at a time. I don't know why I was nervous, either. It's not like my family was going to be unsupportive. It's just a big step for me.

I've worked for the same landscaping company since my junior year in high school, and I've never really looked beyond it. It was a good job, I enjoyed the work, and it was flexible. Or, rather, my boss was flexible.

But lately, I was wondering if it was going anywhere.

If *I* was going anywhere.

Suddenly, Delia's comment about broadening my horizons made a lot of sense.

I haven't really done much of anything other than work and school since coming back from LA. Two weeks ago, I got a postcard from Portland, Oregon, from Lindsey.

Thinking of you, it said, in a neat, female cursive script.

That was it. Three words on a postcard from Portland, Oregon.

Thinking of you.

Four months of silence, and I get three words on a postcard?

And why was she in Portland?

After Sunday dinner, I ambled down to the dock, sat in one of the Adirondack chairs, lit a joint, and stared at the postcard. A form settled into the chair beside me, and I, assuming it was Dunc, handed the joint over.

The fingers that took it were slender, and the nails painted a pale, matte pink.

"DeeDee," I said, coughing. "Not who I was expecting."

She puffed on the joint, exhaled, and handed it back. "I know. You were lost in thought." She snatched the postcard from me. "'Thinking of you.' No signature."

I didn't answer.

She handed it back. "Lindsey?"

"Yup."

She sighed. "How are you handling all that?"

I didn't bother asking how she knew about all that—there were no secrets in this family, and we love us some piping hot tea. I shrugged. "Fine, I guess."

Delia laughed. "Bullshit, brother."

"Fine. I'm still pissed, okay? Like...well..." I shook the postcard. "I haven't heard a peep from her in *four fucking months*, and then I get *this* bullshit outta the blue? You're thinking of me? What does that even mean? Thinking of me how? And why is she in Oregon?" I shook my head. "I just...I've been trying to move on. Trying to not think about her. Staying busy. I even tried going on a date."

"Hooking up, you mean."

"No," I said, my tone firm. "A *date*. It didn't even get past the date part. I got through the appetizer and then realized it just felt wrong, so I made my excuses and left."

"What was your excuse?" She asked.

"I, um..." I winced. "I didn't really make an excuse. I just told her I was sorry and that I had to go."

"Good. Shitty excuses are always transparent. Better to just be honest." She took the joint from me. "So you're still in love with her."

"I mean, I guess. I don't know. I don't want to be. She doesn't feel the same way. Or maybe she does, I dunno. It's all fucked up, and there's nothing I can do about it except just deal with it." I glanced at Delia. "Should you be smoking that?"

She frowned. "I'm not pregnant."

"Aren't you breastfeeding?"

She shook her head, smirking at me. "No, actually. We switched him to formula because he has a fussy tummy. But thanks for looking out for me." She sounded more amused and affectionate than offended, mostly because she knew I was coming from a loving place, not a judgmental one—I knew she was a damned good mama.

"Oh."

"If she showed up tomorrow and wanted to be with you," she asked, "what would you say?"

"I honestly can't even imagine. I'd probably get all tongue-tied from having too many things I'd want to say that they'd get all tangled up."

Delia flat-out laughed at this. "You always have something to say, Dane."

"Exactly."

She puffed on the joint again and then handed it back. "You've got it bad, huh?"

"I...y'know, Delia, the honest to god truth is that I'm more worried for her than anything. Like, right now, yeah, I feel shitty about everything. I care about her. I miss her. I want to talk to her. Laugh with her. Other stuff." I hurried on past that part. "But I know that in time, if I never see her or hear from her again, I'll be okay. I'll get over it, someday, somehow. But

Linz? God, she's a beautiful person. On the inside, I mean. Obviously, she's gorgeous, but I mean, who she *is* is beautiful. If it's not me, it's fine, but I just hope that she learns how to let someone love her someday. She deserves it."

"Don't we all?"

I shrug. "Maybe not the assholes of the world. Fuck mean people."

Delia makes a *well, I don't know about that* face. "Maybe if the assholes of the world had been loved better, they wouldn't be assholes. Maybe not being loved is why they're assholes."

I groaned. "Can't you just let me hate the world's many assholes in peace?"

"Nope. Hating assholes makes you an asshole. The only way to beat assholes at their game is to not be an asshole."

"Wow, DeeDee, thanks for that stunningly brilliant piece of advice."

"Stunningly brilliant…but surprisingly difficult to do regularly."

"Yeah, you're probably right."

"So, choir, huh?"

I shrugged. "I literally just picked it because it filled the hole in my schedule and eliminated a missing elective credit."

"But?" Sis knew me too well.

"But…I'm finding I like it a lot. It's…I dunno. New? Different? I dunno. I highly doubt I'm gonna, like, follow in Canaan and Corin's footsteps and become a musician or anything. I just like singing in the choir, I guess."

She exhaled smoke at the sky, glancing at me sidelong. "Purpose is a funny thing, huh?"

"But you've always had one."

She nodded. "That's what I mean. We were all raised by the same parents in the same house, but yet…"

I snorted. "But yet you, Dunc, and Sunni all have a distinct sense of purpose, while I'm out here stumbling around aimlessly like a dork."

"You've always been a late bloomer," she said.

This got a cackle out of me. "Wow, Dee, you're just really making me feel great about myself, thanks! Not only do I not have a fucking function in life, I'm *SLOW*!"

"That is *not* what I meant, Dane, Jesus fucking Christ. Take things the wrong way, why don't you?"

Her ire was intense enough to give me pause. "Well, how else am I supposed to take it, Dee? You've always known who you are and what you want out of your life. Same with Dunc, same with Sunni, same with Ella, same with Jax. I can go on."

Footsteps thunked on the deck, and we both turned to see our Uncle Lucian striding down the dock toward us. Second youngest of Dad's brothers, he was tall and lean, built more like Duncan where I was more like Uncle Bax, shorter and denser. He had shoulder-length hair tied back low on his neck—a style he'd kept pretty much his whole life—going gray at the temples with a few strands of silver sprinkled through it. He had a week's worth of stubble on his jaw, his hair bound back and tied low on his neck.

"Uncle Luce!" Delia and I said in unison—there were two ways of pronouncing his name: *LOOSH-an* and *LOOSE-ee-an*. He would answer to either and refused to say which he preferred, so some people in the family shortened his name to *LOOSH* and others to *LOOSE*; Delia used the latter while I used the former.

"Hey, kiddos." Uncle Lucian has always been the epitome of laid-back cool.

He moved slowly and with purpose, stayed quiet unless he had something important to say, and was almost always even-keeled, soft-spoken, and easy-going. He and Aunt Joss owned The Garden, a bookstore-cafe a few doors down from Badd's Bar and Grille that had a pretty big following online. Lucian was also a fairly well-known nature macrophotographer, and his work was displayed at The Garden, as well as being sold online and in galleries around the country. He, Joss, and their two kids were also inveterate travelers who spent a good portion of the year out of the country—their kids were homeschooled online to accommodate their travels.

He perched on the arm of Delia's Adirondack, took the joint from me, and took a long hit. "Came down here to say hey and couldn't help overhearing you two."

At that moment, there was a shriek, a smack, and a wail—Delia's head whipped around toward the sound as if yanked by a string. "Ooop, that's mine. You can take my spot, Uncle Luce, Sebastian is gonna need a nap, and he's in this phase where he'll only let me put him down. Hunter just winds him up, no matter what he does, and Harry is…well, she's just impossible."

Harry was Delia's and Hunter's youngest child, Harriet, affectionately known as Harry to everyone; she was named after Hunter's second-in-command, a tough old battle-axe of a woman who was a regular at Badd Clan shindigs and was known to all as Grandma Harry. She pretended to hate the nickname, but it was clear to all that she secretly loved it. She was particularly enamored with her namesake, who called her "Mamaw Rarry."

Delia hustled off to sort out her kids, and Lucian settled into the vacated chair, taking another puff before handing it back. "Purpose, huh?"

I groaned. "A topic I'm getting almighty sick of, honestly."

"I know exactly how you're feeling, kiddo." He extended his long legs, ankle crossed over ankle. "It's a tough row to hoe, not knowing where you want to go in life, who you want to be."

I frowned at him. "You're a famous photographer. You own a cafe that's a beloved tourist landmark."

"Yeah, but that's just where I ended up. I grew up feeling *exactly* how you're feeling. Think about my brothers, Dane. Bast was the heir apparent to the bar. Zane was a SEAL. Brock was a hotshot pilot. Bax was an athlete—a football star and then an MMA god. The twins were musical geniuses, and Xavier was…well, Xavier. I was the only one who didn't come out of our mother with a predefined purpose in life." He was quiet awhile, as if speaking so much at once required a reset. "I left home to get away from the feeling. I only did photography because it amused me. I never thought of it as art or a possible career—your aunts Tate and Eva were the first to see my talent. And The Garden was Aunt Joss's dream, not mine. I ended up in photography almost by accident. I met Joss by accident. I bought the retail space because I wanted to give Joss her dream, and discovered that it was my dream, too."

"So I need to hope for an accident to give me my purpose?" I puffed and passed.

He laughed. "No, man. Good lord, that's idiotic." He took the joint—now a roach—and took one last little puff before pinching out the cherry. "My point is that it'll happen on its own. As long as you're moving, you'll find your way. You're putting too much emphasis on the idea of purpose, like everyone is supposed to have some sort of, like, holy, god-given mission. It's just life, kid. Do the things that bring you joy. Get a job that pays the bills and that you don't hate, a job you can wake up and not mind doing most days. Have a hobby that fulfills you. Do good things. Love people. Have fun." He shrugged. "It's pretty simple, really."

I stared at nothing for a few moments. "But... but I..."

"Your sister and Dunc grew up wanting to follow your dad in the family business," he said. "Emerson has a natural talent for soccer. Ella is a born entrepreneur. Jax is a tech god like Xavier. They were born that way."

"And I was born without that built-in value."

"*Value?*" he repeated, incredulous. "You equate *purpose* with *value?*"

"Well...yeah?"

He shook his head. "No wonder you feel so trapped, kid. Jesus."

"What?" I asked, genuinely lost.

Didn't everyone feel that way?

"Is someone who *only* works as a bartender as their career—Elias, for example—less valuable than... say, Emerson, simply because Emerson was born, through no effort of her own, with a talent and passion for soccer?"

"Well, no, but—

He cut in over me. "Is a plumber less valuable than a painter? Is a retail manager less valuable than a corporate CEO?"

"Uncle Luce, I get your point, but—"

"But what, Dane?" His tone and gaze were both sharp; this was a rare glimpse of strong emotion from Uncle Lucian. "It doesn't apply to you? You're special, somehow? You're less valuable for not having a prede-termined life path, but that only applies to you? I'd call that inverse hubris."

I cocked my head, considering the meaning be-hind his statement. "I mean, I guess I see your point."

"I love photography. I love macrophotography in particular—I love seeing a whole new world through the lens. I do it because I love it—I just happen to be fortunate enough that I can make a decent living doing it. But I'd do it anyway, even if I never made a dime from it. Joss's dream of owning a place like The Garden was born out of her life experiences—it wasn't some-thing she wanted from the jump. You can do things you enjoy just for the enjoyment of them. And you can work a job that's…just a job. That's okay. There's nothing wrong with simply working to pay the bills and finding your fulfillment in life elsewhere. Your family, when that happens. A hobby. A sport. Art. A commu-nity choir or theater troop. Whatever. *It doesn't fucking matter*. You're putting an expectation on yourself that's unfair and unrealistic. Not everyone in this world is going to be born with a predetermined purpose or mis-sion. Joss and the kids are my purpose. Photography is my passion—making money from it is just gravy."

My mind was reeling. It was a stunningly simple shift in perspective, but a massively significant one.

We sat in silence for a while as I processed this. Eventually, Uncle Lucian spoke again.

"You don't need to know exactly where you're

going, Dane. You just gotta be moving. Living. Seeking. Creating. Stagnation is the enemy, not a lack of purpose. You're not stagnant—you're *searching*. And right now, maybe that search *is* your purpose. Take the pressure off yourself, kid. Stop thinking you need to be like Delia, Duncan, and Emerson. You're not them. You're *you*. I know your parents, and I know they want you to just be happy, whatever that looks like."

"I think that's the most I've ever heard you say, Uncle Luce. Like, combined, across my whole life."

He chuckled. "Don't be a turd."

"So you're saying I just need to do what I've been doing?"

"You're a smart, hardworking young man. You'll figure it out. Why do you think your parents aren't worried? They know you'll figure it out."

I nodded, sighing. "That actually does make a massive fucking difference."

"I felt like a fraud for years," he said. "Even when I was starting to get some name recognition in the area, I felt like people would see through me. I didn't see my photography as a career. It was something I loved doing, and people just happened to want to spend money on it. Running The Garden with Joss was the same for a long time—I felt bad for getting so much meaning from it when it wasn't even my idea. But eventually I realized what I'm telling you. Hopefully, I can save you some heartache by sharing my experience."

"I think you have, Uncle Luce."

"Then it was all worth it. Now. C'mon. You, me, Goldeneye. Like the old days, huh? Whaddya say?"

I followed him up to the house, but paused before we went inside. "Got any advice for how to convince someone who's scared that it's safe to let herself love me?"

He paused with his hand on the sliding glass door handle, thought for a moment, and looked at me. "Be there when she comes around. If she's scared of it and actively running away from it, then it means she has real feelings; she's just fighting them. There's no guarantee she'll come around, unfortunately, but if she does, be ready."

"Hurry up and wait, huh?"

He nodded. "Wish I had better advice, but yeah, basically. You can't make someone do anything or feel anything or want anything. Someone can love you but be too scared to act on it, and there's nothing you can do about it. I've never been one for thinking 'Ohhh, it's fate, what's meant for you will come to you,' or whatever. That's not always true, in my experience. But I *do* believe that on the whole, things have a way of working out. Sometimes, it just sucks along the way." He clapped a hand on my back. "Now that I've used up my quota of words for the month on you, it's time to kick your punk ass with Odd Job."

ELEVEN

Lindsey

*B*WAAAAAAAAHHHHHH! THE FERRY'S HORN LET OUT a deafening blat, startling me. I was behind the wheel of my Neon, windows open, engine off, legs crossed ankle over ankle out the window and resting on the side mirror as the ferry took us toward Ketchikan.

I couldn't quite believe I was really doing this. I was almost there: Ketchikan. My new home.

After leaving the hospital, I'd gone back to my apartment and spent the rest of the day in a daze, lost in thought, processing everything that had happened. Not just with Danny, but with everything.

Dane.

Our first liaison.

The wedding. How he'd held me when it was all I needed.

The way he'd pleasured me. Taken care of me.

Listened to me. Let me push him away when he obviously and desperately wanted the opposite.

He'd stayed silent, giving me the space I'd asked for...demanded, really.

The horn blatted again, and the ferry rocked over a choppy section of water. I spaced out a bit, exhausted from the last forty-eight hours of driving up here from Seattle.

I'd landed on the realization that I was done with LA. Rune was gone. Raquel was gone. Rune's folks were gone. That should've been enough impetus to push me toward Ketchikan, but it was Danny's shock reappearance in my life that had been the final straw. He'd been in my workplace. He'd walked right up to me. He'd *touched* me; he'd been in LA, which meant LA was tainted. The bar was tainted. I know it's ridiculous, but even my apartment felt violated simply by his existence in the city, as if his arrival had brought with it a miasma that fouled everything a hundred miles around it. I swear my apartment just *smells bad*, even though I spent four hours deep cleaning—baseboards, under furniture, behind furniture, crevices, everything. And the more I deep cleaned, the more I found myself discarding or boxing up—trophies from college, old textbooks and notebooks, clothes that don't fit or I never wore, kitchen stuff I never used.

A four-hour deep-cleaning binge turned into a weekend-long purge of my belongings, and by the time Sunday evening rolled around, I had the majority of my life already boxed up and sorted into donate, toss, and keep piles; the donate and toss piles were the biggest.

I'd stood staring at the piles, realizing that there was absolutely nothing keeping me in LA—not just that, there was nothing for me here. I looked at the piles of my shit and realized that all I needed to do was box up the rest of the stuff I was keeping, pack it up into my POS car, and I could bust out of LA. My lease was month-to-month since the last two-year contract had expired, and it was the end of the month. I had a little money set aside—I'd been saving for a new car.

So that's what I'd done—packed up my rattling, wheezing, dying Neon with my suitcases and duffel bags of clothes and toiletries, a few contractor bags of bedding and pillows, my laptop, a plastic bin full of purses, another of shoes, and a few small boxes of knickknacks—our championship trophy from the year we took nationals in high school, a creative writing award, my psychology degree, and a few photos of Rune, Raquel, and me.

I'd rented a pickup from Home Depot for an hour and dropped the donated stuff at a homeless shelter and the garbage at a dump, did one last very thorough cleaning of the apartment, and left. I'd stopped by to tell Saleh of my decision; he'd been sad that I was leaving, but he understood and gave me two grand in cash as a going-away gift.

I'd meandered slowly northward over a period of a couple of months, stopping here and there in little towns, picking up shifts at diners, bars, and clubs, hanging out with locals, and trying to put Danny behind me.

I had a dream journal, now. In it, I wrote down every nightmare I had, every awful, vile, nauseating, graphic detail. Every flashback. Every waking memory. I wrote it all down as it came up, and I faced the feelings. I had bi-weekly online sessions with Dr. Mitra, my therapist, who applauded my decision to leave LA and to keep a dream journal. We talked about the things that came up—which was new stuff all the time, now that I'd opened the floodgates.

But along the way, despite waking up most nights in a cold sweat, sobbing as a new memory resurfaced, I found myself feeling a little lighter each day, feeling more hopeful, more joyful. More able to face the nights. Panic attacks came less frequently, and when they did strike, I was able to get out of them faster. It was almost as if by purging myself first of my ties to LA—where I only now was realizing I'd long felt trapped—and then of my hoarded and suppressed memories, I was removing the chains and shackles, I was shrugging off the burden tied to my shoulders.

By the time I made it to Portland, after eight weeks of intermittent travel, I felt like a new woman. I was sleeping through the night without nightmares. My dream journal entries were farther apart. During the day, I had *so much* energy; I felt...*alive*.

The sun seemed brighter, the air seemed clearer, and the sky seemed bluer.

It was in Portland that Dane first began entering my dreams.

I'd been consumed by the past up until then—finally processing all the shit I'd kept suppressed for the last decade. Now, I could finally, even if only subconsciously, look toward the future.

I'd picked up a two-person pup tent from a second-hand shop in Eureka, along with some other camping supplies—a quality sleeping bag, propane cookstove, a cooler, a few other odds and ends. My car was now packed to the roof, leaving only the driver's side open. I even had stuff ratcheted onto the roof, despite my junker car's lack of roof rails. I'd never been camping, not really. Rune, Raquel, and I went "camping" once, our junior year at Stanford, but that had been in a rented RV, and we'd gone less than an hour from LA.

My first attempt at putting up the tent was...well, let's just say it's a good thing I was alone. If it had been filmed, it'd have won an award on *Funniest Home Videos*. And then, after I got it up, I immediately realized I'd forgotten to stake it down; a gust of wind blew it halfway across the campground before I was able to catch it and stake it down properly.

Starting a fire was another learning curve. Same with using a camp stove. And electric lanterns. And sleeping bags. I didn't realize you had to lock food up, and woke up to a loud snuffling sound outside my tent, and the backlit silhouette of a giant bear rifling through my stash of hot dogs and potato chips.

By the time I got to Seattle, I was a camping expert. I could put up my tent in fifteen minutes, start a fire, cook my food, keep bears out of my stuff, and sleep like a baby. I still hate using outhouses, though.

I dreamed of Dane all the time, and put those in my dream journal as well. Some dreams were just weird—Dane riding a purple unicorn that was somehow also a robot that spoke flawless Japanese? I dunno. Other dreams were intensely emotional—him gazing at me, sad, brokenhearted, and lonely. Guilting me for pushing him away. More than once, I dreamed he was a GI leaving for the front, and I'd run along the platform for one last kiss; I never made it, in those dreams. Other dreams were the expected fare: sinful, sexy, dirty dreams reliving the magic of our two sexual encounters. I woke up orgasming from the dreams more than once. Thank god for car chargers that let me recharge my toys while I drove, because those things were getting *a lot* of use. More than once, I know I scared a bear away with my screams of climax.

I sent him a postcard from Portland; I'd sat in a cafe for two hours after a shift, staring at that postcard, trying to figure out what to write.

In the end, all I could come up with was *Thinking of you*. It was lame and way insufficient, but what else could I say that would fit on a fucking postcard? I knew damn well when I sent it that he'd receive it and be like, *WTF is this and WTF am I supposed to do with this after all these weeks and months of nothing?* I convinced myself that it was better than nothing, and also, I'd see him face-to-face soon.

I just hoped he'd be receptive. I was upchucking my entire life, after all. Not for him, per se, nor because of him. I hadn't been thinking about him at all when I decided to leave LA.

BWAAAAAAAHHHHHH! Dude, with the fucking foghorn. Good grief. Why do you have to honk the thing every few minutes? It's a giant boat; no one is going to miss us.

The boat docked, and I waited for my turn to drive off the ferry, and then I was officially in Ketchikan with everything I owned in my car. Which was most assuredly on its last legs…or leg. The gauges didn't work at all now, the AC blew hot, the heat blew cold, and the oil leak under the car every morning would make Exxon executives uncomfortable.

But it had gotten me here.

I hadn't told anyone I was coming. I'd spent a week on Raquel's and Hamish's couch, so she obviously knew I was heading up that way, so I guess what I mean is I hadn't told Rune or Dane I was coming. I wasn't trying to surprise them, I just wasn't sure what kind of welcome I'd get from the Badd family after the way I'd hurt Dane, and I knew that Rune would lend me her couch until I figured out a plan.

I also didn't have any addresses, didn't know where anyone lived, or where the bar was that she and Duncan

lived above…I did have Waze, however, and it knew
where Badd's Bar and Grille was.

I found a parking spot not far away, locked my
car—for the stuff in it, not the car—and walked to
Badd's.

It was eight in the evening by the time I reached
the doors—which were standing open despite the fall
chill—and an acoustic duo was playing a cover of "Mr.
Brightside" in a gritty, bluesy tone, which was an interesting choice. The bouncer was a mammoth man with
long jet black hair, who was covered in what looked
to my extremely sheltered white girl eyes to be actual native, tribal tattoos, but the real kind, not the
shitty douche-bro type. He was wearing baggy Adam
Sandler-style gym shorts and a tee that could fit two
of me and still have room for activities. He looked me
over, asked for my ID, scanned it, and scrutinized me.
"Lindsey Snelling from LA." His voice was so deep my
ribcage rattled.

"Uh, yeah, that's me. Hi." I grinned nervously,
even though I was obviously old enough and had no
reason to be nervous; this guy was just so big he could
yeet me back across the Inside Passage from here.

The giant man checked the time on his phone
and then looked at me. "You can make it if you hurry."

I blinked at the non sequitur. "I…what? Make it
where?"

"The concert."

I shook my head. "I'm sorry…I feel like we're

having a conversation, but you know what we're talking about and I don't."

He leaned in through the door. "Kaylee!" The volume of his shout left my ears ringing. "I'm going to the concert. Have Brian come to the door."

"GOT IT!" A female voice answered back in a shout.

The giant lumbered to his feet, towering at least six inches over me. "C'mon, Lindsey Snelling from LA. You can ride with me."

"Ride with you where? And no offense, but I don't know you, and you're kinda scary."

He grinned down at me. "Name's Ink Isaac."

"Ink…?" A penny dropped. "*Ohhh*! You're one of Dane's six billion uncles."

He nodded, grinning at the exaggeration. "Sure am."

"I remember seeing you at Rune and Duncan's wedding," I said. "I was…a little distracted that day. Plus, you looked way different with your hair down and wearing a suit."

He just nodded again. We reached a vintage Suburban, and he lowered his bulk behind the wheel—the whole vehicle sank a few inches. I hesitated, and then got in on the other side.

"So, uh, where are we going? A concert of some kind?"

"You'll see."

I swallowed hard. "How—how is he?"

He sighed, tipped his head to one side. "He's okay. Finding his way." He looked at me. "He doesn't know you're here?"

I shook my head. "No. No one does. I mean, my friend Raquel knows I was headed this way, but I haven't told anyone up here that I was coming."

He didn't answer that, either, beyond a nod. Man of few words, I guess.

He pulled into the University of Alaska Southeast, Ketchikan campus, and parked near the Performing Arts Center.

Color me baffled. He ambled unhurriedly toward the building and led the way inside. The last of the crowd was filing into the auditorium, and we joined them. Ink stopped just inside, scanning the rows—the Badd family wasn't hard to find, as they'd taken up an entire section near the back, with a few seats still saved. I spied Dane's Dad, his mom, Delia and Hunter—sigh, swoon—with their kids on their laps; there was Rune in an aisle seat, rubbing her giant belly, Duncan beside her, arm around her as he leaned forward to exchange jokes with a female cousin. My god, so many cousins— it was a sea of absurdly good-looking humans. My god, what did that family *eat*? PHAT pills? I know, I know, no one uses that term anymore. Shut up.

Ink spied a short, dark-haired woman with four kids, a seat saved between her and the kids. He glanced down at me. "No one is mad at you."

I swallowed hard. "I…"

He patted my shoulder with a paw the size of a Kodiak bear's. "You look like you're about to shit yourself. I can't speak for Dane, but I know the rest of the family understands how things go. You did what you had to do. No one is mad at you."

My heart *was* clamoring and clattering in my chest, and my anxiety was trying to feed me ideas that the Badds would all hate me for hurting Dane.

"How do you know?" I asked.

"Cuz we ain't like that, darlin'. He didn't tell us much, either. But he's not mad, so we're not mad."

"He's…he's not?"

A shake of his head. "Nah. Hurt, maybe. Confused, definitely. Angry? Dane's not an angry guy."

I looked around. "Thank you, Ink. But…why are we *here*? What is the concert?"

Rune had seen me with Ink and was valiantly struggling to her feet. I scuttled over to her and knelt beside her. "Don't get up, don't get up."

Sinking back down with obvious relief, Rune twisted to hug me over the armrest. "Linz! You're here!" She pulled back and fiddled with my hair, sniffling. "Why are you here?"

"Long story," I said. "Short version is fuck LA and I had nowhere else to go. Also, ummm." I gave her a simpering grin. "Is your couch available?"

Duncan heard me, whipped around, stared at me, exchanged a meaningful look with Rune, and then tipped his head to one side. "Couch? No. Spare room with a bed where you can stay as long as you need? Yes. We're about to have this baby any second, though, so I hope you either sleep soundly or have earplugs."

My eyes burned. "I don't want to get in your way or anything. I won't stay long, I just—"

Duncan interrupted. "Linz, you're my wife's best friend. Regardless of anything with my brother, you're her family first."

Rune leaned into her husband. "See why I love him?"

My throat was tight. "Yeah, I do. So, um…obviously, Dane doesn't know I'm here either. I sort of just showed up."

The lights dimmed just then, and the orchestra in the pit—which had been warming up with a dissonant racket—quieted.

"Lindsey!" A voice hissed.

I twisted around and saw Ella, one of Dane's cousins, who I'd chatted with a bit during the wedding reception, was waving me to an empty seat next to her in the next row back; I patted Rune's arm. "We'll talk more after whatever this is."

She nodded and turned forward as college kids filed onto the stage from the wings. The guys were wearing tuxedos, and the girls were wearing plain black dresses—which, honestly, weren't the most flattering. More than one poor girl could have used a tailor to either take in or let out the dresses. One girl was about to bounce out of her dress if she failed to hold her cleavage down, while another could have hosted a Christmas pageant in the bodice of hers; it was so loose.

They all filed onto the risers occupying the stage in a semicircle, and an older woman in a tailored black pantsuit stepped up onto a podium and tapped her wand thingy against the edge of her music stand. The choir—for such it was—rearranged themselves in a single shuffle, some stepping up, some down. Why, I don't know; choir things, I guess.

Silence.

Tap-tap.

The orchestra started a melody—I recognized it but couldn't place it until the choir started singing— it was a classic hymn I don't remember the name of, but it was standard choir fare. They sounded fantastic, but I still wasn't sure why I was here—why the whole Badd clan was here.

I scanned the faces on the risers, looking for a familiar one, but we were in the back and I am sort of nearsighted; I've just never bothered with corrective lenses. It's only in situations like this that I notice it; this and night driving. The hymn ended. Pages were turned. A few people on the risers moved positions, again for reasons that were opaque to me.

Tap-tap.

A broad-shouldered figure stepped down from the back row and made his way to the mic stand at the front of the stage.

Dane.

His tux had tails, and he looked fucking stunning. James Bond who? Hunter who? The man was a god. The way he filled out that jacket? The white bowtie? A lot of dudes look dumb in bowties. Dane? Hot.

"Fuck me," I whispered. "Dane?"

Ella looked at me in shock. "He has a *solo*?"

"He's in a *choir*?" I shot back.

"HUSH!" Someone behind us hissed.

Dane was laser-focused on the director, waiting for the cue. The orchestra started "Hallelujah" by David Buckley, as made famous(er) by *Shrek*.

Dane took a deep breath, wiped his hands on the front of his trousers. Poor guy was so visibly nervous, I was nervous for him.

And then the cue came, and he opened his mouth, and…

The man could *sing*.

Like holy shit.

I don't know fuck—about baritone or tenor or soprano—that one's girls, I think?—I just know his voice was rich and smooth and expressive as he began the low, quiet opening, his voice growing in power and richness as the song built. When it crescendoed at the chorus, the choir joined in, weaving a harmony around Dane's voice. The song went slow and quiet again, and the choir faded until it was just Dane again, finishing the song.

When it was over, I was crying.

Not sure why.

But when I looked around, pretty much every Badd in the house was looking emotional. Ella was literally open-mouthed as a single tear trickled down.

"Did you know he could do that?" I asked as the crowd lurched to its feet, applauding.

"No!" she hissed back. "Did you?"

I could only shake my head.

Dane looked as stunned as the rest of us, as if he couldn't quite believe what had just happened, either.

That was Dane's only solo, but the rest of the concert, now that I knew why I was there, was amazing. They did some current pop numbers, some classics, and an obscure piece in Latin I've never heard of that was haunting and gave me shivers.

Dane was glowing. He moved with the music, swaying, eyes closed, looking so full of light and life I almost didn't recognize him.

My favorite part was when the majority of the choir filed off stage, leaving Dane and seven others, evenly split between boys and girls, to occupy the bottom center of the risers. Singing *a cappella*, they did a stripped-down rearrangement of "The Boxer" by Simon and Garfunkel, a truly inspired take on "Empire State of Mind" by Jay-Z and Alicia Keys—with certain lyrical adjustments made—and a soaring, gut-wrenching version of "Wicked Game" by Chris Isaak.

When it was over, the Badd Clan made its way out

to the lobby to wait for Dane to make his appearance. Rune found me, and we hugged properly.

"You're here?" she whispered in my ear, clinging to me. "Like, for good?"

I nodded. "All my shit is in my car. The little that I kept, at least."

"Why were you in Portland?"

I shrugged. "I left LA more than two months ago. I spent almost two weeks there. I spent nearly two weeks in Seattle with Raquel and Hamish. I spent a week in Eureka."

"Doing what?"

I shrugged. "Not being in LA? What were you doing when *you* left LA?"

She grinned. "The same thing."

"So where do you think I got the idea?"

Her grin faded. "Dane is...putting on a brave face, but he misses you." She examined me. "Please tell me you're here to talk to him."

I nodded. "I am. Of course I am. It's...he's not the only reason I came, though."

"You look...different," Rune said. "I can't pinpoint why, though, or what it is."

I grinned, shrugged. "Probably just the fact that I've spent the last two months since leaving LA finally confronting my demons."

Her eyes instantly went misty. "Really?"

I nodded. "I'm not, like, *healed*. That's a lifetime

process, I think. But I'm…" I let out a deep breath. "I'm okay. Like, actually *okay* for the first time in my life."

She scrutinized me. "Something happened."

I nodded. "Yes. But I'd like to tell you and Dane at the same time, so I only have to tell it once."

"But you're okay? Whatever happened?"

I clutched her close again. "Yes, Rune. I'm okay. More okay than I've ever been. I just…I guess now I just have to hope I can salvage things with Dane." I blinked hard. "Is it…is it salvageable?"

She looked over my shoulder, a grin spreading across her face. "You tell me."

Dane was there in the crowd, staring at me. The crowd seemed to swirl around him, leaving space around him as he stood beneath a light as if spotlit. Hands in his trouser pockets, debonair in his tailed tux.

"DANE! WHAT THE FUCK WAS THAT?!" Duncan was yelling, rushing for his brother. "Since when are you Josh fucking Groban?"

The tableau broke as his family surrounded him, and I faded into the background, knowing they and he needed this first.

I watched as his brother and sisters hugged him, and his mom gave him a single rose, and his dad clapped him on the back gruffly, muttering something while looking emotional. Aunt, uncles, cousins, they all swarmed him.

It was a massive crowd, his family, taking up the majority of the lobby outside the auditorium—and they drew a lot of looks, being a massive clan of tall, hot, loud Alaskans. They just…stood out.

I leaned back against a window, watching, and the joy on Dane's face as he joked and laughed with his family was enough to make me emotional. Albeit I was always emotional, these days. I'd spent so long hiding it all beneath vulgarity, cursing, and inappropriate humor that I was having to adjust to letting myself feel other stuff. It was hard, but good.

After a good thirty minutes, the Badd Clan finally filtered out—for Dane's parents' house, I heard, which was apparently the go-to spot for family gatherings.

The lobby was empty by then, except for a few stragglers, a janitor, and a tiny girl hauling a giant cello case around.

And Dane.

I stayed where I was; he came to me.

Stopped a few feet away, expressionless—carefully so. "Lindsey."

I pushed away from the window and moved a few inches closer, expecting him to back away. He didn't, but he did visibly tense at my proximity. "Dane. I…" I halted, swallowing hard. "You have an incredible voice. I had no idea."

He laughed. "You and me both. Came as a shock to me too."

This got a laugh out of me. "So then…how'd you end up in a choir, if you didn't know you could sing?"

A shrug. "Needed an elective credit, and this fit

my schedule. Turns out I love choir." He licked his lips, cast his gaze down. "You're here."

"I am."

He shifted his weight restlessly. "For how long?"

I shrugged. "I dunno. I gave up my place in LA, and everything I own is in my car back at your family's bar."

"So…you're staying?" I still couldn't decipher what he was thinking or feeling.

I gulped, hands shaking. "That was the idea."

"Where are you staying?" he asked.

"With Rune in the spare room. Until I find my own place, at least." A long, tense, awkward silence ensued. "Say something, Dane," I whispered.

"Why'd you come?" It came out hoarse.

"I had to get away from LA. There was nothing and no one there for me. Rune's parents are in Europe for the foreseeable future, researching her mom's new book. Rune is here. Raquel is in Seattle." I saw his face shift. "I…I was also hoping there was still…um…another reason for me to be here."

"Lindsey, I…" he looked away. "We have a lot to talk about."

I nodded. "We do. I have a lot to say." I dropped my eyes. "What you said before you left my place."

"Yeah?" It was a ragged whisper.

"Do you…do you still feel that way?" My eyes burned, and tears fell despite my best efforts to stop them, and I couldn't breathe. Couldn't see for the haze of sudden salt burning my eyes.

I felt his hands on my waist. "That doesn't just go away, Linz."

"I hurt you."

"Yeah. But not on purpose. You were hurting." He touched my chin, tipped my head back so I was looking up at him. "Do you still hate me?"

"Yes." I choked back a laugh. "'But mostly, I hate the way I don't hate you, not even close, not even a little bit, not even at all.'"

"Really?" he said, laughing. "You're *really* gonna quote *Ten Things I Hate About You* at me?"

"Yes, I am."

He was close. Eyes big and dark and deep and liquid, the color of the richest hot chocolate.

"You get my movie quotes," I whispered.

"I love movies. I do it all the time. Drives Dunc nuts."

"You get my sick, twisted, inappropriate humor," I whispered.

"Takes one to know one."

"You see me," I whispered. "Not just my T-and-A."

He chuckled, which didn't feel like *exactly* the right response. "I see your T-and-A, and I'm obsessed." He brushed a thumb over my lower lip. "But yes. I see you. I see your big heart. I see the sweetness you try to hide. I see how much love you have to give, and I want it for myself." He smirked. "I'm a selfish dick like that."

"You're not selfish, Dane," I said. "Not even a little bit, not even at all."

He extended his hand to me. "Wanna get out of here?"

"And go where?"

"Well, everyone is gathering at our house, apparently, and it seems I'm the guest of honor, so I kinda have to be there."

"Your whole family?" I asked in a whisper.

"You scared?"

I dropped my head, eyes downcast. "Yes, Dane, I am. You and your family have every reason to hate me." This got another laugh, which again felt like the wrong reaction. "Why do you keep laughing at me?"

He cupped my face. "I'm not laughing at you, Lindsey." When I arched an eyebrow in sarcastic disbelief, he snorted. "Okay, sure, fine, but not in a mean sense." He kissed my forehead, which did a number of significant things to my metaphorical heart and literal stomach. "No one hates you. Why would anyone hate you?"

"The way I treated you?"

"Do I seem mad about it?"

"Maybe you're a good actor?"

He snorted again. "Linz. Was I hurt? Yes. Confused? Also yes. Have I felt moments of anger at you out of that hurt and confusion? Yeah, I have." My heart twisted again, my stomach lurched again, my eyes went hot and hazy again; Dane bisected my lips

with an index finger, silencing me. "But Lindsey, I always, *always* understood where you were coming from.
I see the outlines of what you went through, and I
know there is absolutely no way I can even begin to
fathom how that's affected you your whole life. How
could I? I may not be able to empathize, but I can
sympathize."

"But your family—"

"Understands. No, I haven't shared very much
with anyone except Jax, Dunc, and Dad, and only the
vaguest outlines, for context. I don't know enough to
tell anyone anything anyway. They know I was hurt
that you couldn't be with me, but it wasn't malicious.
You were doing what you had to do to take care of
yourself. So yeah, it hurt, but...so what? It's not about
me."

"Dane, *what*? How is it not about you?"

"I have the world's greatest support system.
Legitimately. Who do you have? Rune and Raquel. And
Rune is now my sister-in-law. Whatever happens, I'll
get through it. I'll be okay, somehow, someday, even
if that means saying goodbye to you." His gaze drilled
into mine. "I don't need to know the details to understand that you've been through hell and need understanding and support."

My heart twinged. "Dane, god." I shook my head,
sniffling. "I don't know what to say. If you don't want
to know, that's fine, I just—"

"I said I don't *need* to, not that I don't *want* to. I

want to know everything about you, but only if and when you're ready to share it."

I sighed. "It's not a fun story."

"I can only imagine." He took my hand and led me into a walk. "That's for later. For now, let's get out of here and go hang with my family."

"Yay," I muttered.

He chuffed a dismissive laugh. "Oh, stop. You're being ridiculous. You have nothing to worry about, I promise. You'll see."

He led the way to his car and drove us to his parents' house, and I could only hope he was right.

TWELVE

Dane

I FELT LIKE A DUCK: ON THE SURFACE, I KNEW I SEEMED COOL, calm, and collected, but under the surface, things were paddling frantically.

She was here.

She'd come to Ketchikan indefinitely. She was looking at me, talking to me. She seemed…different. It was hard to explain how, exactly. I knew I'd have a chance to talk to her at length later, but I wanted to talk *now*. My family was expecting me, and they'd all shown up to support me, so I couldn't ghost 'em in order to talk to Lindsey.

She was here and not going anywhere…hopefully.

We arrived at home, but Lindsey sat in the car, staring straight ahead, visibly shaking.

"Linz, you're *that* scared of what my family thinks of you?"

"Just…scared."

I circled to the passenger door and took her hands, pulling so she had to stand up and out. "There's nothing to worry about. Rune ran from Duncan, and my parents love her."

"Yeah, but that was different."

"Oh? How?"

She glared at me. "Shut up."

I just laughed and led her in through the garage. We entered the kitchen from the back, and were greeted by a cacophony of voices—the usual clamor of a Badd gathering.

Lindsey tensed as we entered, her hand crush-gripping mine.

"Hey," I heard Mom's voice exclaim. "It's the man of the hour!"

I sighed. "Here we go."

"Don't sound so excited about a celebration of you," Lindsey muttered to me.

"I wasn't expecting all this," I said. "I thought it'd be Mom, Dad, and my siblings. Not, like, literally *everyone*."

"Seems like *everyone* is your family's default setting."

I shrugged and nodded. "It's true. It's great, I know, and I don't take it for granted. It can just be a lot sometimes. I wasn't ready for the whole crew. I was already shitting my pants."

"You looked nervous," Lindsey said. "But you were incredible."

Mom had plowed her way through the scrum of milling Badds to me and was already wrapping me in a hug.

"I'm so proud of you, Dane! I had no clue you could sing like that." She kissed both of my cheeks, European style, her eyes misty. "My boy."

I resisted the urge to pull away. "Mom, you're nuts. I sang *one* song."

She held me tighter, cackling through her tears. "I'm *proud of you!*" she shrieked, squeezing me until I groaned, laughing. "*ACCEPT IT!*"

"Okay, okay," I wheezed. "You're gonna break a rib, Jesus."

She reluctantly let me go, dashing fingers under her eyes and holding me at arm's length. "Fine. But only because you can't sing for me if I crack your ribs." Her gaze went to me. "Lindsey, hi. Welcome."

Lindsey faked a smile. "Thank you, Mrs. Badd."

Mom waved a hand. "Call me Dru. I've never identified as a missus." She glanced at me and then at Lindsey. "You caught his surprise performance?"

"I did," Lindsey said. "I couldn't believe what I was seeing."

Mom smiled. "Me either! I didn't even know he was taking choir until last week." She guided us further into the kitchen, shooing me away. "Dane, you have cousins to talk to. Lindsey, let's introduce you around."

Lindsey looked at me with a plea in her eyes. I just laughed, shrugging. "Mom's got you in her grip, babe. No one can help you now. Best to just give in and follow along."

Mom rolled her eyes. "Because you're *so* good at that, Dane."

"I never do anything the easy way," I said.

"Well, ain't that the truth," she deadpanned. "Lindsey, I'll bring you back to Dane in a minute."

I watched Mom drag Lindsey around the house, introducing her as my friend from LA and Rune's sort-of sister. I was half paying attention as I made the rounds of my cousins, thanking them for coming and fielding the shocked congratulations. I wasn't sure how I felt about how surprised everyone was that I didn't sound like a dying goat, but I suppose it's nice. The other part of me was watching Lindsey. At first, she was tight and tense, shoulders up around her ears, whispering her answers, but when she gradually realized that no one seemed to hate her—and that, in fact, everyone seemed to accept her presence without question, she began to relax.

I did notice that Lindsey was refusing alcohol, instead opting to nurse a can of Diet Coke. When I finally managed to pull away from the crowd of family members, I found Lindsey in a conversation with my cousin Ella.

Ella saw me approach and leaned forward to hug Lindsey. "I think Dane the Pain wants to talk to you."

I rolled my eyes. "You and your stupid nicknames."

I glanced at Lindsey. "She calls Duncan Donkey, and he fucking *hates* it, let me tell you."

Ella widened her eyes at Lindsey. "You can't call him that—he'll get pissy."

Lindsey smirked. "Well, now I'm going to. Making people pissy is my favorite hobby."

Ella cackled. "In that case, he *really* loves it when people call him Dunky Punky."

I spluttered. "Oh fuck. This is gonna get interesting." I glanced at Lindsey. "The one thing you have to understand about my family is that we've elevated insult-based humor to an art form. So if someone starts verbally fucking with you, hit 'em back with your best shots."

Lindsey's eyes lit up. "Oh, *reaaaaaally*?" She drew the word out into a multi-syllabic sing-song.

Ella and I exchanged looks, then burst into laughter. "Yeah, she'll fit in just fine," Ella said, and then looked at Lindsey. "Have you met my dad, yet?"

Lindsey widened her eyes and shrugged. "Maybe? I've met like forty people so far, and I've been driving for the last two days."

Ella tipped her back. "DADDY!"

"Yo!" Uncle Bax called.

"COME OVER HERE!"

Bax's broad form swaggered toward us. "You bellowed, dear heart?" He jutted his chin at me. "Dane. I'm impressed. I thought Canaan and Corin were the only musically inclined ones in the family. Was startin' to wonder if Mom and Dad adopted 'em in secret."

The twins were nearby and overheard. "If anyone was adopted in secret, it was you, you overgrown gorilla," Corin quipped. "They got you from the zoo."

Ella glanced at Lindsey. "See?"

Lindsey was grinning. "I do. That's definitely a game I can play."

"Dad," Ella said. "Have you met Lindsey yet? Dane's…friend?"

Uncle Bax shook her hand. "No, not yet. I saw Dru making the rounds with you, but she managed to skip me. Guess I'm not important, AM I, DRU?"

"Nope!" Mom shot back without looking, and it wasn't at all clear whether she'd heard what was said or not—not that it mattered.

Bax laughed and then turned his attention back to Lindsey. "So, Lindsey. You're the one who turned our boy Dane's world upside down, huh?"

"DAD!" Ella hissed. "What the *fuck*?"

Lindsey visibly flinched. "It wasn't my intent."

Bax frowned. "I was fucking with you. Please don't cry. Eva'll kill me if I make you cry."

Lindsey snickered at this. "Afraid of your wife, are you?"

He nodded. "Oh, absolutely. I posit that in any healthy marriage, the man should be a little scared of his wife." He grinned. "Just a little bit, though. Enough to keep you on your toes."

"You're more than a little scared of Mom, Dad. The last time she used your full name, you hid in the garage."

"I did not *hide*," Bax said, his tone jokingly prim. "I selectively avoided detection."

Lindsey laughed at that. "I think that's the same thing, my dude."

"Have you *met* my wife? She's scary!"

Lindsey shook her head. "Maybe? I dunno. I just told Ella and Dane that I've met a lot of people."

"Uncle Bax," I interrupted. "I was gonna take Lindsey for a walk."

Bax arched an eyebrow. "Take her for a walk? Is she a poodle?" He pretended to scrutinize her. "You don't look like a poodle."

Lindsey shrugged. "Definitely not a poodle. More like some sort of really fucked up mutt. You know, the type you adopt at the shelter because they just look so pathetic?"

Bax laughed. "My kids tried to get me to adopt a dog like that, once. There was some adopt-a-dog thing happening at the park, and there was this super fucked up little thing. Tongue hanging out, one eye was all milky, and it needed to wear diapers. They were like, ohhh, it's so cute!"

"It *was* cute!" Ella insisted. "Ugly-cute, but cute."

"It was *not* cute," Bax argued. "It was goddamned horrifying."

Ella gave Lindsey a droll look. "He got us Tamagotchis instead."

Lindsey cackled at this. "Tamagotchis don't shit the carpet."

Bax flung his arms wide. "*Thank* you! Someone gets it! Even my wife was like, awwww, Bax, c'mon, everyone needs love."

"Not yappy, drooling little shit-monsters," Lindsey said.

I frowned at her. "Are you anti-dog, Lindsey?"

Lindsey shook her head. "No. I'm anti-annoying dogs that never shut the fuck up and shit and piss everywhere."

Baxter held out his fist, and they tapped knuckles. "I like you. I feel like we're kindred spirits." He narrowed his eyes at her. "Pop quiz: Is the word fuck a verb, noun, adjective, or adverb?"

"Yes," Lindsey answered without hesitation. "It's also a conjunction and…other, um…grammatical… things."

Bax nodded sagely, as if she'd deposited a nugget of wisdom. He looked at me and clapped me on the shoulder. "Approved."

Lindsey bit her lip to stifle a laugh, and then shot me a look. "Come on, puppy. Time for walkies!" She patted her thigh and whistled twice.

"Woof." I pronounced the word deadpan. "How did *I* become the dog in this situation, though?"

Bax shoved me playfully. "Get outta here, young pup. Go on, git."

I snagged Lindsey's hand and led her out of the house. She exhaled a long, slow breath once we were away from the noise and chaos of the house.

I laughed. "Same. Like I said, my family is fucking amazing, but they can be overwhelming at times." She hesitated as if thinking about saying something, and then clapped her teeth together, clearly reconsidering. "Well, don't start filtering yourself now, Linz."

She sighed. "I'm kind of jealous. Or, a lot jealous. Under different circumstances, I'd love to hang out and get to know everyone. Right now, though, I…selfishly, I just want to talk to you."

We strolled across the back lawn toward the beach and walked along the water's edge just out of reach of the lapping wavelets.

I sensed she was putting her thoughts together, so I let the silence stand. She stopped after a quarter mile or so and sat down in the grass on a bluff overlooking the Passage. I sat beside her and waited.

"I have a brother, Larry," she said, eventually. "He's ten years older than me, and he's technically my half-brother. He's also a piece of shit."

I barked a laugh. "Wow, okay."

"No, for real. He was always a fucking hooligan. Always in trouble for stupid shit. He didn't get arrested for dealing drugs; he got arrested for trying to sell drugs to a uniformed officer."

I spluttered. "No. No fucking way."

"No, for real. He knew the guy and thought they were buddies. He offered him a dime bag of heroin."

I stared at her. "You aren't for real. No one is that stupid."

"Larry is." I shook my head. "He pulled shit like that all the time. He also had an uncanny knack for getting himself *out* of trouble. He never saw charges for that stunt with the cop, somehow. Never went to jail at all, actually, despite all the terribly illegal shit he pulled."

"You're saying 'had.' Is he dead?"

"No, just in the Navy, apparently."

"I take it you're not close to him."

She snorted. "Not even a little, for reasons that will be obvious shortly." She inhaled, held it, and let it out slowly. "Larry was an obnoxiously, shockingly stupid person, but we generally got along okay. If Mom was gone at work, he'd make sure I at least had a PB-and-J or something."

I frowned. "Don't much like the sound of that."

Lindsey shrugged. "Mom wasn't exactly the most attentive mother. Not the point. My problem with Larry wasn't really so much Larry as it was his friends. They were all uniformly fucking awful. Just jerks and assholes. I always hated it when he brought his friends around because they were just the worst assholes in the world." She paused, sighing. "And then there was his friend Danny. Daniel Cohen. I hated him from the moment I met him. He was greasy, smelly, and un-washed. He was *mean*. Not just an asshole or obnox-ious, he was flat-out mean. And the way he'd look at me?"

My stomach lurched, sank. "Shit."

She stared out at the water, painted silver by the bright curve of the waning moon, just a few days past full, and the numberless stars. "I was twelve when Larry started bringing Danny around. It was always at night when Mom was reliably going to be out get-ting wasted."

"Your mom left you at home alone with a drug dealer brother?" I asked.

I actually laughed. "Dane, she left me alone *with-out* my drug dealer brother when I was *eight*. It was better when Larry wasn't there, honestly. I was safe when I was alone. By twelve, I knew how to take care of myself. I already did my own laundry, made most of my own meals, got myself to school, all that shit. Mom had already gone to work by the time I had to get up for school."

I feel my heart shred. "Jesus, Linz."

She shook her head. "Don't. Not for that. It taught me independence."

"No, it taught you that you can't trust anyone," I said. "That you can't rely on anyone but yourself."

She nodded. "True enough, I guess. Anyway. Danny Cohen. He and Larry would come over and watch TV, play video games, get wasted, the usual twenty-year-old boy bullshit. School was an escape for me, so I actually liked going. It was safe. There was food. Sometimes Mom would forget to pay a bill and we'd be in the dark until she got paid, or the gas was out so our showers were cold and the stove didn't work, or we didn't have water so I had to shower at school. Didn't happen all the time, but it happened."

Another long pause; I got the feeling she was delaying getting to the hard stuff.

"April 5th, four months from my thirteenth birthday, I went to bed early because I had a math test the next morning, and I really wanted to do well on it. I'd studied my butt off for it, and I was excited to show my teacher how hard I'd worked." Her eyes watered, shimmering, and she dropped her gaze, head hanging. "Fuck."

I took her hand. "I'm here."

"I know," she sniffled. "It's just hard to talk about." Another long pause. "I woke up to the sound of my door opening. It was Danny. He closed the door and locked it. He was drunk. He…I had a nightlight that was just bright enough to let me see his face clearly, and the look on his face? Dane, it made my blood run cold. I started crying before I knew what he was gonna do, because I just knew nothing good was about to happen. It was this…*evil* expression. Not just evil, but, at the risk of sounding Biblical, *delighting* in evil. He knelt on the bed and covered my mouth with his hand. He carried this pocket knife, one of those fancy box cutters. Not the cheap plastic ones. It looked like a folding pocket knife, but it was a razor blade."

"I know what you mean."

"He opened it and pricked my lip with it. He told me if I made a sound, he'd cut my tongue out. And the look in his eye, Dane? I believed him."

"Linz," I whispered.

She shook her head. "He also told me that if I co-operated, he wouldn't hurt me. But if I gave him trouble, he would. And I…" she blinked hard, looked away, yanked her hand away, and dashed at her eyes with the back of her wrist. "I didn't want to be hurt. And I didn't really understand what he was going to do. I loosely understood what sex was, but only vaguely." She sniffled as tears began to fall. "He showed me. It hurt *so* bad. I bled. Not just because I was a virgin, but because I was only twelve and he was twenty-two. And because he was violent about it."

Hate burned inside me, seared my eyes, and stained my cheeks. "I don't know what to say."

She looked at me, sniffling a sad laugh as she wiped at my face. "You can't do that, Dane, or I won't be able to get through this." She brushed a thumb under my eye. "You don't need to say anything. There's nothing *to* say." She collected herself and began again. "That was the first time. It wasn't every day after that—he and Larry were too busy being hoodlums to waste every day playing *Call of Duty*, because despite their many, many faults, they *were* hard-working—they were just hard-working fuckhead criminals." She sighed. "Sometimes he'd just come in and fuck me and leave. Other times he…he wanted to….to play."

"Ahhhh god, fuck," I snarled. *"Play?"*

She nodded. "His favorite game was to play tonsil hockey with his dick. He thought it was hysterical to shove his dick so far down my throat that I would retch. I barfed a lot before I learned to control my gag reflex."

I felt sick to my stomach, especially thinking about the day she freaked out. "Linz—*fuck*. No wonder you had a panic attack. I would never, *ever*—"

She clapped a hand over my mouth. "Hush, Dane. I know. Just let me talk."

I nodded.

She removed her hand and gazed back out at the water. The wind picked up, tossing her blonde locks this way and that. A strand of hair stuck to her lips, and she scraped it behind her ear. "The question everyone asks is, *Why didn't I say anything?"*

"He threatened to kill you."

"He threatened to cut out my tongue, actually. Threatening to kill me came later." She paused, started again. "He convinced me that if I told anyone, I'd get in trouble. Sounds dumb to an adult who's never been molested as a kid, but when you're twelve, scared, alone, being brutally sexually assaulted multiple times a week by a strong, violent 22-year-old, it's hard to think rationally. And you can't see what's right and wrong from there. You know that what's happening is very,

very wrong, but you can't stop it. You know it's wrong because it makes you feel so fucking awful. You wonder why it's happening to you. And he's telling you that you'll get in trouble, you'll go to jail, and it hurts, and you want it to stop, but it doesn't ever stop, and you wonder what you did wrong, why you deserve to have that done to you. You start to believe that it *is* your fault. That you *do* deserve it."

I couldn't summon a single syllable. What was there to say? *I'm sorry? That sucks?* Words are useless, sometimes.

She searched my face for a moment, gave me a sympathetic smile—tearful, but understanding. "Don't look at me like that, Dane. I'm okay, now. Or, I'm getting there."

"I just…" I swallowed hard. "How could anyone do that to a little girl? To *anyone*, let alone a twelve-year-old?"

"Predators and pedophiles," she answered with a shrug. "Dudes with no soul. I dunno." She cupped her chest. "I developed early. I got my period at ten and had C-cup boobs by twelve. I figured it was that—that if I hadn't had such big tits, maybe Danny wouldn't want to rape me. I tried taping them down. Wore too-small bras. All sorts of dumb shit in an attempt to be less…whatever, to him and guys like him. I got nasty comments from more than one male staff member at school. I knew no one would believe me, though, so I didn't bother telling anyone."

"Jesus," I breathed. *"Disgusting.* Men like that oughta have their dicks chopped off, sauteed, and fed to the hogs."

"I don't disagree," she said. "I did tell my mother about Danny, also. But her only response was to ask what I'd done to ask for it."

"Your own mother said that?" I asked, incredulous. "I can see sexist old men saying shit like that, but a woman, and your own *mother?*"

"Ironically, when it comes to rape and sexual assault, women are just as likely to be judgmental and victim-blame as men. Which is super weird to me. But yeah, my mom figured I must have been a little slut whoring herself out to her brother's best friend. Didn't do a damn thing. I told my brother, and he just laughed. He may have even kept watch in case my mom came home—not that I think she'd have done anything, mainly because she was always so drunk when she got home that all she could do was pass out in bed." A shake of her head. "That's my mother."

"When did it finally stop?" I asked.

"When I was sixteen. It's honestly a miracle I never got pregnant. He might be infertile or whatever, honestly, because he never used a condom." She was quiet for a few moments. "He got arrested for rape and went to jail. I ran away not long after that and moved out here to go to Stanford as soon as I could."

"A homeless girl who spent four years being

molested earned a full ride to Stanford," I said. "Fucking amazing."

"I've never wanted to let that define me." She swallowed hard. "I still don't. I refuse to be a lifelong victim. I refuse to let *that* be the defining element of my life and who I am."

"I think you've succeeded," I said.

She shook her head. "No, I haven't. I hid from how I felt. I hid how deeply I was hurting. I've seen therapists for years, but I never let anyone in far enough to actually help me heal. I suppose that's why I've been through six therapists in the last four years. I just couldn't talk about it. I mean, I *did*, but only in general terms, and I always downplayed the severity of my feelings."

"Why?"

A shrug. "I wish I knew. Fear? The intensity of the pain is scary. Not just pain—shame. Guilt. Anger. Even if you intellectually know that it wasn't your fault, your heart doesn't know that, and neither does your body. And when I say pain, I mean emotional pain. I almost wish it *was* physical, because physical pain you can deal with easily. Sure, it sucks, it hurts, but you can focus on it. You can take a pill for it, and it gets better. Break a leg? Take morphine or Vicodin or Percocet or what-the-fuck-ever. But *this* shit? What do you do? Talk to a therapist? Did that for fucking years and got almost nowhere. Sure, I've developed some coping mechanisms for panic attacks, but until I got up the fucking courage to figure my shit out myself, nothing ever changed. And yeah, maybe some or most of that is on me for being unwilling to face it head-on, head up. It's just... there's no pill you can take for a broken heart or a screwed-up childhood."

"Hey, here you two are," I heard Rune say behind us.

Lindsey twisted, reaching for her best friend. "Oh, hey you. Perfect timing. I just finished giving Dane the awful truth of Lindsey's...Tragic...Past." She framed the last three words with her hands, miming a newspaper headline.

Rune waddled and shuffled to where we were sitting and stood over us. "Yeah, I'm not getting down there, ya'll. You just don't sit on the ground when you're nine months pregnant."

Lindsey and I stood up in unison and we strolled slowly toward the gazebo in the corner of the yard a few dozen feet away from the back deck—it was Mom's favorite place to be, with benches lining the perimeter, lots of hooks from the underside of the roof where she could hang all sorts of potted flowers and such, and one of those gas firepits with the glass rocks in the middle.

Rune settled onto the bench with a relieved sigh, puffing as she rubbed her giant belly. "Much better." She peered at the firepit—it wasn't actually a pit, per se, though, being raised up a few feet on a pedestal that served as a ledge for resting drinks, plates, and feet. "Fire?" She gave me a wide-eyed look, saying the word in the same silly falsetto someone would jokingly say *"Cheep-cheep!"* like a baby bird.

I snorted, opening the false-front compartment where the controls were and turning on the fire. It caught with a soft *whump,* and blue-yellow flames danced in the gentle breeze. "Need anything else, oh pregnant one?" I asked, grinning at her.

"Um. I'm craving Skittles and potato chips." She bit her lip. "Oh. You were teasing me. No, I'm good."

I shook my head. "Skittles and potato chips?"

She shrugged. "Pregnancy does some seriously weird shit to you, my friend. The other day I just *had to have* a peanut butter and grape jelly sandwich and it *had* to be on sourdough bread, and I *had* to have *specifically* Cool Ranch Doritos with it."

Lindsey stared at her incredulously. "Grape jelly? What the actual fuck? You hate fake grape flavor."

"I KNOW!" Rune shouted. "I tried to ignore the craving for like an hour, but I couldn't get it out of my fucking head. I *had* to have a grape jelly PB and J. I don't think I've had a PB and J since I was like seven, let alone grape fucking jelly."

Rune cackled. "And when you ate it? Did it satisfy the craving?"

Rune huffed, nodding. "Yes, yes it did. Which honestly pissed me off a little. Now, if I had a grape jelly PB and J right now, I might barf. But a bag of Skittles and some ridged Ruffles? Fuck yes."

I sent a text to Duncan with his wife's request,

and a few minutes later, he appeared with a bag of Skittles, a bag of ridged Ruffles potato chips, and a can of Diet Sunkist.

When she saw the can of orange soda, Rune squealed and clapped her hands. "Orange drink! How'd you know, baby?"

Duncan sputtered a laugh. "I mean, you've gone through almost a case just today, so it was a solid bet you'd want one with this weird-ass fucking combo." He handed her the two bags and then looked at me and then Lindsey. "Is this a you-three conversation?"

Lindsey shook her head. "I'd never ask Rune to keep anything secret from you, Dunc." When Duncan sat down beside his wife and helped himself to the chips, Lindsey spent a moment fiddling with a fold of the fabric of her leggings before speaking. "Dunc, I'll let Rune fill you in later on the details of this because I don't have it in me to go into it again. Suffice it to say, I was sexually abused by my brother's friend for a period of four years from the time I was twelve until I was sixteen."

Duncan's face took on a furious cast. "Fucking hell, Lindsey. I'm so, so sorry you had to experience that. I hope you know that our whole family is here for you, no matter what you may need. If the fucking asshole piece of shit scumbag is still out there—"

Rune clapped a hand over his mouth. "Baby, hush. Let the woman speak."

"Sorry," he said, still muffled by Rune's palm.

I rolled my eyes at him. "You think I haven't said that?"

Lindsey smirked at me. "Well, actually, you haven't." When I opened my mouth to protest, she just laughed and spoke over me. "But I know. I don't need you to say it, because I already know—I can tell. I think if the rest of your family, your eight hundred gigantic, muscle-y, intimidating uncles, especially, found out?" She winced. "They'd form a torches-and-pitchforks committee."

"But he's in prison, isn't he?" Rune asked. "Danny?"

"That's why I wanted to talk to you both at the same time. I have...an update." She inhaled a shaky, shuddering breath. "He showed up at my bar."

Rune sucked in a shocked hiss. "No! He did?"

Lindsey nodded. "Hasn't changed a fucking bit. I didn't know it was him at first. I was rolling silverware five minutes before close and heard someone come in and ask for a drink. I knew it was him the second I heard his fucking voice and I...I was..." she trailed off, voice cracking, breaking. "I was there. Back in Boston, in that house. For a second, I was...he was holding me down and..." she shook her head. "He didn't know it was me. He was just...*so vile*. He made these awful remarks. And I...I sort of...um, lost my shit."

Rune covered her mouth. "What happened?"

"I hope you did a secret murder," Duncan said. "Or gave him a really bad papercut on his dick-tip or something."

Lindsey snickered. "I stabbed a fork through the middle of his hand so hard it pinned it to the bar. And then, I, um, sort of kicked him in the balls so hard so many times he had to be hospitalized and will never reproduce again, and most likely won't ever get an erection again either."

Rune clapped. "Excellent!" She gasped, hands over her mouth. "Wait, did you get in trouble?"

Lindsey shook her head. "No, I did not. And, um, actually, I sort of snuck into his hospital room by pretending to be his girlfriend."

Rune popped Skittles into her mouth like a caricature of a rapt moviegoer with popcorn. "No! Shut up! You *did not*!"

"I one hundred percent did. Some seriously spiffy acting on my part, I gotta say."

"Why?" Duncan asked. "Why go see him?"

Lindsey raked flyaway hair out of her face. "I had to. I know you can't…grasp it…and that's not a dig, I promise. He just…he'd haunted me every day and every night for fucking *years*. Talk therapy, EMDR, hypnosis, I tried it all. I had fucking nightmares, flashbacks—I've been fucking *haunted* by hiss ass. He was never far from my mind. What he did to me. The helplessness. The fear. The guilt, the shame. The anger. No matter how brave a face I put on, no matter how much I tried to bury it all and not think about it, I just…he… it never went away. Dating, hooking up, he was always the invisible third person. Tainting every facet of my

life, my love life especially." She huffed a laugh. "Love
life—what a fucking joke. I avoided love like the goddamn plague. How do you love someone when you
see someone raping you every time you try to sleep,
when you feel him violating you every time you're in
bed with someone?"

I felt bile in my throat. "Linz…"

"You were the exception," she whispered, her
voice wet and hoarse. "Dane, *you* were the exception.
Why do you think I was so freaked out? I know…"

She shot to her feet and paced to the steps of
the gazebo, head tipped back, breathing with slow
deliberation.

Started over. "I know it seems like that should be
a relief, but it's just terrifying. To suddenly have silence
when you're used to this endless mental noise? Arguing
with yourself. Trying to silence the monster inside.
Trying to pretend you don't hear his sick fucking voice
in your head telling you he'll cut your throat if you
tell anyone, he'll make sure I go to jail, and you know
what happens to little girls in jail, right? Hearing his
voice calling you a good little whore when you choose
to lay there and take it instead of fighting it. You hear
that shit—it's *all* you hear. And then suddenly you meet
this guy, and he's sexy and funny and interesting, and
he's attracted to you and…and…you think it'll be like
all the other times you've hooked up. You'll get a little
pleasure out of it, and if you're lucky, your fucked up
brain will shut up for two fucking seconds."

I moved behind her, and she didn't look at me, just shook her hands at her sides. "Please don't touch me right now, Dane. I can't keep my mind straight when you talk to me, and I need to get all this out of my fucking head."

"Okay. Can I at least stand near you?" I said.

"Please, yes." She turned to peer up at me, eyes wet and shimmering and wide and sad and hopeful all at the same time. "I need you—" a choked sob, a shake of her head. "I need you close. I just…I'll fall apart if you touch me, and I can't fall apart yet."

"I'll be there when you do," I told her. "No matter how, no matter when, no matter where, no matter why."

"I know, Dane. I know." She shook her head and blew out a short breath. She glanced back at Duncan. "I went to see him because I had to look him in the eye, face-to-face, without flinching. I had to face him. I would never have gone looking for him if this hadn't happened. I guess I thought he was still in jail. Naively, perhaps. It's not like I went to the trial or knew how long he'd gotten, I'd just been told by fucking Larry, my shit-eater of a brother, that he'd gotten popped for raping some poor girl."

I was standing behind her, and I heard her swallow, saw her shoulders lift and lower as she controlled her breathing. She leaned back against me, head on my breastbone, drawing strength from me—I hoped. After a moment, she straightened.

"I told him I forgave him. Not for him—for me. I…I just…I knew I had to try to let it go. Let him go. Move on. Be free. So I looked him in the eye and I fucking forgave him. I said the words, at least. I…said a lot of shit that's honestly gonna stay between him and me. And then the best thing in the whole world happened."

She paused for effect.

"Two LAPD officers showed up to arrest him for violating the terms of his parole and for violating a restraining order."

It was Rune who pointed out a discrepancy Lindsey had apparently overlooked. "He was on parole in California? I assumed he served his prison sentence in Massachusetts."

"Oh," Lindsey muttered. "I hadn't thought about that. Yeah, he was in a state pen in Massachusetts. So clearly, he got out, moved to Cali, got arrested again there—I assume for something to do with the girl who had a restraining order against him." She blinked. "He said he'd been on oil rigs for the last few years." A shrug, a wave of the hand. "Whatever. Doesn't matter."

"So he was in the hospital with literal busted balls and he got arrested?" Duncan said, laughing. "That's fucking fantastic."

Lindsey turned and grinned at us. "Oh, it gets even better." She rubbed her hands together gleefully. "They hadn't even finished saying what he was under arrest for when the fucking *FBI* shows up saying they've got him for drug possession and transportation, possession of a firearm without a license, and witness intimidation."

"On oil rigs, my ass," Duncan said.

Lindsey shrugged. "He's always been a two-bit criminal, but he also always had a job." She let out a breath. "So yeah. I left the cops and the feds to figure out who got to take him away first. But even if and when he gets out again, I'm not living any more of my life trapped by the memory of him. In my mind, he was still this huge, strong twenty-year-old with all the power. He's not that anymore. He's wasted away. He's old. Drug-addled. He's…he's no one. He's gone. The thing I was so afraid of—who he used to be and the things he did to me—it's in the past."

Rune appeared beside her. Leaned against her, head on her shoulder. "Linz, honey. I'm *so* proud of you."

Lindsey laughed. "For what?"

"Oh, I dunno…everything? Surviving. Coming through all that. Not actually murdering Danny Cohen."

Lindsey twisted her head to kiss Lindsey on the crown. "Thanks, babe."

Rune straightened. "So then you left LA?"

"More or less. I tried to go back to work, but…I kept seeing and feeling Danny behind me. I kept having little panic attacks. I'd feel him behind me in the parking lot. In the store. At home. Everywhere I went, I felt him. I knew he was in jail and not getting out for years at best, but it felt like LA had been contaminated. Like, he'd been there for how long? He could have shown up at any time. What if he'd found out I was there? Plus, everyone I knew in LA was gone. I didn't even have Mom and Pop Rigby to drop by and talk to."

"And a home-cooked meal," Rune added.

Lindsey grinned. "That too." A shrug. "I woke up one morning and just knew. At first, I was like, maybe I just need a new apartment. I dunno. I started cleaning my place out with the idea of maybe moving somewhere else in LA, getting a new job. But then I started boxing up shit to give away and bagging up shit to throw away, and I realized there wasn't a single reason for me to be in LA. Your parents weren't coming back. Raquel wasn't coming back. You weren't coming back. All I had were memories, and a lot of those weren't good ones. LA, for me, has been…difficult. I got my degree, and I'm proud of that. I met you and Raquel, and you guys saved my life. You're my best friends. Rune, you're closer than any sister ever could be. But there's also just so much shit. So much weight. And knowing Danny had been in LA at the same time, even for a fucking day, I just…*felt* him there. The whole city just felt…slimy."

Duncan cackled. "It feels that way to me all the time."

Rune whacked him. "Hey, I still love things about LA."

Duncan raised his hands in surrender. "As long as

you understand that while I have no problem visiting, I'll never, ever live there."

Rune laughed. "No, no. I know." She blew him a kiss across the gazebo. "I'm an Alaskan now, anyway, sweetheart. And happily so."

Lindsey leaned back against me. "So, I gave up my apartment, got rid of most of my shit, and started driving north. I wasn't even sure I was coming here at first; I was just getting out of LA. And I…" She closed her eyes, sighing. "I faced things for the first time. When I had a nightmare about him, I wrote it down. Every detail. Everything I thought and felt. I wrote down my flashbacks. Memories. Everything that happened, I wrote it down. When I had a panic attack, I'd write about it. Figure out what triggered it. I didn't try to bury what I was feeling."

"That sounds…rough," I said.

She laughed. "Oh, it was. The first month or so was really, *really* fucking hard. I barely slept at night because the more I faced the shit, the more came up. I remembered things I'd suppressed or forgotten. Things he'd done to me. I'd forgotten how he used to literally dick slap me in the face when he was done fucking my throat."

Duncan growled like an angry wolf. "Fucking hell."

She turned to look at him. "Yeah, that's the kind of guy he was. He'd dick slap me and call me his good little whore."

"Fuck," Duncan mumbled. "I'm gonna be sick."

I turned in time to watch him lurch across the gazebo and lean over the railing, head hanging, breathing hard.

Rune went to him. "My sweet, soft-hearted man," she whispered, rubbing his back.

Lindsey turned to face me, her hands resting flat on my chest. "I'm not, like, all better. What I went through, what he did to me, it'll have its effects on me my whole life. That's not something you ever really, truly get over. But I'm…I can honestly say that I'm… maybe not okay, but on the way to okay."

"Linz," I whispered; I wasn't sure what else I was trying to say, and so managed nothing else.

She rested her forehead on my chest. "For the last month or so, you're all I can think about. I dream about you. I think about…" she buried her face against me. "You know."

"I do," I murmured.

I heard movement, but my focus was exclusively on Lindsey.

She sighed, pulling away to look up at me again. Her eyes were fraught and wet and searching me. "I want to try."

"Try?"

"Us," she whispered. "I…I don't know how to… how to be a good girlfriend. How to…how to love someone. There may be some things that will always trigger me. But I—"

It was my turn to shush her with my hand. "Linz. If I'd known even a *hint* of what you'd been through, that you had some kind of issue with—"

She tugged my hand away. "I never told anyone. I knew going down often triggered me, but I did it anyway."

"Why?" I asked. "Why do that to yourself?"

A shake of her head. "I felt like...like if I let the panic stop me from doing sexual stuff, he'd won. He'd be taking that away from me. I felt like if I let him win, I was weak, and I'm not weak, so I refused to let him win. I refused to let him ruin sex for me. Because it wasn't—it's not all the time that sucking dick gives me a panic attack. It's always seemed random. Sometimes it does, sometimes it doesn't."

"But Linz, at all is too much. If it causes you any kind of...anything negative, I don't want you to do it. No matter what it is."

"But I—"

"No," I cut in. "Please try to hear me. Yes, it feels good to get a blow job. Really fucking good. When you were doing that, it was great. But I don't need it. Your peace and happiness are the only things that are important to me. If you can't have sex at all, only kiss me and let me hold you, that's okay. I'll be okay."

Her eyes shuttered, and her body shuddered. "Dane. I *want* you. I *need* you. I've stopped having nightmares and flashbacks almost entirely. Now all I dream about is *you*. The things we did together. The way you made me feel." She opened her eyes and gazed up at me, ice-blue eyes soft and warm and deep. Her fingers fisted into my shirtfront, rumpling the button-down. "I still don't want to let the past dictate what I can and can't do, but I…I guess I'm willing to stick with what I know is safe until I feel able to experiment with you and see how things feel."

I brushed her cheekbone with a thumb. "Just communicate with me, Linz. Be honest. No matter what you're thinking or feeling, just talk to me about it so we can handle it…*together*."

"I'm not good at that, historically, but I'll try my best."

THIRTEEN

Lindsey

DANE TOOK MY HAND AND LED ME TOWARD THE HOUSE. "Where are we going?" I asked. "I...I don't know if I can handle your whole family right now, Dane. I'm too emotionally raw."

"I can't either," he said. "We're not going home." He paused. "Well, only long enough for me to change outta this damned monkey suit and grab my keys."

My heart pitter-pattered. "Maybe, um...just grab a change of clothing?" I whispered, feeling oddly nervous to express the totality of what I was feeling.

He smirked at me as we reached a sliding glass door on the side of the house that opened onto a hallway. "Oh? Why's that?"

I bit my lip. "I like the tux."

His smirk morphed into a full grin. "Ohhh, I see."

"You see what?" I demanded.

"You don't want me to take of the tux because *you* want to take it off me."

The pitter-patter became a swirl of fluttering things in my belly. "Maybe."

"I thought we agreed you'd be honest with me," he said.

"No, you told me to be honest with you, and I said I'd do my best." I swallowed hard. "I guess I'm having trouble believing that after everything, I can just show up here unannounced and be like, 'Okay, I'm ready,' and you're just…fine with it? With everything I've done? How I've treated you this past half a year or whatever? You're not bitter? No part of you is like, fuck that bitch?"

He glanced to the left, where you could see a glimpse of the kitchen, filled with a milling crowd of family, and then tugged me the other way down the hall. We reached the very end of the hall, and he pushed open the last door on the left. His bedroom was neat and tidy. A queen bed took up the middle of the room; there was an ensuite bathroom on the right with a walk-in closet next to it, a bureau, and a desk on the right.

Still not answering my question, he popped into his closet, found a duffel bag, and went to his dresser, shoving a few changes of clothing into it, a few toiletries from the bathroom, and a charger and block for his phone.

That done, he turned to me. "Why would I be

mad or bitter, Linz? You didn't do anything to me. You did what you felt you had to do for your mental health. And honestly, I think you did the right thing. Not just for you, but for us."

My legs went wobbly. "*What?*"

He guided me to his bed, and we sat side by side at the foot. "Look, I know you have feelings for me, Linz. I don't need you to tell me or to say anything. It was obvious you felt things from the get-go. Just like I did. But you…you couldn't handle those feelings. You had too much unresolved other shit. You had no room for your feelings for me. When you told me to leave, I understood that it wasn't because you didn't care about me or want me. You weren't ready. I got that. So yeah, babe, you can show up here unannounced. I wasn't, like, sitting around crying and waiting for you. I mean…" He frowned, tugged at the bowtie around his throat. "I suppose I was, in a way, but not, like, actively waiting."

"I didn't expect you to wait for me," I said. "So if you, y'know, had a thing with someone else, I'll understand."

Dane looked away, and my heart sank. Despite what I'd said, I would be pretty upset if he had hooked up with someone else.

So much for honesty, I guess?

Dane turned his gaze back to me. "Linz, this won't work if you're not being truthful with yourself and with me about things."

I huffed. "What are you, a fucking mind reader?"

He chuckled. "No. But if you were harboring any ideas of becoming a professional poker player, maybe don't. You have zero poker face."

I snapped my fingers. "Well, damn. There goes that career." I sighed. "Fine. You want the honest truth?"

"Always. Fuck me up, fam."

"If you did hook up with someone since we saw each other last, yes, I would be…upset. It'd hurt. But I know I have no right to expect you to have, I dunno… been faithful to me when I threw you out of my house the way I did."

"In the spirit of honesty," Dane said, "I went on a date with a girl I met at school. We chatted in the cafeteria for an hour, she asked me to lunch the next day, and I went." My heart twisted in my chest, rose to sit hot and acidic in my throat. "I didn't make it past the appetizers. I had precisely three mozzarella sticks, realized there was absolutely no chance of anything with her or anyone else, and left."

"Oh no! The poor girl," I exclaimed, trying not to sound too happy. "What did you tell her?"

"Just that I was sorry, it wasn't going to work, and I had to go." He grinned. "If you were trying to look or sound sad about that, you also should give up any dreams of being an actress."

I sighed. "You really can read me like a book, huh?"

He took my hand, entwining our fingers. "Yes. I can."

"I don't know how I feel about that."

"You should feel good about it. I don't mean that I'm a mind reader or that I know everything there is to know about you. But I can see things on your face. I can see what you're feeling. I may not be right, but I can see the feelings, and honestly, that's an improvement. You were pretty hard to read, before."

"I didn't want to be seen," I said.

"Well, I see you."

"I know you do." I licked my lips, watched his eyes follow the path of my tongue.

"I'm glad you showed up," he whispered.

"I wasn't sure you would be. I don't feel like I deserve to—"

"I'm gonna stop you right there," he said. "Because that's bullshit. You were taking care of yourself. You couldn't be with me. You did the right thing by me—if you'd tried to force the issue, tried to just gut through all the shit you'd never dealt with, eventually, even if things maybe started out good between us, it'd have fallen apart."

A shadow slid across the doorway—his mother filling the space. She was dressed in a pair of navy slacks and a pale gray fitted sweater, her auburn hair loose and wavy around her shoulders. She was beautiful, Dane's mother. Classy, sexy, and beautiful. Intimidatingly so. I felt frumpy in my three-day-old leggings, a crusty sports bra that doesn't really support the girls, and an XXL hoodie with Eeyore on it. Yes, Eeyore. I love me some depressed donkeys; that motherfucker keeps it 100 all the time. We should all be more like Eeyore.

She smiled at me. "Hi, Lindsey. I saw you at the concert but didn't have a chance to say hi."

I gave her a small, shy smile and a tiny wave. "Hello, Mrs. Badd."

"Call me Dru." She entered the room, eying Dane's bag on the floor at his feet. "Going somewhere, son?"

He nodded. "Staying in the spare room at Dunc and Rune's for a night or two."

She arched an eyebrow. "Which means pulling a French exit on your own party?"

He shrugged. "Mom, I didn't want it to be a whole thing. It was my first time ever singing in front of a crowd, I was already nervous as all fuck, and I only wanted the immediate family in case I totally fucking bombed. Imagine my surprise when I go out and see *literally everyone*. So yeah, sorry, I don't feel an obligation to hang around at a party I didn't ask for."

His mom blinked at this. "Oh. I see. We just wanted you to feel supported, Dane."

I elbowed him. "Don't be an ungrateful turd, Dane. Be glad you have a giant family to support you. I've got Rune and her parents, and that's it."

Dru gave me a long look I couldn't entirely decipher. "I don't think that's entirely true anymore, sweetheart." She perched on the edge of the bed beside me, sandwiching me between her and her son. "Lindsey, dear. Whatever's going on between you and my son is between the two of you. I am very close to my boys, and I like to think they tell me most things. So I know that things happened between the two of you. That's life, that's relationships. Shit happens. I overheard the last thing Dane was saying, and he's absolutely right. You shouldn't feel bad about making the decision you did. We can't give anyone else our heart if we're a disaster. Love can heal, and it does. But if you're too much of a broken mess, there's nothing to heal. You did what you had to do to put yourself in a better place. That's admirable. It was the only thing you could have done. And now you're here. My boys are not perfect, but I like to think they *are* understanding. And so are we." She took my hands and gave me a long, hard look, making sure I was really listening. "You are welcome here. Always, no matter what. Rune is my daughter, now. We don't differentiate between daughters and daughters-in-law. By that same logic, you're Rune's sister. So even if you and my son don't end up together, you'll always have a place at our table."

My eyes burned. My throat was tight and hot. Is it dusty in here or what?

"Dammit." I lurched to my feet and paced across the room. "What is it with you people and making me fucking *cry*? Jesus."

I felt a presence behind me—by the vanilla-floral

perfume I smelled, it was not Dane, unless Dane was suddenly into women's perfume. "Don't run away from what you feel, Lindsey. That leads you nowhere good. Trust me."

I laughed. "Sounds simple, doesn't it?"

"No, it does not. It's not simple at all. It's neither easy nor simple. All of us have struggled with something like what you're going through. It's really, really, really hard to trust your heart to another person even if you *don't* have emotional damage."

I snorted. "I've got a fuck-ton of emotional damage."

"So it's gonna be even more difficult to let yourself be vulnerable," Dru said. "We get that. And I know Dane does. But the first step, since I'm handing out unsolicited advice, is to just let yourself feel things. Which I know is hard when you're used to shoving all that shit aside."

I stared out the window at the rippling, shimmering waters of the Passage, swallowing hard, eyes burning—I let them burn. Let tears slip out. "I've been on my own my whole life. The closest thing to a family I've ever had is Rune and her parents. And they are, quite literally, the only reason I'm…" I shook my head, at a loss for the right words. "They fed me, clothed me, and helped me when my car took a shit. Paid for therapy. But at the end of the day, you get in bed alone, and it's just you and your thoughts, and I…I sometimes feel ungrateful for feeling lonely or whatever when I know I had—and have—Rune and Mom and Pop Rigby. I just…" I sighed. "I don't know what I'm even trying to say."

"That's okay," she said. "Maybe you just need to express all that stuff that you haven't let yourself express. All those thoughts and feelings that we label as ungrateful or spiteful or whatever…the sadness, the loneliness, the anger, the bitterness. We lock all that up in a vault somewhere around our stomachs and ignore it. And you know what happens? It turns physical. It makes your back hurt. It makes your stomach hurt. It fills you with this bubbling, festering, fermenting sea of nastiness inside that has nowhere to go."

A strange, high-pitched keening sound erupted from my throat, a tight, teeth-gritted half-scream of raw emotion too potent for anything so prosaic as mere words.

"I'm so *angry*!" I hissed through my teeth.

"I never had a mother. I never had a father. My brother was a nightmare—a useless troublemaker at best. And it was his best fucking friend who ruined me. I've spent my entire life running, hiding, suppressing, pretending…hating him, hating myself, hating my brother, hating my mother for not protecting me, for blaming me when I was the fucking victim. I've tried to…to be okay, and I'm fucking not. I'm tired!" My knees wobbled, and I sank to the ground, to my hands and knees, gulping ragged hot breaths. "I'm so fucking tired of fighting. Of being sad. Of being scared. Of hating. It's so exhausting, hating. It's exhausting trying to act like you're not a fucking zombie on the inside."

I felt hands on my back, body heat on either side of me, hands holding my hair back, stroking my back.

It felt like vomiting. You know the feeling: you've had too much to drink and the earth is wobbling unsteadily and whirling around you, so you lay down on the couch with one foot on the floor hoping to steady the universe a little bit, and your stomach is sour and boiling and acidic and hot and you don't *want* to vomit but you know you'll feel better once you do but you still fight it back until it's a hot flood surging against the back of your teeth, and then you finally lurch and stumble to the bathroom and let 'er rip. It sucks, the process of emptying it all out. But then once you're finally done, fuck, you feel so much better.

"Why me?" I rasped, my voice a hoarse whisper. "Why me? Why did Danny have to pick me? It's not like I want anyone else to go through what I did, but I just...I can't help asking why me? Wasn't it enough to not have a dad? It wasn't enough that my mother was a useless piece of fucking human garbage? It wasn't enough that my brother was mean, cruel, vindictive, troublemaking fucking cunt? I had to be sexually abused every fucking day for four fucking years? And now I have to live with that! Where's the goddamned *justice*?"

My phone rang, just then. I dug it out of the pocket in the thigh of my leggings and glanced at the screen—it wasn't a number I recognized, but a niggling feeling in my gut told me to answer it.

"Heh—" I had to clear my throat and try again. "Hello? This is Lindsey Snelling."

"Good evening, Miss Snelling. My name is Special Agent Cameron Urie. We met briefly in Los Angeles."

"You arrested Danny Cohen," I said, recognizing the voice—the Patrick Warburton lookalike had a similarly recognizable voice.

"Yes ma'am." A pause, a clearing of his throat. "I thought you would like to know—Daniel Cohen is dead."

The world tilted; it was a good thing I was already on all fours or I would have fallen down. "I…he…how? In prison?"

"Yes ma'am. We don't have too many details other than he was shivved in the food line. We aren't certain who or why, but such things are, unfortunately, all too common. It could be as simple as a disagreement over cigarettes or a card game, or it could be he made an enemy who got to him on the inside."

"Honestly, Special Agent Urie, I don't care who or why. He got exactly what he deserved, and I will not be wasting a single second mourning him."

"No one will, ma'am. I'm not supposed to say things like this in my offical capacity as a law enforcement officer, but Daniel Cohen was a real piece of shit."

"He sexually abused me for four years, starting when I was twelve."

The silence, then, was profound. "I'm sorry to hear that, Miss Snelling. He did indeed get what was coming to him."

"I'm tempted to send an edible arrangement to whoever shivved him," I said. "They did the world a favor."

"I am inclined to agree, ma'am. Well, I've got to go. I just wanted to make sure you were aware. You don't ever have to worry about him again."

"That's the best news I've had since you showed up to arrest him."

"Glad I could provide at least some kind of comfort, Miss Snelling. No one deserves what that creature did to you. Speaking as a father of a daughter, I don't know that I could have stood in a room with him and not committed murder."

I sniffed a laugh, now sitting on my shins as if I were Daniel-San at the Cobra Kai dojo. "I thought about it. But I...I wasted way too many years hating him. If I'd been the one to kill him, even if I got away with it, it wouldn't have brought me any peace."

"I can guarantee you it wouldn't have, Miss Snelling. I've seen a lot in my line of work, as I'm sure you can imagine. I've seen the aftermath of revenge, and it's never pretty. Revenge is a game with no winners, only losers."

"Glad I chose the other path, then," I said. "Thank you for telling me, Agent Urie."

"Of course, ma'am. Take care."

"You, too."

I tossed the phone to the floor, tipped my head back, and blinked at the ceiling. "He's dead."

Dane was beside me, sitting cross-legged, close enough to touch but very carefully giving me space. "Are you relieved or…?"

I nodded. "Honestly, yes. I know you're not supposed to be happy when someone dies, but…I am." I laughed. "Is it terrible that I feel lighter and freer knowing both my mother and Danny are gone?"

Dane shook his head. "I don't think it is. I didn't know your mom had died."

I shrugged. "I didn't either. Danny was the one who told me, ironically. I guess she got some kind of super-aggressive cancer and was gone within a few months. Good riddance to the old bitch, and good riddance to Daniel Hezekiah Cohen."

I looked at Dru, on my left. "Thank you, Dru."

She wrapped one arm around me. "Anything, any time. You're family now, no matter what happens."

I sagged, hunched over. "It may take me some time to lean into that."

She squeezed me with that arm. "That's okay. We've got a lot of big personalities in this family, and all of us have been through some shit. You have a support system in place, now, Lindsey. I know it won't come easily or naturally, at first, but just try to let us help you if and when you need it."

I let myself lean against her. She was soft and warm and comforting. At first, I just leaned sideways, but then something dissolved inside me and I twisted toward her.

My eyes burned again, but I couldn't find the courage to fight them. I couldn't remember the last time I'd had a motherly hug—Rune's mom, a few months ago, probably. I wasn't a platonic huggy sort of person, generally. But just then, with Dru's arms around me and her warm spirit and calming, soothing energy surrounding me, I just…collapsed into her, sobbing hysterically.

"Oh, oh, oh," Dru murmured, gathering me against her chest, petting my hair, and rocking me like a baby. Which, to my eternal mortification, was wonderfully and inexplicably comforting. "There we go, there we go. Let it out, sweetheart. It's okay."

The world evaporated as I let go of the last strangling bonds of restraint, of emotional suppression. I'd wept for the child I was, and I'd wept for what Danny did to me, but I'd never wept for my lack of a mom. I'd never wept for the ache of loneliness I'd always felt, even when I had Rune and the Rigbys and Raquel. I'd never wept for how fucking hard life could be, even without trauma.

I let Dru Badd hold me, and I let myself go. With the amount of crying I'd done over the last two months, you'd think I'd be all cried out, but apparently not.

When my tears finally cleared up, I straightened, sniffling, and wiped at my face. "I'm sorry. I just—"

Her hand covered my mouth. "No ma'am. No apologizing. A mama knows when someone needs a hug and a good cry."

I nodded, glancing at Dane, who was sitting and watching, a soft smile on his face. "Not the reunion you were hoping for, huh?"

He shifted closer to me, resting a hand on my knee. "It's what you need. All I care about is you."

I shook my head. "I don't understand how you can be so understanding when I did everything I could to push you away."

"Because I love you."

Dru moved my hand to rest on Dane's and stood up. "I think that's my cue."

I snagged her arm. "Dru? I…"

She leaned down and kissed my crown; I barely knew the woman, and she was showering me with more love and affection than I've ever known. It was tilting my world on its axis. "I know, sweet girl." She put her lips to my ear. "Love him back, Lindsey. Take a risk. Just jump."

"What if I hurt him again?" I whispered back.

"You will—and he'll hurt you," she said, in a more normal volume. "It's life, it's marriage, it's love. What matters is what you do next. Do you forgive him?

Does he forgive you? Do you approach the problem together? I'm not a big churchgoer kinda gal, but at weddings they always read that one chapter about love. You know what I'm talking about?" I nodded, and she continued. "The part I always remember is where it says, 'love keeps no record of wrongs.'" She squeezed my shoulder. "I've tried really hard in my marriage to not be the wife that drags out old arguments or trots out that stupid thing he said six months ago during a different tiff. As long as you remember that loving someone is a choice, not an emotion, you'll be fine. You'll make it."

I frowned. "Not an emotion?"

She smiled, nodding. "The feelings come and go. Don't get me wrong—I'm just as hot for my man now as I was twenty-three years ago when I met him. But when he pisses me off? I'm not so hot for him. I still love him, though, because while I may not always be *in love* with him, as in feeling the whole gamut of squishy, gooey, heart-eyes, I-love-you-baby stuff, I will always *choose* to love him… even if that just means not murdering him in his sleep like I sometimes want to. And trust me, I've lain awake beside him more than once and considered smothering him with his own pillow because he did or said something monumentally idiotic…and honey, he's a man. He's gonna. So is Dane. What matters is making the choice to love even when you don't feel the emotion of love. Make sense?"

"I...yeah? I think so." I looked at Dane. "It's just hard to picture what that looks like."

Dane smiled. "Stick around, watch my parents, watch my aunts and uncles. You'll see it in action. We don't hide our messes. I've seen every couple in my family get in fights on any number of occasions, mostly in private but occasionally in public. And I've seen them resolve it with love and forgiveness one hundred percent of the time."

"All I ever saw was dysfunction, abandonment, abuse, addiction, and selfishness," I said. "Sorta made me cynical about relationships, I'm realizing."

Dru squeezed my shoulder once more. "Honestly, Lindsey, just tuck all that aside for now and focus on what's in front of you. Which is Dane. Figuring out what being together looks like. The rest will come in time."

I nodded. "I think I'd like to be alone now, Dane," I said.

He sighed, smiled, and nodded, rising to his feet. "Of course. Take all the time you need."

Panic hit like a lightning bolt when he started to walk toward the door. "No!" I scrambled to my feet, lurched across the room, and slammed into him. "I meant with you."

"Oh," he mumbled. "Thank god. Leaving you alone right now would have been—"

"Don't leave me alone!" I protested over him.

"Please." I clung to him, fists in his shirtfront. "I need you."

Dru laughed. "I think maybe you two should head over to the bar. I'll keep Dunc and Rune here for a while so you two can have some privacy."

I blushed furiously, but Dane only pulled me against his chest and held me; I let him.

Dru left, then, and Dane snagged his duffel bag.

"I don't know how to feel about your mom knowing why we'd need privacy," I said.

He just laughed. "We're all adults, here, babe."

"I know, it's just weird. She's actively encouraging us."

He laughed again. "Stop thinking about my mom for a minute."

"That's a big ask. That was more mothering in... what? Fifteen minutes? Than my mother ever showed me my whole life."

"That's fucking pathetic."

I just shrugged. "Not everyone is as lucky as you in the parent department, Dane. I hope you know how incredibly fortunate you are."

"I am, but never more so than right now."

A thought occurred to me. "You're not gonna, like, get jealous if your mom ends up loving me more than you, are you?"

A cackle burst out of him at this. "Tell me you don't understand how love works without telling me you don't understand how love works." Before I could get offended, he laughed again and kissed my temple as he led me back outside toward the garage. "Love is infinite. I love Mom, Dad, my sisters, Dunc, my cousins, my aunts, my uncles...but I never run out. I love Mom in a different way than I love Dad. So, Mom can love me and everyone else and still love you just as much." He snickered. "Besides, I'm her favorite."

"I was kidding about the loving me more. Sort of."

"I know. But the concern behind it was valid. I'm not insecure, Linz. I know my mother will never stop loving me. Her loving you won't take away from how she loves me. The opposite, if anything. She'll see how you love me and how happy I am with you, and she'll love you all the more."

"I'm not sure that's the opposite of the first part of what you said, but I take your meaning," I said. "I guess I have a lot to learn, huh?"

"Maybe," he said. "But you've got all the time in the world."

We arrived back at Badd's Bar and Grille. I stopped at my car and grabbed the suitcase containing my core wardrobe and a smaller duffel bag that had my toiletries and makeup; Dane insisted on carrying them for me.

I resisted at first. "I'm perfectly capable of carrying my own luggage, Dane," I protested.

"Well, of course you are," he said. "That's not the point."

I frowned. "Then what is?"

"I want to do things for you, Linz. I want to take

care of you—not because you need help or taking care of, but because I enjoy doing that stuff for you."

We were on the sidewalk outside my car, a few doors down from the bar's main entrance.

He took my shoulders and held my gaze. "I want to take your car and fill up the gas tank for you. I want to change your oil for you. I want to buy you stuff just because. I want to bring you breakfast in bed. I want to carry your purse for you while you bore me to tears, dragging me around the mall. I want to rub your feet while we watch TV after a long day of work."

Fuck my eyes for getting burny and watery again. "Awww, for fuck's sake, Dane." I hissed, tipped my head back, and sniffled. "What do I do for you?"

He gave me a look of incredulity. "What do you do for me? You love me. What does that look like? Whatever you want it to. Hugs and kisses. Make love to me. Let me be the little spoon sometimes. Do things for me. Like what? It doesn't matter. Domestic shit. Affection. Gifts. Tell me I'm handsome and buff and smart—I'm sure you can find the right lies." He grinned and snickered, making that last part an obvious joke. "It doesn't matter. I don't need you to *do* anything but be who you are and let me love you. If you let me love you, you'll find ways to love me back." He cupped my face. "That doesn't mean sex or being barefoot in the kitchen making me a sandwich, by the way."

I cackled. "Good, because a domestic goddess I am not."

He brushed a thumb over my lips. "We're getting ahead of ourselves, baby. We just gotta learn how our relationship is gonna look. We do that together, and we do it by being honest with each other about what we like and don't like, need and don't need, want and don't want."

I bit my lower lip, bunching his shirtfront in my fist. "Right now, I need to be alone with you." I dropped my voice to a whisper and lowered my eyes from his to his mouth. "I've been jonesing for your kisses since I sent you that postcard from Portland."

His sweet smile shifted to a hot grin. "Is that so?" He wrapped a big, hard fist around my hand clutching his shirt. He lifted the hand, kissed each knuckle in turn, one by one, without taking his eyes off mine. "Like that?"

I let out a growl which, embarrassingly, sounded like nothing so much as a tiny kitten trying to be fierce. "Unless you want to get arrested for public indecency, Dane Badd, you'll take me upstairs and kiss me properly."

His hand curled around the back of my neck, which sent shivers down my spine. "To be clear, you're asking me to take you upstairs so I can *take you*… upstairs?"

"Yes," I breathed. "That's exactly what I'm asking."

"As you wish."

FOURTEEN

Dane

I PRECEDED LINDSEY UP THE STAIRS. I FELT HER BEHIND ME, felt her gaze, her attention, her tumultuous emotions.

I was feeling a pretty wild variety of shit myself—sorrow for all that she'd been through, fury and rage and hate for everyone in her life who had victimized her, whether through simple neglect or active, outright violation; I felt an upwelling of love that made me so intensely protective that if the Cohen motherfucker wasn't dead already I'd be tempted to go take care of him myself. I felt a deep, driving desire to make sure she never felt pain ever again. I knew I couldn't protect her from the vagaries of life, but I could sure as hell try.

"I can feel you brooding up there," Lindsey said, a few steps below me. "Stop it."

"I'm not brooding," I muttered as we entered the apartment over the bar.

I carried her stuff into the spare room, set it down, and moved to reach for Lindsey. She was already in my space, tugging at my tie.

"You were hating. It was palpable," she said.

"You had no one to protect you. Everyone in your life failed you. It makes me angry." I toyed with the strings of her oversized Eeyore hoodie.

She looked up at me with wet, wide eyes. "You don't know how it makes me feel, Dane, hearing you say that. But I refuse to waste any more of my life, my time, or my energy on hate, especially now that he's dead. And I won't have you hating him either. He's not worth it." She unknotted my tie, tugged it free, and let it flutter to the floor at my feet. "Instead of being angry and hating, spend that energy on me. Please?" I sighed, nodding. "Yeah, I can do that. I just needed to be angry for a minute. You've had your whole life to come to terms with what happened, Linz, I just found out an hour ago." She gave a head-tilted nod. "I suppose that makes sense. I just…I want to put it all behind me. I want to be all in on you—on us."

I dipped to kiss her—a soft, dry kiss, a quick touch of the lips. "That sounds pretty nice to me."

"You know what sounds nice to me?" she whispered, pushing my jacket off my shoulders and letting it, too, hit the floor at my feet. "You, naked."

"Just me naked? Or us naked together?"

She bit her lip, smirking. "Let's start with just you. I'll let you get me naked after I've had my fun."

I smoothed my hands over her hips as she unbuttoned my shirt. "Just don't do anything that will trigger you. Don't ask, don't try, don't even think about it." I palmed her ass, feeling my zipper tighten just from the soft weight of her glorious ass in my hands. "You are all I need."

"You have me." She had my shirt undone, and it hit the floor too; my white tank top was next, leaving me in slacks, shoes, and socks. "You have all of me, Dane. I promise. I won't run again. I won't push you away again."

"No freakouts from pushing yourself into sex stuff that's gonna set you off."

"I promise." She swallowed hard. "Won't you miss blow jobs?"

I shrugged, shook my head. "Not really." I gazed down at her, tugging at her lower lip with my thumb. "Just a hypothetical situation, okay? Let's say you had no issues with giving oral, and let's say you were feeling generous, you wanted to do something that makes me feel good. If you were to tell me I could pick a blow job or sex with you, there wouldn't be a decision to make. I'd always, always pick connecting with you, being intimate with you, whatever you want to say. A blow job feels great, yes. We've talked about that. If you could do that without it causing you any problems, I'd be all for you giving me that once in a while, or as often or seldom as you wanted. But if you can't ever do that again, I won't be trudging through life all heartbroken or whatever because you can't nom my knob."

She snickered. "Nom your knob? That's a new one." She sighed, tugging at my belt. "I want to, though. I want to be able to. For myself, not just for you. I want my life back. I want my sexuality to be my own, not held hostage."

She opened my slacks, and they slid down my legs, pooling on the floor at my feet. My cock pulsed in my underwear, thickening, unfurling, tenting the front of my black boxer briefs.

I toed off my loafers, stepped on the fronts of each sock in turn, and stepped out of them, hissing as Lindsey palmed my package. "Linz, I'm here for you, okay?"

"I know that," she murmured. "I don't wanna be all gooey and emotional anymore, though."

I cupped her chin, tugged her face up so she had to look at me. "No, what I mean is that I'm here for whatever you want, whatever you need. You just have to honestly tell me what you're feeling and what you want, what you need." I searched her trembling, shimmery blue eyes. "And as for being gooey and emotional? Linz, that's not something to avoid. It's okay to be… soft…with me. Vulnerable. Emotional."

She dipped her chin, looking down and away. "There's nothing sexy about a weepy woman."

I pulled her focus back to me. "I don't need this to be sexy, sweetheart."

This got her eyes flicking up to mine in surprise. "But...but...Dane, we haven't...I haven't—" she shook her head. "This is our big reunion, though. We've been avoiding each other—or I've been avoiding you, I should say, if I'm being honest—for months. I've dreamed of you. Of us. I've..." she swallowed hard. "I've fantasized about this moment—finally getting to be alone with you, all my cards on the table, all my fucking baggage out in the open...hoping you'd..." her eyes misted, dripped. "You'd still want me, even after knowing how much fucking work I'll be."

My throat closed, hearing her grit out these fearful truths, seeing the depth of her fear, the power of her insecurities.

"I just want to feel sexy," she whispered, "I want to feel...desired. I don't want to be a fucking basket case or a charity case, where you give me sweet little kisses because I'm so fucked up you don't—you don't see me as...as..." a gruff growl of frustration escaped her. "*Fuck*! See? This! This is exactly what I didn't want!" She turned away from me, pacing angrily toward the window.

I followed her, sliding my arms around her waist, locking my fingers together at her belly as I murmured in her ear. "There's something you're missing in this scenario, sweetheart."

She stiffened. "There is?"

"Yup."

"What would that be?"

"I'm not in this just for the sex."

Already tensed, she turned into a statue. "I know that, Dane."

"I don't think you do. I think you *think* you do, I think you *want* to believe that, but deep down, you don't trust it."

"Dammit, Dane." She sniffled. "I'm trying to seduce you!"

"I know that. I don't need seduction." I cut over her protest. "Don't misunderstand me. I want you to seduce me all the fucking time."

"Then I don't understand the problem?"

I turned her in place, tipping her face up to mine. "Do you want to be with me?" I asked. "Do you want to live life with me? Explore what a real, lasting, long-term, committed, monogamous relationship with me looks like. One with no escape clauses or secret ways out just in case it doesn't work."

"Yes," she whispered. "You've had that modeled for you your whole life by literally dozens of people. I, on the other hand, have only ever seen one positive relationship in my life. So I just…I don't know what that looks like."

I smiled. Whispered my lips across hers in a ghost of a kiss. "That's what I'm talking about, sweetheart. You haven't seen what I have, so I know something you don't."

"Then enlighten me, please."

"You've had to be strong for so long, Lindsey," I

said, holding her eyes as she tried to look away. "Don't look away. Stay with me, honey. *You don't have to be strong.* You don't have to have it all figured out. You don't have to be sexy. You can be messy. You can be emotional. I'm not scared of or threatened by your emotions or by tears. I don't just want you when you're all made up and wearing sexy lingerie and feeling hot. I want you when you're down, when you're scared, when you're pissed off, when you're...I dunno, whatever you're feeling. And right now, baby, what you're feeling may not be sexy, but it's real. If that's gooey and emotional, that's okay. Be that. Show me that."

"You're saying you can get hard for me even if I'm all weepy and sad?" she said, arching an eyebrow at me.

I laughed. "The funny answer is yes, I can always get hard for you. The real answer is that I love you, and sometimes, that may not look like seduction and heavy breathing and drawn-out foreplay. I can feel a desire for you that's not just hot, sexy passion. It can be something else."

"Like what?" she whispered.

I danced my mouth against hers. "Like this." I kissed her, slowly, softly. "It can be a love that's gentle and sweet. It's not *less than*, honey, it's just *different*."

"I'm not good with that kinda stuff, though," she muttered, resting her fingertips on my waist.

"That's fine. We can figure it out together." I pulled her hood up onto her head, laughing when she glared up at me from beneath the hood. "Fuck, you're cute."

"I don't want to feel *cute*," she grumped. "I want to feel sexy."

I lifted the hoodie up and off, leaving her in a white baby doll tee and tight black leggings; she wasn't wearing a bra, and her heavy tits bulged against the confines of the shirt, her erect nipples standing out hard.

"No bra, huh?"

"Nope," she whispered. "I like wearing baggy hoodies so I can go braless."

"Can't you just…I dunno…not wear a bra and fuck what other people think?"

She snickered. "Sounds nice, but no. Not with tits as big as mine. Men get weird, and women get judgmental. It's just easier to keep 'em in titty jail for the most part. But since I was just driving alone, I went for comfort. I'd expected to have a few minutes to change before I saw anyone, least of all you."

I touched her lips. "You're babbling. I'm a fan of the no bra look."

She smirked. "You just like looking at my giant bazingas."

"Facts," I whispered, peeling the tight white stretchy garment up and off, baring said bazingas. "But not just looking at them."

She blinked hard, looking away and crossing her arms over her chest before backing out of my reach. "Sorry, I…I'm not—I don't feel—" she shook her head, stepping past me away from the window with her arms crossed. "I know I must be giving you emotional whip-lash. I'm horny, I'm crying, I'm confident, I'm insecure, I'm needy, I'm bitchy, I'm pushy, I'm sweet…" A shrug as she trailed off.

I stayed where I was, giving her space. "Linz, try to hear me, please."

She turned her head in my direction, looking at me over her shoulder without turning around. "I am, Dane."

"No, you're hearing me with your ears. I need you to listen to me with your heart."

She swallowed. "Trying."

"I love you as you are. Right now. If that's all over the place, that's okay."

She took a deep breath and held it. Tipped her head back, blinking tearfully at the ceiling. "Fuck. You're too good to be true."

"I'm not. I'm just this guy, Linz. I just happen to be in love with you. I promise, live with me long enough, and you'll find more than a few things about me that will drive you absolutely fucking bananas."

"I want to feel sexy, not…whatever this bullshit is."

"You don't need to be sexy all the time."

"It's all I'm good for, Dane."

"Oh, fuck that," I snapped, angry, now. "What the fuck is *that*?"

"What else do I have? What else am I good at?"

"Being a good human?" I said, not bothering to

hide the anger in my voice. "Being a good friend? You're smart. You're kind. You're courageous. You're fucking hysterically funny. You're a hard worker."

"Yeah, but..." She shook her head. "What am I... what am I doing? Where am I going? Why am I here?"

I laughed. "God, Linz. You think *I* know any of that? I don't fucking know! I don't know the answers to that shit myself. I wish to god I did, but I don't. I don't need you to have all that together, babe. All I need from you is you! All of you, all in, no matter what. We can be confused about life and purpose together. We can figure out where we're going together. We're not always going to feel sexy. I think..." I sighed. "I'm not sure how to say this."

She barked a sarcastic laugh. "Bluntly. And now I'm scared."

I closed the distance between us by a few feet but stayed out of touching distance. "I think you hide behind sex."

She huffed. "I don't even know what that means."

"You're used to being able to use sex to shift the focus away from feelings. Instead of being vulnerable, you make it sexy. And guys being guys, we fall for it every time. Mostly because we're just as scared of big feelings as you are."

She huffed again. "You—that's—"

"I'm not falling for it." I moved closer. "Not because I don't want that with you, obviously I do."

"*Is* it obvious?" she asked, still facing away from

me but looking over her shoulder at me, watching through her peripheral vision.

I stepped up behind her, crushing my hard-on against the swell of her ass. "I don't know, honey. You tell me. Is it obvious?"

"I think I might be a little worried that you're erect right now, given the heaviness of this conversation."

I laughed, slipping my arms around her waist again, my hands now sliding over her bare, warm skin. "Don't be worried."

"Do you have some kind of emotional kink? like, you're turned on by tears or some shit?"

"Lindsey."

She sighed. "Avoidance through humor again. I'm sorry." She rested her head back against my shoulder. "What am I supposed to be feeling, right now?"

"Complicated. There's no *supposed to*, that's my point. There's no right or wrong. There's just what *is*." I kissed her cheek, caressing her belly between her diaphragm and waistband. "I can feel desire for your body at the same time as I feel empathy for the complicated emotions I can see you wrestling with. They're not mutually exclusive, babe. You can want me and touch me and need me while feeling…shit…I dunno, honey, everything you're feeling right now. Feel it all, Linz. You can kiss me while you're crying, as long as I'm not the reason you're crying—in a negative way, at least."

She sniffled a half-hearted laugh. "God, Dane."

"I love every facet of who you are, Lindsey,

including facets I know I haven't seen yet. Cranky in the mornings? PMSing and ready to kill me for chewing too loudly? Silly and weird for no reason? Melancholy and in need of a long bath?"

She snorted. "A long bath? You mean sitting in bacteria soup?"

I frowned. "You don't like baths?"

"Gasp!" She literally said the word. "A woman who doesn't like baths? What is this world coming to?"

"Have you tried a relaxing bath lately?"

She rolled her eyes, shaking her head. "No. I tried a few years ago and just got sweaty and felt gross."

I pivoted, taking her with me so I was walking backward, pulling her after me by the hand while she covered her chest with other. "C'mon. You clearly have no idea what you're missing."

She snorted. "And you're the expert on baths, are you?"

"I'll have you know I have been known to take a bath on occasion. I get bored and get out before long, but it's a nice way to just relax, breathe, and...I dunno...just be." I pulled her into the bathroom. "You ever take a bath *with* someone?"

She shook her head. "No. You?"

"Nope." I twisted on the hot water and let it run. "But it sounds like fun to me. Try it with me?"

She dropped her arm. "Fine. I'll light some candles. I think I saw some in the kitchen."

While she was hunting down candles, I sent a

quick text to my brother, asking a question—I was over here a few weeks ago with Rune, Duncan, Jax, and a few other cousins, just hanging out and watching TV. This bathroom had been in use, so I used Rune and Duncan's, and happened to spot some of those bath bombs in a little ceramic bowl by the tub. I asked him to ask Rune if I could steal one. I received a thumbs up and a winking emoji. I sent back a rolling eye and a thanks.

I popped over into their bathroom, took one of the chalky-looking, plastic-wrapped balls, opened it, and tossed it into the tub. It fizzed pink and red and pink again, spewing foamy suds in a rainbow of colors. I adjusted the water temp to be tolerable for human flesh.

Lindsey came in then with a handful of tealights, which she scattered around the bathroom and lit. She noticed the sudsy, colorful, foamy, lavender- and rose-scented water. "Where on earth did you get a bath bomb?"

"Rune. Happened to know she had some in their bathroom and asked Dunc if I could have one."

She bent and sniffed the air over the water. "Smells pretty girly. That doesn't bother you?"

I snorted. "Smells nice to me. I don't really go in for all that genderized bullshit. As a straight man, I see no reason why I can't enjoy certain smells or whatever. I don't need to smell like gunpowder and whiskey and shit in order to be a man. I like the scent of lavender, and I like the scent of roses, and yet…" I sidled up behind her as she straightened and caressed her belly, cupping her breasts. "I feel pretty confident in my heterosexuality and masculinity."

She exhaled slowly, softly. "I feel pretty confident in your heterosexuality and masculinity, too."

I kissed her nape. "Glad we agree on that."

She exhaled again, this time with a quiet whimper as I rolled her nipples between my fingers; she reached up behind her head to clasp my neck, scraping and sliding her hands down my arms, rotated her hands down to slide her touch down my waist, and reached behind herself to run her hands over my thighs. She arched her chest into my touch, whimpering again as I caressed her tits, cupping and lifting and squeezing and kneading the soft, hot weight of them, and then pinching and rolling her hard little nipples.

I palmed her jaw, turned her face to the side, and claimed her mouth. She whined into the kiss, opened her lips, and gave me her tongue. Slid her fingers under the elastic of my underwear and over the angles of my hipbones, her touch barely missing the hot rigidity of my aching cock.

"Dane," she whispered. "I want you."

I mirrored her action, slipping my hands down her belly and under her waistband, pushing my hands down her thighs, taking her yoga pants with them. I sank to my knees as I dragged her leggings down, leaving her thong in place, kissing my way down her nape, dotting kisses along her spine until I was kneeling behind her. I grabbed her ass, filling my hands with her generous curves, kissing my way around her left cheek, the dimples above each side. She stepped out of her leggings, tugging her feet free.

Kneeling, I reached up and pinched her nipples. "Bend over, baby. Grab the tub for me."

She huffed in shock. "Okay." Complying, Lindsey spread her feet wide apart and bent forward at the waist, grabbing the lip of the still-filling tub. "Like this?"

"Yes." I caressed her ass. "Just like that."

"I want to touch you, Dane."

"You will." Reaching between her thighs, I traced her seam over the silk of her thong. "Eventually."

"Dane—"

I pinched her nipple hard enough that she yelped, and that's when I tugged the gusset of her thong aside and slipped a finger inside her. "You're soaked for me."

"Oh god." She pushed her ass backward, gasping. "You make me wet."

"You're gonna come for me, aren't you?" I demanded.

"Yeah."

"Say 'yes, Dane.'"

"I'm not a submissive," she snapped.

I slid my finger out of her. "I'm not asking you to *be* submissive, or to be *a* submissive," I emphasized the article to differentiate between the noun and the adjective. "I just want you to trust me. To do what I tell you, knowing all I want is to make you feel good."

"I trust you."

I traced her seam again, over the fabric. She whimpered, tipped her hips. "Now. Tell me what you want me to do to you."

"I thought you wanted emotional vulnerability. This is feeling pretty damn sexy."

"I want it all. I just want you to know that you *are* sexy even when you're emotional."

"Touch my pussy, Dane. I want you to make me come."

I traced her seam yet again. "I *am* touching your pussy."

"Take my thong off." I slid the strings down over her hips, past the bubble of her ass. It dropped to the floor, and she toed it aside. The tub was almost full, so I cut the flow. Steam skirled and twisted in lazy, scented curls from the surface.

I traced her seam again, and her knees dipped. "You're gonna come for me, aren't you, Linz?"

"Yes, Dane," she whimpered, and then huffed a soft laugh. "Okay, that *is* pretty fucking hot."

"Put your fingers inside yourself," I told her.

Bracing on the tub with one hand, she slid her ring and middle finger inside her channel, gasping. "Oh god, oh *fuck*."

"Again."

"I want you inside me," she hissed, sliding those fingers back in.

"Deeper. All the way."

"Oh god."

"Get 'em covered," I said, palming her ass and watching her touch herself.

"They are."

"Show me. They better be dripping."

She withdrew her fingers and held them out. I turned her by the hips and she perched on the rim of the tub, offering me her fingers—which were slick and glistening with her juices. "Wet enough?"

I slipped those two fingers into my mouth and devoured the taste of her, groaning. "Fucking perfect."

She gasped as I licked her fingers clean. "Dane!"

"Spread your legs for me."

"Yes, Dane," she whispered, spreading them as wide as they'd go. "Now what?"

I fused my mouth around her clit and devoured her, sudden and aggressive—she shrieked, arching and throwing her head back, clasping my head in her hands, holding me to her sex. I licked and sucked and swirled my tongue and flicked it against her clit until she was panting and thrusting. "Now...you come for me."

She whimpered through gritted teeth as she started to come, shaking all over as the orgasm seized her. "Oh—ohhh—oh god. Dane!"

"Come for me. Right now."

"Yes, Dane!" She shuddered, spasming, legs

stiffening out straight as she nearly slid off the tub, arms out wide to either side as she gripped the tub rim in both hands. "Dane! Oh—oh fuck! Dane!"

"Are you coming for me, Lindsey?"

"Yes, Dane," she whimpered. "oh god, oh god, yes! I—I'm—oh god. I'm coming for you."

"Good girl," I praised, curling two fingers inside her pussy, and then plunging them in and out, hard and fast.]

She came on a scream, shattering and shuddering and spasming. "DANE!"

When she couldn't spasm any harder, hips thrust forward as the orgasm reached its zenith, I took her clit in my mouth and sucked hard, and she screamed, heels scrabbling on the tile as she lost control over her legs. Still sucking on her clit, I slid my slick fingers out of her pussy, trailed them over her taint. Pressed a fingertip against her asshole.

"Say yes," I murmured.

"YES!" she panted. "Yes, yes, yes. Do it. I want it. Please."

I slid that finger gently past the initial resistance, slowly applying pressure. I felt her tense, resisting, and then she overcame the resistance and relaxed, and my finger slid deeper.

"Oh fuck, Dane."

I flicked her clit with my tongue. "Come again.""Dane, fuck."

"Come for me."

She swayed on the tub, toes curling as she rocked in rhythm with my swirling tongue. "Dane!"

I pulsed my finger inside her. "Does this feel good?"

"Yes, Dane!" She arched her back, tits shaking beautifully as her climax ripped through her. "Dane! Oh fuck, fuck!"

"You want more, baby?"

"YES!" she screamed. "More, more, more!"

I gave her more, little bit by little bit, tonguing her clit wildly and then slowly, gently, and then roughly, all the while pressing my finger a little deeper inside her.

Her scream cut off with a ragged shudder and her heels scrabbled at the floor, and she teetered precariously on the edge of the tub, arched backward as she writhed through her orgasm with silent intensity, mouth open in a soundless scream as I began pumping my finger faster and faster inside her, thrashing her clit with my mouth until she sucked in a shaking breath and went paralyzed, sliding off the tub, now only held up by her grip on the rim. She found purchase just in time, re-seating herself on the edge, panting, eyes delirious and unfocused as the last paroxysms of climax left her whimpering and staring at me in stunned ecstasy.

"Jesus, Dane," she breathed.

I very carefully removed my finger, nuzzling her cheek with mine. "Get in." Her lips touched my ear. "Yes, Dane."

"You like being my good girl, don't you?"

Her voice was tiny. "Yes, Dane."

She slid into the tub and sank down until she was submerged to the chin, gazing at me, watching me as I washed my hands thoroughly.

I turned from the sink toward the tub, the tip of my cock peeking up over the waistband of my underwear. With just her eyes and nose above the water, now, she locked her eyes on me, a slow grin spreading across her mouth, reaching her eyes, turning her gaze seductive and hungry as I stood outside the tub.

She lifted her face free of the water. "My turn."

I stood where I was. "As you wish."

She dropped her mouth below the waterline again, but her hand left the water, rested on the edge of the tub, and then reached, dripping, for my underwear.

FIFTEEN

Lindsey

Fuck, I was so mixed up I didn't know if I was coming or going, emotionally. Dane was wreaking havoc on me, emotionally, mentally, and physically. One second, he was getting me all worked up emotionally, and then he made me come and had me saying "Yes, Dane," like some sort of…I don't know what.

Fuck, it was hot, though. I've never been that girl. I've never even *considered* being that girl. Because I mean, what man would I ever trust enough to put that kind of faith in him?

This man, apparently.

Dane Badd.

He stood outside the tub in his tight black boxer briefs, the outline of his cock bulging and straining against the fabric, a hint of the pink tip sticking up over top of the elastic. My heart was pounding wildly from the exertion of orgasm, and I couldn't believe I'd not only *let* him put his finger in my asshole, but I'd *begged* him to. My nipples ached, standing hard and turgid and sensitive in the hot water, and my pussy was slick and hot and aching emptily. Yet, despite my physical, sexual arousal, I was still an emotional mess. He'd said a lot, and it all rattled around in me like marbles at the bottom of an empty coffee tin.

I use sex to avoid my feelings? Okay, first of all, rude.

Second, I do not.

Do I?

I…

Fuck.

I totally did.

A riptide of past occurrences zipped through me like a movie montage of Lindsey being a thirsty, emotionally-avoidant slut: guy after guy that I went on a few dates with, got to know a little, slept with, and then as soon as I sussed out that he was starting to actually get near my spiky walls of emotional defense, I'd hop on his cock and distract him from investigating those feelings any further.

And then I'd bolt.

Dump him and run—usually to Mom and Pop Rigby's for emotional support and repair.

Yeah, that was a pattern.

So was the fact that I avoided facing my emotions. I stuck with being funny or horny or annoying instead of letting the fear or pain through the walls.

He saw *me*; he *saw* me.

It was fucking terrifying.

He saw that I was vulnerable and scared, and he didn't shy away from it. He accepted it, leaned into it. He didn't push me to another emotional breaking point, though. He gave me the physical release I needed and took the burden of decision from me at the same time. He took charge and showed me that I could trust him, that I could sort of…turn off, mentally, and just relax into his care.

I hadn't realized that's what was happening, but that was the downstream effect, whether he'd done so on purpose or not.

He loved me.

He'd proven that multiple times and in multiple ways.

So, I lay submerged in the tub, considering all this as I gazed at him. His posture was relaxed but alert, watching me, waiting for me. The ball was in my court, now.

Did I want sex? Did I want emotional intimacy? Both, somehow? I wasn't sure how both could exist—they never have, in my world.

It's what I wanted, though.

Not just sex.

Not just "Insert Tab A into Slot B and repeat" for a few seconds or minutes of feel-good time.

Not that that's what it had ever been with Dane, but still, I knew there was more than that between us.

I held his eyes as I rolled toward him in the water, holding onto the rim of the tub with one hand and hooking my fingers in his underwear with the other. I pulled his underwear away from his body and tugged them down inch by inch, running my hand from left hip to right without touching his cock, easing them past the hard swell of his taut ass until they slid free and dropped to pool around his feet.

My first instinct was to put my mouth on him—his cock was just so fucking pretty. So long, so thick, so straight and hard, standing ramrod stiff against his belly and begging for sloppy wet kisses.

I examined myself, and I recognized, in a wild burst of brand-new self-awareness, that I was too emotionally on edge for that. I'd get triggered and break down, fuck everything up.

So…no. Not yet.

I decided to be nice to myself. Don't push the envelope just yet. Maybe in time, when I was more settled into whatever this was or would be with Dane, I could experiment.

Instead, I focused on what I *could* do, what I *could* enjoy.

I clasped his cock in my fist, rested my chin on the back of the hand gripping the tub's rim.

He hissed, jaw tensing. "Linz—""I won't do anything triggering," I promised him. "This won't."

He gritted his jaw. "Linz, I…"

"Shush," I whispered. "Let me have a little fun."

He hung his head, breathing with slow intention as I caressed his length. "Do your worst, then."

I giggled, biting my lower lip. "Careful what you ask for, big boy. You really want my worst? Or my best?"

"I, um…" he broke off with a groan as I twisted my hand around the plump head of his lovely cock. "Fuck, that feels good."

"What if my worst involved teeth?" I asked.

"You like my cock too much to bite it," he said. "Plus, we aren't doing anything that might involve teeth, right?"

"We? Or me?" I asked.

"You know what I mean," he said, and then dipped at the knees, hissing, as I gave his fat, hot cock a nice, firm squeeze.

"Just get in here with me," I said, letting go and sitting up and scooting forward to make room behind me.

He stepped in and slid down behind me, gingerly, so as to not overflow the tub, which was now, with both of us in it, precariously full. Once he was seated behind me, we gradually adjusted our positions until I was reclining in the open wedge of his thighs, which were conveniently placed to be perfect arm rests. His firm chest was a lovely pillow, and his heavy, brawny arms draped over my chest, crossed at the forearms, his hands lazily cupping but not quite holding my breasts in a familiar, possessive way that somehow managed to be more affectionate than sexual. His erection, however, was an undeniably sexual presence pressing somewhat uncomfortably into my spine.

Overall, with the hot water and Dane's embrace surrounding me, cocooning me, I was more comfortable and relaxed than I can ever remember being.

I began by counting moments—not literally counting seconds, just…hyperaware of the moment, of the silence, and more than anything, of the fact that I was luxuriating in the delicious glow and hazy contentment of post-orgasmic bliss.

And he wasn't.

I'd gotten him all rowdy and ready to go, and then abandoned that effort. Guilt over this was acidic and shame-inducing.

"Dane, I…" I was at war with myself—I prided myself on not being a cock-tease, and a significant portion of my being was attuned to his desire, his need, and wanted nothing more than to satiate his desire and meet his needs; yet, at the same time, another just as significant portion of myself was in desperate need of exactly and only this—intimacy without expectation.

He tilted my chin up and to the side, and his lips met mine. "Hush. It's fine," he whispered.

"I'm not a tease, Dane, I promise," I said, hating how tearful I sounded.

The bastard had the gall to *chuckle*. "You think I don't know that?"

"But you gave me an orgasm, and I haven't—"

"I'm not keeping score, Linz. I did what I did

because I wanted to. Because I enjoy making you come." His lips ghosted over mine, teasing kisses even as he whispered to me. "I go down on you because I love the way your pussy tastes. Because I love the sounds you make when I lick your hard little clit." His fingers slid and danced and tripped and walked down my torso to my navel, to my pudendum, and then to my clit, feathering soft, gentle touches to the bundle of already-sensitive nerves. "I go down on you because I love the way you move when you're about to come for me."

He had me gasping, had my hips tipping forward as he circled my clit, pushing me up toward the peak of yet another climax.]

"I make you come because there's nothing on this earth that gives me more joy and more pleasure than *you*," he said, his lips moving on mine, kissing and whispering, touching and sliding. "I don't need *anything* from you, my love. I'm not keeping track. I'll never, ever keep score. I'll make you come a hundred fucking times and never once stop to wonder if it's *fair*." He laced the word with such vitriol as to make it almost a curse word.

"But you're all…" I wiggled against him, rubbing my back against his hard-on. "I know that has to be uncomfortable."

"Sure, a bit, but don't worry about that. I know we'll connect that way soon enough. I have absolutely zero doubt that at some point in the very near future, you will show my sad, neglected penis all the attention I could ever want or need." He cupped my cheek, brushed my cheekbone with a thumb. "I ask for nothing. I expect nothing. I'm not sitting here pissed off because I have a hard-on that you're not fixing right the fuck now. I can handle being hard and not doing anything about it. And to be perfectly honest with you, any guy that tries to guilt a woman into doing something for him because he happens to have an erection is a sad, selfish, pathetic piece of shit."

"But Dane, I do *want* to—"

"I know," he interrupted. "I know you do. But I also know that right now, this is more important."

"All we're doing is laying here, though."

As we spoke, his erection was subsiding, and with it, my stupid sense of guilt that I wasn't doing anything about it.

Which made me realize that I may have a fucked-up sense of obligation. He saw it, but I didn't, until now. He chose to forgo his own release to free me, in a way, from my sense of obligation.

"Exactly," Dane said. "Just breathe, honey. Let me hold you."

Panic took hold, because of course it did. "But I'm…you're…fuck." I couldn't breathe for a moment. "I have to earn it," I whispered, the words tumbling out unbidden.

"Earn what?"

Earn what, indeed? Why had I said that? What did I think I had to earn?

I examined myself and found the answer right there, top of mind, like a Maraschino cherry resting on top of a melting swirl of Reddi Whip.

"You," I whispered through gritted teeth. "Being happy."

"Why would you have to earn being happy?"

"If it were logical, I'd understand it myself." I squeezed my eyes shut. "I'm so fucking sick of all this shit inside me. I just want to fucking...*be*."

I realized he'd stopped touching me. I didn't mind—in this moment, that's not what I wanted anyway.

"Just let me hold you, Lindsey. No expectations. I don't want or need anything from you right now other than to lay here in my arms and just fucking exist with me. You don't have to earn it, honey. I love you for free."

"Your love doesn't cost a thing?"

He snorted quietly. "Deep cuts with the facts."

"That's not a deep cut, that's a classic banger."

He covered my mouth with a wet palm. "Hush, you."

I hushed.

Now that his erection had gone bye-bye, I was finding myself slowly relaxing, slowly releasing the guilt, slowly exhaling the sense of obligation and expectation. I breathed. I luxuriated. I wiggled my toes in the hot, scented water. I lay against Dane's chest and felt his breathing and the soft, slick firmness of his body behind mine and the gentle strength of his arms around me.

I felt his love radiating from him in palpable waves, and I soaked it up.

I didn't have to earn it.

He'd love me even if I couldn't suck him off every day—an unspoken but implicit expectation in my relationship with Damian. He never said it outright, but he found ways of making it clear that he needed to get off every day, and it was my responsibility to make sure that happened, and also, he just happened to prefer getting oral to having sex.

Maybe my relationship with Damian had been a little more uneven, if not exactly toxic, than I'd thought. I'd had to push through my discomfort with that act more often than I'd like to admit to myself— and I did for him. Because I cared for him. I wanted to make him happy.

But also…

Because he expected it.

It was insidious, though, the unspoken but clear sense of obligation.

I was free of that with Dane.

And I hadn't even realized I'd harbored that feeling until just now.

My god, I loved this man.

I lay in his embrace, content and happy and free

of the dread of the past, free of the weight of obligation—whether imagined or real, because let's face it, it's entirely possible that I'd invented the expectation I felt with Damian, not that I was eager to confront my ex about it and find out. My heart swelled, filling and burgeoning with a lightness I couldn't describe, a bone-deep joy I couldn't entirely contain.

It needed expression.

Instead of acting on it right away, though, I held onto the feeling. Examined it, faced it, felt it, absorbed it.

I wanted to give Dane this sense of joy. I wanted him to—no, I *needed* him to know how much I loved him. I needed him to know how grateful I am for his patience, his understanding, his courage in the face of my craziness, his willingness to walk at my side even when I was actively trying to push him away.

"Why do you love me?" I asked. "What have I offered you other than problems?"

He didn't answer immediately, but I felt his attention and knew he was taking time to consider the question. I liked that. I knew I'd get the truth and not just something that sounded nice.

"I love how I feel when I'm with you," he said, after what felt like at least two minutes. "You make me feel interesting. Funny. Strong. Attractive." A sigh. "I might be wrong, and this may just be me, but sometimes it seems like there's this expectation on men to just be confident and feel good about themselves without ever being…I dunno. Validated? Like, we rarely get compliments, you know? Women tell each other all the time, 'Oh you look so cute, I love your outfit, your hair looks so nice.' Men tell their girlfriends and wives and sisters and moms that they look beautiful. It can be a platonic thing or a romantic thing. But unless I do something special, like accomplish something, no one really says anything complimentary to me. No one tells me I look nice just because—unless I'm wearing a suit or dressing up somehow. But I need validation, too. And you give that to me. You make me feel good about myself. You look at me like I matter. Sexually or not, you touch me in a way that makes me feel…wanted, and there's something vital about being touched nonsexually. Feeling wanted but not for sex, you know?"

"Oh, I know," I whispered. "Believe me."

"I love your sense of humor. You make me laugh. I always have fun when I'm with you, and I love that, too. You laugh at me—when I'm being an idiot, which I need, and when I'm being funny, and that makes me feel good."

"Dane—"

"Shush, I'm still answering your question," he said over my protestation. "I love how strong and brave you are."

"I'm not," I whispered.

"Yes, you fucking *are*," he said, intensely enough it almost felt like a snap. "You fought for a better life for yourself, and you worked your ass off to get there. You fought like hell to overcome not just the shitty hand you were dealt in terms of family and home life, but the awful, evil, disgusting thing that was done to you. You didn't just overcome it, Lindsey, you did so without losing yourself."

"I don't know if I agree with that."

"Because you can't be objective about yourself, babe. You have PTSD. You're dealing with it. You've done the work to process, heal from, and cope with what was done to you. You're kind to others. You're generous. You may have bitterness and anger or what-ever toward the fuckstain who abused you, but that's normal. You haven't let what one man did to you make you bitter and angry toward everyone, men especially, which would be totally understandable. Yeah, you may trust issues, but how could you not, when everyone in your life utterly failed you?""I…I guess I hadn't thought of it that way," I admitted.

"I could sit here and keep coming up with differ-ent things, Linz. But when it comes down to it, I love you because I love you. I love the person that you are, and I love the person I am with you. You don't need to *offer* me anything, even though you do."

"What do I offer?"

"Happiness."

My eyes fucking misted again. "I…I do?"

"Yes."

"But…how?"

"By being *you*, sweetheart."

"But…" I blinked hard. "But…but how…but how is that enough?"

"It's all there is." He sat upright, lifted me in the water, and rotated me; I took the guidance and shifted to straddle him face-to-face. "You're enough, Lindsey. Who you are is what I want."

"Just being who I am is enough?" I asked.

"Yes."

What a radical fucking idea.

But then, looking at Rune and Duncan, I knew that this was the truth I'd been missing, or overlooking, or just hadn't considered. Duncan was enough for Rune, and vice versa. He didn't have to achieve anything or be anything, and neither did she. The same applied to Mom and Pop Rigby—the only healthy relationship I'd ever seen, until Rune met Duncan and I started to see how the rest of Dane's family operated.

I am enough.

He was searching my face. Searching my soul. "Talk to me, Linz. What're you thinking?"

"I'm enough."

"Yes, you are."

"It shouldn't be such a radical concept to me, yet it is."

He ran his hands up my thighs, ending with his thumbs pressing into the soft concavity where my thighs bent to meet my hips. "You weren't raised to feel that way."

"I may need some reminders, now and then."

"Every day of your life, I hope."

I sat astride him and knew, in that moment, that I'd finally found my home. The place where I belong: here, with Dane.

I felt the last of my many shackles fall away, then, because I looked at Dane and knew that I was enough, exactly as I was. I didn't need to do or be or become or have anything more.

That freedom was intoxicating.

Arousing.

My heart pattered in my chest as I felt my new-found freedom spread through me. It was a palpable, physical feeling, a literal epiphany.]

I am enough.

I would be enough, with or without Dane. Even if, for some horrible, tragic reason, he and I didn't end up working out, I would still be enough. The thought of not being with Dane, however, made my entire being recoil in horror.

I had to show him how I felt. I had to make him understand the gift he'd given me.

Sex wasn't enough.

Tab A into Slot B would never be enough.

But...there was more to it than that, wasn't there? Tab A into Slot B was hookup culture. It felt good, yes. With the right person, it could even feel pretty fucking amazing. But what did it *mean*? Nothing. And that's okay. There's nothing wrong with that. But at a certain point, one just needs…*more*.

I needed more.

I needed Dane.

I rested my hands on his wet chest, eyes downcast as I searched myself. I found no hesitation, now. I didn't want to run. I didn't want to avoid him.

The opposite.

"I love you," I breathed.

Dane turned to stone. "Will you say that again?" he whispered. "And look at me when you say it, please."

I forced my eyes up to his, knowing I'd cry yet a-*fucking*-again. His eyes were molten and tender at once. Full of understanding and love and…

Unmitigated, unhidden, undisguised need.

"I love you, Dane." My heart swelled as I said the words I'd once have sworn on a stack of Bibles I'd never utter.

And I meant them down the last atom of my being.

Fiercely.

Passionately.

I was only seeing the surface of how fiercely, how passionately I loved him, I realized. How deeply.

It would take a lifetime to explore it, to plumb those depths.

"I'm sick of thinking and feeling and crying and talking," I said. "I just want to…"

Dane smiled up at me, gaze never wavering from mine. "What, baby?"

"Make love with you." I winced. "That still sounds awkward as fuck to me, but I don't know how else to put it."

"It's not awkward, it's the truth. But we don't need to *say* anything." He kissed the tip of my chin, and his hands roamed my thighs, caressing from knees to hips below the water. "In fact, maybe the only thing you need to say now is my name."

"Dane," I breathed.

"Kiss me," he commanded.

"Yes, Dane." I brought my mouth to his, tasted his breath, and then kissed him.

My heart swelled yet again, cracking and expanding, shedding layers like a snake's skin. I clutched his jaw in both hands and kissed him harder, deeper, groaning as my heart and soul seemed to burgeon infinitely, tangling and fusing with his, and all from a simple kiss.

I needed more.

"Take me to bed, Dane," I said.

"Yes, my love."

He stood up with me in his arms and stepped out of the tub. I snagged a towel from the rack as he walked us into the bedroom. I tossed it onto the bed as we approached it, and he tried to straighten it without losing my mouth, but that wasn't working. I wiggled out of his arms, and he fixed the towel while I dripped on the floor, and then he picked me up again, claiming my mouth with a greedy grunt. My breasts crushed against his chest, and his hands dug into my ass, and my skin tingled, and my pulse hammered.

I was desperate for more of him, for all of him. I knew how he felt inside me, and I needed that more than anything.

Yet, at the same time, I was in no rush. I didn't want to hurry this process. I wanted to savor every millisecond.

So I clung to his neck with my arms and toyed with his hair at his nape, and clutched his hard, narrow waist with my legs, and I kissed him. I gave him my tongue, and I took his; I gave him my breath, and I took his.

He growled into my mouth, and I growled back, earning a rough laugh from him.

"Bed," I mumbled, breaking the kiss.

He set me on the edge of the bed and stood in the V of my thighs and he cupped my heavy, aching tits in his big hard hands and his thumbs stroked my nipples and flicked them and he pinched them and twisted them and I whimpered and arched into his touch.

His cock bobbed between us, hard and thick and still growing. I raked my fingernails up his thighs and back down, and then briefly clutched his jaw as I sucked on his tongue and tilted my face up and opened my mouth and demanded he kiss me harder, kiss me deeper.

He groaned softly at this and gave me what I

needed—he kissed me harder, kissed me deeper. My soul soared, and my pussy wept.

I scored my nails down his chest, over his belly, and down his thighs. Again. And again.

Finally, I let myself take his erection in my hands, sighing into his kiss as I filled my hands with his hardness. He moaned as I caressed his length, and his kiss stuttered, broke off.

"Fuck, honey," he breathed. "*Love* the way you touch me."

I shifted to the edge of the bed until I was almost falling off, and I pulled him closer to me, hooking my legs around his waist. The kiss broken, his eyes fixed on mine and held there. I stroked his hot cock and felt him respond, pushing into my hand, needing more. I bit his lower lip and sucked on it, and then claimed his mouth and took his tongue, heart hammering wildly as I guided his cock to my seam.

This wasn't our first time togther, but in a way, it felt like it.

"Linz," he whispered as I notched his tip between my lips. "Fuck."

His eyes fluttered, closed. I kissed his closed eyelids. "Look at me, baby." It came naturally, then, calling him baby. "Look at me."

His eyes opened.

"Watch us," I said.

Our gazes moved down together, and I tipped my hips to take a little more of him. Dane groaned again at this, and I whimpered. I ached for him, ached at the emptiness which could only be satiated by having all of him inside me.

He was giving me the lead, right now. But I knew that wouldn't last—I didn't want it to.

I clasped one hand at his nape, snaked my legs low around his, so my feet were hooked around the backs of his knees, and I palmed his taut, hard ass in my hands and pinned his eyes with mine…

And I took him inside me.

He entered me in a slow, hot slide, filling me by aching degrees, splitting me open with his immense size until I was breathless from the burn, mouth hanging open and shuddering as he pierced me inch…by… inch.

"Dane!" I gasped.

He bent at the knees and then straightened, standing up with me. His hands clawed into my ass as he held me aloft, his eyes hot on mine. "Lindsey," He breathed. "Fuck, you feel…"

"How? Tell me, baby. How do I feel?"

He lowered me, letting gravity do the work, and filled me so full that I couldn't breathe, couldn't move.

"Oh—*FUCK!*" I cried as he bottomed out inside me, buried to the hilt.

"My love," he gasped. "Oh god, oh god. Linz, baby, you feel—oh *god*." He lifted me, dragging his cock out of me until only the tip was left inside me, and I clung to his shoulders and used my legs to grip his hips while he supported my weight, his knees against the side of the bed. "*So* fucking perfect."

"Take me, baby," I whispered. "Make me yours."

"Oh god, thank fuck," he breathed. "I need you so goddamn bad."

"Take me," I breathed. "Please, Dane, take me."

He shifted onto the bed, fell forward, so I hit the mattress. In a movie, this would have happened without us losing our connection, but reality isn't always so smooth and effortless.

I whimpered as I lost him, but it wasn't for long. He crawled past me and flipped to his back, grabbed me, and pulled me to him. I crawled over him, straddling his long, hard body. He cupped my jaw and kissed me, and with the other hand, he stroked my pussy, petting my lips and rubbing my clit until I was whimpering and gasping. I only lasted through maybe sixty seconds of this before I was quaking and at the edge of climax, rocking on my hands and knees and kissing him and gasping open-mouthed as he swirled his fingers around my clit, and then lightning was flashing blue and white behind my eyes and heat was crashing in my belly and need was ferocious within me, but I was lost to climax and shuddering and shaking and rocking and empty and wailing as he made me come, yet again, with no more than a few swipes of his talented fingers.

Lost in the throes of orgasm, I reacted with instinct as he lined himself up against me. I felt his cockhead press against my pussy lips, and my entire being lit up, knowing I was about to get him back. "Please, please, please," I panted. "Dane, fuck, please, *please!*"

"Tell me what you need, Linz."

As soon as he was notched inside me, I rocked down onto him, squealing in ecstasy as his huge, hot, hard cock speared into me. "This!" I wailed. "I need you. I need your cock, Dane. I need you to fuck me."

I felt each vein and ripple stuttering through my tight-stretched channel, and I ached around him as he slid deeper and deeper, and I felt my orgasm making my walls clamp and clench around him. My ass settled onto his thighs and hips, then, and he was home, filling me totally, his hips nestled in the cradle of my thighs and his beautiful, muscular body beneath me, and I wept for the beauty of this, of us, of having him, of being his.

"Linz," he breathed.

"I'm yours," I whispered.

He pulled back, hesitated, and thrust into me, dragging another tight, keening wail from me. "Say it again, baby. Please."

"I'm yours," I gasped, tilting my hips to meet his next thrust. "Dane, my love—I am totally, utterly yours."

He hunched, driving into me hard. "Mine," he grunted. "You're mine."

"Yes!" I answered, rocking forward onto all fours above him. "Yours. I'm yours. Everything I am, my love."

I felt something break, then, and I gave up whatever vestige of restraint I may have had. I rolled my hips to take him, rocking backward onto his cock, feeling him cram deeper into me with each successive drive, and he grasped my hips and showed me the rhythm he wanted, the pace he needed. He took control even as I let my body and my heart and my soul merge with his.

We found our perfect union together.

He palmed my ass in both hands, spread me open so with his next thrust he could fuck even deeper, dragging a raw, ragged scream from me. I fell forward, then, arms clinched around his neck and my tits flattened between us and my face buried in his throat as I rolled and rocked and rode him, and he bucked and thrusted, gripping my ass with powerful, greedy fingers, keeping me spread open for his thrusts.

"Linz!" He growled, his voice ragged with tension. "Fuck, baby—oh god, oh fuck!"

"Dane, yes, yes!" I rocked back into his thrusts, and an orgasm like no other rose up like a phoenix from the ashes and shattered me, dissolved my voice, ruined me, destroyed me, crushed me.

It began deep within, and each time Dane fucked into me it grew hotter and wilder and more potent. I found my voice for half an instant, and screamed hoarsely as he fucked, harder and faster, and our bodies met with loud slaps and wet squelches, and my orgasm blistered and detonated and I lost the air to scream, couldn't weep, couldn't breathe, couldn't move—all I could do was take his fucking and come through it.

"Dane!" I rasped. "Please—pl-please, baby!" I begged.

He found my mouth and kissed me—it was a ragged, desperate, sloppy, gasping kiss. "What, love?"

"Come!" I ordered. "I need you. I need you to come inside me."

"I'm close," he growled. "Oh fuck, you feel good."

"Dane!" I felt my pussy clenching around him, felt him slow his pace.

I needed to take it from him.

I sat up, braced my hands on his chest, held his eyes, and rolled my pussy against him. "Stop moving, baby," I breathed. "Let me do it."

He was panting, sweating—he'd been fucking me hard and fast for long minutes. "Fuck, Linz, I—"

I covered his mouth. Bent forward and draped my breasts over him. "Suck on my tits while I fuck you," I told him.

"Yes ma'am," he breathed, and suckled my nipples into his mouth, ripping a soft wail from me as a bolt of heat shifted through me.

I started slowly.

Just rocked against him, keeping his cock buried to the hilt, rolling and rolling with slow, sinuous movements of my hips. I felt him throb inside me, and knew it wouldn't be long.

Faster.

Faster.

Still just my hips rocking back and forth on his belly, smearing my wetness all over him, my pussy aching and clenching as the last of my orgasm left me. He began moving with me helplessly, pumping up into me, and I started using my legs, pushing with my thighs, lifting up so I almost lost him before sinking on him, still with measured, deliberate movements.

His hands roamed my back and shoulders, toyed with my hair, caressed my ass, and the backs of my thighs. He suckled on my tits and licked them, kissed here and there, pausing now and then to growl and pant as I moved on him.

"Ah fuck, Linz," he panted. "I'm—oh god, oh god, ohgod—oh fuck oh god ohgodfuck!"

"Yeah?" I breathed. "Is that what you need?"

"Yeah, baby. Just like that."

I sat upright on my shins and rode him for all I was worth, then, slamming down on him as hard as I could. He reached up to palm my tits as I rocked on his cock, and then as orgasm seized him, he gripped my hips and crushed me down onto him.

"Oh fuck, Linz! Lindsey!"

I felt it happen, felt the moment he let go. His hard, stroking thrusts faltered and he shouted as his cock pulsed inside me, and his cum filled me in a hot, wet flood. I cried out in ecstasy as he came inside me, weeping and sobbing as his release triggered yet another of my own.

This one, however, was unlike any other. And yes, I know I've said that before. But I really, really mean it, this time, and it's been true every time I've said it.

It's just that this climax was one of union—soul with soul. He came inside me and I came around him, and our eyes were locked and we were both breathless and we moved in perfect synchronicity, meeting each other stroke for stroke and I felt his very soul wrap around mine, felt his heart shatter as mine did and the pieces of our hearts and the fragments of our souls united and shifted together and matched and puzzled until there no end to me and no beginning to him, no seam between our souls. It was perfect oneness as I had never known could exist in this universe, and now it was ours.

I fell forward onto him and he claimed my mouth and crushed me to himself and fucked into me as he came, filling me with rush after rush of hot wet seed, and I braced on one arm over him, fingering my clit with the other to send my orgasm to renewed heights—another orgasm, and another, or wave after wave of the same one; I didn't know and cared less. He cupped my face in one hand as he kissed me, all tongue and teeth, and with the other he palmed my ass, and then his fingers splayed over my crack, and I arched my back into him.

"I want it, Dane," I whispered. "Give it to me."

He growled and fucked me harder, and his middle finger slid against my asshole. "You want this?"

"Yes!" I cried.

His finger vanished and I heard him spit, and then hot saliva smeared my asshole and his finger pushed against me and then he was fingering me, his thick digit sliding into me slowly as he fucked me.

I couldn't manage words, then—I could barely summon the oxygen to let out a scream as the new sensation poured jet fuel on the inferno of my climax. My whole body shattered, shuddered, and shook, then, and he was unrelenting, pounding his cock into me while slowly, carefully sliding his finger deeper into me until his knuckles finally met my ass cheeks.

I couldn't breathe, and I could no longer even move—I was coming too hard, shaking too helplessly. I was bent double over him, my mouth open against his throat as I rasped wet, sobbing breaths, and he was panting and gasping and groaning, making small soft desperate noises that had no neat categorical descriptions, thrusting into me with ragged, powerful thrusts, each one pouring a new hot wave of cum into me, and then finally, at long last, he stopped thrusting and the longest, hottest, most intense orgasm of my life began to subside, and then I was a boneless puddle of very well-fucked woman on top of him, leaking cum and shaking like a leaf.

He still had his long, thick middle finger planted firmly up my ass.

I liked it.

A *lot*.

Alas, he had to remove it eventually, and he did so even more carefully than he'd put it in. Next, I lost his cock.

This made me sad.

I mewled pathetically when he slipped out of me. "No," I whimpered. "Give it back. I need you."

His laugh was low and pleased. "You sure know how to make a man feel ten feet tall."

I used the fact that my mouth was already pressed against his throat to kiss him there, and then his jaw, and then his mouth. "And you sure know how to fuck a woman so good she forgets her own name."

"Lindsey Snelling," he supplied.

I giggled. "Oh, right. Thanks."

He lifted me off of him and deposited me next to him, cradling me against his chest. His heart beat rapidly under my ear, and his skin was hot, and his muscles firm, and his arm was a protective, enveloping weight over my low back, his hand resting on my ass—the clean one; the other was out to the side, dangling over the edge of the bed.

I don't know how long I lay there, barely able to draw breath for how overcome I was in that moment—so fully sated by orgasm, so filled with and consumed by love that it surely was oozing from my pores and leaking out of me.

I wept.

"Ah god, Linz," he breathed. "Tell me those are good tears."

"The best," I whispered. "I just…I love you so fucking much, Dane. I finally get it."

"Get what?"

"Mom and Pop Rigby. Rune and Duncan. Raquel and Hamish. Your parents. I finally understand."

"Me too. I saw it, but until you experience it…?"

"You can't understand it," I finished.

My eyes burned—from crying, from having been awake for who knows how long.

I yawned. "I need to clean up, but I can't move."

"I got you, baby."

I gladly stayed in bed and watched Dane's ass jiggle as he went into the bathroom, peed, washed his hands—three times, and then put on hand sanitizer—and then wet a washcloth and came back to me, that big, thick, beautiful cock of his swaying heavily.

He parted my thighs, wiping the warm, wet washcloth down my seam, pressing in a little; he folded it and did it again, and again, until I was clean. He tossed the washcloth into the sink from the doorway and then climbed back into bed with me.

"C'mere, you," I said, reaching for him the instant his body hit the mattress.

He tossed aside the blankets and climbed in, and I curled up half on him, half against him.

When his hand rested on my hip instead of my ass, I made a sleepy, grumbly noise of irritation and moved it down where it belonged—on my ass.

This got me a soft laugh.

Silence.

I felt him fading, felt myself drifting.

I sought his mouth with mine, found it. Kissed him gently, tenderly. "I love you with everything I am, Dane," I whispered. "Thank you, so, so, so much for not giving up on me. For not letting me push you away."

"I love you."

It was his only answer. It's all the answer I needed.

I fell asleep, then, and the only dreams I had were of the man holding me.

SIXTEEN

Dane

GRAY LIGHT MET MY EYES AS I LET THEM SLIDE OPEN—I knew without looking that it would be within ten minutes of 6:30 am, because I'd woken up within ten minutes of 6:30 am every single day, no matter the events of the preceding evening, since I was ten years old; mostly, it was a good thing, but sometimes I hated being unable to sleep in. This was one of those times—I just wanted to stay in bed a bit longer.

I didn't have to get up, though, I realized with a drowsy half-smile—I had the day off of work today.

So, I let myself be sleepy and content.

The ceiling wasn't that of my bedroom at Mom and Dad's…

A smile spread across my face as the night before reclaimed my memory.

Lindsey.

As her name washed through me, the woman

herself stirred. We hadn't moved all night—she was still in my arms, cradled against my chest. Her naked body was hot and silky against me, her thigh draped over mine, her hand resting low on my belly.

God, I loved her.

It filled me with a soul-deep peace and with an intense, wild, primal possessiveness; the two were a dichotomy within me, but I didn't question it.

I normally couldn't fall back asleep once my eyes opened, but with Lindsey sprawled out on me, her hair tickling my nose and her hand teasingly close to my dick and her breasts against my ribs and her breathing soughing on my skin, I found myself drifting back into a light sleep.

I woke again to a pink-yellow light from the sunrise bathing the room.

"Hi." Lindsey's voice was a delicate whisper.

I looked down at her, smiling. "Hiya, Gorgeous."

She blushed. "Thank you for last night, Dane. It was…" her eyes misted, blurred. "It was the best night of my life."

I brought her up for a kiss, intending it to be a quick soft closed-mouth good morning peck, but she had other ideas. The moment our mouths met, she moaned and opened her mouth to mine, and while I knew we both had to have morning breath, I didn't care, didn't notice. All I knew was the glory of her mouth, the heat of her kiss, the wildness of her need, the depth of her love.

She pulled away first, looking a little dizzy—which did wonders for my ego, knowing I could make her dizzy with a kiss.

"Best night of my life, too," I whispered.

She searched me. "Dane, I…" she buried her face in my chest, blushing.

"What, baby? You know you can tell me anything, ask me anything."

She nodded slightly, sighing. "Yeah, I know. I just…" another sigh, and then she lifted her head to look at me again. "I don't ever want to be apart from you again. I know this is maybe, like, zero to sixty, but I just…I woke up with you just now, and I slept so good, and I'm so happy, and I love you so fucking much it kinda scares me, but I…I just can't bear the idea of not falling asleep with you." She cupped my cheek. "I don't care what our life together looks like, Dane. I'll live in a shack or a van down by the river or a mansion on a hill. I don't fucking care, as long as your face is the last thing I see at night and the first thing I see in the morning."

My heart flipped, burned. "My god, Linz." My eyes stung unexpectedly, and my throat felt tight. "I couldn't ask for anything more."

She leaned on an elbow. "Dane, are you…*crying*?"

I cleared my throat gruffly. "Yes. Dunno why." I sniffed a laugh. "That's a lie—I do know. I've loved you since we first met. That night, while we were fuck-ing, I knew. I just *knew* that you were it for me. I knew then that I'd never want anyone else. I'd never be with anyone else."

She shivered. "For real?"

I nodded. "Absolutely for real, honey. I knew I was in love with you then. I may not have been willing or able to admit it to myself or put it into words, but I knew, deep down, what I was feeling. I've seen it enough to know what it looks like."

She settled back down onto me. "Can I tell you something kinda weird about me?"

I chuckled. "Please do."

"I think diamonds are stupid."

"Okay." I wasn't sure what to do with that information or where it was coming from.

"And I reject outright the gender norms regarding marriage proposals."

My heart clattered in my chest as I began to grasp a glimmer of where she was going with this. "Linz?"

Her hand covered my mouth, and she wriggled upright enough to lean on my chest, gazing into my eyes. "Hush, Dane. Let me talk."

I nodded.

She removed her hand, resting it on my chest while gazing at me with such open and blinding love that I almost wondered who this woman was—she was utterly transformed from the person I'd known just yesterday. She was bright and free, light and wild, joyful. Her eyes sparkled like sunlight glittering through icicles hanging from the eaves of a roof.

"Be mine forever, Dane." She swallowed hard, emotional but unafraid. "Please? I don't want or need a ring. I don't care if we ever get married. I just want you. I want to wake up like this every single fucking day until I die in your arms."

"What if I said I wanted to marry you?" I asked. "What if I said I wanted you to be my wife, to become Lindsey Badd? What if I wanted to buy you a ring? It doesn't have to be a diamond."

"I'll marry you tomorrow," she said. "I'll wear any ring you give me. I'll take your name. I'm just saying it can look…however. I don't care. Just please, Dane, promise me that I'm yours forever, starting right now."

I palmed her ass, getting a sly grin from her. "You're mine forever, Lindsey. You're mine, and I'm yours. You have my heart. You have my soul. You certainly have my body. You have my past, my present, and my future."

She let out a shuddery breath. "Oh god, Dane. I swore to myself I was done crying."

"Don't. Cry when you need to cry." I cradled her closer. "I've got you."

"You've got me."

"Forever."

"Forevah evah?"

"Forevah evah," I promised.

"I'm sorry, Ms. Jackson…ooooh! I am for *reeee-aaaal!*" She sang the chorus under her breath. "I love that you always know what I'm referring to."

We drowsed together, then, not quite awake, not quite asleep. I was on the verge of dropping back into a surface-level snooze when I felt her shift a little, sliding her thigh lower down mine, draping more of her body on top of mine. Her hand, resting on my belly, slid south.

"Mmmmm," I hummed, pleased at the direction this was going.

"Mmmmhmmm?" she murmured wordlessly.

"Mmmmmhmmm."

She curled her fingers around my cock, which was, until that moment, flaccid and soft, laying off to one side. "Mmmmmm-hmmmmmm."

At first, she just held the soft little fella in her hand, and he responded gradually, swelling slowly. Once she felt him start to unfurl, she stroked with her thumb, gently petting. This lasted…oh, I don't know. Minutes. Long, slow, wonderful minutes of unhurried affection.

Eventually, I was erect in her fist, and she was lazily pumping me, stroking me, twisting around my head, rolling her thumb over my tip.

Eyes closed, I breathed slowly and just enjoyed her touch as she toyed with me, caressing my cock as much for her own pleasure as mine.

More long, groan-inducing minutes of slow strokes and soft caresses had me arching and writhing under her touch, feet scraping at the sheets, spine arching and bowing.

I didn't want it to end. I didn't want to come.

I fought off the urge to push into her touch, the urge to move, to thrust.

I felt the sheet and blankets move and cold air wash over my naked body, and then Lindsey was kissing me, taking my mouth and demanding my breath, stealing it, leaving me breathless and aching and swollen and desperate.

She broke the kiss, and her soft small hands were both caressing my cock and I was throbbing, helplessly bucking into her fists as they plunged down my shaft.

"Fuck, baby," I whispered. "I love how you touch me."

She didn't answer.

Not in words, at any rate.

She kissed my mouth again, this time quick and soft, and then kissed my chest, rested her cheek on my pec for a moment, and then kissed my diaphragm. I had inkling where she was going, but for the moment, it felt too fucking good to stop her.

She kissed my belly. My navel.

My hipbone.

"Linz?" I murmured. "No. Please don't."

She kept one hand plunging down my cock, and the other slid up my torso as she kissed my belly again, and then my other hipbone, and then my thigh. Her upward-wandering hand patted my face and then clapped over my mouth.

I tried to protest again, but she muffled anything

I would have said, and her lips ghosted over my thigh, and I felt her breath huffing hot on my shaft.

And then her mouth was on my balls, softly suckling, tongue flicking, sliding. "Holy fuck," I gasped. "Linz!"

"Mmmmmhmmm!"

Her mouth slid upward, stuttering sideways along my shaft, tongue dragging against my skin, and my cock was throbbing and aching so hard it hurt, and every fiber of my being wanted her to take me into her mouth.

"Lindsey, wait," I said, instead. "Don't. Please don't. I don't need it. Just make love to me."

She didn't listen.

Her mouth slid up my cock, oh so slowly, lips and tongue wet against my flesh, and I arched my back and gasped as she covered my weeping tip with her lips, and her tongue slithered against me as she tasted my precum.

"Linz," I growled, trying again. "Don't. There's nothing to prove."

"I know," She whispered. "I'm not proving anything."

"Then—"

"I'm doing exactly what I want to do."

I opened my mouth to argue, but she chose that exact moment to take me into her mouth.

"FUCK!"

I had no clue what to expect next. Knowing

Lindsey, in the back of my mind, I still half-expected her to stop and freak out, or, alternatively, to realize no freakout was coming and to go crazy, giving me a blow job for the ages...and *then* freak out.

She didn't freak.

Not yet, at least.

It felt fucking amazing, obviously. Her mouth was wet and hot, and her tongue eager, swirling soft circles around my cock. This wasn't just a blow-job; this was cock-worship.

She held me in her fist and wrapped her lips around me and made slow, hungry love to my cock. She never took more of me than up to my glans, but holy fuck. She'd open her mouth wide and swirl her tongue around me, flick it against my tip and taste my precum, and then suction her mouth around me again, working my length slowly and gently, and all the while her hands plied me, circling my base and squeezing, palming my balls and teasing them with her fingertips, caressing my length up to her chin and back down, doing as much with her hands as her mouth.

I held absolutely still, barely daring to breathe, not moving a muscle.

"Lindsey," I gasped, when I could form words and summon breath.

She kept going, unhurried, slowly caressing my cock and playing with my balls, suckling and licking and swirling with her tongue.

I felt climax bubble up inside me, rising and

boiling, and there was no hope of holding back. She suckled and sucked, eager and greedy and hungry, pumping my shaft until I was groaning and growling, and finally I had no choice but to move, to give in to the need to thrust.

That's when she stopped. I left her mouth with an audible, cartoon-like *pop*. Before I could so much as groan at the sudden loss, she was rolling to her back and pulling me over her. She guided me into the cradle of her thighs and slid me inside her tight, hot, wet pussy. All the way in, all at once, no hesitation, no lead-up, just a long, slow, hot slide into heaven, and she was so fucking tight, so fucking wet, I couldn't breathe again, overwhelmed and overcome.

"Lindsey," I whispered.

Her mouth met mine, silencing me, claiming me with a hot, hard kiss, and this time she didn't stop; it was a kiss to fuse our very souls.

Her hands dug into my ass, and her legs hooked around my thighs, and she pulled at me, whimpering into the kiss. "Please," she breathed. "Please. Please."

"Lindsey, my love."

She arched, rocked against me, taking me deep—I lost my voice to a loud cry as her soft wet heat swallowed me, enveloped me, and I thrust into her, once, hard

"YES!" she screamed. "AGAIN!"

I thrust into her again, and she screamed while biting my lower lip—hard enough that I grunted, but she licked the hurt away, and I forgot the sting instantly as she bucked up to meet my next thrust. Her hands clawed into my ass and pulled me to her.

Her lips slid up my cheek to my ear. "Please, my love. Please." She nipped my earlobe, breath hot. "Fuck me. Please. I need you. I need your cock. I need your cum. Please, Dane. Please, please fuck me as hard as you can, baby. Fuck me. *Please* fuck me."

I groaned at her words, at the raw desperation as she begged and pleaded.

How could I possibly refuse a plea like that?

I took her mouth and gave her what she wanted—slow at first, driving deep with slow, hard thrusts. She gasped softly with each one, and her eyes stayed fixed on mine, filled with love, sparking blue heat with each crash of our bodies together.

"Harder, Dane," she pleaded. "Harder!"

I built the pace gradually—or rather, that was the intent. The reality, however, was that I had no such restraint. She begged me to fuck her harder, and I could only give her what she wanted. I fucked her harder. Her huge tits sloshed in wide, quivering circles as I pounded into her, and she wailed desperately each time I drove into her, and she gripped my ass with fierce strength, and even as I fucked her, she clawed at me and pulled at me with her hands and legs and shrieked and wailed, and begged for more.

"YES! Dane, oh god, Dane, yes! YES! Fuck me, baby, fuck me just like that!" Her voice was raw and ragged and raspy and breathless, and she cried out wordlessly as I crashed into her, aching with the orgasm that I couldn't bring myself to give in to.

"Come inside me, Dane," she panted. "Come for me. Fuck me until you come. Fuck me as hard as you can and never, ever stop."

"You want me to come?" I growled.

"Fuck yes. I want you to fill me with your cum."

I pulled away, slid out of her with a groan. I rolled Lindsey to her belly and she eagerly gave me what I wanted, what she knew I needed—she went on all fours, presenting that big, plump, round, juicy, perfect ass to me.

"Is this what you need, my Dane?" she demanded, her voice sultry and low and aroused. "You wanna take me like this, don't you?"

"Fuck yes, baby. You always know what I need."

"Take me, sweetheart," she whispered, looking back at me over her shoulder, ass high, shoulders low. "Fuck me."

I gripped my cock and guided myself to her entrance—she took over, notching me in her wet seam; the instant I was there, she rocked back into me and her pussy swallowed all of me, all at once.

I lost it, then.

Whatever shreds of control I may have had were utterly erased when I took her in that position. It's what I'd fantasized about, needed, dreamed of—the one position we hadn't done together yet.

"DANE!" she cried as I thrust into her, my hips slapping loudly against her ass. "FUCK! Yes, fuck yes, baby. Give it to me, my Dane. This is so good—so perfect."

Her Dane.

I liked that.

My heart sang and my soul soared, and I watched the woman I love arch and writhe as I fucked her—I poured my love into her, thrust after thrust, and I should have come right away, but I didn't. Couldn't. I needed her, and I needed this to last forever. Her ass cushioned each thrust with soft, beautiful give, and I gripped her curves and drove in, leaned back as I thrust and smacked her left cheek with my right hand, and she cried out at the spank, pushing back into my thrust in a way that told me exactly how much she liked being spanked.

I don't know how long we fucked. Minutes? Hours? Time lost any meaning or flow. But when at last I felt the orgasm reaching a crescendo inside me, I went willingly to meet it, knowing it's what she wanted, needed, had been begging for.

"I'm gonna come, Linz," I warned. "Fuck, baby, I'm gonna come so hard."

"Yes, Dane, yes, yes, *yes*! Come for me, honey. Give it to me, give it all to me." She rocked back to meet me, and I palmed her ass cheeks, pulled them apart so I could fuck deeper, and she cried out, guttural, as if

I was fucking her so deeply she was choking on my cock from the inside. "DANE!"

Harder, then. I gripped her hips and yanked her back against me, fucking her roughly, each thrust so hard she was rocked forward, her ass quaking with each slapping thrust, creating hypnotic rippling waves as I pounded, pounded, pounded.

Orgasm ripped me apart.

Destroyed me.

Ruined me.

My shout left me hoarse, throat sore and aching as I poured into her and roared, fucking her through a climax that left me momentarily blinded, deafened from the howling of my blood in my ears, thighs burning from exertion, gasping ragged breaths as I came and came and came.

When I slowed, still hard but too shattered to keep going, Lindsey collapsed forward, mewling as she lost me, and guided me to my back, where I lay, panting. She caressed my cock as she lay beside me, milking another lazy dribble of cum out of me to trickle down her knuckles.

She licked it, grinned at me...

And went down on me again, taking my cock in her mouth and sucking another little spurt out of me, making me arch, shocked and gasping.

She popped back up after a moment, wiping her lips on her wrist as she settled on my chest.

Neither of us spoke for a long time.

"Holy fucking shit," I gasped, eventually—the length of time it took me to regain anything like coherence.

"I love you," she said.

"Holy fucking shit," I repeated.

She giggled, rolling to her belly on me, mostly on top of me. "I just fucked your brains out."

"Yes," I said. "Yes, you did. You absolutely fucked my brains all the way out."

Her grin was happy. "I sucked your cock."

"You did." I wiped an errant drop away from her lips. "Was it…were you okay?"

She nodded. "More than okay." She leaned up to kiss my jaw. "I wouldn't have done it otherwise. I just…I wanted to see. To try. Because I woke up wanting you, and…I remembered how much I liked going down you before…you know, I lost my shit. And I realized that it's not oral itself that makes me freak out, it's certain things that…were done to me, during it."

"What things, honey?"

"Deep throat," she whispered. "I don't want to talk about it. I won't ever say that name again. I'll never discuss it again after this. But that's what he did to me. He used my throat. I gagged on it. *That's* what I hated. And with you, that first night, it was fine until I started going too far. I…I was getting into it, and I thought that's how…I thought that's what I was *supposed* to do. But I don't have to do it that way. It actually seems pretty simple, now."

"I don't think it's just that, Linz."

"No, probably not," She agreed. "But that's a big part of it. Most of it, though, is that I fucking love you. That beats everything else all to shit. I know you'd never..." she stopped, shaking her head. "You love me. I'm secure in that, Dane. It gives me peace and confidence. I woke up in love with you, happier than I've ever been, and I just knew I could do that, and I wanted to, and so I did." She grinned at me. "And I stopped because what I needed was you. Us. I needed exactly what you gave me."

I shook my head. "Linz, I..."

She covered my mouth. "Just tell me you love me."

"I love you."

"Last night," she began, hesitant. "The stuff about rings and..."

"I meant every word, Linz," I interrupted. "I love you. I want to do life with you. As long as we're together, it can be whatever we want it to look like."

She rested her cheek on my chest. "Could we... um...stay here?"

"Like for today?"

"No, like, to live."

"Oh." I frowned, thought about it, and shrugged. "Yeah, for sure."

"Because I'm gonna need to fuck you at least once a day, loudly and lengthily, for the foreseeable future." She cleared her throat delicately. "And I don't think your parents want to hear that."

"No," I said, shaking with laughter, "probably not." I hesitated. "When you say at least once a day…?"

She turned onto her chin, smirking, an erotic gleam in her eyes. "You've unleashed a beast, honey. I am one horny ass bitch, and you're *mine*."

"I see."

"What's your refractory period like?"

"Short."

"Not short enough."

"Shower with me?" I suggested.

"If you promise me an orgasm while we're in there."

"At least one," I promised, rolling off the bed.

She reached for me like a toddler asking for uppies. "My legs don't work. Carry me."

I scooped her up and carried her into the bathroom. Set her on the closed toilet lid and started the shower.

While it heated, she gazed at me. "Dane?"

I smiled down at her. "Linz?"

"I love you."

I smirked. "I know."

EPILOGUE

Tea

IT TOOK ALL MY NOT-INCONSIDERABLE SELF-CONTROL TO not fidget with my clothing—civvies. I was starched, pressed, and polished in a brand-new pantsuit…and nervous as fuck. I'd feel better if I were at least wearing service blues, or better yet, a flight suit, but this wasn't the type of function it was acceptable to wear a uniform to, so here I am in brand-new civvies, feeling like a poser, and nervous as fuck.

Which was kind of silly, considering the contents of my CV: Fixed-wing PPL at 17, helicopter PPL six months later; commercial pilot's license for fixed wing at 18, joined the Navy at 19, and flew just about every kind of aircraft, fixed wing and rotary, across a ten-year career. I flew dozens of combat missions in Afghanistan as a helo pilot, flew transports during the clusterfuck that was the evacuation, and spent the last couple of years flying helos in an elite SAR unit. I have extensive

survival training, including cold weather, water, desert, and woodland environments. I've been shot down
behind enemy lines and made it back to base, on foot,
injured, and alone.

Yet I'm nervous for a fucking interview with some
soft billionaire tech lord?

Get it the fuck together, Tay.

The environment wasn't helping. It reminded me
of my grandfather's office, which was unsettling. My
grandfather was an Admiral. My great-grandfather? Rear
Admiral. My father? Commander, legendary Navy test
pilot, a combat pilot with three kills during the Gulf
War. Yeah, I'm a legacy brat. And my grandfather's office? It's where you went to get chewed out for subpar
performance. Such as when I made a mistake soloing
with Dad when I was ten. Or when I got a B- on a cal-
culus exam sophomore year of high school. Or when
I scored less than perfect on a written exam for Navy
pilot school. Or…well, you get the idea.

In my family, less than perfect equals abject failure,
as adhyducated by Admiral James M. Tiernan.

This office—or, the reception area thereof—was
a spitting image of Granddad's office: dark wood pan-
elled walls, plush crimson thick-pile carpet, bookshelves
lined with dense hardcover tomes on weighty, serious
subjects, low lighting, and above all, *silence*.

Oppressive, thick, heavy silence.

You didn't speak unless spoken to, here.

You didn't fidget.

Or cough.

Or sniffle.

You certainly didn't look impatiently at the dour receptionist who looked like she could swallow a lump of coal and shit out a diamond three days later.

I've been sitting in this wingback chair staring at the floor for twenty minutes. There are four other men waiting, each decades older with thousands of hours more flight experience than me. They're wearing expensive three-piece suits. Rolexes. Brogues and Oxfords. They're serious men with stolid names like Robert and Gregory and Thomas.

And then there's me.

Tea.

Five-five, with a feminine build, even my tailored pant suit can't hide. They'll look at me and forget my CV. Happened before, and I'm fully prepared for this dick—Linus Magnus Thorvaldsen, founder and CEO of LMT Enterprises, a tech R&D firm worth sixty billion—to dismiss me upon sight, even though I guarantee I'm at least *as* qualified as anyone he's interviewed and *more* qualified than most.

One by one, the men around me were called in for their interview. Thirty minutes passed. Forty. An hour.

Two.

Some of the interviews lasted more than half an hour each.

Finally, I was the last one left, despite being the

first one there; clearly, interviewees were not called back based on order of arrival.

Figures.

The door to the inner sanctum opened, and the previous candidate walked out, looking peeved. Forties, graying, slim, and serious with the air of a man who runs marathons for fun, he paused as he passed me. "Good fucking luck, sweetheart," he said, sounding ready to chew nails.

Yikes. Okay.

The door closed again. So…not my turn?

Sweet.

Fifteen minutes passed. Twenty.

I'd taken my walking papers from the Navy a couple of months ago, which in itself was a family sin—Tiernans were *career*, dammit. We were Navy lifers. You didn't leave the Navy. You didn't work for civilians. Yet here I was, in civvies, out of the Navy, interviewing for a position that wasn't even a government contractor job, which would have been at least *acceptable* to my family, if not *preferred*.

Finally, three and a half hours after I entered this place, the door opened, and a skinny kid in a suit worth more than everything I own stood just outside the doorway, peering at a tablet.

He peered harder.

Here it came.

"Tea?" As in the hot beverage.

Dick.

I ignored him.

"Tea?" Louder, as if I somehow hadn't heard him the first time. He also wasn't looking at me.

He cleared his throat ostentatiously. "Tea Tiernan?" Still mispronouncing my name and omitting my hard-earned rank.

I looked up and met his eyes, and I gave him the Tiernan Terror: our family's ability to stare at someone and make them feel tiny, stupid, insignificant, and inferior. It can't be taught or explained, only experienced, survived, and internalized until you can replicate it yourself on unsuspecting ensigns; I'd perfected it to the point of being able to make grown men cry. Literally, once.

He quailed, paled, and glanced at the tablet again. "Lieutenant Commander Tiernan?"

I stood up at perfect parade attention. "Good afternoon." I emphasized the afternoon slightly to point out that I'd been waiting since morning.

"This way, ma'am." He gestured through the doorway, as if I'd somehow take a wrong left turn at Albuquerque and end up in someone else's office.

I strutted past him, hating the feel of the leather ballet flats my sister insisted went best with this outfit. You can't strut properly in flats, dammit. You need heels, at least, but preferably a good pair of heavy shitkickers. Nothing says "don't fuck with me" like a stomp-heavy strut.

Walking into the inner sanctum felt like walking

into a different world. The reception area was Serious Business; this was…Tech Bro Playground.

Two walls were entirely glass, revealing a breathtaking view of Seattle's skyline and the Puget Sound. There was a putting green—not a strip of fake grass from Menards with a little plastic cup. No, this was actual grass, indoors, complete with undulations in the "terrain". It occupied a whole corner of the office, which itself was most of the floor. I could land a Huey in here. There was an 80" flatscreen TV on one wall with a PS5 and a couch facing it. A foosball table. A table arrayed with junk food.

The desk was bigger than the USS Princeton, my first berth. The man behind it totally shattered what I'd been envisioning. I'd imagined some doughy, pencil-necked dork in coke bottle glasses, or a stodgy old fart who paid other people for his ideas.

This guy was, objectively, hot. Six feet even and fit, he was wearing khakis and a seafoam green polo. Messy, curly blonde hair, and yes, glasses, but chic designer ones that gave Clark Kent more than pre-Microsoft Bill Gates. He was older than he looked, though, I knew that. I'd done my research—he was notoriously reclusive and never gave interviews, never attended public events, and had never been publicly photographed. The only known pictures of him stopped at college. So, while he looked to be late thirties at best, he was, in reality, past fifty. Which was, in my estimation, a combination of good genes and the longevity care that comes with being a billionaire.

He was doing the classic Important Businessman Pose: standing at the window behind his desk, hands clasped behind his back, looking pensive and thoughtful and busy, as if he had a million things to do, but his current train of thought required Gazing Pensively While Thinking Deep Thoughts. Yes, the capitals are necessary.

He had nice arms, I couldn't help noticing.

He wasn't my type, but I am straight and single and in possession of excellent eyesight, and he was attractive.

I crossed the veritable wasteland that was his office to stand at attention between the two wingback chairs angled toward each other in front of his desk.

"Mr. Thorvaldsen," I said. "Good afternoon, sir."

A lengthy, posed pause, and then he turned to face me, scrutinized me closely, silently. Head to toe, twice. He noted the cut of my suit, I'm certain. My chin-length black razor bob, long enough to pull back if necessary, short enough to fit under a flight helmet comfortably without getting in the way. My makeup-free face. And, most certainly, the irritation I knew I was failing to hide—I have a shit poker face.

"My apologies for the long wait, Commander Tiernan." His voice was quiet, smooth, and placid.

I didn't answer that—I'm not in the habit of saying

"oh, it's fine" when it's not, and a three-and-a-half-hour wait when I was one of six candidates was absurd.

An intentional slight, as I saw it.

For some reason, Thorvaldsen smirked at me, and then gestured at the chairs. "Please, sit."

I sat—on the edge of the chair, knees together at an angle, feet under me, spine straight, chin high: seated attention.

More smirking. This guy was starting to irritate me with the knowing smirks.

He flipped open a manila folder—my CV. Perused it slowly, line by line, page by page.

"Impressive," he said, when he'd finally closed the file.

This didn't merit an answer, since it was objectively true.

More smirking.

"I've interviewed eleven men and three women for this position," he told me. "All of them have impressive qualifications and resumes."

At some point, he *was* going to ask me a question, right?

"None of them have been even remotely interesting."

This got my attention. "*Interesting*, sir?"

A full grin, this time. Dazzling. Megawatt. "Yes, *interesting*, Commander. You'll find the things I value are not always…what you'd expect."

"Such as qualifications for a personal pilot?" I said, my tone arch and wry.

He laughed. "Precisely, Commander." He leaned toward me, shoving my file aside. "I could throw a rock and hit forty excellent pilots. Every one of the fifteen pilots I've interviewed over the last month, has been more qualified than the last, regardless of which order you put them in."

"Fourteen, sir."

That smirk. "Quite right." It didn't reach his eyes, though—those were calculating, assessing, not quite cold but not exactly nice or warm. "I'm looking for more than just a pilot, Commander."

"Oh?"

"I travel a lot. I have ventures in some remote places—research stations in the Arctic, satellites in the jungle, office buildings in Dubai, server farms in the desert, that sort of thing. I don't trust just anyone, however, so when I hire a pilot, he or she is not just flying my Gulfstream from airport to airport. My pilot must be willing and able to fly in all conditions. Fixed-wing and helicopters. Sandstorms, windstorms, blizzards. I might get a call at four in the morning and have to fly from Seattle to Nome on a moment's notice."

"Sounds like an adventure," I said, honestly.

"I've been in three crashes, Commander. The first was a hard landing in a puddle jumper in the Caribbean, just got a little jostled when the landing gear gave out. I went down in a helicopter during a freak sandstorm in Africa, and then, most recently, a very bad landing during a blizzard in Siberia. Chances are I'll crash again, and I need to know my pilot will keep me alive."

I kept my face blank. "I make no promises, sir. Flight is dynamic. We think we're in control, but we aren't. But if survival is possible, I'll make it happen. I've been through a few myself, sir."

"A few, eh?"

"I've been flying since I was a little girl and soloing before it was strictly legal. I've put down hard plenty of times in all manner of aircraft. I've ditched at sea, crash-landed behind enemy lines, bailed out, skidded off runways." I shrugged. "I can land a C-2 on an aircraft carrier, sir. I can keep a helo hovering over a pitching deck. I can handle whatever you care to throw at me, sir."

This got me a long stare. "Crash-landed behind enemy lines?"

"Details are classified, sir," I said. "I wasn't the only survivor of the landing, but I *was* the only one who made it back—through no fault of my own, I feel compelled to point out."

He flipped through my file again. "So you've flown in combat?"

"Yes, sir." I gestured at the file on the desk. "Not everything is in there, sir. I was attached to some heavily classified ops."

"Juicy."

I frowned. "Pardon?"

"I said that's juicy."

"Juicy." I tried to process what this could mean in this context and didn't quite make it.

He grinned. "So you've got some great stories to tell, but you're not allowed to tell them."

"Correct, sir."

He nodded, standing up and turning away from me. "I have two children, Commander Tiernan. A son who is, in a word, a wastrel. Charming, fascinating, and immensely cool, but a wastrel, currently. He can charm the pants off a nun, Commander. The other is a daughter who's getting married soon. She has, for reasons I cannot fathom, chosen to have a destination wedding and honeymoon in Ketchikan fucking Alaska, of all places. Now, I like Alaska. I've got a research station up in Nome. But I wouldn't get married there. Helena, however, is…unique, and she's my baby, so I spoil her."

"I see." The man liked his non sequiturs.

"Gunnar, however, my son…I worry about him. More to the point, I worry about his influence on my employees. He has slept his way through my secretary pool, twice, and several of my PAs. That's why I hired Albert, there." He pointed at the skinny kid who'd brought me in. "He's…what are you, again? I'll remember, eventually."

"Abrosexual, Mr. Thorvaldsen."

I frowned. "I don't know what that is."

"Fluid, essentially," Albert answered. "Who I'm interested in is…changeable, depending on a variety of factors, but I tend to be more interested in men than women."

Thorvaldsen grinned. "See? It's foolproof! My son is very firmly heterosexual, and likes his conquests with a lot of silicone and not a lot of brains."

"Well, sir, he won't be interested in me, then." If he saw me in a bikini, that might change, but that wasn't happening. "You can consider my pants firmly up and me immune to his charms."

This got me a nod. "You're single?"

"Yes sir."

"Do you drink?"

"Seldom, and never within twelve hours of flying."

"I take my privacy more seriously than even my business."

"I have Top secret security clearance. Or, had. I'm very good at keeping secrets."

Silence.

"You're hired."

I blinked. "Excellent, sir. When do I start?"

He turned to me, grinning. "No nonsense, I like that. But I wouldn't hate it if you loosened up a bit. Tell a joke. Banter a bit. In time, I suppose." He turned to Albert. "Get her processed, paperwork, all that mess." To me, then. "Can you fly me to Ketchikan tomorrow?"

"Ketchikan?"

"It's in Alaska."

"I know where Ketchikan is."

"Does it matter why I'm going there?"

"No, sir. Just curious."

"I'm interviewing a candidate for a special project, and he lives in Ketchikan. He doesn't know I'm coming. I've been putting him through several rounds of interviews with various subordinates, and now I need to meet him in person. It's a surprise. I'm unconventional, you see." A pause. "I also have wedding details to iron out in person."

"I'm noticing that, sir."

He sighed. "How long will it take you to stop saying 'sir' every time you address me, Commander Tiernan?"

"As long as it takes for you to call me Tea." I glared at Albert as I pronounced my name: *TAY-uh*.

He winced, avoiding my gaze.

He rounded the desk and stuck his hand out to me. "Call me Linus, for now. If we decide we like each other and get along, you might eventually end up calling me Mags, which is what my inner circle calls me." He glanced at Albert. "The candidate, Albert. I've forgotten his name."

"Jax Badd, Mr. Thorvaldsen." *TORE-vahld-son.*

"Right, right. Jax. Jax. Jax." He glanced at me. "I'm great with faces but not so much with names sans faces." A shrug. "Anyway. Welcome to LMT, Tea."

Jax Badd? Really? He's probably a douchebag.

I shook Thorvaldsen's hand, putting the odd name out of my mind—I'd fallen into a weird name portal, clearly, and I was used to being the one with the weird name, so I wasn't sure how to feel. "Thank you for the opportunity. I look forward to flying for you, Linus."

He glanced at me. "Would you like to know when I knew I'd hire you?"

I nodded. "Sure."

"When you corrected me."

I wasn't expecting this. "Really?"

He nodded. "Yup. I made that same, simple addition error in every interview. No one corrected me. You did. You're not afraid to speak your mind, to tell me if I'm wrong. I need that in the people closest to me." He sat behind the desk. "You'll drive for me, too, as needed. Is that an issue?"

"I can handle that. I don't have a defensive driving cert, but I could get it easily."

He laughed. "You're very serious, aren't you, Tea?"

"Except when I'm not, Linus."

Another laugh. Despite everything, I was starting to like this guy. He was weird. I like weird. He didn't take himself seriously, but he also did. Not sure how to explain that any better, but it felt true.

"Albert will onboard you, introduce you to the relevant people, show you the office and garage, and introduce you to my aircraft. We're wheels up for Ketchikan tomorrow morning."

"Time?"

"Eight…ish. I'm not the most punctual man, you'll find."

I was, but no need to mention that. "I'll see you tomorrow, Linus."

"See you tomorrow, Tea."

I waited until I was alone in the back of the Uber on the way to my hotel to do a self-congratulatory fist pump—I'd gotten the job: Private, personal pilot for Linus Magnus Thorvaldsen, billionaire and professional weird guy. I'd get to fly to cool places, and, if the rumors about his fleet were true, I'd get to fly some of the most cutting-edge aircraft on the planet.

If he had a Roth jet, I'd shit my pants. I'd read that Thorvaldsen had a personal relationship with Valentine Roth, who designed the very best luxury jets money could buy—each one was bespoke, hypersonic, invisible to radar, some with VTOL capability...I was salivating to get my little mitts on the controls of one.

And rumor had it, Thorvaldsen had *three*.

I hadn't been this excited in a long, long time. I'd needed a change of life after what happened, and this was definitely that. No more arrogant superiors, no more saluting and all that shit, no more bullshit orders from out-of-touch brass.

No more watching entire fireteams get mowed down.

No more SAR missions that went horribly, horribly wrong.

Hopefully, this would be interesting and fun and challenging but not traumatizing.

See the world, fly cool shit, make bank.

Fuck yeah.

The dog tags hanging between my breasts felt cold for a moment—I had two sets. Mine and...*his*.

Not going there.

I pushed memories aside as I followed Albert around the building into a private little office where I filled out reams of paperwork, signed releases and a viciously ironclad NDA, received the badge that would get me where I needed to go, and then was shown the rest of the office, the garage—filled with Rolls Royces and Mercedes-Maybachs and Rezvanis—and then I was taken to the LMT private hangar.

Roth jets—three of them! Sexy and sleek, they made my blood race.

A Roth helo—stealth, silent, and faster than anything the military could put out, according to the scuttlebutt.

There are more prosaic craft as well—Cessnas, Gulfstreams, regular private helicopters, a replica WW1 biplane, a genuine Spitfire...oh, *man*.

I was in heaven.

We approached Ketchikan, and I radioed the tower, got permission to land. It was an easy, smooth touchdown. I taxied the Gulfstream, parked it, and ran through my post-flight checklist while my new employer did whatever he was doing back there.I was driving him around as well, so once I was done, I met the courier who had driven Linus's Range Rover up here from Seattle.

We took a ferry, which was weird but kinda fun.

I expected our destination to be a fancy hotel, or, barring that, a high-end Airbnb.

"Badd's Bar and Grille, Tea," Linus told me, once we'd left the ferry.

I put the destination into the GPS. We arrived a few minutes later.

I eyed the place. "Linus? You sure this is where you wanna go, sir?"

He laughed. "Yes, Tea. We're meeting my possible hire here."

"Should I circle the block? Park?"

"Park and come in with me. It's dinnertime, after all."

This was feeling more and more like I was an additional PA who just happened to also be a pilot…and a driver. Considering how many zeros were in my contract, I was fine with this arrangement, as long as I didn't have to cook, clean, pick up dry cleaning, or anything gross, like clip toenails; my sister had moonlighted as a PA for a low-level exec in Silicon Valley right out of college, and she'd had to clip her bosses toenails. Fuck that.

We entered the bar—it was early afternoon, so it was mostly empty. He'd told me eight this morning, but we hadn't actually been wheels up until almost noon—his delay. There were a few regulars at the bar, a few tourists at tables, and a young man by himself in a booth near the kitchen.

Linus consulted his phone—a one-off he'd designed

and was testing out, apparently—and then looked at the young man.

I followed a few feet behind Linus as he approached the guy—not a kid, just younger than me by five or so years.

"Jax Badd?" Linus said.

Jax held up a finger and went back to typing. "Yeah, one sec. Just gotta…" he trailed off, frowning at his laptop, tracing a line of code with his finger. "A-*ha*! Got you, little fucker." He entered a single keystroke, triumphantly, and shut the laptop. "Sorry, sorry. I'm Jax."

He stood up and turned to us.

Jesus…*Jesus*.

He was…

His eyes were—and his jawline? Fuck me.

The *eyes*—so brown, so warm, filled with humor and curiosity and kindness.

His mouth? His jaw?

His *shoulders*?

I was dry-mouthed and clammy-handed just looking at him.

And then he looked past Linus, directly at me.

Grinned.

To say my underwear combusted would not be an understatement. They combusted and went wet at the same time.

Good thing I was just the pilot, because if I had to talk to this guy, I couldn't guarantee I wouldn't jump his bones.

People talk about dry spells?

I wasn't in a dry spell, I was in a *drought*.

A long, *long* drought.

And this guy?

He was a tall, sexy, hunky drink of water.

And I was very, *very* thirsty.

They'd been talking while I was daydreaming.

"Tea?" Linus's voice. "*TEA!*"

I startled. "Sorry, sorry. Yes, I'm…yes. What?"

Linus laughed. "I just wanted you to meet my newest acquisition—Jax Badd."

His hand was rough—not a computer nerd's hand. His eyes sparkled, twinkled. "Tea. Nice to meet you."

"Yes." It was all I could manage.

He grinned. "I hear we're gonna get to know each other, soon."

"Excuse me?" I almost choked on my spit. "What?"

Linus was grinning at me knowingly; I was caught. "You're flying Jax to my project. You'll be in close quarters with him for the next few days while I deal with wedding plans here."

Oh.

Oh god.

Good thing I have an indomitable will and iron self-control.

Right?

ALSO BY
Jasinda Wilder

Visit me at my website: **www.jasindawilder.com**
Email me: **jasindawilder@gmail.com**

If you enjoyed this book, you can help others enjoy it as well by recommending it to friends and family, or by mentioning it in reading and discussion groups and online forums. You can also review it on the site from which you purchased it. But, whether you recommend it to anyone else or not, thank you *so much* for taking the time to read my book! Your support means the world to me!

My other titles:

Forbidden Fruit

Wild Ride: Biker Billionaire

Delilah's Diary

Big Girls Do It:
Big Girls Do It
Married
On Christmas
Pregnant
Rock Stars Do It
Big Love Abroad

The Falling Series:
Falling Into You
Falling Into Us
Falling Under
Falling Away
Falling for Colton

The Ever Trilogy:
Forever & Always
After Forever
Saving Forever

From the world of *Wounded:*
Wounded
Captured

From the world of *Stripped:*
Stripped
Trashed

From the world of *Alpha:*
Alpha
Beta
Omega
Harris
Thresh
Duke
Puck
Lear
Anselm
Sigma
Gamma
Delta

For a Goode Time Call...
Not So Goode
Goode To Be Bad
A Real Goode Time
Goode Vibrations
A Very Badd Christmas
Badd Apple
Badd Baby

Dad Bod Contracting:
Hammered
Drilled
Nailed
Screwed

Fifty States of Love:
Pregnant in Pennsylvania
Cowboy in Colorado
Married in Michigan
Christmas in Connecticut

Billionaire Baby Club:
Lizzy Goes Brains Over Braun
Autumn Rolls a Seven
Laurel's Bright Idea

Club Sin:
Rev
Kane
Chance
Silas
Saxon
Solomon
Lash
Inez

Blood Heir
Blood Heir
Blood Rising
Blood Bonds
Blood Reign

Three Rivers
Into the Light
Light in the Dark
Light Up the Night

The Cabin:
The Cabin
Christmas at the Cabin

Standalone titles:
Yours
The Parent Trap
Wish Upon A Star
Big Hose

Non-Fiction titles:
You Can Do It
You Can Do It: Strength
You Can Do It: Fasting

Jack Wilder Titles:
The Missionary

JJ Wilder Titles:
Ark

To be informed of new releases and special offers,
sign up for
Jasinda's email newsletter.